Realms

By

Maureen Ungar

In a Cowslip Press LL

For information on the author's upcoming works, please
see her website:
http://thewritersrealm.wordpress.com/

'*Realms*'© 2012 by Maureen Ungar is
Book One in the **Realms Series**, which includes Book
Two '*Realm Lost*', and Book Three '*Old Realm*.'

ISBN-13:978-0615628608(In A Cowslip Press LLC)
ISBN-10: 0615628605

DEDICATION

My writing is not possible without the support of my loving husband Bennett and our wonderful children Jennifer, Stephen, Adam and Shaina. I am grateful for the love of this crazy crew.

CONTENTS

ACKNOWLEDGMENTS

I have found generous encouragement through friends I made learning this craft. Many of you were also readers that helped me sift wheat from chaff. Thank you,
Karina Berg Johannsen, author of **'Synvilla/Delusion'**,
Annette Bosley-Boyce, educator and author,
Susan Bangheart, illustrator and aspiring children's writer;
and author of **'Pure**,' Julianna Baggott, who also writes as
Bridget Asher and N.E. Bode.

I also wish to thank Eckerd College's Writers in Paradise Conference and Wesleyan Writers Conference for their excellent programs, and everyone in the Litchfield Writer's Guild for listening.

All chapter headings in this story are taken from Edmund Spenser's classic, **'The Faerie Queen.'**

Chapter 1

What if within the Moon's fair shining sphere?
What if in every other star unseen
Of other worlds he happily should hear?

The glass splinter changed everything for May, though
she would not understand how until long afterward. Her
mother shuffled into the kitchen that morning, like usual, still
in her nylon nighty.

"I'm making eggs and toast," May said.

Her mother groaned and poured a glass from the orange
juice container on the counter. She left room for a shot of
vodka from a bottle in the freezer. "Toast," she said. "Dry."

May popped down a slice, but before it browned, her
mother's glass was half-empty.

"You're up early," May said.

"Got to look for work…your father's taking me."

She finished her cocktail and left waving the toast. May's
mother hadn't looked for a job in months. Since they had
forgotten May's last birthday, her parents might use job-
hunting as an excuse to go out and make up for it today. Her
parents returned late afternoon. May had broiled chicken,
mashed potatoes, and heated canned beets for supper. No
cake-in-a-box, no present wrapped in a bow appeared. Her
mother managed to find wine when they were out though, kept
filling her glass while her father drank beer.

"You could take the job at the hotel," her father said.

"Manning the counter?" Her mother might not realize she shouted.

"It's a start, you can work up to night manager," her father said.

"I'm a book-keeper, I make thirty-five bucks an hour," her mother said. "They were paying minimum."

Her father was on his feet now. "Were book-keeping, were making thirty-five an hour. You blew that off spiking your coffee on the job."

Her mother screeched. "Screw you!"

She grabbed the now empty wine bottle, threw it at May's father. It missed, hit the wall, shattered. A shard pierced May's hand.

"What the hell was that?" her father asked.

May pulled out the glass, put it on her plate and watched the cut bleed. She whispered, "Happy birthday."

May left dirty dishes, uneaten food, and shut her bedroom door without saying goodnight. She wrapped the cut with tissue and played her radio to drown out shouting. The next morning, she fixed her hair and quizzed the mirror.

Would she pass for eighteen, nineteen with her hair up? She left the braids down, then quickly packed a battered suitcase, tiptoed outside and hid it in the garden shed. It wasn't going to hold everything she needed to bring, so she dug around the attic and found her father's old backpack. She washed it and hung it outside with other laundry, a chore May handled most times because her mother liked vodka.

Afterward May studied the wooded hills across the way. Should she leave?

The silence answered her. No one was coming to her rescue. Acting as if it was any other day, before she started her hike, May carried the kitchen trash bag behind the garage. She stepped on an empty waffle box in the grass. It was almost impossible to find a clean spot on the back lawn. Skunks and raccoons had been at the garbage pile growing there, one way to recycle banana peel, potato skins, leftovers scraped from plates. For months now, her parents found better things to do than drive trash to the local dump. May would bring the garbage there, but couldn't since her parents wouldn't take her to get a driver's license.

Just another task her parents had no time for, though Granddad had taught May to drive. She left the bag with the others and walked away. This was not going to be her problem. Decided to take the wood's trail, May passed her secret refuge, the old apple tree. Its tangled branches were intricate as lace. A few of last season's shriveled leaves still clung to it. The realization this would be her last time here hit. She sank onto tree roots facing away from her house.

Her bottom lip quivered. "I hate this."

May didn't know when she started talking out loud when she sat in this spot; it was far enough away from her parents to catch a break, but close enough to rush home when she had to. Somehow it helped.

"They didn't come when I got a lead in the junior play...

they won't sit without a drink long enough for me to get a diploma either. No one asked me to the prom, but did either of them wonder why? Who will date the daughter of the town drunks? I should get away, I should."

A tear slipped down her face. "What could be worse than this?"

Granddad had understood. He stayed at a local bed and breakfast every summer since May was ten, got her each day so they could do things together. He asked questions, listened to her answers, and shared his stories too. There would be no visit from Granddad this year. He passed away last September. May had not, as her mother urged, gotten over him. Granddad did not forget her either, in fact, he bypassed his absent son and her mother to will May his bonds and stocks. Of course, May could not take legal possession until she was eighteen, but her parents were expressly forbidden any use of his property. This surprised everyone but May.

"Not that I wanted anything from him, but he was a damned old fool, giving that to a kid," her mother said when the will was read.

"He should have left it to you, so you could invest the money for May," her father said.

Granddad's lawyer oversaw the trust fund; his daughter got nothing but a personal note from her father, which she threw in the lawyer's trashcan. May got a sealed envelope too, but folded it and stuck it in her pocket. Later, alone in her room, May had opened it.

'Honeybug,

I hated to do that to your mom, but it had to be. If things don't get better with those two, well, the money should help you move on. Sure will miss you, Honeybug, the best thing to come into my life in a long while. Bless you.'

Granddad always said not to rely on strangers. In the envelope with his letter had been a check. He knew she would need cash right away. May would rent a room, already had a list of places downloaded from a school library computer. Recently she recopied her birth certificate and other papers she needed, fudging a year so she could get a job. Next year, when her trust was open to her, May would get her license and a second-hand car. She'd be alone, but that would be a whole lot easier than being here. Tonight, she would buy a bus ticket to Vermont. May stood.

She listened to bird calls, breathed in the sun-warmed grass scent and said, "I'll miss this," to the tree.

She put her palm on the trunk, felt wetness, and lifted her hand. The glass splinter cut re-opened. Bright blood beads stood out on the rough bark and then, strangely, seeped in. She rubbed the area with her fingertips and felt a weird tingle. The old bark was awfully dry to soak up such moisture. May dug a tissue from her pocket and put pressure on her wound. She was calm now she had made up her mind. That changed when she returned from her hike.

Her mother was in her room. A cigarette pinched between her fingers filled it with its stink. Something was behind her on the bed.

"What's this?" her mother asked.

May's stomach clenched. Did she find Granddad's check?

Her mother slid May's laundry toward her with the backpack on top. "I was hanging underwear and needed clothespins. If you've got some boy thinking you're running off with him, miss, you'd better disappoint him before he does you."

May flushed.

"I suppose you're too good for any of the boys around here. Keep thinking that way." Her mother smirked. "You're better off."

Her mother took a drag. White streamers flew from her lips. "You think I don't know what it's like to fall for a guy? Your father was a real looker, met him at the lake. He owned a pricey boat he restored. I wanted a nice wedding. He sold that boat to make sure I got what I wanted."

What was her mother trying to say?

"Huh. You think you won't make my mistakes?" her mother asked. You'll make 'em. Just don't get silly ideas about how it'll turn out."

Her mother snorted. "You're not so different from me."

"I like to hike," May said. "I wanted it to carry a drink and a sandwich, maybe a book. That's all."

"Watch who you talk to when you're out there," her mother said, gripping May's arm to get up. "Stay away from that big bad wolf."

Her mother went downstairs.

May brushed ash from her faded spread and said softly, "I didn't make you have me."

The free calendar tacked to her wall showed a full moon tonight, perfect for finding her way. She smelled dinner. Since May had been out, her mother cooked because her father expected food on the table at five-thirty. It was strange to sit down with her parents, a last meal. Her father had ale at hand, her mother, vodka tea. So far dinner was drama-free.

"It was my birthday," May said.

Her mother lifted her head. "Oh, right, how old are you now?"

"Seventeen, Mother. I'm seventeen."

"Well, happy birthday," her mother said, swallowed tea.

"Yeah," her father said as he lit his after-dinner cigarette. "Why didn't we have a cake?"

"Don't look at me," her mother said.

"You should have said something." Her father gestured toward May with nicotine-stained fingers. "We could have had a cake."

"You know I don't bake," her mother said. "If you gave me enough household money, I could go to a bakery, get whatever we need."

Her father shoved his chair aside. "You already stock the freezer with enough vodka."

He stalked out of the room.

Her mother hurried after him yelling. Much later, their argument cooled down. When they were silent for a half-hour, it was eleven-forty-five. May slipped out with the backpack and got the suitcase from the garden shed. She went across the road, stepped into the field. Moonlight poured over boulders and brush. May headed for the woods to follow a logging road, a shortcut to the next town, where she would get a bus ticket. When she reached the apple tree, she slowed, turned for a last farewell glance.

Good riddance, her father would say, to bad rubbish. She hadn't turned all the way back around when she smacked into an apple branch, wasn't hurt but startled. She set down the suitcase, shifted her walking stick to that hand, and grabbed the branch with the other to move it aside. *A pins and needles feeling prickled in her palm.*

The sensation engulfed her arm, instantly spread into her entire body. The ground heaved, the sky turned to pitch. May's stomach lurched as if she'd hit the deepest dip of a tall roller coaster. A strangely hollow, disconnected feeling replaced it—then the world snapped like a giant rubber band. Impossibly, she sensed her body flew forward, her mind at war with what her eye could not see; that this occurred with incredible, unimaginable speed.

Chapter 2

*Why then should witless man so much misdeem
That nothing is, but that which he hath seen?*

May's stomach settled. Earthquakes were rare in Connecticut. She never thought she would experience one. At the same moment, the moon must have been covered by clouds because she could not see anything. Her suitcase had the flashlight she used to read in bed. She felt about for it, brushed a tree root. The ground shivered a second time.

Was that an aftershock? Forget the suitcase; May huddled close to the tree. Dawn was hours off, but as soon as there was enough light, she'd get moving again. At times, she heard sounds. Skunks, raccoons, and possums were regulars around here. May pulled off her backpack and curled up beside it, head on her arm. She did not know she had fallen asleep until something tickled her cheek.

She rubbed it, felt a crunch, and opened her eyes to a crippled ant on her fingers. Suddenly May felt others crawling in her hair, spied an ant hill where she had laid her head. She leapt up, tugged the compact brush from her pocket, flipped her hair over and brushed until she was sure no ants could be left. She straightened, shook her shirt and wiped her neck, glanced up.

"What—"

Her parent's house, cars, the barbed-wire fence, and the road were gone. May ran flat out, stumbled once, twice, but when she reached where the street should be, paused as if unseen cars might run her down. Where the house's front steps were not, May dug her fingers into the dirt, felt cool, crumbly soil. She touched her finger to her tongue, tasted, and spit. It was all real, of course it was, but the absence of everything she was running from was bizarre. Her anchor was the old apple tree.

May raced to her tree and scanned the woods, no, forest. It had trees of great heights and thick girths, nothing like the tame woods she knew. Dark beneath because of its mass of leaves, it was also too quiet. That pond was bigger, probably deeper than the pond May had skated, fished, and rafted on. At least the apple tree was the same.

No, it wasn't. Instead of little green apples, there were pink buds; this tree had not blossomed. Her stomach grumbled. May checked, yes, there was her pack, but where was the suitcase? Gone, though she'd set it by the tree. She spied the branch she grabbed, part of it was on the ground, perhaps it snapped when she fell. She touched the broken branch and gasped as a current sparked off her fingers. That wasn't as strange as the stick itself.

Midway down the bark was tiny offshoot with two apple blossoms. Above them was a small red apple. Below the blossoms, three tiny green apples. She'd never seen anything like it, so she tucked it in the pocket of her pack. Then she took out peanut-butter crackers and a can of soda. When done with breakfast, she shouldered the pack, took a deep breath.

Seeing how little food she had worried her. May didn't want to leave the one thing that felt as if it belonged to home, but she could not live under this tree. She must find other people, ask for a phone, and call her parents. Decided, she braided her hair to keep it off her neck as she started toward the pond. Closer to it, she stepped on grass tussocks and jumped stretches of mud. A rill escaped this end of the pond. May bent, washed her face, and then brushed her teeth. Flashing silver, tiny fish disturbed by her darted away. She got up, moved around several boulders near the shore.

"How fare you, sir? Forgive me, I misspoke, lady."

Frozen, it took several seconds before May glanced toward the speaker, a young man bent over in an exaggerated bow.

"Don't fear me, lady. I'm harmless, though some may not believe it. The name's Kester. Might I have yours?"

She took a step back. Was that a sword? Yes, and its scabbard, next to a bow and arrow quiver on the grass. May's skin goose-pimpled—he had a knife sheathed on his belt. A hunter, or was he a re-enactor? A group from area towns dressed in uniforms to play out battle scenes. Kester had to be eccentric to participate, but surely he would help her. While she studied him, he did the same to her.

"I believe you'd bolt like a hare could your legs carry you," he said with a smile.

His smile had charm, so she relaxed a bit.

"My name is May," she said in a shaky voice, "May

McKinny. I'm lost."

Kester considered her. "Where were you when you first thought so? It's meet to start at the beginning."

She looked back the way she'd come. "I thought over there, but," she said, "I don't know...somehow that's really far away from where I came from."

Her lower lip trembled.

"I was just going to brew té," Kester said. "My mam held everything looks better for a cup. Join me . . . May?"

All she wanted was to get home. Kester at least, seemed to know where he was, so she nodded. Acting on his invitation, Kester bent to the pond to fill a battered pot. He went round a huge rock. She followed. Here was his camp. A fire held glowing coals.

Once he propped the pot on its stone ring, he shoved in more wood. "Ready in short order. Pray, sit and rest."

She removed her backpack. As he measured out leaf for the pot, he watched her. The day was warming. May took off her jacket. Kester glanced at her chest, back up to her face, gave a choked-off cough and looked away. She never got that reaction before. Stealing a look down, she made sure her T-shirt covered what it should. Kester kept his face bland as he stirred the pot. Seated on the grass, she opened her backpack and drew out a baggy.

"Would you like some?"

He took the bag from her outstretched hand. "What would this be?"

"Raisins," May said, "dried grapes."

Kester looked over the bag, took raisins and tasted them, nodded. "Dried grapes, but what carries them?"

He dumped the rest on the ground and held up the baggy.

"Hey, don't waste my food. I don't have much with me."

Ignoring her, he sniffed, pulled, and poked.

"It's plastic. You've seen plastic before. It's everywhere," she said.

It ripped. "Not strong," he muttered.

"Look, I hope you're just acting in character," May said.

"What of my character?" Kester asked. "What have you heard? Does someone question my honor?"

"I'm not, that's not what I meant," May said. "I was referring to this role you're playing. Are you supposed to be a spy? Is that why you're alone in the woods?"

Kester lost his humor. He stood and pulled her pack from her, started to rifle in it. The sudden change alarmed her so, she didn't protest. He held up her plastic soap container, thumped it.

He opened it, sniffed. "Soap, but this box that holds it, what wood is it?"

"You know it's plastic. Stop acting weird," May said.

A light filled his face. "You... you're one of them? So young too, yet it must be. Nothing else can explain your outlandish garments and foreign goods. What other wonders do you bring with you?"

She snatched the soap box from his hand. "Just drop

your act for now. What do you think you look like to someone who doesn't get what you're doing? You're wearing a knife; you've got a sword. Don't know what plastic is."

Kester stepped back. "Perhaps you're more dangerous than you appear. You have no visible weapons. How do you defend yourself? Do you hide a threat in that sack? Or do you use your staff? Are you a mage?"

With speed, he was beside the spot she left her walking stick leaning on the boulder and tossed it aside. May rocked on her feet.

"Don't stir." Kester slid the knife out of its scabbard. "I have deadly aim."

He dumped her pack's contents and examined everything with suspicion, except for the bras and panties thank you, which he had the decency to ignore. When he shook a can of soda, she snapped.

"Don't do that."

"Nah!" Kester dropped it as if it bit his fingers.

May picked it up. "It's soda."

She shook it gently by his ear, "it's a drink that's fizzy. If you shake it hard, it'll burst out."

Kester steered clear of soda cans, but dug into every pocket in the pack, stopping to study her dad's old compass. The pointer jittered back and forth over its face.

May put her hands on her hips. "This is getting ridiculous."

He'd found the side slot with the branch. Kester frowned

over it longer than she did. Finally he poked at her toothpaste.

She snatched up the tube, opened the cap, and waved it under his nose. "It's mint."

"I know this herb," he said. "We use it in té when the stomach needs soothing."

"Can I take my things?"

He nodded grudgingly.

May stuffed the pack with Kester intent on her every movement. "I...I'll go now."

Kester put his knife back in its sheath. He crouched by his fire, added a lump of what looked like sugar to the pot and poured two mugs, setting one at arms' length.

"I meant no harm, Lady. Please...the té...join me."

She picked up the mug and sat as far as politeness allowed. If she acted normal, perhaps he would calm down.

"Thank you." She blew and sipped.

"You understand I'm not playing a part in what you're doing?" May asked. "So why should I carry a weapon?

"Your claim is strange, Lady. Everything about your person gives you away. You must be powerful not to hide your nature. Perhaps it's inexperience? If that is the case, Lady, you're in for more trouble than you might wish."

She ticked her head saying no without words. "I'm just lost. That's all. I hate to ask what you think I'd be doing out here."

"Why, Lady," Kester said reasonably. "It's certain you're a rover. You can be naught else. Though I've never met one before, I'm versed in the signs. I must say it's more interesting to meet one than to hear the tales."

She'd had enough of his weirdness and slowly rose.

"It's been nice…talking, but I… should leave. To get home, nice to meet you," she added, as she pulled on her backpack. "Will you give me back my compass?"

"This?" Kester took it out of his pocket. "Why does it move so?" He looked intently at the compass face.

It was like speaking to a child. "This is a directional finder. See, the N stands for north; the compass will always find true north. It helps you find your way."

Or it should. "I'd like it back, please."

Reluctant, Kester handed it to her. "Perhaps you might tell me its secrets?"

"Sorry. I'll go now. Alone."

"You think to go about in those garments, unarmed, you say, alone?" He shook his head. "If that is your wish, I'll not keep you from your journey. Press on, Lady. Fare you well."

Going to her walking stick, May picked it up, expecting any moment Kester might try to stop her. Relieved when nothing happened, she walked up the hill above the pond, twisting about to check on him several times, but all he did was watch. As she walked, confidence returned to her.

If she'd gotten disoriented last night, then the state forest was over the hill. The town of Chester lay northeast of it. She checked the compass and adjusted her path toward the field's right corner. There was a tangled border of brush and then trees. Her earlier fear of the forest beyond it was replaced by her desire to put distance between Kester and herself. An hour later she had to worry about her sanity, because if trees like these existed in her part of Connecticut, they would be as celebrated as California's Redwoods. She'd just made her way around a trunk wide as a house. As this sank in, her body trembled.

She could be hallucinating or crazy. May tripped and banged her elbow hard landing. Tears of pain turned into sobs.

Chapter 3

Approaching nigh, he never stayed to greet,
Nor bandy words, proud courage to provoke,
But pricked so fierce, that underneath his feet
The smoldering dust did round about him smoke

When the mysterious rover passed over the hill, Kester raced to keep up with her. The steep slope leveled into a meadow of grasses taller than he. Through the funnel she'd trampled though them, she disappeared into the forest. He did not dwell on what or whom she rushed to meet, though when she named him a spy, Kester barely hid his shock. She marked him for a scout, but how? He must find out, so he picked up his pace.

A rover was no one to trust, especially with his responsibilities. Kester plunged into the woods. Light stabbed the undergrowth at first but dimmed further in. He soon found her by the sounds she made huddled crying. With a flush of sympathy, he helped her up, put his arm about her. May stared with reddened eyes, but didn't pull away. He led her back to the high field.

"N-nothing. . . I remember." Her voice wavered. "My house was down there."

He barely understood what she said.

"Cars, planes, electric poles…where did they go?" she asked. "Nothing's right, nothing."

She suffered shock.

"You're not alone," he said. "You know Kester now. If you wish, I'll not leave your side. You're lost, more so than you can accept, I'm thinking. Perhaps you'll allow the truth of what I've said? You're a rover gone far off your mark. If you stick with me, you'll soon find I've not lied. Your garments will cause problems though. I've not met a lady who'd go about in the manner you've arrived here in. I must find something fit for your sex."

When she didn't respond, he kept quiet until they reached his camp. "We'll stop here. I don't think you could walk further this day."

He helped her to a tarp stretched between saplings, his blanket spread under it, bade her take a seat. Instead, she lay down and closed her eyes, perhaps the best way to escape. He shouldn't have promised to help her. No matter her distress, she represented a danger. As a scout, it was Kester's duty to bring her before the King to be examined. If the King agreed she was a rover, she could be imprisoned. Of course, Kester was far from court; he might find a way to do something for her well before it came to that. When she woke, it was early evening.

"There's hot té," Kester said.

She jerked about, moaned, and said, "You're still here."

"I gave an oath."

"Sorry," she said. "I didn't mean…I hoped it was all a bad dream."

Kester poured her té and stirred his stew.

"Smells good," she said.

"Oh, aye," Kester said, "I've done my share of cooking in the wild."

She sipped from the mug he'd handed her.

"I measured your position while you slept," he said. "I should share what I know of rovers. I believe it will help you appreciate the dangers you face on this world."

She stiffened when he mentioned danger. It was certain fear could overwhelm her again. Still, she nodded for him to continue.

"Rovers appear on Illynd in times of upheaval. Some argue they're sent to keep the powers of Illynd in balance. I don't credit that notion. Power comes to those who seek it for good or ill. In the past, rovers allied themselves with those who've caused much ruin, and yet, they've helped others who've done some good."

"You're not making sense," she said. "I have no powers. I was running away from home. I don't know what you're talking about."

"Running? Earlier you argued you were lost."

"I was… I am lost. I don't know how or why I'm here. The only thing that's the same is the apple tree, well, it looks different but everything else, everything that used to be where I came from is gone."

"Show me this tree," Kester said.

She got up, walked around the stone and pointed.

"There in the field."

"Take us to it."

May led while Kester watched all about, his hand at his dirk. The apple tree was a dark spot before the shadowed woods. Close up, Kester said, "Looks like any 'orphan' apple tree, most likely started by a passing bird."

"I just crossed the field heading for the pond when I fell," she said, almost to herself. "That's when everything went strange. I thought it was an earthquake."

"A what?"

"The earth, the ground shakes," she said.

"I've heard such happens farther south," he said.

"You were here yesterday. You felt nothing?" she asked.

"No."

"But it happened," May said. "The moon was bright and its light just . . . went out all at once, at the same time as the shaking started. No. First, I brushed away a branch, then I fell, and this tree...it's—"

She shook her head. "It hasn't flowered yet. The one I left had green apples."

She faltered and her eyes filled up.

"Somehow, someway your actions caused you to land here," he said. "They might send you back."

Kester hoped she grasped his meaning, took it to heart. He must harden himself to indifference for her plight.

"But I was just walking," she cried. "I'd been here...there, hundreds of times. None of this makes sense."

When they settled back at the fire ring, Kester 'baked'

camp bread on a rock heated by the coals, shared that bread and the stew he made earlier. Afterward, May readied herself for sleep, pulling ties from her braid. The wealth of chestnut hair about her head altered her.

Did she know how it looked sliding over her shoulders? She should. There was not a female her age who didn't understand her appeal. He busied himself scouring pots while she brushed that hair. When next he glanced her way, she'd wrapped her hair in a scarf and knotted it, yawned.

"I guess I'll go to sleep. I don't have a blanket though."

"Mine must do," Kester said. "Many a time I've made a grassy bed."

"Thank you, Kester."

"If you wake in the night, do not wander far," he said.

"The last thing I want to do is to bump into anything in the dark," May said. "Good night."

Kester listened to night sounds as the campfire glowed. Soon the twitches and adjustments of his guest settled into even breathing. The night sky crowded with bright pinpoints. One moment he watched stars, the next he was asleep. Chill air woke him. He could use a blanket. Other lights caught his notice, too low for stars, buoyant specks trailing down the hillside. They were bright in their centers and hazy at their edges, captivating the eye while cavorting to music he did not hear. He glanced across the red embers of his fire. Gone!

A dark shape stood between him and the beckoning lights. Springing up, he ran calling her, but May ignored him. The glittering dots hovered under the forest's canopy. Almost out of hearing, Kester detected mirthful music. He shouted.

"May! May! Come to my voice. Don't follow them."

Almost in reach, he shouted another warning. Hesitating, May looked over her shoulder but turned back. The lights skipped up and down. She took another step, and a cloud of spores enveloped her like smoke. He reached out, but May disappeared from mortal sight.

"Fool!"

He cursed.

Chapter 4
Which else could not endure those beams bright,
But would be dazzled with exceeding light.

The music was barefoot in green-grass, stars rippling
across a pond, the moon's face so close May could kiss it
enchanting. Her body swayed, dipped, and twirled. Arms
wide, she danced, danced, and danced. Then someone took
her hand, held her waist, a dancing partner. He tugged
something from her head, her hair flew about. He smiled,
bowed. May beamed back. The dance went on, but not for
her.

May was led from the dance firmly, her partner's hand
pressed into the small of her back. Colors reflected off a
multitude of mirror-bright surfaces to overload May's vision.
Stepping uncertainly, she blinked. A golden chair stood
nearby. Her partner offered May the seat, which she took.
Only then did she realize great weariness in all her limbs, as
though she had danced for uncounted time. A goblet was put
in her hand. Parched for drink, she did. It was refilled for her
as soon as it emptied. The liquid tasted like ripe berries,
honey, and herbs. Strength coursed through her. Three
glassfuls and she was renewed in body but confused. She sat
straighter, gazed at her surroundings.

May's bewilderment grew on seeing gold walls etched
with woods, meadows, and mountains. Gold tree-trunk
columns rose to support a silver ceiling incised with clouds.
Too brilliant to stare at, so she glanced down. The floor

sparkled like diamonds whose facets threw off sparks so fiery they made her blink tears—she shut her eyes.

"Sweet," her dancing partner said.

At that moment, May opened them and was immediately ruled by his glittering blue gaze. There was a force in her incredible dancing partner kin to soaring granite cliffs. She was the sea washing their feet.

He touched her cheek with a finger. "Tell us your name. We will proclaim it to all present."

"May, my name…May McKinny," she said, unwilling and unable to resist his request. Other striking males and exotic females pressed close. Suddenly May knew how a caterpillar invading a gathering of glorious butterflies felt. Her partner lifted a glass and saluted.

"Let all present learn the name, May, of clan McKinny. We are fallen under her spell, and proclaim her our new consort."

On hearing his baffling assertion, May recalled everything that happened to her. Leaving her parents, the uncanny disappearance of all she knew, meeting Kester, and then following the extraordinary lights. What did her dance partner want from her? Under her spell, who did he think he fooled? In spite of the overwhelming beauty surrounding her, May knew whatever this was all about, meant everything just got worse for her.

"Let us drink to May! May and Prince Aidan!"

While they were toasted, a group broke away and

disappeared among those crowded at the rear of the large chamber.

"Escort our consort to the Rose Rooms," her dance partner, Prince Aidan said. "See she's groomed and suitably attired."

Several childlike females came up to May, but one took her hand. Where was Kester? She had not fully trusted him, but his company was sound and sober compared to what she faced now.

"Come along, come along," coaxed light, musical voices. "Don't be shy, Pixies don't bite. That would be Imps. They bite."

They giggled. The little female steering May urged her away from the others. "Come to your rooms. They're lovely rooms. No need to fear. You're out of the dance. Lucky to be free, come away with me. I'm called Bri. I'll look after you. This way, this way."

Like a stick in a stream, May allowed Bri, a diminutive creature half as tall as she, to pull her along. Golden-brown hair tamed to a knot at the back of Bri's small head. Her wide yellow eyes upturned, Bri smiled encouragement as she led May along gold corridors. The air left a spicy-sweet taste in May's mouth—from incense? She might be mad, but she'd created a rich environment to enjoy it. Bri stopped in front of a door etched with pink-tinted, gold roses.

She pushed it open onto a sitting room with a pearly radiance. May went closer, stared at its walls. "Are those crushed pearls?"

"What else, my lady?" the pixy said.

Sure, pearl walls were nothing after walking on diamonds. Rose-velvet seats were arrayed about the space. The fireplace was picked out by glittering green tiles and a rose-gold mantle.

"Your bed," Bri said as she drew May into the next room.

Bed? It had gold arches entwined with living white roses. May discovered that because she plucked one, smelled it, and bruised its petals in her fingers. The arches supported a sheer curtain that trailed down the back, across the top, and over the bed's front. Piled with silk pillows, a dove-white blanket folded at its foot.

"Here is the water closet," Bri said.

"That is the bathtub?" May asked of a golden pool set in the floor, long and large enough to float four.

"Bathing pool, yes," Bri said.

The pool faced a smaller fireplace similar to the one in the sitting room, its tiles—emeralds? May didn't doubt it. As if a bloom on its stem was a sink, petals opened to make a bowl. Behind its private door, the toilet's gold tank hung overhead Victorian style. How could so much wealth exist in one place? Why was she seeing this? Was it because of her real home?

May's farmhouse bedroom had paint curls over every inch of it. Before her father bought the house, fire boiled the room's paint before it was fast cooled by fireman spraying water. Worse, those curls were lead paint. Her parent's room was gutted and redone, but not hers. Drinking killed her father's fix-it ambitions. May left the past to consider her current situation.

Did she hallucinate this? She could be in a coma, her mind creating this elaborate fantasy. She pinched herself and then poked Bri's arm.

Bri giggled. "Prince Aidan offers the best for his consort."

"I'm no consort," May said. "This is a mistake."

"Don't fear, my lady. You'll be merry in our fairy realm. For terrans it is a life of delight."

Fairies—here was a twisted version of the most pleasant memory May had of her mother. She'd taken her on a picnic, and while her three-year-old self nibbled her sandwich, her mother convinced May fairies lived in flowers. Ever since May investigated any new flower she saw; silly, but that day was the high point of her childhood.

"My lady, I must leave. I'll return shortly," Bri said.

May sat in the first room and sudden pain hit her stomach. She was starved. Bri must know, as she returned with a tray, which she set by May. Fantasy food perhaps, but May tried hot biscuits with a wedge of cheese. Little boiled eggs sliced alongside dainty vegetables. Bites of cake topped with spun sugar, and water, ice cold fresh. She could taste, eat, and swallow. Perhaps she did not imagine this.

If not, did this place have something to do with Kester's vague warnings? May went to the door, opened it. The hall was empty. If this was more of wherever she ended up by mistake, then she must find a way out, though she'd seen none on her way to these rooms. The idea of doing anything at all fled. Drained, May managed to wash up before she collapsed into dreamless sleep.

Bri shook May awake. For several heart-tumbling moments, May struggled to understand why she was in trouble.

"How do you feel?" Bri asked.

May, certain she'd only snatched a few minutes rest, said, "Like someone who's lost her mind."

Bri laughed, dumped yards of material across the bed. "You'll find it, my lady. Meanwhile, take wine to recover. Here," she said, handing her a glass.

This stuff was fairy caffeine on steroids.

Bri slid over the fabric pile. "After you bathe, we will fit your gowns. The Prince expects the finest for his consort."

"Please," May said as she got off the bed, "no consort stuff. Who is he prince of? Where am I?"

"Even for a terran, you know so little," Bri said with a shake of her head. "Prince Aidan is the head of the Guilly Clan, the most powerful in the Realm of the Daoine Sidhe," Bri said.

"The *deenee shee*?" May said. "I thought you were fairies."

Bri hooked an errant curl beside her ear. "Fairy is a newer name for our proud ancient race."

"Alright, then why would this Prince bother with me?" May asked.

Prince Aidan discovered your glorious red hair and proclaimed his passion for you. There'll be trouble out of it, I said to Lia, a friend from the kitchens. No one crosses Princess Kerriena, not even a great prince such as Aidan. I was right...Princess Kerriena took a terran out of the dance not long after you were chosen. He'll pop up, I told Lia, when the Princess can use him to advantage."

"Wait, wait," May said. "I have reddish hair, so this prince decides he loves me? Nothing here makes sense. I'm just a lost girl...a man was helping me. I must get back to him."

"Red hair is rare among fairies. They chase it, though Prince Aidan never had before," Bri said, "but be glad of yours. Some are never let free of the Dance 'til their limbs lock up. I hope your friend isn't there."

May had to find out. "I don't need any prince. I don't want to be here. I'm going back where I came from. I can handle another year before I can be on my own."

"You'll be cared for here," Bri said as she patted May's arm. "The legendary Guinnemara adored her fairy lover, gave him offspring before her beauty faded. She went back among Terrans rewarded by treasures her lover bestowed on her."

"You mean," May said, "fairies and hu...terrans can have children?"

"Yes, but they are changelings and so must stay with the

Realm," Bri said.

"They made her leave her children? That's horrible," May said.

"Why?" Bri asked as she waved her arms about. "The Realm is comfort, luxury, the finest of everything. You've been selected, a great honor. Prince Aidan is more handsome than any fairy."

Bri studied May. "He chose well. You're fine-boned, fresh. When I'm done, you'll not know yourself. See the gowns I've brought. This blue enlivens your gray eyes. The gold picks out red lights in your hair."

May touched them. "They're too thin. I couldn't wear these."

"Oh, child of earth." Bri giggled. "This is spider silk, pixy weave! Feather soft and steel strong, you will see. Now, I've drawn a bath. Use the bottled decoction for hair and smooth the jarred balm over all your skin, even your face. Mind, wear these after," she added, handing over what must be fairy underwear.

After seeing the gowns, it was nice to know they wore them. May was glad to bathe, feared it was days since she'd been in the wild with Kester. She eased into the pool's scented water. A fat sponge completed a decadent experience that was lost on her. She kept wondering where Kester was now. If he was caught in the dance, could she get him out? Frightening at first for his strangeness, his kindness offset that. Not that he was scary in himself. Sun-streaked hair, tied with a leather string, framed a well-cut face. Expressive brown eyes sparked with humor and intelligence. He might be a few years older than she was. In any other circumstance, she would have not have spoken to him.

A loner at school, May never dated, never held hands with, let alone kissed a boy. She slipped further into the water. Though their first meeting seemed mad, Prince Aidan wasn't someone to take lightly. Not with his intense, under-her-spell nonsense. Shaking off thoughts of Prince Aidan, May soaked as the hearth fire crackled. This was nothing like her run-down home, but right now she would trade every comfort here for it. She reached for the bottle.

Even as she washed with whatever was in fairy shampoo, her hair felt incredible, like silky threads. Out of the bath, May wrapped in a towel, then opened the jar and sniffed. Flower fragrant, but light—she rubbed it into her face, neck, body, even her feet. It made her skin shine. She drew on silk underwear and then, there was no other word to describe it, bound herself with the deceptively pretty silk corset. It had no straps, but pushed up and in with an iron will not evident in the design or material. When done, she peeked out the door. There was a robe on the bed. She came out, pulled it on and tied it. A gilded table held a silver brush and comb set. She sat on its seat and finished her hair when Bri came in. The pixy picked up the comb and put it to work.

"I just did that," May said.

Bri clucked, pulled out drawers to reveal combs, pins,

strands of crystals, and other accessories May didn't recognize. Bri smoothed cream from a new jar that made her hair shine. It was soothing to be fussed over.

"Lovely," Bri said when she'd finished putting in combs. "I've brought another tray."

"Bri," May said as settled in the other room to eat again, hungry though she'd eaten before her bath. "Could you show me about? I'd feel better if I could look around."

Even better if she found a way out.

"Of course, my lady, after we've done your gown," Bri said.

"If you've cleaned my clothes, I'll wear them."

"Those won't do here, my lady, not now you're Prince Aidan's consort," Bri said.

"I am no one's consort, Bri."

Bri hung her head.

"All right…if I like the gown, and only so I fit in. For now," May said.

So it was her own fault May stood in a silk corset and panties telling herself they covered more than her bikini, while trying on gown after gown so Bri could decide which style suited May. Finally she let May wear a gold, sleeveless gown gathered near the bosom.

"The fit could be better," Bri said. She opened a packet May hadn't noticed before, took a pinch of something in her fingers, and blew it at the gown.

May sneezed, but the gown glowed as its material pulled

tighter to her shoulders, back, everywhere it lay near her skin, and then the glow faded.

Bri said, "Done," and led May to the mirror.

"You're kidding—" May lifted the cloth, dropped it.

"The spider silk reknit itself to your shape. All natural matter falls under the influence of fairy powers," Bri said.

Of course they do.

"Very graceful you are," Bri said. "The Prince will approve."

May stared, for where was she in that reflection? Certainly the creams she used were more fairy magic, because she had never seen this self. Mirror-May's figure was enhanced by the fitted gown. Her image's hair was tumbled-down sensual, her features luminous. Bri held out sandals for her to slip into. May turned away, put them on. Then Bri rubbed a fragrant ointment over May's arms.

"Flawless." Bri beamed when she was done.

When Bri ushered her around, May felt stranger. There was no knowing if it was day or night. The female fairies had one style, gowns, glorious hair, precious jewels, and the males were just as formally beautiful. Oddly, not one fairy appeared old or even middle-aged. She saw no fairy children. They passed under blown-glass chandeliers, moved alongside massive mirrors in gold frames and walked by whole rooms veneered with marvelous tiles.

"They're sliced gems," Bri said when May stopped to study them.

One room was copper sheeted, its lower half hammered with an attractive pattern. Its pillars mimicked trees with gold, silver, and shining copper leaves. Yet May grew more concerned. Nowhere did she see a window showing the real sky or a door leading to the outside, so how did she get in? How would she get out? Many rooms had tables laid with platters brilliant as iridescent insect shells. They displayed little cakes, tiny sandwiches, and delicate vegetables with sauces, teeny eggs in speckled shells, and fanciful fruits. Alongside them were carafes of herb wine and crystal glasses. Fresh herbs and flowers filled vases. May went from bouquet to bouquet; each flower was a flawless bloom. Small trees blossomed in urns. Flowered swags twined with silk ribbons hung on walls. So dazzled was May, she bumped into a teeny fairy.

"I'm sorry, forgive me," May said.

She'd made the fairy tip a tray of used goblets. May helped right the glasses while trying desperately not to stare. His, her, hairless head was shaped as sort of a cap, smooth over the top with a sharp-edged jaw. The fairy's eyes were slits, the nose merely an opening in its cap-like head, the mouth barely visible.

Bri came up; the fairy was half as tall as Bri, wore like others working nearby a top, pants, and boots. They had pale, dark, or reddish skin. The fairy May jolted had orange spots on brown skin, and kept up a steady mumble-grumble just loud enough for May to catch. As Bri led her away, May asked,

"What sort of fairy is it?"

The irritable sounds the fairy made rose.

"What, the grumby? Pay no mind," Bri said. "They're like that. Fairies kindled them, but they've never stopped complaining since. They wanted to stay planted, breaking forest into soil. You'll see that lot doing the dirty work, as they complain. Of course, Pixies do the finer work here."

"What do you mean, the fairies kindled them?" May asked. "What were they before?"

"Mushrooms," Bri said shaking her head. A curl popped free, and she tried but lost the battle to tuck it in her bun. "Fairies stirred them from sleep."

"How do they do that?" May said. "I don't understand."

"Fairy power is not to be meddled in. They did it is all you need know. Here's the Hall of Dance."

People twirled, swayed, skipped, their faces blissful. Some were humble farmers in heavy boots. Several were brawny young men. There were mystified children waving thin arms. Others had frail, withered limbs, garments pitifully worn. Here was the boil on this fantastically rich realm, the visible one at least.

The music called to May. She held her hands over her ears. These people capered away their lives to amuse fairies who sat, stood, ate as they watched, or in most cases, ignored the dance. What evil creatures was she caught up with? Kester said so little of Illynd. Why didn't he give her more warning? May turned away. A hand grasped her arm hard.

Chapter 5

Of Faerie land yet if he more inquire,
By certain signs here set in sundry place
He may it find

Kester grabbed for her a hair too late. May was gone, perhaps forever. Panting, he cursed himself for letting her fall asleep before he properly frightened her with tales of this forest. Where she'd been was an irregular circle of faintly glowing mushrooms. He cursed again. There was no other way. He stepped into the ring. A fresh wave of spores hit.

"Fool," he snapped.

Even a great fool wouldn't tempt what Kester was getting himself into. Haunting notes overwhelmed him. A kaleidoscope whirl of winking lights and pulsing colors dazzled him. He struggled to keep hold of his senses while he strained to discover May. This blasted fae trap doomed them both unless, perhaps she was a lure to bring him here? All his life he'd thought he was too wise to be caught; yet pretty May snagged him through his honest efforts to help her. The mistake was his. He had responsibilities, important ones, and now who would take them on? Kester capered to the poignant music, hating it, unable to resist it. Others were alongside him, dancing to amuse those unseen beyond the fae glamour that bound them. A soft hand touched his.

It came with a face fine beyond measure, cool, elegant, the fairest creature ever, and she danced with him. Hair so pale it silvered above violet eyes, whitest skin with a touch of

43

rose, her filmy shift swirled about her flawless form. But when she pulled Kester from the melody puppeting his legs and fogging his brain, he knew only reluctant relief.

A drink was thrust into his hand. Several times Kester held the cup out for more. Exhaustion fell away from him. His surroundings focused. The stunning fae who singled Kester out paid him no mind, but watched something at the far end of the great hall. Damned faes; what sort of trouble were they brewing up? His fae made a gesture, and faes hovering nearby moved Kester along with her. Several minutes and many twists and turns later, Kester found himself in another chamber.

This hall's great door shut with a bolt once they all gathered inside. The fae who chose him sat in a silver seat, then jumped up and began to pace. Sensual energy sizzled in a charged circle about her. Kester was mesmerized by her long throat, the curve where her waist nipped in, couldn't tear his gaze away when her lips parted to expose her brilliant teeth.

"Peace, Princess Kerriena, peace, all will come right in the end. This is but a ploy to try your patience. All will come right," one of the males at the Princess' side said.

The Princess; of course she would be, stopped pacing to pout at Kester. "He's fair enough, but will he cooperate with our plan? Let us see what wit he may possess."

She stepped right in front of Kester. Deep down he understood hers was the kind of beauty that could make a man hopeless and helpless, but added to this was fae glamour. He must reject her appeal, tell himself what he saw was a shell that covered something foul.

"My lady," Kester bent his head. "You've honored me by choosing me from the dance. How may I please you?"

"You seem an intelligent fellow for your kind." She sniffed. "You may do us a service, but not at this moment. You will rest and refresh yourself until we send for you. What are you called, boy?"

"I'm Kester, my lady, no boy among my own, but a man."

"Just Kester? No clan name?"

"No, my lady. I'm too humble to claim a clan."

"We see. Very well, you're dismissed."

The Princess stepped away and was immediately surrounded by advisors that followed her through another door. He started to follow just to watch her, that was all, but a male pixy placed himself at Kester's elbow, tugged his sleeve.

"Please come with me, sir. I'm to be your servant."

"What are you—" Kester shook off the pixy's hand, realized he'd tripped into the enchantment the Princess cast. He'd have to fight harder to keep his wits. Kester studied the pixy's upturned, grass-green eyes and wildly curly hair.

"Well, what do they call you?" he asked, amused.

"Call me hey you, come here, do this or do that, sir, it's no mind to me."

"You have a name," Kester said.

"If that's what's needed, call me Con, sir. Simple and

sweet that. Her highness has spoken. Please follow me."

They went down a corridor until Con opened a door onto a room faced with silver. Its silvered bed was draped with a blue coverlet. A fire glowed in the fireplace, though it was said faes felt no cold. Perhaps fire was used here for how it looked, which made as much sense as anything in this cursed place. A crystal table was nearby. On it was food and a pitcher of herb wine.

"See, sir, here is the water closet," Con opened a panel in the wall. "As an escort of the Princess, you'll want proper garments. Tall for a terran, sir, you'll look elegant groomed. Please eat, drink. I'll come by after with all you'll need."

"Thank you, Con."

Con bowed. "No thanks to me, sir. I'm your servant, after all, sir."

As soon as the pixy left, Kester sank with trembling legs onto a settee. No telling how long he was stuck in the infernal dance. It could be anywhere from hours, months, or worse, years. He didn't feel older, but badly needed a shave. He was fair famished too, so first things first. He tucked into the food, craving meat. The fae aversion to blood fare meant he must do without. His hunger cured, the desire to payback May for luring him here was uppermost.

He didn't have the luxury of revenge, much less the means. His da, did he ever hear of this folly, would be unsympathetic. He had wanted Kester to wed any one of the more suitable young women Kester flirted with, stop rambling, and work alongside him. Con reappeared

"I've your bath ready, sir," Con said.

Kester was finished feeling sorry for himself. While he soaked, Con came in with new garments for him. Out of the bath pool, he sat in a towel and allowed Con to shave what looked a week's beard off his face.

"Here sir," Con said as he raised scissors. "Sit still, sir, and you won't lose an ear."

Kester knew Con followed orders, so he let the pixy trim his hair neat. He begrudgingly wore the velvet tunic and fancy trousers, but felt a fool in black leather boots, slippers, Con called them—useless for tramping in the wild. Afterward there was another tray waiting, as if to make up for what he'd missed in that damned Dance.

Fae food was tasty, yet unsatisfactory. Kester wanted the savory meats and heartier breads of home. He must get back, not for the food, but to give his king a full report of his stupidity. For now he would get round this place, spy out its secrets. The Dance of Fools would be where to start, but he'd eat these silly slippers if he found May anywhere near there. He should let thoughts of her go.

Duty didn't send him into this snare. Still, he couldn't be sure she fell into the fae ring by accident or design. That distinction meant all the difference, a fool's errand indeed if she lied to him. Con bustled about the room putting things right while humming.

"Con, I'd like to walk the halls. Is that possible?"

"I don't see why not, sir. Her highness will want you happy."

"Good," Kester said. "I'm off."

"I'll show you about, sir. Otherwise, you'd never find your way. That could cause trouble. Can't have that, sir."

"Fine, let's get on."

Con led him to the Hall of Dance. Since neither night nor day existed for them, many faes were about. Kester wondered where to go next when he spotted her. Shorter than these tall faes, May stood out for another reason. Done up in their fashion, May's shining hair was more of an adornment than the rich jewels these females' wore, her youth more tangible than their ageless veneer. After taking a circular route to be unnoticed, Kester seized her, said, "How at home you appear."

Her wide eyes sparked with recognition, relief, and gladness he was hoped wasn't false, considering he'd snuck up on her. He kept hold of her arm and escorted her to a chair away from the pixy shadowing her, and as far from the other faes in the room as he could get.

"Oh, Kester, I've never been so glad. I was afraid you were in that forced show they call a dance. I was there until this prince, Aidan, led me out. What's happened to us?"

Kester wondered that she played naïve still, but it did not appear she wielded a rover's weight among these creatures. Nor did she act as if she'd been dosed with fae glamour to make her insensible to her true self.

"I should have warned you about Fools' Lights, you so

green to this world, I'm to blame," Kester said. "When I saw you caught up, it was only right I go after you. I was taken out of the dance by Princess Kerriena."

He let go of her arm, and she rubbed it. "We're in danger with this lot. They're proud and powerful. Tell me, why did this prince take you from the dance?"

May took a deep breath and spoke all in a rush. "It's ridiculous. Said he was under my spell. They've even tried to do me up like one of them. How do we get out of here? These fairies, they're horrible. They make sport of those poor people, it's awful."

His doubts about her eased another degree. "Bad as that looks, I suspect we've landed in the midst of clans fighting for control, which means we're involved in things we must get free of. I'll see what I can discover about this power struggle and how to get out to the world. In the meantime, be contrary with this Prince, and take care what you eat or drink."

"I already ate." She looked as if she'd faint.

He inwardly cursed himself. "You're alright, I can tell. I meant to say, if you find yourself alone with this Prince, that's the time to take care. If you haven't heard of fae glamour, the short of it is, they use their powers over us, to bend us this way and that. Most times I imagine these creatures expect their celebrated beauty will work for them, but if a fae takes a fancy toward you—"

"They wouldn't care what I think, you mean."

"It's more of what's done to that lot," Kester said, with a

gesture at the unfortunate dancers. "Nothing is what is seems here, May."

He studied her moist eyes for several seconds. "They must not discover how you came to Illynd."

Again, her fair face drained. She breathed fast, fought to control herself. If she were a liar, she was accomplished.

He put his hand on her arm, lightly this time. "I'll look for you again later. Stay alert, pry into everything, but don't get caught. Between us we'll find our way out of this fae warren."

From her expression, she mustered all of her resolve to go back to her pixy, who led her away. Perhaps it hadn't been a mistake to go after May, or at least, not too big of one.

Con was at his side. "The Princess asks for you, sir."

Before he was escorted to her, Kester snapped a rose from a vase, sniffed it, and tucked it in his pocket. Princess Kerriena sat at her crystal table, advisors all about her. She'd changed into a shift shimmering with sapphire beads; a be-jeweled spider spinning webs to catch the unwary. Con led him to an empty seat. Bowing first to the Princess, Kester said, "My lady."

"Princess or your highness is the proper address, oaf," a fae to her right said.

Princess Kerriena intervened, her tone sweet. "Kester, isn't it? My lady has an intimate touch…we allow it between us. We have a function to attend, Kester. We require you at our side."

"If I am to help you, my lady, I should be taught," Kester said.

She frowned at her advisors. "Leave us."

Her courtiers did so reluctantly. Princess Kerriena poured fey brew for Kester and herself.

"Drink," she said when he didn't take his glass.

"I'm not thirsty, my lady."

She smiled and took a sip from his. "We don't employ a fairy charm."

"A certain prince would see through such devices?" he asked.

Her eyes narrowed for a brief second. Then she laughed. "Quite intelligent for a terran, we've made a good choice; not one of these rube farmers or pig-butchers. One to catch any lady's eye, as you caught ours."

She placed a delicate hand on Kester's.

"No need to play lover for me, my lady. I'll help make your prince jealous. All I ask is to be let go when my usefulness is done. And if I please you, with a small reward?"

"You fear to love us, terran? Perhaps a clear head is what's needed. Stay by our side. Look on no other. Dance only with us. Let us see where this game will take us."

She withdrew her hand. "Prince Aidan's tedious courtship play will end. He will renounce his new poppet too."

She stood and smoothed her gown. "Give us your arm."

Kester bent his elbow. When they joined the revel, the Princess Kerriena spotted May and hitched in her stately glide.

Prince Aidan kept May close, though she appeared annoyed with him. His opinion of May skipped up several notches. For his part, Kester danced with, smiled adoringly at, and otherwise acted devoted to the Princess, but the farce had no visible effect on the Prince. When the Prince made a show of giving May a priceless gift, Princess Kerriena and her entourage left. Freed, Kester went to his room.

First thing, he sucked the wound he got from the rose thorn he'd hid in his pocket, buried so deep into the pad of his hand now, he had to pull it out with his teeth. It had been worth the pain. He'd pressed the thorn every time he needed reminding he did not adore the Princess. When that wound stopped bleeding, he pulled on his own clothes. He slipped out alone to look about.

The halls and rooms held knots of faes, a pixy here, and grumbies everywhere doing cleanup. In each space, he sought a door or opening. If the room was empty, he wasted no time searching for a way outside. Not once did he come across any. He had an idea when he spied grumbies with dirty trays.

They ended up in a large kitchen. Numerous grumbies worked under few pixies, cleaning gold and silver plate. Breads and cakes baked. Fruits were washed and cut while sweet butter churned. Kester couldn't see where the supplies came from. However, he noted pixies in charge wore keys.

One pixy entered a storeroom filled with barrels and sacks. They came in at some point. They didn't conjure foodstuffs from the air. Before the pixy noted him, Kester left for his room, unexpectedly craving down to his bones its bed. The span of a fae's life may wear down stone, but time had no patience with Kester. He had to get out of this accursed realm soon.

Chapter 6

Dear Lady how shall I declare thy case,
Whom late I left in languorous distress?

Following Bri, May counted the halls they passed on the way to the Rose Rooms. There were seven, but she couldn't keep up with all the turnings. Bri left. May collapsed on a cushion and struggled not to cry. Kester left a lot of out of his warning, but she did not doubt the necessity for those he managed to impart. Every fiber of her wanted someone to protect her from this place, but unused to saviors as she was, it felt stupid to long for one now. Kester had done more than anyone; he'd come here for her. They had to get out.

She had to. Though she'd ended up in an Oz of extraordinary beauty, just as Dorothy knew, there was no place like home. May stared at the fire a while, got up and examined the rooms for something to do. There were no books to read, but the best writing would not distract her for long.   At home she would paint, draw, write; May would welcome a sink full of dirty dishes. How did fairies occupy themselves when they weren't torturing humans? Unexpectedly weary, she went to lie on the bed. Bri bustled in with another gown.

"My lady, the Prince invites you to his table. We must hurry."

"Now? Isn't it late?" May asked. "I could sleep for days. Don't you ever rest?"

"Things move differently here. Take more wine, you'll

feel fine," Bri said.

Afterward, Bri had May change because of course, everyone had just seen her in the gold gown. Bri led May back to the Hall of Dance. At the door, she urged May go where the Prince waited, but his great beauty hit her. Bri only created a mask for the May that shrank from this overwhelming fairy. He was a perfect male in his powerful, youthful prime, didn't appear older than nineteen, but his expression and manner were supremely confident. She felt Bri give a push from behind, which made her stumble. Embarrassed, May forced herself to continue across the floor. The Prince sprang from his seat, took her hand prepared to kiss it, but May pulled it back.

"I don't know you."

He laughed. "You will."

His eyes were sapphires with sharp edges.

"We commend ourselves for excellent taste. Agree with us, Rais," Prince Aiden said to a nearby fairy.

Rais, whose remarkable looks stunned May speechless, brushed golden hair off his shoulder. "Quite the little morsel," he said.

The Prince laughed harder. May swung around to leave, but Prince Aidan swept her up.

"It's delightful you're so timid, little sweet. We'll dance and get to know each other."

He nodded his head. The music swelled. With one hand on hers and the other at her waist, he started them dancing. He was too close, too possessive.

"I don't like it here," she said in a hiss. "And I don't want to dance with you."

"Hah. We've made an amusing choice. Little sweet, we won't eat you. We won't do anything to you."

"What do you mean by catching me then? You've no right to keep me," May said.

His ignored her protest.

"Does this party ever end?" May asked. "I'm already bored with it."

"Enjoy our company, little sweet, and we'll have much to keep us occupied."

May renewed her efforts to pull out of his grasp.

"Stop; we won't tease. There's more to our realm than the eye reveals, little sweet. Yet all we ask of you is to look exquisite and stay by our side. Not too difficult?"

The Prince spun her out and back in again, and again. Her heart banged inside its cage; did he smile because he heard it and that amused him too? Finally, he waved his hand and the music changed. With her arm in his, he led her to sit beside him. A grumby offered herb wine, but thirsty as she was, she didn't drink. When the Prince's attention shifted toward a party of arriving fairies, she took a sip out of his glass, certain his drink was safe. Kester was among the newcomers, elegant in fairy garb where she played dress up. Yet Kester kept close to an exquisite fairy, his eyes never straying from her face. May worried. Did this fairy bewitch him?

"That's Princess Kerriena of Clan Maich," Bri whispered to May, having come up with a plate of sweets. "Offer one to the Prince."

May did as Bri asked. The Prince thanked her. Though he appeared not to, May was sure Prince Aidan watched Kester with the Princess.

After a time, he stood. "We have a gift to bestow."

His clear voice didn't rise, but the Prince caught the room's attention. A grumby handed him a velvet bag. "This string of Mere pearls is set in raw gold. They're but a token of our regard for our new consort."

To May's dismay, when the Prince set them about her throat, his warm hands lingered on her neck. All eyes fixed on her, to measure what she hoped were the pearls. A murmur enlivened the room, the Princess leaving with her followers and Kester.

"I want to go to my rooms," May said.

"But of course, little sweet," the Prince said. "We've been seen together long enough."

Bri was nowhere in sight, but the Prince guided her. He reached the door first and pulled it open. May hesitated.

"Good choice of color," he said from the sitting room as she stepped in. "The rosy hue warms your fair skin."

"Get out," May said.

The Prince chuckled. "Not even a taste, little sweet?"

He bent and grazed her cheek so quick May felt helpless. "Of course, we should stay here. She will set spies to see how long our devotion toward you lasts."

"No you won't," May said. "I don't want you here."

"You're certain?"

The Prince tilted her face and in one smooth move his mouth was on hers. With that touch, May felt an inrush of all the room's oxygen. Dizzy, only his hands holding her shoulders kept her from falling. Though May had no experience of kisses, she understood this wasn't a kiss, but a seduction she felt in her soul.

The sensitivity he employed sent captivating currents through her body. Every part of her trembled on the edge of total capitulation except for the tiny piece of her brain that whimpered no. To feed that spark, May formed weak fists and beat at him. He pulled away.

"We'll leave, little sweet, but soon enough you'll beg us not to."

He left the door ajar when he went. Bri came in sometime later, and May was in the same spot. "Please, leave me alone," May said.

She went to the bed and leaned back against its pillows. The Prince was hateful. He expected to subdue any bit of sense May had, to use her to make Princess Kerriena angry, jealous or both. Even considering all she suffered through with her alcoholic parents, she never felt so helpless. She'd landed in a nightmare.

How would she get out of it? She pulled over a pillow and hugged it. As for Prince Aidan kissing her, her responses to him were just physical. She wished she'd slapped his face. Unable to sleep, May drew on her old garments. Out of her room, she counted the turns and the halls until she was back at the Hall of Dance. Something had occurred to her.

What about the draft of the hall's great fireplace? The dance continued, its music played by pixy musicians behind a gold screen. Circuitously, as if it wasn't her destination, she reached the fireplace. The fire was embers, its box so tall she could have walked into it. May bent as if she'd dropped something and while feeling for it, gazed up the flue. Wide enough for someone to fit inside it, though she couldn't see where it ended. How to get up there and what to do afterward must be discussed with Kester. A grumby came up to clean out the ash and stack a fresh fire. May had done what she could for now. When she opened the door to her suite, she had a shock.

Grumbies were everywhere, cleaning the carpet, buffing surfaces, and replacing old flowers with new. The one nearest her, who'd been polishing the stone floor where she entered, lowered his tuneless string of grievances and shuffled out of her way.

"I'm sorry; I didn't mean to disturb your work," May said. "I'll go to the bedroom."

As a group, they bowed, and then turned back to their chores. Would the little fairies give her wanderings away? Prince Aidan would press her for her reasons, would easily see through her. The idea of standing up to the Prince was tiring.

Suddenly she wanted nothing but sleep, days of it, though day or night was all the same here. There were no clocks, windows, or any way to learn what passed out-of-doors.

"My lady," Bri said.

The pixy had popped up beside her. "You'll want to bathe before you change."

"After I sleep, you mean," May said.

"Oh, but the Prince expects you at his hall soon. Here," she said, having filled a glass with the fairy concoction that went farther than coffee dreamed.

"Is this herb wine bad for humans?" she asked Bri. "I mean, we're used to sleeping."

"I've never heard so," Bri said. "Perhaps the Prince could tell you."

After she downed it, May was glad to bathe, because it gave her time before she must face the Prince again. Next she donned a blue gown whose narrow skirt was fairy-dusted by Bri so it skimmed her body. Bri tried to fasten Prince Aidan's pearls about her neck, but May refused. Instead, Bri pinned May's hair with jeweled butterfly pins. A soft knock sounded at the door.

"Come in," Bri said when she opened the door, "do your best."

The same troop of grumbies entered to work on the bedroom. Stealing herself, May waited for a mention of her ramblings. When nothing of the kind occurred, she guessed they were not inclined to share them. Relief filled her.

"You do marvelous work," May said to the grumbies. "Thank you."

Tittering that May took notice of the humble fairies, Bri led her to the sitting room.

May whispered, "Do they eat, drink?"

Bri laughed. "Oh yes, my lady, scores belong to the Gathering Clans Conclave. When not at work, they play in the woods. They're well rewarded too. The grumbling is a sham. Neither pixies or grumbies are slaves to fairies."

She crossed her tiny arms and tried to look severe. "Low Fairies are free. Long ago, Pixies lived rough in woods and fields. But we learned to prefer luxury. To be sure, there's a wild pixy or two living as they had in the Old Realm."

"Where's that?"

Bri had a rueful smile. "Nowhere now…we lost the Old Realm long ago."

Wishing to hear more, but decided to make use of any free moment, May said she'd take a stroll before she must meet with the Prince, assuring Bri she wouldn't get lost.

"Certainly," Bri said. "I'd find you anyways."

May returned to the Hall of Dance, relieved Prince Aidan wasn't there. Kester should be. She waited near the fireplace, hoping he would hurry.

"So, the little sweet's fancied up."

Princess Kerriena stood in front of May in a flowing gown, her rare beauty palpable.

"Your highness," May said.

She curtsied in what she hoped was the proper manner, certain the Princess heard the not-so endearing term 'little sweet', from the source. Why wouldn't the Prince tell his princess everything? She was exquisite.

"Do you love him?" the Princess asked.

May must assure her otherwise. "I am nothing, no one."

The Princess fingered May's gown. "Hm-m. Yes, but he's promised you jewels, sumptuous surroundings, elegant garments. We saw what you were used to, poor little sweet. No wonder you ran after Fools' Lights. Be warned; a little sweetness soon sours."

May nodded. "Yes, and I'm too young."

"How young?" the Princess asked.

"Seventeen, Highness."

The Princess flounced off.

"And her two thousand if she's a day," a grumby working nearby said in a low rumble.

"You can speak," May said.

The fellow resumed fussing to himself, buffing in a circular motion as he moved away.

Chapter 7

To see sad pageants of men's miseries,
As bound by them to life in life's despite

When Kester entered the hall, May exhaled. She'd acted a fool, almost slobbering to please Princess Kerriena. She was marveling over this as Kester took a random route toward her.

"How are you faring?" Kester stopped by the fire, held up his hands as if to warm them. "You appear so fine, I thought you fae."

May didn't want to hear flattery from Kester, not after her first dose of fairy glamour. "What did you learn?"

"Nothing useful yet, but watch yourself with Princess Kerriena. She's betrothed to Prince Aidan for all he's unfaithful to her. Recently, a wedding contract was nearly agreed on. Then Prince Aidan pulls you from the dance. It's rumored he seeks more control over Princess Kerriena before he'll seal this bond with her."

He paused. A fairy had come close, moved away. "I haven't found a way to the outside, but if I learn how their food supplies are brought in, it could help us."

"There's this fireplace's flue," May said. "Maybe we could climb up and out."

"Clever of you," Kester said. "I'll investigate it later."

More fairies entered the hall, some lingering nearer now. Kester leaned to whisper.

"I'll meet you later at your room is so we can talk privately. You've done well for Prince Aidan. Kerriena's livid. Before we attract attention, we should part. Be wary with the Prince."

He walked toward a table, picked up a tiny cake, and left the hall. Against her will, May studied the hideous dance again. One man, bent almost double with age, seemed barely able to lift his feet. A young woman, motherly in her apron, moved about with a frozen smile. May had to get away. Bri found her in the corridor.

"With me, please," Bri said.

"Why?"

"We're late!"

A flustered Bri led May to the gallery where treelike pillars were crowned with leaves. Tables were covered in shining cloth, flowers overwhelmed vases. Crystal candleholders blazed. The biggest drawback to being stuck in this whimsical setting waited on her—Prince Aidan. Before May reached the table, he was up, helped her to her place. She would pull away if he wouldn't laugh at her again. He looked especially striking in black velvet with silver piping. As if he knew she thought so too, he smiled.

"What are we playing at now?" she asked, though she glanced at the table and not him.

"We wished to see how you fit our grand surroundings. You're quite lovely, little sweet, fresh as a flower in that gown."

He'd delivered this speech in a self-congratulatory way. His arrogance was huge. Unused as she was to male attention, the Prince overwhelmed her. Just then the elegant Kerriena arrived with her clan. Kester held a seat for the Princess; she kissed his cheek.

"Now you've been seen with me, I'll leave," May said.

"Ah, but the Conclave speculates about our little sweet, so you must not," Prince Aidan said.

He didn't exaggerate. So many fairies studied May that her face flamed.

"Don't any of you have better ways to occupy yourselves?"

Nearby, Rais made a sound that could be called a chuckle, but he drowned it with a sip of wine.

"Our little sweet has a passionate temperament," Prince Aidan said.

"I don't exist for your pleasure," May said.

"But you do," he said.

With a gesture, he ordered foodstuffs brought over. The rest of the meal was torture. The Prince poured her herb wine, made much of cutting and offering her half of each tidbit on his dish after tasting it first; perhaps to prove he need use no glamour with her, and then he brushed a crumb from her lap. His warm fingers burned through the thin cloth. After an interminable time, he rose to escort her to her rooms once again.

Swept off, her arm held firm by the Prince, May caught a glimpse of Kester's honest face. The besotted mask slipped to betray concern for her before it went back as before. Once again, the Prince came into May's rooms. This time he ensconced himself in the sitting room and ordered drink and desserts. Bri bustled out for them. May sat as far away as she could.

"Still untrusting, little sweet? We find it charming you don't fall into our embrace like that." He snapped his fingers.

"You're not sick yet of having everything you want?" May asked.

He laughed. "We do believe Princess Kerriena jealous. She nearly let the wine glass slip when we kissed your hand."

"Huh," May said. "Princess Kerriena is exquisite. She's just angry you don't fall for her like that." She snapped her fingers.

The Prince took her hand and drew her up. "You're delightfully...tasty."

She was drawn into an embrace that the larger part of her waited for. His mocking mouth sent tremors through her. May felt things she had no experience of, wanted to learn more about, and run away from at the same time. She'd gone from jeans, braids, and high school anonymity into a super-charged atmosphere where this incredible fairy prince was supposed to be mad for her. Of course it wasn't real, but the sensations she had to deal with were. Prince Aidan parted her lips with the tip of his tongue. Kester's words, 'resist the Prince, it might even amuse him,' helped her break out of his arms.

He laughed. "Still wary, but you warm up nicely."

Bri came in to set a laden tray on the low table.

"You may take our leave," he said. "Your lady will not require your services."

Bri curtsied and left. Did the Prince think May's reactions an invitation for him to stay?

"You look like you've been caught in Fools' Lights. Take a cake. We'll even sit way over here," he said with a smile.

May picked up a wine glass but couldn't drink. She curled her legs on the cushion. Sipping his, Prince Aidan watched her and the fire alternately.

"Tell us about you," he said. "We often wonder what sort of life terrans' lead."

His question surprised her. "Well," she said, as she cast about for a way to describe life on Illynd. "I did things pixies and grumbies do…prepare food. Clean house, make beds, sweep." She hesitated. What else could she say?

"Fascinating," he murmured. "Tell us of your sire, your dame."

"You mean my father and mother? I have no sisters or brothers. It was lonely."

With nothing else to speak of, she resorted to personal issues.

"My parents drank too much alcohol, but nothing like this herb wine. I don't know if you understand what that sort of drink will do to a . . . terran, but it makes them very unpleasant, loud, fighting, throwing, and breaking things."

She gestured at her elegant surroundings.

"My parents stopped caring about our home. They spent

more on alcohol than food. I was running away from them when I got caught by fairy lights in the forest."

He was silent for so long, she feared she'd overdone sharing.

"If your life was that unpleasant, why do you fight us? We offer you pleasure and ease. You will want for nothing."

"I don't love you," May said. "I barely know you. You say I'm pretty. A great prince such as you settles for so little? I won't. I have feelings, a mind of my own. You treat me the same way you treat those caught in your dreadful dance."

She leaned forward. "Did you ever consider the lives you snatched those poor souls away from? Their families mourn their loss, have children who miss them. They've a right to own their lives. It's terribly cruel to make them dance the time they have away to entertain you. I can't bear it."

"So we're cruel? That's ugly, isn't it, little sweet?"

The Prince crossed the room, snatched May's arm, and led her out the door. As they passed others in the corridors, the Prince told them to follow. He moved at a great pace, half-dragging her. Finally, he stopped in the Hall of Dance and held up his free hand. The room full of fairies hushed and drew near.

"Hear me, Clans fairy," Prince Aidan said. "Clan Guilly proclaims the Dance of Fools is ended. We need not amuse ourselves at the expense of hapless terrans. If asked, many a terran would come willing enough to our court. When we wish such diversions, let us seek them out in that manner."

The hall stood in shocked silence a moment, then broke out all at once with many voices, some protesting, some agreeing. The Prince pushed aside the screen covering the pixy musicians, grabbed a violin and broke it on his knee.

"The spell is done. Go home to your lives."

All as one the dancers stopped, dazed, and then looks of comprehension slowly dawned as they realized where they were.

"See they're compensated for their troubles before you send them off to their homes," Prince Aidan said.

Pixies and grumbies lead the exhausted dancers away, offering herb wine, food, and a place of rest.

An elegant female fairy protested. "What will we do now?"

"Why, Enira," the Prince said. "Take a fairy partner of your choosing. You're a more sophisticated dancer than any of that poor lot."

With that, Prince Aidan accompanied May back to her rooms.

She could not hide her pleasure over his decree. "Thank you, that was wonderful. Those poor folk will be so grateful. You really can be kind."

He put his arms about her. "We can be so much more for your sake, little sweet, but for now, we'll take our leave."

She'd expected another kiss, but he let her go. Why did he end the dance? Was it to make Kerriena jealous? Or did his act mean something else?

Chapter 8

Which when the vile Enchantress perceived,
How that my Lord from her I would reprieve

Princess Kerriena rushed in near the end of Prince Aidan's announcement in the Hall of Dance. Kester was just behind her. It was easy for anyone to note wonder and gratitude in May's face as the Prince spoke. Princess Kerriena turned about and left with her retinue, Kester momentarily forgotten. He followed anyway. Once back in Maich Hall, the Princess picked up crystal glasses and smashed one after another at the floor. Kester dare not go too close.

"All to please her!" The Princess cried. "Just to favor . . . this, this nothing—"

Cutting short suggestions and commentary of her hovering courtiers, she dismissed them. Kester, she told to wait. For several minutes she surveyed the damage she caused, chest heaving, and then calming. She moved close to Kester and laid her hands on his arms.

"You're fine-looking this evening," she said in a purr. "We've become quite fond of you. You've done all we could wish to show devotion to us."

"It's no hardship playing your consort, my lady."

"Why play, Kester?" she said with lowered eyes. "We would take you to our rooms. We're certain you would be well satisfied in our bed."

Kester, thorn-less, had to call on self-will. Her incredible body was outlined by her clinging shift, her mouth pink, moist;

no! He could not do this. Many a mortal had been driven mad by unrequited fae affections. He spoke honestly.

"My lady, your beauty is legendary. Lost in it, I would become insensible…and of little use in furthering your plans. Instead, let us play our parts and both gain what we wish, I my freedom, you, your great prince."

For the first time since he met her, Princess Kerriena laughed. "You're such a relief. We are sick to death of our supporters fawning, never being true with us."

"May I ask something, my lady? If I'm too bold, please forgive me. Why do you fight to marry this Prince?"

"You see no love in the match?" She stopped smiling. "You are bold…and correct. What we desire is more intoxicating than adoration. We crave power. If Clan Maich is joined to Clan Guilly, then for the first time on Illynd there will be a King and a Queen. Such is the strength of both our clans if united. We were made for such a role."

The princess lifted her sapphire pendant, let it fall. "We have many plans for our queen-ship. Aidan yearns for control as we do, but he will have it under his terms. He seeks to wear us down, but we will not yield. We are his match in every way."

Her tone changed, once again seductive, drawing him in. "We do like you. Kiss us."

Seeing no way to avoid the request, Kester backed her against the wall, his kiss rough. Her mouth was everything he feared, provocative, rich with the promise of surrender.

"My princess—" He struggled for restraint and the right words. "Will…it not," he drew a breath to steady himself, "be better to dangle me before Prince Aidan only? Wouldn't this…injure his pride?"

"So we fear deep down." She moved away with a sly smile. "Though fairies are wont to take a comely terran to their bed when they will, Aidan is proud. What others do, he does not. This terran, she's the first he's ever chosen out of the dance. Aidan's lovers were always fairy, but never his equal in rank as we are, and so inconsequential to us. This time we can't read him. What he's done is out of his character."

"Perhaps to throw you off," Kester said. "Surely, this ploy is part of his bid for the upper hand in your betrothal. No one could choose a terran over you."

As there was no answer for the truth of his statement, Princess Kerriena made a small smile. "You have our leave."

Relief coupled with regret for what he must resist hurried Kester from her. Seeking new diversions, the clans left for an outdoor hunt that left Kester and May behind, so Kester risked going to her suite. Her pixy was not there either. May was cuddled on a bench, sleeping off the exhaustion of being forced to live as faes did, relentlessly making time move as they willed. Prince Aidan was clever to dangle May before Kerriena, though May appeared unaware of her charms. If this pose was a different sort of trap, Kester was already in it. He tapped her shoulder. Her look of drowsy surprise said she forgot his promise to visit her rooms.

"Oh." She struggled to sit up. "Sorry."

"No need," he said.

She poured and drank fae wine, immediately became alert. They went back to the Hall of Dance. It was truly empty with no musicians or dancers, the fire on its great hearth burnt to cold ash.

"Keep watch," Kester said. "I'll see how far I can go."

He pulled a chair into the fireplace box, stood on its seat, and used its back for a step. Soon he could barely see the grate below. As he climbed, he strained for sounds. If they were discovered here, what might happen to May could be harsher than the consequence to him. Kerriena would release him, but this Prince would not let May go gladly, if at all. After a tense time going up, he headed back down the flue. At the bottom, he dropped onto the chair, streaked with black soot. May had wide, nervous eyes.

"Come, we'll speak in your rooms. We risk fate here," he said.

Once in her sitting room, she lit candles. Kester washed off the ash and joined her by the fire she built up.

He took the fae brew she offered, sipped and said, "The opening was narrow, so I braced my back against one side and set my feet against the other. In that manner, I pushed myself up. The outer vent was large enough to pass through, but it was pitch dark. I fear the forest floor is a long fall. Still, it's a way outside, the first we've known of, thanks to you." He paused.

"What happened earlier? Why did the Prince stop the dance?"

May flushed. "I told him it was cruel. He up and ended it straight away."

"Princess Kerriena was furious," Kester said, "stamping and flinging things. He had more in mind than pleasing you, though it was good he did it for those poor souls' sake. He's tormenting her. She'll bend in the end. Kerriena pretends not to, but she fears a rival."

Turning his head slightly, he searched for a way to phrase his next question. "Before I left her hall, I heard her spy say the Prince spent time with you...alone."

May colored. "I couldn't get rid of him. He asked me about my life. I was careful, and I think he knows little of how your people live. He didn't seem suspicious."

Kester let out a breath. "If he ever, ever, learnt you are a rover," he said, "you'd never get free. He'd want that power for himself. Already you make too pretty a package, you being so fresh. They've lived everything many times over. You see how they occupy themselves. You're green air here."

Fear washed out her face. "We have to get away."

"We will," he said.

Yet Kester had meant to frighten her. She must be wary, must keep fighting the Prince. He left for his room, though he briefly considered going back to the fireplace with rope and leaving without her. May had no notion if she came with him, she risked trading one prison for another, and if given the choice, she might prefer this one. If he was a friend, he'd give May the truth. Duty denied him choices in the matter.

He obeyed his king. When they escaped, he had to bring her to court. The time they'd spent together here was not wasted however. Kester gauged much of May's character from how she behaved since they were taken. If she were on Illynd to further murky ends, she would have won allies in the Realm. When Kester warned her not to reveal she was a rover, he'd expected her to do just that. Once at court, he would be her advocate, take full responsibility for her. But first he must get her free. How long would she be able to keep the Prince at arms' length?

The sooner Kester got her away from here, the better. Rover she might be, the more time he spent in May's company, the more he believed her telling of how she fell into the vile profession—by accident.

But it was no accident Kester went running after her.

Chapter 9

And thou, O fairest Princess under sky,
In this fair mirror may behold thy face,
And thine own realms in Land of Fairy

Not long after Kester left, May changed with Bri's insistence into a lavender gown with iridescent straps. Prince Aidan's flirtations sent thrills through her, but Kester's faithful face lingered in her mind's eye. As if she needed convincing the deed was done, May returned to the Hall of Dance. With no dancers present, the musicians played a different tune, fair and melancholy. It recalled sunshine and the wind on her skin. Bri rushed toward May.

"My lady, the Prince requests you in his hall."

What was wanted of her now? Prince Aidan sat with several members of his clan. He stood when she was next to him.

"Our little sweet is more charming at each meeting," he said. "Join us."

Since she could not say no, she took a seat and a cup of what he called honeyed nectar from his hand. She nearly sipped it too, but set it down. "I was just in the Hall of Dance," she said to cover her lapse. "A new melody played. It put me in mind of the outdoors."

"And this makes you sad. We don't like this frown, Rais," the Prince said.

Before Rais could make a cruel quip so they could have their laugh, May spit out, "You've taken away my freedom...of course I'm unhappy. My life wasn't easy, but at least no one kept me in a cage. I used to walk every day even if it poured down rain, or snow blinded me. The outdoors was the one thing not ruined for me....I miss it terribly, not that you'd understand."

Rais shrugged his broad shoulders. "And you expect what?"

The Prince frowned at him.

"We enjoyed the great woods earlier ourselves," Prince Aidan said. "We'll consider another outing. To see you in starlight is an enchanting idea."

She couldn't help it; she smiled at Prince Aidan, even grinned at Rais. To get out might allow a chance to escape. When the Prince graciously dismissed her, she hung about the Hall of Dance hoping to catch sight of Kester. When he didn't show, she went back to her rooms famished. She had not dared eat her food and couldn't tell when she should eat anyway.

Shut in this tricked-out warren, not even thirst, hunger, or tiredness could tell her what hour it was. Before she sent her pixy to bring her a tray, Bri asked excited questions of the outing the Prince planned in May's honor. A tap came at the door. Bri answered it. Kester stood there.

"Please, come in," May said. "Bri, would you go for my tray?"

Bri left reluctantly, clearly not wishing to leave her lady unescorted in this male's company.

"I heard the news," Kester said when they were alone.

"So I chanced a visit. I can't be sure I wasn't followed. Kerriena would have me gutted if she found I'd come to you. She's already livid over this outdoor revel."

"It was my idea," May said. "I thought we might use it to escape."

"It's likely a hundred eyes will be on you outside, but it was a good try," he said. "These favors the Prince bestows on you provoke Princess Kerriena. Her people plan overtures to Prince Aidan's clan. She may surrender a measure of her power yet. Don't go about alone. I fear she'll do you an injury, or worse."

"I'll take Bri. She's very sweet to me."

"I should leave before she returns. I'm looking into something my pixy told me," Kester said.

May wished he could stay. Being with someone who cared what happened to her was such a relief.

"You've done well," Kester said, as they both stood. "Not just anyone could handle all you've had to since you've come to this place."

He gave her a brief hug. "Pray be careful when you're with the Prince. Farewell, Lady May."

He left as Bri returned with food. No way was May going to wait for the Prince to call on her for some new torment.

"Bri," May said. "I'd love to see where my lotions and creams were made. My skin was never this soft, or my hair so smooth. Is that possible?"

"Yes, my lady, though I've not had the request before.

Mostly it's the work of pixies. If you wish, I'll take you when you've done with your meal."

"I've lost my appetite. Let's go now."

Bri led her to an area May didn't see on the first tour. Here the halls were paneled wood. They entered a workshop with tables covered with bottles, pots, wood boxes. Pixies' ground with mortar and pestle, mixed, measured. She watched fascinated as a pixy put pinches of green powder on a glass circle. He set a glass tube in a copper holder over it. A flash off the pixy's finger and the powder sparked into a green flame, the liquid started to boil. The hall was science lab as run by fairies. Open doors revealed closets filled with bags, sacks, and pots. Dried herbs hung from wood racks overhead. Bri stopped at a table where a male pixy, curls cropped short, measured ingredients into beakers similar to those in a chemistry class.

"This is Goll," Bri said. "He's quite the expert."

Goll wiped his hands on a cloth and bowed. "My lady, how might I assist you?"

"The Lady May," Bri said, "is Prince Aidan's consort. She asks after the unguents and balms made here."

"We follow recipes writ by High Fairies," Goll said. "We merely mix, measure, and prepare them. See, this is a bathing decoction. The herb I just added is comfrey. Once all the ingredients are in, I'll boil it to the proper consistency, then cool and jar it for use."

Goll led them to a closet. "For instance, Princess Kerriena

requests this face cream. Would you like to try it, my lady?"

"Thank you, Goll, I would," May said, "but how do I pay you? I have no gold or silver."

"Take it, my lady," Bri said. "The Prince will insist on it and be glad to pay the price too. I wish I'd thought to ask Goll's advice before I secured your potions. He's that knowledgeable. You couldn't get a better suggestion than his."

Goll ducked his head before he picked up a jar and handed it to May. She lifted its lid and smelled geraniums. "Thank you, Goll."

Just as they were to leave the closet, Rais and Prince Aidan entered the hall. Unwilling to be seen, May held back, and drew Bri with her. The Prince would not be as easily fooled as her pixy was by her reason for coming here. Goll covered for them by going out and leaving the door cracked. May peered through it, barely breathing, as Prince Aidan went into a closet across the way. He came out with ingredients, worked with them until he appeared satisfied, and then gave Goll precise instructions on how to finish his creation. He said he'd return to check on it later. Rais in tow, he left the hall. As soon as Aidan was out of sight, Bri and she exited the closet.

"Thank you, Goll. I didn't wish to be discovered," May said.

"No fear. A lady keeps her beauty secrets close," Goll said.

Even more curious now she'd seen the Prince here, May made a general inspection of every station, especially interested in the closet where the Prince got his materials. All the while, she tried not to seem to pay it more heed than she did the rest. There was no way she could understand what Prince Aidan was making short of asking, which she didn't dare do.

"My lady, we must prepare for the outing with the Prince," Bri said.

Escape; hope lifted May before doubt weighed her. How dangerous would an attempt be? The thought hadn't occurred to her before. They were back in the Rose rooms again.

"My lady, try Princess Kerriena's cream," Bri said.

"I'd need to bathe, and we don't have time," May said.

"Then this, my lady, please?" Bri said.

Bri had brought back a balm Con also recommended. It surprised May by making her lips rosy and fuller. She was beginning to like fairy 'beauty secrets', as Goll put it. Wearing a new gown whose layers of spider silk shifted color when she moved further lightened May's mood. Would Kester notice? In spite of his admonition, they just might see a way of escape during this outing.

If they failed, she could not believe the Prince would punish her for trying—he let those poor dancers go. In the Hall of Dance, May joined Prince Aidan's party. Princess Kerriena was there, striking in a sheer, silvery pink. Kester wore a wine tunic, no doubt meant to complement her outfit.

Everyone waited on something.

"Now," Prince Aidan commanded as he clasped May's hand. Just then, pixies' showered everyone with glittery dust. *Full dark, her breath suspended in her chest,* and the next thing May noted was insect sounds, grass rustling. The air was fresh. Lights bloomed inside glass globes. When her surroundings sharpened, she gasped.

Just like that, they'd come outdoors using pixy dust. It was the opposite of what happened with the mushroom ring. A thrill went through May at having gotten her way. Then her attention fixed on flowers larger than she was. Towering overhead was a tree so tall she couldn't see its top. It struck her; the flora wasn't abnormally big, but every one of them was so very small. Black specks grew in her vision. She swayed.

How could this be? How did she get this way? When she turned to ask what was happening, she was jolted to her toes. A set of iridescent blue wings unfolded from the Prince's back. Completely unfurled, they were fantastic sails long as Prince Aidan was tall. Bright red, shimmering yellow, violent violet, hundreds of wings popped like telescoping umbrellas from every fairy, pixy, and grumby. May did the only sane thing. She fainted.

She came to on a cloth spread on grass. The concerned face of the Prince moved into view. Many fairies crowded close. To her right was Princess Kerriena, silver-white wings tucked tight, glaring. Behind her, Kester shook his head as though he was trying to tell May something.

She frowned in his direction. He mouthed no. No.

Bri rushed up with a wet cloth and wiped her temples. The Prince held a cup to her lips. May took a shaky sip.

"What's wrong with our consort?" Prince Aidan said sharp to Bri.

Before Bri could speak, May struggled to sit up. "I'm fine, really." She took another sip of herb wine and spoke again.

"It's my fault, I haven't eaten. I'm sure that's why I felt weak."

"Foolish pixy," Prince Aidan said. "Take more care with our consort's delicate state. Bring food straightaway."

Bri went to the picnic baskets and filled a plate. The drama done, the bulk of the revel's fairies lifted, floated, or soared skyward. Bri flitted just above the ground with sheer pink wings. Grumbies' flights stuttered in a manner that reminded May of lady bugs. While she forced herself to eat what Bri brought, she studied the wings to see how they were connected whenever a fairy's back turned toward her.

They jutted from below the shoulders. Somehow, they must end up small enough for tunics and dresses to cover them, as May didn't see a sign of wings on any fairy before now. Why would she, when they were all inside and couldn't use them? Thank goodness, she didn't make the mistake of asking the Prince questions that betrayed her ignorance of Illynd. One wrong word would have given her away.

A native here would know fairies could be small as a grasshopper. It was what Kester tried to warn her. After she improved from her shock, which she covered by taking time to eat and drink, May's fear turned to delight. Against the backdrop of this ancient forest flew fairies, her mother's tale made real. Some, like the Prince, had wings with crisp iridescent colors, while others were muted powdery hues. Many sets mimicked bird, insect, or butterfly wings. They were wide or narrow, their edges defined by darker shading or fluttery fantails. She got to her feet.

Prince Aidan broke from his courtiers and came to her. "Are you well, little sweet?"

"I am...I was busy today with Bri. I'll be more careful when I eat in the future," she said.

"We have a treat for you, if you feel up to it."

Prince Aidan was being solicitous, so she was wary. "I, being out in the air was all I asked for, thank you," May said.

"We see you wear our gift."

Bri put his pearls on May as they were leaving. If it wouldn't ruin what she was hoping to do here, she'd pull them off.

"They are much better for lying near your skin," he said. "Come, time for our surprise."

He led her apart from the others, his arm about her waist before she realized what he was doing.

"I have you," the Prince said.

His wings beat, and May's toes lifted from the ground.

She clung tight as he glided up and up, so high above the party's glows they soon looked like firefly lights in summer grass. He flew past branches and leaves until he cleared the canopy. Bright stars winked overhead. A freeing, delightful energy possessed May.

"What do you think of our surprise?"

"It's wonderful, a dream," May said.

The Prince flew faster. Treetops flashed by. The breeze made her shiver.

"Cold?"

"Yes," she said breathlessly. "But don't stop. It's unbelievable."

Laughing, he lowered them until they were beneath a cover of leaves. He settled on a branch wide as a room and rubbed her arms to warm her up. Flight was intoxicating, but suddenly May was aware of how alone they were.

Catching her closer, the Prince whispered, "A taste, little sweet," and kissed her, his warm mouth welcome on her cool lips for more than their heat.

Unthinking, May fell into his kisses. The slant of the tree trunk made her body lean against his. Every place their skin touched grew hot. His hands slid over her back in a way that made her aware of herself as she never was. His touches made her long to caress his back, arms, dig fingers into his hair.

"We can enjoy this at our ease," Prince Aidan said. "But we must return to the revel first."

As they fell back toward the ground, May was panicked at

the signals she sent to the Prince. This could not happen. She must get away from Prince Aidan and his realm, not be trapped by his allure. He would keep her at his side until her prettiness faded and then send her away. The best part of her life would be gone and for what? Add to that the spiteful Princess Kerriena, already furious over the Prince's actions. Back at the party, May noted Kester's expression of relief on seeing her return. Princess Kerriena acted as if she didn't notice them together.

That was impossible, for as soon as he set them down, Prince Aidan declared the party done. Once more pixies dusted partygoers. All went dark. When the light returned, they were in the Hall of Dance. The Prince whispered something to Rais, never letting go of May's hand until they were alone in her sitting room. Something seemed to clog her throat. It was awkward to rebuff him after her lack of good judgment, but she must.

"I, need to rest," May said as she took a seat.

Politely, the Prince ordered wine and then dismissed Bri. He handed May a glass. "You're trembling. Is something amiss?"

"Still cold," she said.

He took her glass, set it down, and came beside her. "We have the remedy for that."

He titled her face to capture her mouth. She liked his arms around her, his mouth on hers too much. "Don't."

The Prince had moved his lips to her bare shoulder. May

pushed at his head and stood. "I'd like you to leave. I want to retire. Alone."

He smiled. "That's impossible. And we're very sure you don't want us to leave."

He gathered her up and carried her to the bedroom, where he dropped her on the bed.

May scrambled up. "Get out," she said. "I know all about you."

He appeared amused. "What can you know of us, little sweet? We're curious. Tell us."

May slid off the bed to plant her feet on the floor. "You couldn't care less about me…you're using me to make Princess Kerriena jealous. But I want my life back. I was brought here against my will."

"If we don't love you, then do you believe we love the Princess?"

"No," May said. "If you did, you wouldn't hurt her by using me. True love means you care for someone's feelings enough to consider them. You don't respect her or me. If you did, you'd leave when I ask you to."

He frowned. "Well," he said at last. "You're very right and very wrong at the same time."

Again, she was in his arms, up tight to his chest before she could squeak. "We care about what you can do for us, and we won't be leaving you this night. We could force your real feelings, but instead, little sweet, we'll leave you to consider them."

He let her go and closed the door after him.

She wanted to lift the nearest candle stand and heave it after him. He was vile. He was doing something to her, making her weak. It was only when he was near, oozed whatever at her that she caved. That could not happen. She wasn't naïve.

On one level May was wondering why not make love with Aidan, but just below that, was terrified to let go and let it happen. He would own her soul if she allowed how she felt with him to triumph over her common sense. She shuddered. Worse, there was no sign of any protection against her getting pregnant she'd seen, nor had the Prince brought up the subject. She had to get out of his grasp, be in control of herself again. She didn't care if he heard or what he thought; May wrapped herself in the bed cover and sobbed.

Chapter 10

There to his subtle engines he does bend
His practiced wit, and his fair-filed tongue

A rustle made May come full awake. Someone was next to her. Her throat squeezed in when she spied the Prince's dark head. The blanket slipped to the dimples above his buttocks. Folded, flat and compact between his broad shoulders were his wings. She'd wanted to see how they fit on a fairy's back, but regretted that curiosity now. Could she get up without waking him?

With care, she moved to the side of the bed. Painfully slowly, she slipped out of it, instantly sorrier she'd changed into this thin nightgown at one point. She crept to the water closet to lock herself safely inside.

Prince Aidan sat up. "Ah, awake so soon?"

He'd caught her with her hand on the door, smiled and said, "And after such engagements as we enjoyed last night."

"Nothing happened."

"Dear little sweet." He laughed. "If anyone saw us now...who would believe it?

Bri would know the Prince was in her bed, everyone would learn he spent the night. Her skin felt scorched all over. What would Kester think?

"Though we appreciate that confection you wear, please do bathe. We will order a tray to share."

"Oh!" She yanked open and slammed the door to the water closet behind her.

"Damn!"

She forgot fresh clothes. No way she'd come out wrapped in a towel in front of him. She rushed back out and riffled through the closet for something demure, as if any of these filmy dresses could be prim. Grabbing the green gown she'd worn before, she stormed back into the water closet, this time slamming the door on the Prince's laughter. By the time she emerged, damp hair loose about her shoulders, Prince Aidan sat in bed, tray on his lap, wide, bare chest above it. There was no shame in him, but May couldn't look his way for fear she'd stare. Bri was busy at the grate building up the fire.

"Little sweet, your hair is exquisite tousled, so seductive we wonder if you mean to tempt us."

May ignored him to sit at the dressing table. Bri started to comb her hair.

"Good morn, my lady." Bri kept from her usual smiling self.

"Please," May said. "Nothing fancy today. I'm not a Barbie doll."

Bri wasn't immune to the undercurrent in May's tone. "Yes, my lady. What is a Barbie please?"

"A toy," May said, "that looks like a woman. You can dress it up, do what you like with it, but it has no feelings. Just the sort of thing needed here."

Prince Aidan laughed. "Bri, we're done with our tray. Draw our bathing water, very hot."

Bri did as bid and left the bedroom when she was done.

"Unless you desire to see more of us, you'll take your leave too," the Prince said.

May hurried, but the door to the water closet clicked before she made it to the sitting room. When the Prince finally left, May stayed in. She had no wish to hear gossip whispered about Prince Aidan and her. Most of all, she dreaded facing Kester. The Prince played on her inexperience. Part of her was seduced by what his beautiful body, along with his fairy charm, did to her senses. After a long while where she called herself idiot, fool, and then switched to name-calling the Prince, she calmed down. When Bri came in, May asked what was being said about them.

"My lady, everyone talked of how the Prince didn't go to his rooms after the revel, and fresh garments were sent here for him. Oh, my lady, isn't he the finest fairy? It is whispered Prince Aidan will sire a child with you. Such an honor is usually reserved for contracted unions."

"Oh, Bri!" May started to pace. "I can't stay here. I have to get away, please, you must help me escape."

Bri appeared shocked. "I thought you pleased with the Prince, my lady. If you're afraid of Princess Kerriena, don't be. Prince Aidan is formidable. The Princess can't touch you. Don't forget she has her new consort.'"

She stopped pacing, faced the pixy. "You don't understand, Bri. I don't care about Prince Aidan or Princess Kerriena's problems. I want my life back. To me this isn't a real place, it's a dream world. I hate it here…I have to get away."

Helpless tears shook her.

Bri patted her back. "My lady, I didn't know you felt so. It was certain you'd adore Prince Aidan. I thought you young and shy."

Bri gave her a handkerchief. "I wish I could help, my lady. I wish I could."

May dried her eyes. These rooms were luxurious but prison was prison, stifling and confining no matter how anyone dressed it up. After a long while, she curled on the couch. Bri woke May from a headachy sleep.

"My lady, the Prince requests you come to Guilly Hall."

May drank herb wine to energize herself. Then Bri fussed with her hair and clasped the Prince's gift about her neck. If she must enter a room full of speculation about her relationship with Prince Aidan, Bri appeared determined to give them something to see. When May stood at the door to Guilly Hall, those standing nearby fell silent.

Eyes' followed her to where the Prince stood. Afraid she was not to up the pretense, May moved up on her toes and gave a surprisingly steady kiss to his cheek; she'd rather claw it. Across the way, Princess Kerriena sat as if carved of ice. Kester's face bore a hurt look that bruised May. When food was served, May continued playing the besotted girl, sipping from Aidan's glass, feeding him from her dish, smiling as if she had everything in the world because he was at her side.

"We have an announcement," Princess Kerriena said. Her

tone captured the room. "The Maich Clan concedes the dowry required by Clan Guilly. Midsummer is chosen to join Clan Guilly with Clan Maich."

Cheers went up around the hall. It was not lost on any present Princess Kerriena's betrothed sat with his new lover and not with her. However Kerriena fixed her smile, she'd given in. Prince Aidan's pleasure and triumph were evident in the flash of his eyes. May acted as if she didn't care.

Well she didn't. The Prince kept busy with courtiers, who whispered comments in his direction or congratulated him. May left as soon she got the Prince's nod she was excused. She was determined to get a message to Kester. She must explain why she went along with Prince Aidan. After she pleaded with Bri to send to Kester in secret, she waited in the sitting room a long while, her head growing heavier. Someone shook her; Kester.

May rubbed her eyes. "It's you, thank goodness."

Kester spoke low. "I almost didn't come...in case the Prince—"

"You believe the lie too?" she asked as she went to pour herb wine. "The Prince arranged this fantasy to make Kerriena jealous. You know that better than anyone."

"Yes, but I hoped you wouldn't fall so hard for his designs."

"He was out here, Kester, while I was in there. He got into the bed before I woke, but nothing happened between us. It was a ploy to break down Kerriena. You saw how well it worked."

"I believe you because you tell me so but, May you gave a good show at his side."

"On purpose, Kester. I wanted his plan to work. He wouldn't leave me alone otherwise. Get me away from this hateful place, please. Did you find anything that will help us?"

"Possibly, but preparations for the union will move quickly. Princess Kerriena will be wed and queen before Prince Aidan can regret capitulating. Everyone had the rumors of pregnancy…If you gave the Prince an heir, it would be before hers in the line of succession."

"Kester, I've done nothing to risk that."

"I believe you, but she can't. I worry for you. We must get free of this place. Princess Kerriena is spite-filled. I fear Prince Aidan hasn't lost interest in you, or to placate her, he'd move you far from here."

"I never mattered to him. He was playing a part, Kester. Forget him for now. I've found a work hall where fairies do up potions. It must be where they make powders used to transport us into the wood. Can you find out?"

To her surprise, Kester scooped her up in his arms, whirled her around, and set her down.

"You've done it again, May. This is a thorny spot to be in, yet you're handling it so well. I'll go to this hall, but I shouldn't risk coming here again. Even now she doesn't need me, Kerriena would peg my ears to a door for going anywhere near you. Meet me when you can in the Hall of Dance."

Kester left, and May felt tears well up. She saw him so differently since their first meeting. He was decent, brave, and she needed him a lot more than he needed her.

"Why do you look sad, little sweet?" the Prince said softly.

May started. "What are you doing here?"

He put his arm about her and played with her hair. "Our revelry is just over. It's a long time in coming, this match. Our supporters and clan celebrate well. You did it for us. Princess Kerriena would never fall in with our demands if not for your acts. Why did you help us?"

May ignored what stirred inside her, shifted away from him. "To be done with you. I can't have you sneaking into my bed, or worse."

The Prince leaned in and breathed into her hair. "Worse? Would it be terrible to take what you desire?"

Before she could answer, he had his mouth on hers. The need to run melted into the heat that spread through her. He should have forgotten her, why didn't he? She should push back, get away, but he was here, he wanted her. Tears ran down her face. Drawing away when he felt moisture, he gently touched the wetness on her cheek. Then he kissed her again, using his lips like delicate fingers. They touched her neck, shoulders, one breast while he slid her gown off the other. She quivered.

"Little sweet," he whispered.

"My lord prince, this has gone on long enough."

He blocked May with his body while she hastily pulled up her gown. Princess Kerriena's stare was unflinching. "A bargain's been struck, but it can be undone still. We will not be crossed on this."

Prince Aidan marched to Princess Kerriena, grabbed her, and thrust her ahead of him. The sudden withdrawal left May in shock at what happened between the Prince and her. Strange to owe the Princess for barging in when she'd lost all resistance. She'd never sleep in this place again. May locked the water closet, soaked and scrubbed with plain water, didn't use any creams, dressed in her own things, braided her hair.

"My lady," Bri said when she came out. "You're busier than a grumby. Hungry?"

"No," May said. "You're excited. What's going on?"

"It's almost midsummer, a favorable time for the ceremony," Bri said.

"So quick...I guess it will be grand."

"Oh yes, my lady," Bri said, "The clans will stage battle, but one side will yield. That will be Clan Maich. The mediator will declare pax. Then the union of clans is cemented by the marriage. There hasn't been such a match for ever so long."

A knock sounded. Bri opened the door, spoke with someone, and shut it. "The Prince sends regrets, my lady, and asks you keep to your rooms."

"I need to go out," May said.

"Don't fret, my lady. It's just the union...he must attend

to it and the Princess," Bri said.

May put her hand on the door anyway; she had to get out. But if she tried to do anything now, she might lose her freedom altogether. Bri could get Kester another message. Strange that she had nowhere to go even if Kester and she escaped. She had not forgotten her panic when she found herself adrift on Illynd. Yet her reasons to flee were overwhelming.

"Bri," May said. "There's something I need you to do for me."

The passionate feelings the Prince roused alarmed May more than any other consideration. If she gave in to them, to him, she could find herself stuck in the half-life being the Prince's lover would be. Once again, she was grateful to the Princess. Kester had been right. Prince Aidan was not done with her.

Chapter 11

Himself he frees by secret means unseen;
His shackles empty left, himself escaped clean.

Kester ran his hand through his hair. He had to get May, get them out of the Realm. Princess Kerriena's using him to make Prince Aidan jealous had no effect. Worse, since the poor thing fainted, and the Prince seized on that to suggest May was having his child, the Princess and her courtiers discussed how to destroy May. How could Kester have failed to forewarn her? Thank goodness, May possessed the wit not to reveal the real reason for her collapse. She was clever and quick, but was her talent for self-preservation proof against Prince Aidan's allure?

May falling to the Prince shouldn't be Kester's main concern. Seeing May flushed when she returned from that picnic flight, Kester knew neither one of them could linger in the Realm and come out unscathed. When he risked running into the Prince in May's suite, he felt greatly relieved to find her alone. But there was hurt in her voice as she spoke of the Prince; she was in greater danger than she realized.

The Prince's spellbinding aura had done its work on her. Thank goodness May might have found what they needed to escape. Yet when they did, Kester must obey the claim duty had on him. After winning her confidence, he would destroy it. Even if he managed to help her with his king, May would be right to hate him. He hated just thinking of it. Kester never gave his word lightly; yet he'd sworn to help May pretty quickly. Now he had longer knowledge of her, he couldn't regret that hasty vow. After breaking fast, Kester asked Con to show him the work halls.

"I heard crystal is created there…I'd love to see how it's done," Kester said.

"Pleased to, sir," Con said.

One work hall should be near another. As they walked, Kester undid his tunic collar, sick of dressing up. It was with no pretense Kester enjoyed watching pixies create glass from glowing, hot lumps. They pulled, tugged, pinched, and cut the molten glass until like a miracle, crystal goblets formed. After a time, he excused Con, saying he would stay.

"Thank you, sir," Con said. "There are heaps to be done before the union."

The other pixies paid Kester no heed. He looked in on several work halls. In one, metal smiths burnished armor and polished swords. In another, Kester caught a glimpse of exquisite jewelry before a pixy ushered him out, saying the hall was closed. Finally, Kester chanced upon the one he sought.

Just as May said, pixies mixed decoctions. Liquids bubbled over flames. Doors to the storerooms stood ajar, as pixies were in and out as they worked.

A pixy stood at his side. "May I assist you, sir?"

"Princess Kerriena sent me for new soap. Something special," Kester said. "Can you help?"

The pixy's face lit up. "Oh yes, indeed, come this way. We've just made these." The pixy handed Kester a cake in paper tied with string. "Smell this, sir."

The aroma was of a flower that grew in the deepest woods. "I'm sure the Princess will approve," Kester said. "May I tell her who recommended these?"

"Goll, sir."

"Thank you, Goll."

After this, he asked questions about the work he saw, glanced into the storage closets he passed with Goll. Kester walked back to his room sure what they needed was in that hall. Yet how would he recognize it? He might be allowed to leave now his usefulness was over, but not May. She'd end up Prince Aidan's consort for real. That shouldn't happen to someone as naïve, as sweet as May. When he got back, much to his surprise, his solution waited for him.

Con had put his tunic and trousers on the bed. "The Princess Kerriena expressed satisfaction with your efforts. She releases you from further obligation. As her reward, you'll be allowed to leave the Realm with this."

A small leather bag lay next to his tunic. Kester poured out its contents. Fabulous diamonds, rubies, sapphires, emeralds, and topazes, each one perfect in cut and carats in size, sparkled at him. He put them back into the bag and pulled the string tight.

"I have powders to transport you outside," Con said. "The Princess wishes this matter to be discrete."

"May I see them?" Kester said.

Con took a package of paper from his tunic. Carefully, he

unfolded it to show Kester its contents. About a teaspoonful of dust, resembling powdered mica, caught light and reflected it.

"That will restore my former size too?"

Oh, no sir, that's a different packet," Con said. "It's used when you're clear of the Realm. Here, I'll show you."

Con replaced the packet with one of blue paper, perhaps to tell it apart. "Just shower yourself with it. Your proper size will rebound."

"This is enough?" Kester said, skeptical.

"More than enough, sir," Con said.

Kester nodded. "I say, Con, might I leave after the mock battle? I've no desire to see the union, but to see faes in armor doing battle would be something," he said enthusiastically. "I'm sure you wouldn't miss it?"

"No, sir, nothing like it's happened in a hundredth year, as we say."

"This is my only chance then," Kester said. "I'll stay well back out of the way, and find you so I can leave right after."

Con slowly nodded his head. "I don't see why you shouldn't, sir. Can't be any harm in it."

"Good. I'll take those packets for later." He held out his hand.

Con shook his head. "Sorry, sir, I can give you this. No one would risk coming full size here."

He held up the blue packet of enlarging powders. "But not this; we've strict rules for this, sir," he said of the transportation powders. "Quite against the rules to allow a terran, forgive me sir, to lay a hand to them."

Kester didn't let disappointment show. There was another way out. "Thank you, Con, you've been a friend while I've stayed here. I won't forget it. I'll take the blue packet."

Con gave it to him and put the white one into the breast pocket of his tunic.

"Oh, after I've gone," Kester said, handing back the bag of gems. "Present this to the Princess. Tell her I don't require a reminder of my service to her. She'll understand."

After leaving Con, Kester hurried to the Hall of Dance, but instead of May, Bri seemed to have been waiting for him and came right over.

"My lady," she said softly, "could not meet you, sir, but will come when the ceremonies begin."

"She's alright?" Kester asked.

"Yes, but sir," Bri said, "Whatever you've planned, please, watch out for her. I don't think she can bear this place longer."

She must be desperate if her pixy noticed. When Bri left, he spotted a crew of grumbies preparing for the merry-making.

"You, fellow," Kester said to an orange-spotted grumby. "Why haven't you put out the fire?"

The grumby stopped his low muttering to tip his head up.

"The fire is to be out for the ceremony," Kester said. "It will be too warm when the room's filled, especially for those sporting armor."

Kester glanced down the hall. "See the moveable wall near the musicians? Put it in front of the fireplace."

The grumby stared at Kester.

"Well, hop to your orders," Kester said.

With a bow, the grumby was off with a resumed complaint. Kester waited until all his directions were carried out. He left for the kitchen, where pixies and grumbies worked at a mad pace, so he found it easy to go to the pantries for what he hoped to find there, rope. Yes, there were lengths of it in a closet filled with buckets, baskets, and other supplies. He coiled the longest one tight as he could, laid it in a basket, and on his way past the linen closet, covered the rope with a stack of tablecloths. Back in the Hall of Dance, he put the basket down near the fireplace and surreptitiously moved it closer to it with his foot. Then he grabbed the cloths, kicked the basket behind the screen, and handed the linens off to a grumby who appeared puzzled over what to do with them. It was hours before the mock battle was to begin, so he returned to his suite.

When it was nearer the time, Kester dressed in his own decent things, and hurried to find the Hall festooned with swags of gold and silver flowers. Faes sipped their brew, gossiped, and danced. Why wasn't she here? Whenever a blasted fae hung too close to the fireplace's screen, Kester wanted to shove them away. So far, they were all too full of what was to come to show interest in him or what was behind the screen. As the start of ceremonies drew nearer and May didn't appear, Kester's unease grew.

If she didn't show, he must leave without her. Could he do that? Kester should be sure, he never wavered before, but nothing had been the same, he wasn't the same since he met May.

Chapter 12

*Him therefore now the object of his spite
And deadly food he makes: him to offend*

Bri insisted on fetching a tray, though May wasn't hungry. When the pixy set it before her, the savory scents changed her mind. May put a spoon in the soup and raised it to her mouth.

"No!" Amazingly, Bri knocked it from her, spraying soup on her arm and the table.

"Poison! My lady, poison in the soup. See the sheen on top, the blue cast?"

May titled her head. There was an unmistakable blue shine glossing the soup like oil.

"That?" she asked, as Bri scrubbed soup off May's arm with the napkin.

May held out her T-shirt. Tiny blue dots against the white seemed to swim. She made herself breathe slow and steady.

"Just a measure, my lady, born of caution," Bri said. "Some were angry over Prince Aidan's interest in you, so I tested daily. A small measure, to be sure, it's rarely used here. A pinch of a powder, and if poison is present, a blue cast will show. Oh! This is terrible, and on the eve of the union. What shall we do?"

Overcome, May hugged Bri. "You saved my life. I was warned about Princess Kerriena, but never dreamed she'd try this."

"Tell the Prince, my lady, you must, this instant."

May followed Bri, unhappy with the glances and whispering her presence in the corridors provoked. They entered Guilly Hall, stopped near a half-open door where fairies adjusted armor. While Bri spoke with a courtier, May was stuck with the supremacy those gold-clad fairies radiated. Bri signaled, and they were ushered into Prince Aidan's study, where he sat an agate desk with Rais. The Prince frowned on spotting May. Rais stalked out angrily, almost slammed the door as he left.

Bri spoke first. "My lord Prince, your consort was poisoned!"

"What!" He leapt up from his seat.

"Peace, my prince, I stopped her in time." Bri said. "I took the old measures against treachery, saw the blue cast."

"Blue—you're certain?" the Prince demanded.

"See," May said. "Drops got on my shirt."

She stretched out the material, but the Prince didn't inspect it. Instead, he slapped his desktop. "On the eve of our union!"

His nostrils flared, his mouth tightened. He visibly mastered himself. Coolly, he asked if May recovered from her shock. She nodded.

He opened the door. "Rais."

"What trouble is she stirring, my prince?" Rais asked. "If the Princess gets wind of her—"

"There's trouble already," the Prince said. "We wonder if

the owner of it is prepared to pay the price."

"What's wrong?" Rais' face became grimmer, if possible, than his prince's.

"Rais, escort our consort to her rooms and guard her. We'll be sending Seg to fetch a tray there. He's to bring it straight back to us."

Rais didn't need to be told more. "Yes, my prince."

"How long will I be kept a prisoner?" May said, sorry she listened to Bri. The insult to the Prince mattered most. Now she must get past Rais to meet up with Kester.

"Pouting becomes you not," Prince Aidan said. "We will come to you when our obligations allow it."

Angry, May went to the door. "Don't. You have what you wanted, I want to be let go."

"Not without our leave, consort," he hatefully reminded her.

Back at her rooms, Rais bid them wait by the door while Seg hovered.

"Where's the tray?" Rais asked.

"On the table," Bri said coming into the room. "It's gone!"

Rais made a thorough search but nothing was left behind. "No doubt a spy was stationed near to see how this treachery played itself out," Rais said. "It's a pity you didn't bring the tray with you. Seg, go back to your master with this news."

"Yes sir."

"You've missed your repast, my lady," Rais said. "No

one would dare to proceed against you now. This pixy will take precautions, just the same."

May sank into a velvet seat. "I feel ill."

Rais' gaze was sharp. "It's nerves, my lady. If you wish, I'll send for a physic."

"NO! I just want to be let alone. Please."

With a slight smile, Rais bowed lightly and left for his station outside the door.

Bri came over to May, fussily putting pillows behind her back. "I'm sorry, my lady, that things should come to this."

"To hate me that much," May said, "to wish me dead. In a way, I understand the Princess. Where I come from couples promise to be faithful. If I loved someone, I wouldn't share them."

May crossed her arms over her chest. She was unable to stop replaying the Prince learning about the poison. Not once did he comfort her, or voice concern for her welfare. Kester was right. Resist him, he warned her. She wished she'd been able to. If he came to her after he wedded the Princess, May would give in, and afterward hate herself. She must get far away from these terrible fairies. This was no time for self-pity, so she got up and dressed in a lavender gown.

She wanted her own things, but she must blend in. Bri braided her hair and wound it amethyst beads. Afterwards Bri went out with the pretext of fetching food, and when she bustled into the suite minutes later with a tray was excited.

"The halls overflow," she said. "I was jostled and

bumped everywhere. Try this."

May finished pouring what she hoped was her last glass of the herb wine that kept her unnaturally alert since she fell into fairy lights. "Did you test it?" she said.

"No need, my lady."

"Not after what almost happened?" May said.

"This is special," Bri said, as she lifted the cover over a dish.

There was a folded paper on it. May snatched it up and read.

May,

The rumor of poison is everywhere. I was sick for you when I heard it. You must slip away during the mock battle. Meet me where we planned.

Kester

She threw the paper in the fire so no one else could discover it. Dear Kester. A tear slipped down her cheek, which she quickly wiped away.

"When will the Mock Battle start?"

"We'll hear war cries," Bri said.

May ran to the bedroom to get the clothes and shoes she'd tied into a bundle and stashed under the bed. How was she to distract Rais at her door? Getting an idea, May left her old clothes and washed her face for several minutes in icy cold water. Then she lay on her bed and called weakly to Bri. Bri fluttered in, laid a hand to her cool, damp skin and fretted.

"My lady, you're ill!"

"Oh-h," May groaned, rolling her head from side to side and clutching her middle.

Bri ran for Rais, who rushed in to touch May's cheek. "I'll get a physic."

May was half off the bed, but fell back when Bri returned, started moaning again. In a panic, Bri said, "Stay here, help will come." She fled the room.

May sprang up and reached for the bundle under the bed, then pulled her hand away. There was no way to hide it, and she was already conspicuous. She cracked the outer door. The passage jammed with fairies. She just joined them when frightening chants sounded; the mock battle cries. May squeezed her way forward. Spectators stood layers deep, so she kept them between herself and the ceremony. Pushing past a knot of ooh-ing pixies, she got a glance of the hall's center.

Arrayed on either side were fairies in silver, fairies in gold, fierce in their armor. Then Prince Aidan and the Maich challenger stepped out, bowed to one another and straitened. The air filled with stinging reports of steel on steel as they struck again, and again. The sounds frosted May's heart—a mock battle included a real contest.

Why did Prince Aidan fight? Princess Kerriena did not. A male fairy took her part. Those swords had sharp edges. The Prince swept his sideways and hit his challenger on his armor's joint. Blood spattered diamonds. The crowd seemed uneasy. They weren't trying to kill each other, were they?

Prince Aidan fought as if enraged, rained blow after blow

on his challenger, relentless. The mediator kept still. The Prince's foot slipped on his opponent's blood. That fairy struck Prince Aidan's helm. The vibrating clang made the crowd sway with excitement. Fingers dug into her arm. Kester half-dragged May toward the fireplace while every eye strained to follow the contest. He got May behind the screen.

"Let's go," he said.

"But how will the fight turn out?"

"As it must, May."

"Please, Kester—"

"May, if you won't leave, I have to. Don't make me go without you."

He meant it. When she was on the chair he'd put in back, she pressed one leg before her, got her back against the flue, put up the other leg up. It was dim, so she pulled the gown between her knees and started shimmying upwards. It wasn't easy pushing against opposite walls while she inched her body's weight up. Kester, rope coiled over his shoulder, was just below. If she fell, he'd take the brunt of it.

"Move over," he said when they'd gone about twenty feet. She did, and he went past.

Minutes later he said, "Take my hand."

Thankful, May allowed Kester to help pull her up.

"We've little time," he said, uncoiling rope and playing it out the flue's opening.

He was right. Rais would know May was missing. Fairies would be searching. Suddenly excited cries from the crowd below swelled. She couldn't bear to think what might be happening. One foot slid. She gasped and caught herself; sweat coated her forehead, her knees felt like pudding.

"I can't do this much longer," she said.

"You can," Kester whispered.

In this dim light she watched Kester take a piece of wood out of his tunic, tie one end of the rope to it, and then fit it crosswise in the opening.

"It might not be long enough," he said. "Wait here until I whistle."

He dropped the other end of rope out of the opening. "If this doesn't work, seek out Aidan. Tell him I kidnapped you in league with the Princess. He'll protect you."

May grabbed Kester's tunic to say no, don't try it, but he would do it anyway. "Kester...I couldn't bear it if anything happens to you."

A swishing sound alerted them they weren't alone. "My lady, I'm here."

"Bri how did you—?"

"My lady," Bri said from just below. "I saw the note and replaced it on the tray. You must go, the Princess will kill you. Tell your friend not to break his neck. I'll take each of you a safe distance. Ask him to hold on just out there."

Bri squeezed past May and hovered near while May climbed to sit dangling over the opening's edge. Bri put her arms about her. Together they flew down and away from what May realized was a tree that hid the chimney's flue.

"You never would've done it, even with rope, my lady. It's too high."

"Bri, you've been a true friend. Tell me. Is Prince Aidan all right?"

"I know not, my lady. It was all I could do to part the crush to reach you. Here, this spot will do."

Bri landed by another tree. May shivered; the gown was thin for the real world.

"I'll be back with your friend."

Hunkered down, May was afraid to move. For one her size, the night held hidden dangers. She made a mouthful for a raccoon. The bite of a harmless spider would kill her. Thankfully, Kester was soon by her side.

"I must go back, my lady, join the search so no one suspects. Here's a gift to remember me." Bri pushed a purse into her hands.

"I could never forget you, Bri. Thank you for your kindness." She kissed the pixy's cheek.

"Bye, my lady, goodbye," Bri said softly, as she flew away.

"Here, we'll do this right quick," Kester said when Bri deposited him and left, taking a packet from his tunic. "I don't fancy being this size."

Kester sprinkled the contents onto them. *Her entire body hummed like a violin string plucked.* She sneezed three times, was suddenly too large alongside Kester. She fell forward onto her hands and knees. Kester, who also toppled, was up first. He helped her to her feet.

"We must run for it. A shame you're stuck in that getup."

"It's worth this," May said.

They were out, free. Now she must put as much distance as possible between the Realm, Prince Aidan and her.

Chapter 13

With living eye more fair was never seen,
Of chastity and honor virginal:
Witness ye heavens, whom she in vain to help did call.

Kester and May ran, walked fast, and even after the herb wine wore off, managed through sheer will to keep moving all night. Faint starlight was their only help. Exhausted, May shivered in the night air. All she could think of was her last glimpse of Prince Aidan. In spite of how he treated her, it was horrible not knowing how the fight ended. Kester had reached a stream.

"This will take us to the river that flows out of the wood. I have a boat cached near here."

Stumbling alongside him, Kester caught her.

"Sit, rest a moment," he said. "I'll be back."

Kester ran ahead around a bend in the water. May's feet burned inside the useless sandals, the thin straps cutting. Ash streaked her head to toe. She leaned over, rubbed her hands in the water, and then cupped them to sip fresh water. All she got away with was the purse Bri pressed on her, which she'd tied about her wrist. Otherwise, she would have lost it long since. Her pack was at Kester's camp near the stream. She was certain she was so far away from where she started out she'd never find her apple tree again. Kester came back into view carrying a pouch.

May wiped her face and stood.

"Where'd you get that?" she said.

"With the boat I spoke of. If you're up to it, we'll be on our way," Kester said.

May glanced back.

"They won't catch us now, May. We're well away from there."

Once in the boat, May collapsed against the wood deck. Kester picked up and placed the oars. She sat up, reached for an oar.

"I'll row. Rest, I can't carry you along on my back, here." He handed her the leather bag. "There's dried jerk. It's tough, but will nourish in a pinch."

May took a piece of jerk, chewed it. It was smoky; suddenly she spat it into the water.

"Had it turned?" Kester asked.

"I haven't eaten meat in so long...thought I'd get sick," May said.

May sat back, twisted to one side, the other, uncomfortable. Fair-weather clouds scudded by.

A jarring thunk woke her. The sun was an hour from the horizon. May slept the day away, the first long sleep she had in who knew when. Kester pulled up to a bank on the left side of the river. A few hundred yards away, the lights of a settlement flickered.

"Where are we? Is it safe?" she whispered.

"Yes, it's Delain, a port town I was headed to before we met,' he said. "I've friends here. If not for your gown, we'd go about openly. One look and anyone would know you've been in the Realm. That alone would cause all kinds of trouble. Faes single out the prettiest girls to be consorts. It's known they're rewarded for such dalliances when they leave. Some will be after you for the gold or jewels you might carry. Others will be after more if they see you like that."

May knew how the gown clung, blushed.

"Come." Kester stepped into the shallow water.

Before she could pick up her hem to step in the water, Kester scooped May up and placed her on dry land. He hid the boat in tall weeds. Kester led the way. Voices drifted out of open windows. The scents of cooking wafted to them. A dog barked. Finally, Kester stopped by the back door of a large building.

"Stay put. I'll be right back," he said.

Kester returned in minutes with a cloak for her. She held it tightly closed.

"All's clear. Follow me."

He moved toward a two-storied building weathered soft gray by sea air. Many windows faced its sprawling garden. Kester opened a door, and they stepped into a narrow hall where a half-door opened on a large kitchen. A roast was spitted over its fire. A table held cooling pies. Loaves of bread stacked at one end. A girl pushed through swinging shutters into the kitchen's farther side, dark hair coming undone from her braid. One hand balanced a tray of mugs, the other grasped a pan of dirty dishes. Smiling broadly when she saw Kester, she set her loads on a sideboard and wiped her hands on her apron.

"Kester, you're way overdue. Moran was asking after you since late spring. Who's this?" she said, suddenly wary when she caught sight of May.

Kester stopped her short.

"Kerys, this is May, a friend of mine. She's seen trouble. I've been helping her."

Kerys came closer. Openly inspecting May, her eyes narrowed. "I can see what sort. You should leave her to herself, Kester. You don't need her kind."

Kester pushed May forward, though she shrank from Kerys' hostile glare. "Kerys," he said, shaking his head, "May is an innocent. We just escaped the Realm last night," he added in a low voice. "You're not like some who'd judge May. She was separated from her family when they caught her. She's blameless, I know, I was there."

"You say so?" Kerys clucked, put her hands on May's shoulders and pulled her away from Kester.

"Poor thing, come along with me. You're done in. We'll soon put you right."

Kerys steered May to the hall outside the kitchen and up its stairs while Kester came behind them.

"This room will do. I'll bring water for a bath. Kester, the inn is fair full. You'll bunk with my brother. He'll give you somewhat to wear while I wash your things. Did the pair of you fall in an ash pile? If you've been in some fae warren, you'll be starved for decent fare. I'll be back shortly with supper."

May had to smile over this girl. Kerys was thirteen or fourteen at most but mothered Kester and her. Hard-working as Kerys appeared to be, perhaps in this society, she was considered an adult. May spotted a wash bowl and pitcher of water. She poured some and scrubbed up. When she was done, the water was grey. The fire in the grate was laid, and Kester worked at kindling it. May pulled out a chair, sat. A wood bed had blankets tucked tight about its plump mattress. Braided rugs covered the floor. Two walls had shuttered windows.

"Does the inn have a water closet?" she asked. "I'm afraid to appear ignorant of what to expect here. I was sure Kerys would turn me out to be stoned or worse when she first saw me."

"You'll find no water closet; these are simple folk," Kester said as he tossed May's dirty water out the window, then refilled the basin with fresh before availing himself of a wash up.

"A little house out of doors is used for the necessary," he said, patting dry. "As to stoning, a virtuous woman hereabout would throw cutting words at a girl who's been a consort. They wouldn't allow any excuse if she were caught against her will. They believe if it happened to them, they'd die rather than yield."

May shivered. "No one would believe I was a consort in the name only?"

"Not as fine as you are," Kester said. "You've no notion of your prettiness."

"It's this clothing, the fairy potions…I'm nothing special."

"Has no one ever told you how special you are, May?"

Kerys' knocked, and Kester went to get the door. She set down a tray with mugs, plates of roasted meat, potatoes, and greens. Bread, butter, and slices of pie finished the offering.

"Eat up. You've lost stone, Kester," Kerys said.

May sipped ale and made a face.

"Can't hold with drink?" Kerys asked.

"I'm sorry. You've been so nice," May said, "but no, I should have said something. My father used to like it too well. So did my mother."

"No harm. Kester can handle his and yours as well. I'll bring up té."

Kerys left and was back with May's tea minutes later. "Full crowd in tonight, can't stay."

May ate of everything but the meat; her stomach wasn't up for more than a few bites anyway. Kester finished his dinner, all of the bread, most of what she left over, and both mugs of ale.

"Ah, that filled the very spot." He leaned back and studied May. "You didn't mention before about your folks liking the drink. Is it why you ran off? Did they beat you?"

"No," May said. "My father would say children are a dime a dozen, which means they're not worth much. They did their drinking and forgot I existed."

Kerys interrupted them, having heard May's answer. She carried an armload of clothes she put on the bed.

"Here you go, Kester, these should do you. You nip down the hall for your wash. Your little friend's had enough. She's to rest. You can get together come morning. Don't worry; I've got her in hand."

Kester thanked Kerys with a kiss on her cheek. "Good night, Kerys, May."

"Good night, Kester. Thank you," May said.

Kerys dragged in a copper tub, May hurried to help her. It had a high back and enough room for a person to sit in it. Kerys half-filled it with hot water. Then she added cold and tested it.

"Get in. I'll scrub your hair," Kerys said.

May was suddenly afraid for Kerys to see her gown. "Thank you, but I can manage."

"Don't be shy. I've sisters. Let me take the cloak, my own it is anyway. Kester was right to borrow it though."

May slipped it off.

Kerys gasped. "I've never seen the like. This is how they dress?"

May nodded.

"No wonder folk take on. It's not decent, but it's fairer than any shift I've laid eyes on. Go ahead, take it off. I'll turn about while you get in the tub."

May shrugged out of the gown and undergarments and

slipped into deliciously warm water. Kerys handed her a cloth
and soap. Kerys undid her hair, laying out the amethyst beads,
exclaiming at their beauty, then rinsed May's hair and set to
scrubbing it. She felt like a child. Finally, Kerys rinsed her
hair and handed her a large towel. It was rough but fresh.
Kerys turned about once more while May stood and wrapped
herself up.

"I'll leave the tub till morning," Kerys said. "Here, sleep
in this shift. Get to bed. You're wore out."

"Thank you, Kerys. Kester told me he could count on his
friends here. I'm so glad you're one of them."

Kerys instructed her to bar the door behind her.
Afterward, May donned a shift that resembled a nightshirt.
She blew out all the candles, got in bed, pulled the covers to
her chin. The room spun. Clean, warm, dry, safe; her legs
relaxed, her arms grew heavy. The Prince was far, far off, yet
his incredible eyes swam dizzily before her. Was she truly
free? He'd loomed so large. Would she forget, and be able to
enjoy a real relationship someday? In her exhausted state, she
couldn't be sure. Eventually, the room stopped twirling.

She woke when sunlight split the shutters' slats. May
peaked out at a harbor view. Fishermen worked at nets. Boats
headed out to sea. Women hung out wet garments. Children
ran, laughed, and played. It was peaceful, normal, nothing like
the Realm. May could see herself staying here a while. When
she got out of bed, her fairy gown, undergarments, and slippers
were missing.

Alarm shot through her until she realized Kerys must have taken them. Other garments waited on the chair. Linen underthings, off-white and gathered at the waist, fit her well enough. A linen shift with a ribbon gathering the material came next. May pulled the ribbon to adjust its neckline. A dark blue dress went over the shift. It flared past the hips, fell to her ankles. The long sleeves slashed to show the shift underneath. The last piece was a boned vest, but May wasn't sure how to wear it. Kerys left her knitted stockings and ankle boots. The boots fit with a half inch to spare for her toes.

A knock came at the door. "It's Kerys."

May undid the bolt. Kerys came in with hot cereal, steaming tea, boiled eggs, and toast. She set down the tray and checked May over.

"I'm not used to these," May said. "My clothes were plainer."

Nothing could be truer.

"It's me older sister's, just second best," Kerys said. "I could use her hands about the work, but she's off nursing our sick aunt. Here, hold out your arms."

Kerys pulled bits of the under-shift through the sleeve slits so they puffed.

"Put your arms in here," she said, showing May how to wear the vest. In worked like a corset. Kerys did the strings in the back, pulling them tight and tying them. When she was done, she directed May to a mirror hanging on the door.

Seeing herself, May felt the same unreality she

experienced in fairy clothes. Still, the outfit was pleasing. "Should I put my hair, up, down?"

"You're of an age to wear your hair down," Kerys said. "Isn't it the same among your folk? Here, sit. It'll not take a moment for me to fix."

Kerys brushed and arranged her hair with a braid on each side, tying them together in back with ribbon from her pocket. "That's fine."

"Thank you, Kerys. I appreciate everything you've done for me."

"Ah, it's nothing." Kerys' shrugged.

"Where's…what I was wearing?"

"Oh, saved the beads—they're worth coin, here." Kerys gave her a cloth bag. "There was nothing else but to burn the rest."

May felt a twinge. The gown was beautiful, but where would she wear it now?

"Kester's off. Said he's back before lunch. I've me chores waiting below. If you've a mind for company, join me when you're done."

When she left, May pulled the table to the window and threw the shutters wide. While she ate, she enjoyed the view. Away to the right, a sandy shore crooked a long arm about a bend. To the left, cliffs shadowed the sea. Birds drifted on unseen currents. It was summery, and if she were on Earth, she'd go swimming. Somehow, she didn't think the locals did anything like that here. She might be out of the Realm, but her fundamental problems hadn't changed. What was she to do? Could she ever get back? Kester seemed the only one who might help her. She went down to the kitchen with the tray, hoping for a distraction. Kerys was peeling potatoes.

"I've nothing to do," May said. "Could I help you?"

"Kester secured the bill. You won't need to work anything off."

"It's just, I like to keep busy," May said. There was a tin pan in a dry sink. "I can wash dishes. Is the water hot?" She spied a large kettle over the hearth fire.

Kerys gave her head a shake, as if she couldn't believe the offer. "It's always ready."

May took the kettle to the pan and poured out steaming water. She shaved soap off the cake as she saw Kerys do in her bath the night before.

"That's too hot. You'll need cold from the well out back," Kerys said.

Back home there were several months when her father waited before her mother insisted he pay a plumber to fix the kitchen sink. May had resorted to throwing dirty water down a dry well in the side yard. She'd wait with the greasy water to be sure no one in a passing car spotted her doing it. The difference was everyone here lived in this manner, and there was no shame attached to it. She carted a bucket of well water in, added some to the dishpan. A pile of dishes waited, likely from breakfast. May started with mugs, rinsing them in water left in the bucket.

"You're used to work, at least," Kerys said approvingly. "No girl worth her keep sits about all the day."

"Kerys, how old are you?"

She laughed. "Fourteen summers, but Da says I boss like an old wife....our good ma has been gone too many years. I've older sisters wedded with babes, but no time for beaus, what with helping da run the inn. My sister Lacey is half out the door. She's with the aunt I spoke of pining to be here, as her beau fishes off Delain. How old are you?"

"I'm seventeen," May said.

"And you not wed? You're too fine not to have a beau lurking. Or is Kester more than a friend?"

Blushing, May shook her head and got busy. When she finished, she found a straw broom and swept the floor. With that done, she looked about for a place to throw away the debris.

"In the dustbin, by the fireplace," Kerys said.

Kerys, meanwhile, dumped the potatoes in a huge pot she hooked over the fire. "What will you do now, May?"

It was the first time Kerys used her name.

"I don't know. Can I help you with lunch? I can cook too."

"That's not what I meant. Kester said you'd lost your folk. Have you other family?"

May sat down heavily on a stool. "No. I don't belong anywhere anymore."

Kerys said nothing, but her concerned face did. May spent

the rest of the morning making meat pasties, as Kerys called them, chopping leftover roast, mixing it with spices, then putting it onto dough and pinching it into triangles, which Kerys put into the fireplace oven. Kerys was a workhorse, her thin arms corded with muscle. May felt tired and a bit ashamed she couldn't keep up with her. When she was done, May washed up, threw the water out where Kerys showed her, and went to her room.

When would Kester return? To spare Kerys, she made up her bed. That done, she sat by the window. The purse Bri pressed on her at their parting sat on the basin table. Curious, May undid the tie, opened it to find folded parchments tucked inside. She pulled them out. The top one was addressed to her.

My lady,

It was my pleasure to serve you. I've enclosed recipes for body, hair and face creams, along with soap and lip balm. I recalled them from our visit with Goll and writ them for you. Tell your friend Con sends good wishes, and leaves his reward in this purse. The Princess wouldn't like her gift returned.

Bri

May opened the purse wider, gasped, and upended the bag. Out poured diamonds, rubies, sapphires, and other colored gems, a fortune. How could he turn down such wealth? What did impress Kester?

Chapter 14

Where she enjoys sure peace for evermore,
As weather-beaten ship arrived on happy shore.

May was taking lunch with Kerys when Kester returned.
She was thrilled he'd come back; she'd feared he might not.

"Kerys, May, good day,' he said. He took a hot pasty
from the platter cooling on the sideboard, put it on a dish and
sat with them.

"You look fine in that shift, May," he said. "A bit too
pretty, perhaps, though that can't be helped. How are you
getting on?"

Kerys poured him a mug of ale. "I'm off to serve in the
dining room."

"Where have you been this morning?" May asked.

"Down at the docks. I lost time in the Realm and must
make up that lack now. By my reckoning, we were there for
weeks while Kerriena and Aidan played with us." He didn't
look easy.

"Something's wrong," May said.

"I'm not certain. The talk about the tavern last night was
that rough strangers have been in Delain of late. So far I
haven't come across any."

He nodded at her. "You didn't answer my question yet."

"Kerys' kept me busy. She's a good person. I like her,
Kester."

She hesitated, looking about to be sure no one would
overhear. "I opened the purse Bri gave me. She left recipes for

fairy creams and these."

May pulled the bag from under the apron.

Kester shook his head, didn't glance at the contents. "I told Con to give them back. That evil fae had nothing to tempt me."

"I know. Bri wrote as much in her letter, but how could you not take them?" May said. "This is worth a lot."

"Kerriena's gift would only trouble me. Keep it safe by your skin. You're stuck here with naught if you can't get back to where you've come from. That could set you up."

"I can't take these," May said. "They're yours."

"Wouldn't it burn Kerriena to know they were helping you?"

May tied the bag shut and tucked it out of sight, unwilling to argue the point now. She would find a way to repay him for his kindness.

"I wondered about something else," she said. "How is it yours is a different accent than Kerys? You're not from this area, are you?"

"No, I was raised to the east."

The swinging kitchen shutters banged open.

"Look at what I've found lurking in dark corners." Kerys laughed.

A broad-shouldered man with a dense beard and rumpled black hair tromped into the kitchen with his arm dwarfing Kerys' waist. His heavy tunic, black trousers, and big leather boots made him even more formidable given his great size, but it was his energy that disturbed May. There was something dark behind his smile. Kerys slapped his arm away.

"Keep those off." She laughed indulgently. "If he wasn't such a good friend to you, Kester, I'd have clouted him sooner."

"Moran! You great beast. It's good to see you." Kester jumped up from his seat and clapped his friend on the shoulder.

"Where've you been?" Moran said. "I'd expected you for weeks' gone."

Moran's gaze licked May up and down. "Who's this?"

"This is my friend May," Kester said. "I've been helping her. May's lost her family. It's a long story. Needless to say, I've been engaged these past few weeks."

"Would I'd been so well occupied," Moran said in a low tone. "You always find the pretty ones, you rogue. It's me pleasure to meet you, lady." Moran made an exaggerated bow. "You're a beauty, May."

"Watch it, you old dog. May's too fine for the likes of you," Kester said.

May didn't like this great brute, Kester's friend or not. Every glance he sent in her direction was a leer. She wasn't used to anyone crude as he was.

"I'll go to my room now," she said, "if you'll excuse me, Kester. It was a pleasure to meet you, Mr. Moran."

"Mister? Moran will do. It's more me pleasure, Lady, me pleasure indeed."

"I'll meet you at supper, May," Kester said.

"Not if I've a say in it, you sly one," Moran said. "We've drink and talk to get through first."

May left the kitchen uncomfortable under Moran's scrutiny. After dull hours shut in her room, she came back down to wait on Kester. She washed more dishes, mashed potatoes, and dished up pie. Kerys was grateful for the help, as the tavern and dining room were full. Finally Kester showed up without his friend Moran, thank goodness. May fixed each of them a plate.

"Good news," Kester said. "The King journeys to Delain for the sea air. I'll introduce you. It may be he can help you."

"A real king?" May asked. "Does he live in a castle?"

"A fortress in the northern mountains, actually," Kester said with a smile. "The King's a sensible man with a charming Queen. They have three fine princes too."

"How is it you know a king?" May said. "Does an ordinary man claim such acquaintances?"

"I've secrets," he said. "It makes my work that easier to keep them. But as I know yours, I should trust you with a few of mine. First, and please, repeat this to no one; Kester isn't my given name. I'm Lachlan of house Mirddyn, nephew of the King."

"You're royalty?" May said, sitting back.

"Nothing so grand in my birth; my da carries the title, Duke Raymore. My older brother and he keep the family estates. For myself, I roam about the kingdom for my uncle and report on various matters. The court is removed from most folk, so no one in the countryside is like to recognize me."

"I guessed right when I met you—you are a spy. Does Kerys know?"

"She knows Kester and I'll keep it that way. Moran's a King's man, a royal guardsman. We never use my real name, even when we're alone. It's safer so."

"Why? Is there some trouble?"

Kester finished his last bite of pie and wiped his mouth. "Mirddyn's a young King, on the throne two years since the late king passed on. He expects a stab at his defenses' weak points. A well-favored kingdom such as this, with its fertile fields, large herds of cattle and sheep, valuable copper mines, and good trade routes is tempting. There are domains on Illynd whose leaders own no scruples. They would grab Mirddyn, and hold tight after, squeezing profit from it and its people."

"Is this the danger you spoke of when we met, or is there more you didn't tell me about?"

"There's always more," Kester said. "And the large part of that trouble is often caused by rovers."

"What kind of trouble?"

He rubbed his head. "Some say rovers take an advantage in uneasy times, but from stories I've heard, rovers heap dry fuel in a landscape poor in moisture. Things look bad before they show, but they're a deal worse after."

"Why do they do it? Are they just bad people?" May asked.

"Greed's their game," he said. "They'll leave Illynd heavier with someone's gold."

"I hope you know by now, Kester," May said, "That I have nothing to do with anyone like that."

He put his hand on hers, squeezed it. "I think well of you, May. How could I not? I was thinking about the life you ran from. If no one's told you this, it's me lucky to be first. You're fine, May, outside and in. Someone should have shown you the truth of that every single day."

Kester left to meet Moran. Once she heated enough water, May carted buckets to her room for a bath. While she soaked, Kester's words sunk in. She'd always tried so hard to love her parents, hoped they could love her back, fearing she was the reason they drank. Now, she started to think they'd been the problem, not her. The realization had been coming on slowly.

It was warming to know Kester approved of her. She rubbed the hard soap, tried to get lather. Right now, May wished for the wonderful lotions and creams she'd used in the Realm. Kester had noticed the difference in her when she used them. She'd like him to see her that way again. Come morning, she'd gather ingredients for Goll's recipes. She scrubbed her arms, rinsed. Prince Aidan came to mind, though she'd kept him at bay all day. How did he fare in the mock-battle? She couldn't believe he'd suffer any real hurt. Having this distance helped May question her attraction to him.

In the Realm, it had become impossible to tell if her physical responses to him were fairy glamour or real. It would never do to love a fairy; she could see that then, knew now it was impossible. Even so, she didn't want to linger over memories of the Prince. Her bath done, she drew on her nightgown, got in bed and she blew out the candle. Now her biggest problem was finding a way home.

May missed few things about her old life except running water, flush toilets, electricity, and heat—when her parents provided them that was. Still, she wished more than anything to find her way back so she could begin life there over. After what she'd been through here, alcoholic parents weren't going to stop her from remaking her life. Losing Granddad must have made being at home more depressing than before. This place, with all its dangers was frightening, but made May realize she was tougher than she dreamed. Kester had a large part in helping her understand that.

She didn't fault him for keeping his real name quiet, but what else hadn't he said about himself? She'd come to rely on him, but was that the right thing for her to do? When he shared with her, she was sure he left a lot out of his telling. Perhaps he couldn't do otherwise. Clearly, he could not take on her troubles too. If and when the time came to say goodbye to Kester, it would be awfully hard. A woodpecker tapping the inn's wood shingles for insects woke her the next day.

Kester left word he'd be back for a late sup.

"Kerys, do you use comfrey, or Wort?" May asked when she'd done up the morning's dishes.

"Are you ill?" Kerys said.

"No…I'd like to make up creams for skin and hair…if I can find what I need, that is."

"Here," Kerys said.

She walked into the kitchen's large pantry and May followed.

"There's dried herbs and such on those shelves. Take what you need. I'll settle any bill with Kester," Kerys said, "if you'll just let me know what you used later."

May was determined Kester accept something from the purse for her expenses.

"We'll look over the kitchen garden to see what's fresh," Kerys said.

After Kerys pointed out and named them, she supplied a peeled stick with a blackened point and a small bottle of sieved ash. "A drop of water will make ink."

May drew faint but perceptible drawings, sketching the leaf and flower if there were any, on the back of the folded recipes. She wanted to identify them in the future, and the parchments were the only papers she had. By noon, clouds piled over the town. She went in to give Kerys a hand. A rowdy crowd packed the tavern.

Kerys came into the kitchen complaining loudly. "If I get pinched once more, someone will lose a finger." She slipped a small blade into her apron before she left with a tray of ale.

May went to the swinging door to peep out. These men weren't like the fishermen she saw about the dock wearing canvas aprons to protect their clothes from fish guts. They dressed as Moran did in dark leather. One, spying her in the doorway, called out.

"Hey, pretty. Come out where there's a cozy lap." His suggestion set the others roaring.

May shrank against the wall.

"I'll come in to warm you up private like, if that's your wish." This got his back slapped.

Kerys hurried in with an empty tray. "I don't like this lot." She grimaced. "They drink too quickly, and they're nasty with it. You'd best go to your room and bolt the door."

"What about you?"

"Don't fear for me. I've Da and me brothers at hand. Kester will be back soon. Just stay out of sight. You're too tempting to be seen."

May went to her room and bolted the door. Kerys' words frightened her more than the behavior of the man from the bar. She sat on the bed listening to muted laughter. Her head nodded, the room grew dimmer, and she fell asleep. When she woke, the only light came from the hearth. Harsh sounds from outside disturbed her. May went to the window. Rain fell, the boats were in, but many figures were visible on the docks.

Those fishermen should at home. It took a moment for her to register one man ran at another with a sword. May's chest sucked in tight. In the distance, a woman screamed.

Dogs yowled. She heard the thin cries of children. May went toward the door, stopped, hands sweaty. What should she do? Where was Kester? He should be back by now. What if he was down there fighting? What of Kerys? May wiped her palms in her skirt. Grabbing a cloak Kerys lent her, she wrapped it about her and slid the bolt aside, wincing at the scrape of metal on wood. Pulling the door slowly, she peered out.

No one out was out there. Resisting the urge to go hide under the bed, May crept down the stairs, cringing with each creak of its worn treads. At the bottom, she paused. A log in the kitchen fireplace popped. May steeled herself to go in.

A tray was upended and mugs of ale spilled, the yeasty smell strong. The puddle spread out toward her. Where was Kerys? The backdoor stood so close. All she had to do was slip out and run. May found a knife on the sideboard and clutched it to her side. Peering over the shutters, she scrutinized the tavern. Tables and chairs were tangled. The reek of stale ale was stronger here. What did she sleep through? Shouts could be heard from the docks. The bar was to her right. May leaned over it. Sick backed up her throat. Kerys' da laid face down, a knife to the hilt in his back. There were black patches in her vision.

Hold on, hold on, don't faint. May stepped back. The door to the inn's left wing was cracked. Pushing at it, she couldn't move it all the way. She looked around it, spotted the bare, slender leg then the body against the door, blood dark beneath it, oh God! Oh Kerys!

May almost screamed her name, but shoved her hand over her mouth and backed away. She stumbled into the kitchen, down its hall, and out the back door. Panting, nauseated, she froze on hearing a noise from inside the kitchen.

"Where's me pretty lap warmer?" said the man who harassed her from the bar earlier.

She ran through the kitchen garden, past the well, and went into a crouch behind the outhouse. When she heard no pursuit for several minutes, she crawled to the stand of trees and brush beyond the inn's yard. A door banged. She was panting, shut her mouth. Light rain still fell. The door of the privy creaked.

"Are you in here?" the brute wondered aloud. He banged the door shut.

Would he see her, hear her breathing? She held her breath. There was rustling, footsteps. He was searching all about, muttering and cursing. His footfalls were closer, too close. When he found her, he would do to her what was done to Kerys. Sweet Kerys, naked, battered about her face, bruised all over because she fought back. May had to get up, run because it was her last chance, but her skin was slick with cold sweat, body shivering so hard she wasn't sure her legs would work right. Someone called out. The footfalls moved away, back toward the Sundowner.

May vomited in the brush, tears stinging, nose running. If Kester already returned, he could well be dead now. Wiping her mouth and nose, she tried to think. She must get to the King. Kester said he was coming to Delain. Surely, he'd have soldiers to protect him? Before she could help Kester or anyone else still alive here, she must get farther away. The boat Kester dragged onto the shore; she could use that. She went along in a half-crouch, taking care not to rustle anything as she moved into the water, around the front of the boat.

In terror of giving her position away, cool water flooding her boots, May slid the boat backwards slow, lifting as much as she could to keep it from scraping. Fires reddened the sky above the harbor. Fishing boats cut loose by the attackers burned down to their hull. Every scream made her bite her lip to keep from sobbing. May went over the boat's side and pushed off the sandy bottom with an oar. She bent low to keep from sight, strove to make as little noise as possible pulling the oar through the water. She headed upstream, away from the terrible things happening in Delain.

It was difficult to make headway. The boat was light, but she must go against the current. She fought to keep close by the shore as well, hoping the shadows there would cover her escape. Rain seeped into her garments, from the knees down she was soaked. After a hundred yards or so, her arms shook with the effort to paddle. Pausing to rest, she dipped her hand in the water, wiped her face with it. She dipped it again.

Just then, a wet hand grabbed her wrist. A sopping head rose next to the boat.

Chapter 15

What war so cruel, or what siege so sore

Leading his old friend from the kitchen and May, Moran and Kester settled in the tavern's darkest corner. Kerys set down a pitcher of sweating ale and left them alone.

"Now, tell me what I've missed," Kester said, after Moran took a deep drink out of his mug.

"The King was uneasy you didn't show at our arranged meeting," Moran said, in a lower voice than he used up till now. "When you were two weeks late, he set me to look about. I could make no report after a month trying, so he decided he'd waited too long. The King let it out he would come for sea air, taking his queen and their bairns, but it was to find you. He'll be here soon."

He had another long swig, wiped his chin. "Where've you been?" Moran asked. "And what has it to do with the lovely little bit you've set up here? Not that I wouldn't find all sorts of ways to pass time with her."

"None of that talk, Moran," Kester said. "She's a decent girl. I won't hear her muddied. I found her lost in the woods, as I said. That part's true enough. By chance, fools' lights caught her. I followed after to get her out. We escaped a few nights ago."

Moran all but drooled. "A consort, she's a consort!"

"Mind yourself, Moran. I was there. She was no consort, I tell you. We found a way out with help from a pixy who befriended us. When King Crovayne comes, he'll have the whole tale. We were in that accursed dance most of the time."

"Ah, we had strange tales not long back of folk released from the dance, sent away with treasures for their troubles. What riches did you take with you?" Moran said.

"We got nothing out of that blasted place but our freedom. Do you know what it is to be trapped in an endless dance by a hateful music that won't let up, day or night? There's no more to say on the matter. I want to know what's happening here about. I've heard around town of strangers in Delain. What do you know about it?"

"And every outsider marked as the wrong sort," Moran said with a laugh. "A farmer brings his wagon-load of turnips to sell, and folk with naught better to do start nattering. I've been in and out of here for weeks. There's nothing amiss."

Kester shook his head. "I was worried the whole while I was away. I needed to be here for my uncle. I'm glad he had you to fall back on, you old dog."

Later Kester joined May for supper and in the morning, purchased a decent mount at the stables. Once equipped, he rode into the country. His uncle would approach Delain from the east. He wished to meet with the King privately about his time in the Realm. It was a fair day, and he enjoyed the ride. Hours later Kester spotted the signs a larger company of horses tramped down the undergrowth. They'd come from the southeast, which meant from the sea.

Recognizing treachery, Kester veered off to the northeast to avoid clashing with the unknown riders and still reach his uncle. He feared he'd not get there first. An hour later, Kester knew the grim answer to his worries. He got off his mount at a narrow pass from the hills. Hacked bodies lay in the brush, on the grass track; the King's party met a grisly end. The killers were already gone. Kester located his uncle's body half shielding his fair queen. His children, all slain, stacked with their butchered governess. Kester, stumbling among the dead, found his father, the Duke, bloody sword in hand. Overcome, he kneeled and scooped the cold form close.

At least he died fighting for his king. He moaned, sobbed and rocked his da. The Duke did his duty. Kester failed, been less than useless. How long he crouched there, he couldn't say. The caw of a crow snapped him to sudden awareness. May! Kerys! Moran!

He forced himself to study the signs and realized the butchers who did this headed back toward Delain openly. There was work for his sword. Giving the cold forehead a kiss, he whispered a goodbye and gently laid his da on the ground. He wiped his wet face, then forced himself to run from the dead to defend what he could only hope were those still living. Spurring his horse, he raced back to Delain. While he rode, he pieced together who orchestrated this evil from the garb of the handful of dead attackers; Dailgre. When he neared Delain, Kester tied off his horse to move closer in on foot.

Dailgre's men overran the town. It was a one-sided fight, battle-hardened men against too few soldiers, poorly armed fishermen, old men, women, and babes. He burned to rush in, but he was one man. He must get help. He went back to the horse, untied it and slapped its rump to chase it away. Then he headed in a circular route to the boat pulled up on the riverbank. All the while his heart tore pieces off itself. Moran stood a fighter's chance, but May, Kerys!

These brutes were taking prisoners. He spied a string of them herded toward a building. If Kerys and May were among them; but Kester couldn't think about that or lose control. He must get help. At the river, only a depression in the weeds showed the boat had been there. He spied footprints on the muddy bank, small feet. He gazed up and downriver. There. Slipping into the water, his heart eased until he counted just one person in the boat. He dived under, came up beside it.

"Sh-h, don't cry out," Kester said.

"You're alive! How did you—?"

"Later," he said as he towed the boat closer to the shore. Where the water was shallow, he got in and took the oars from May. "Let's get upriver."

May turned to gaze at the town, at him, back again, her face pale and strained. Rain pattering the water soon sounded louder than the noise of the fighting they left behind. After a long while where they could see or hear nothing of Delain, Kester pulled the boat under a tree that overhung the water's edge. He took the oars in and slumped.

May's hands fluttered over his. "Are you injured? What happened?"

He shook his head. "I wasn't anywhere near, remember? Was off in the woods. I found, saw…my uncle the king, queen, their…babes, massacred. My da," he choked, "dead. So ends House Mirddyn. I failed, May."

His body shuddered. She held him while sobs racked him, smoothing his hair, rubbing his back. Inarticulate sounds rose from his throat.

"Kerys' is dead, Kester," she said, voice cracking.

Their sorrows ran together, faces wet with tears and rain, salt and sweet mixed. It seemed his heart swelled close to breaking his body to shards but did not, because she had her arms about him, she needed him. When Kester finally mastered himself, he rinsed his swollen eyes with river water. His throat ached.

"Who did this?" May said. "Why?"

Swallowing hard, Kester said, "It looks to be the work of Dailgre, a warlord across the sea. He's wanted Mirddyn a long time. The island he holds, Dail, is a waypoint for seafarers. Ships must put in to load up on fresh water and foodstuffs, paying a pretty price for the privilege. With Mirddyn in his bloody fist, there'd be a source of raw material Dailgre wouldn't have to purchase to resell at a steep profit."

"This is just one fight," May said. "The whole of Mirddyn can't have fallen. Who's in charge now the King's dead?"

"The royal household lies in those hills. I'm the last," Kester said.

"You must have more soldiers? We'll alert them."

"The nearest stronghold is north at the King's seat," he said. "It will take days to reach it, and we're on foot. Dailgre's men have horses. If we don't get there first, surprise may overthrow the guardsmen there. That's where we head."

"Are you able to go on, Kester? I'll take a turn rowing."

Kester sat straight.

"You're strong-willed for so young," he said, understanding what her escape from Delain must have been.

May grasped for his hand. "If...if not for me, Kester...your family, Kerys. I went to help her, but...too late."

"So was I, May, so was I."

They took turns rowing. The rain ended. Kester wanted to go as far to the north as they could on the river. The way through the woods was treacherous. Prince Aidan would be looking for them. Worse, Princess Kerriena's spies might be searching too. They wouldn't know until too late, as faes could fly small and almost unseen. If the Princess laid hands on May, she'd have her dead. How the Princess would view Kester's defection did not enter his concerns. His blunders were harder to face down than any of these blasted faes could be.

On the strength of a brief encounter with an appealing young woman, Kester lost his family and might well lose this kingdom. Charging after May turned out to be the most foolish act of his life. At times, he had to look away from her, fearing she'd read his thoughts and blame herself when the fault lay in him. On top of this, May needed him more than ever. How could he protect her?

Along with his kingdom's needs, he must secure her a place of safety. If only she knew how to get back to her own world. It was the first time since he realized how much he liked May's reliance on him that he thought to be rid of her. Given his current situation, Kester wasn't the one to protect May McKinny. Long before dawn, they left the boat. Kester covered it well, taking the water bag and pouch of dried meat with them.

"Have you the gems from Kerriena still?" he asked.

"Yes. The bag's tied to the slip under my dress."

"Good. We may need to trade for fast horses along our way. This is very near where we first escaped. I doubt any in the Realm would look for us so close by. Go quietly. We make for the camp by the pond. Our packs should still be tied up in the tree where I left them. We need those supplies. This bit of dried meat won't last us."

It was a long while since Kester went into these woods in the daylight. Even he usually kept to the river or wild meadows. Fae rings, like the one that trapped May, grew on the great forest's border, as most shared his view of the dangers of straying here. As they walked, he studied each huge tree with suspicion.

Because of their size, more area was clear about their trunks, which made the forest floor easy to negotiate. Deeper in the wood, trees were hundreds of feet tall, with wide-spreading canopies. The air was green. A layer of decaying leaves from previous years made the ground spongy and deadened sounds they made in passing. Shafts streamed through gaps in the canopy; he made it noon now. The dense atmosphere was like moving underwater. The shock of all he witnessed added to this miserable feeling. He glanced at May.

Her fair face was stony, her gray eyes smudged. Relenting, he reached for her hand. At his touch, she wove her fingers tightly with his. Hand in hand, they moved in silence. The trees ahead began to lessen in size, brush grew, and the going was harder. He led them toward a narrow trail.

"Deer make this track to the water," he whispered.

The path led to a high field. Though glad to escape the close woods, he felt too exposed under the sky.

"It's my field," May said with wonder.

They hurried. The waning sun reflected up from the pond. The lands before them were empty. When they reached his camp, Kester lowered their gear from the tree where he cached them.

"There's time for a quick meal," he said. "I don't believe we could walk further without food and rest. Take these to the freshet and get water while I start a fire."

May filled the water skins and kettle while Kester kindled a small fire, which gave a thin smoke easily erased by the light breeze. He took an iron pan and started frying salt bacon he cut off a rind. In spite of everything, the scent watered his mouth. May watched as he made flatbread. Was it just weeks earlier he did this same thing? How could so much change so quickly? After their makeshift supper, Kester told May to fix her pack.

She must bury food that went green, which was all her store but for nuts. He put out the fire and stirred the ashes with water, spreading them about. "We don't want anyone to read when last someone was here."

"Can we rest a bit longer?"

"Yes. We'll move after night falls," he said.

May settled on the blanket. Her pretty face set stiff, as if any crack would bring fresh tears. Kester sat next to her. She put her hand on his shoulder.

"You did all you could, Kester. It's my fault you weren't…there when your family needed you."

"I might well be long dead," Kester said, the reality of what happened overriding that shame. "This bit of dirty work's been well planned. They scouted the town's defenses. If I was about asking questions in too many places, I might have laid down at the inn one night, to be found with my throat slit by morn." He paused. "Anyway, it can't be undone now."

He made himself hold her gaze. "So you see I can't regret helping you, May."

She laid her head on his shoulder. Kester put an arm about her. They sat like this as the land grew darker. A stick cracked near the boulder to their right.

"Kester?" The urgent whisper cut the night.

"Moran? Over here!"

In the dim light, he could just make out Moran creeping around the rock. "You're alone?" Moran said, as he came closer.

"May's with me," Kester said as they stood.

Moran grasped his shoulders briefly, and then let him go. "You know the worst?"

Kester stood. "I arrived at the killing ground too late. After that, I went to Delain. It was a near thing there too."

"I was away," Moran said, "Scouting west, but back in time to see Dailgre's men carrying off the Kings' seal, his great ring, and the Queen's pendant. The bastards; I wanted to tear hearts open with my teeth."

He squinted in the dark, peered hard at May. "Just you and your little friend?"

As if his regard made her uncomfortable, May made a face and slipped her sack over her shoulders.

"Well," Moran said. "You're King now."

Kester didn't say anything. Moran turned away. When he spun back, Kester caught the glint of steel.

"Kester!" May shouted. "Knife!"

Kester sprang aside. May bent, grabbed, and threw a stone from the fire ring. It connected with Moran's head, leaving a dark mark, but he shook it off.

"Consort!" he spat, backhanding May. She hit the ground. "You'll be consort to me next."

Kester, knife in hand, faced Moran in a crouch. "So you're

the traitorous bastard? I knew someone fed Dailgre morsels that could only come from court."

May did not move.

"I'm bastard for sure. Better than royal pet," Moran said. He spat. "Steps from a throne and you play lap dog and fetch, running after the stick every time Mirddyn tossed it. Well, I gave you a kingship. Now I'll take it away. The line Mirddyn ends here."

Moran jumped, swiped, but Kester jabbed Moran's arm. Grunting in pain, Moran stumbled back.

"I'll make your consort pay for every cut."

He swung up at Kester, marked his cheek. "I'll show her what it's like to spread her legs for a real man."

"A real man?" said Kester, "The sort that kills babes?"

Moran lowered his shoulders ready to bull his way at Kester to knock him down, but having seen him fight, Kester expected this and lashed his boot at Moran's knee.

Moran cursed, faltered, and Kester knocked the blade from Moran's fingers. Moran doubled over, but came up with wet ash from the fire, threw it in Kester's face. Blinded, Kester was momentarily helpless as Moran fell on him. His eyes' watered, vision cleared as they wrestled and rolled around. There were sounds from the hillside of men running, calling out.

"Moran!"

"Down here!" Moran's words were a strangled cry. "I've got the King. Help me, men. He's cut me."

Kester heaved, twisted. Already he was fighting for his life. He must fight for May's too, get them both back into the woods. Maybe then they'd have a chance. Clouds parted, moonshine flooded the field. Moran was over Kester, both fighting for control of his knife. Braced for that sting, Kester saw May raise her walking stick. Crack! Moran crashed on top of Kester.

May pulled at Moran, helped Kester throw off his bulk. The moon slid back under its cloud blanket. Accepting May's arm, Kester headed them toward the forest, winded, his breathing ragged. They skirted the pond and made for the open field. Suddenly, he connected with a solid object. Light sprang forth as a lantern was uncovered.

"A pretty prize," said one of Dailgre's men, the others having closed in a ring about them.

One advanced, long knife in hand, lightning fast, thrusting. Fierce pain flared in Kester's side. He felt hot blood down his side. May's eyes widened with shock. Boneless, he slumped to the ground at her feet.

"Kester!" May's cry was the last sound he heard.

Chapter 16

Or rather would, O would it so had chanced,
That you, most noble Sir, had present been,
When that lewd, wicked person with vile lust advanced,
Laid first his filthy hands on virgin clean

One of the men kicked Kester's side. He didn't even groan. May fell to her knees and put fingers on his neck. His skin was clammy. She couldn't find a pulse. Hard hands pulled her roughly to her feet.

"Come away. The dead can't help you."

May swung her arm and smacked the hateful face. He laughed and slapped her back. Her head flew up and her eyes stung.

"I'll teach her," Moran said bleeding above his ear where May hit him, limping into the light thrown by their lanterns.

"I promised you'd answer for every cut," Moran said.

May struggled when he wrapped her in his strong arm. "You couldn't beat him fair."

Moran put his knife under her chin. "Mind your tongue, or I'll cut it out. A scar or two won't spoil the whole package."

Blood trickled down her neck from where his blade nicked her. The night was shattered by red flashes. A thunderclap knocked May flat. Thick smoke, its odor rank, made her choke. A tall figure showed through its rising wisps, magnificent in golden armor. Prince Aidan. She struggled to rise.

The Prince helped her to her feet. Several of his clan, likewise in gold armor with swords drawn, came into view.

Moran and his men lay all about, slain by Aidan's soldiers. Kester lay where he fell unmoving. May shrugged off the Prince and ran to Kester's side. She took his head onto her lap. His eyes flickered.

"Kester, I'm here."

A groan escaped him. At a gesture from the Prince, one of his soldiers bent over Kester and opened his tunic to assess the damage. A wet, red eye bled in Kester's side, the sight made May blanch. The soldier took out a pouch and made a pad of white cloths. Taking out a packet, he opened it and sprinkled powders onto the cloth, then pressed it into the wound. Finally, he wrapped the wound tightly with a longer bandage. While he worked, Prince Aidan removed May from Kester's side.

"Come," he urged. "Give my physic room to work."

The Prince walked May to the eaves of the wood. He sat her down on a large rock. Taking out a gold flask, he uncapped it and put it to her lips. May sipped and coughed. The familiar mix of herbs and berries coursed through her, warming and strengthening her. Frowning, Prince Aidan turned her cheek to look at the mark made by Moran's man. He took a water flask from his side and uncorked it, pouring water onto a square of silk. Gently, he examined the cut under her chin and washed it first, rinsed the cloth and wet it again, pressing it carefully against May's cheek. Its coolness soothed her bruised skin.

"You saved my life," she said, soft, quietly glad he was

here in spite of her fear of him. "How did you find us?"

"Our soldiers came with tales of armed terrans in our forest. Then one of our clan spotted you with him," the Prince gestured toward where Kester lay. "We had to come. So you love this consort of Kerriena's? This is why you rebuffed us and fled our realm."

May shook her head. "I care for him, very much, but he's a friend, Prince Aidan. When I fell into your dance, Kester came after me. He helped me to escape, but it was to protect me from the Princess. Just now he was injured trying to save me from Dailgre's men."

Prince Aidan glanced at the dead. "We're taking you back with us. You'll be safe as our consort. We vow it."

"I can't go. Please don't do that to me. I can't stay in your realm. Kester needs me. If he lives, even if he doesn't, I have to do what I can to help his people. His king, his whole family was slain. The man who did the foul deed will rape this land, taking everything, the crops, the beasts; he'd level your forest for its wood. Kester knows his reputation. The peace of your realm is threatened too, Prince Aidan. What will you do? Will your fairies fight, or would you let this land be destroyed?"

She twisted to watch the physic checking Kester for other injuries. "Kester is the last of the line of Mirddyn. He'll rally his forces and push Dailgre back into the sea. But first, he must live."

"The Clans do not meddle in terran affairs," Prince Aidan

said. "We protect our own and go our way."

He came closer and lowered his voice. "But you, May, we will have by our side."

The tug of the Prince's allure kept her from meeting his eyes. A part of her found it hard to leave the Realm knowing she'd never see that extraordinary face, feel the way she had in his arms, or hear his teasing, seductive voice. As if the Prince sensed weakness, he bent and captured her lips lightly with his own. Her body hummed at that touch. Kester needed her, but with one kiss from the Prince, she was ready to forget every other consideration.

"You will be our consort and bear our heir," he whispered next to her ear. "We will have no other."

May cringed. "I could never have a child by you."

That he desired this so soon after he'd cemented the union with Princess Kerriena appalled her. "You'd break my heart. I would grow older and you'd send me away. Do you think I'd leave a child behind in your realm never to be in its life?"

Quivering, May stood. "If you really cared for me, Prince Aidan, you'd let me go. Your realm offers nothing I want, no life I'd wish to live. I must be free. Please, please don't do this to me."

The Prince appeared encased in ice. Her impassioned plea hadn't touched him.

"May."

She turned and ran to where Kester struggled to sit up on the ground. "Kester, oh, Kester, you're alright? I thought

Moran killed you."

She burst into tears.

Kester managed to stand with her help, wobbled for a moment, and then stood firm. "The Fae make marvelous medicine. I feel quite good for a man just run through."

Prince Aidan joined them. "What can you say of your flight from our realm, Kerriena's consort?"

"Prince Aidan, I owe you my life. I'll not lie," Kester said; face still pale from blood loss. "I'd sworn to help May. When Princess Kerriena released me from service, I'd already stolen a packet of powders, so May and I escaped."

He swayed, and May put her arm about his waist to steady him. For a long moment, the Prince considered them both, an unreadable expression on his perfect face.

"You will guard her and keep her safe?" Prince Aidan asked at last.

"I will," Kester said. "We're making for my castle in the north. Messages will be sent to allies. May will be safe there, or I will send her to where she will be, this I swear."

The Prince nodded slowly, as if this answer satisfied him. "Set out at once. The way behind you is clear. None of your enemies will get free of our forest this night. Take this gift to aid you."

He handed Kester the flask of the herb wine he'd given May to sip from.

"Prince Aidan?" Kester said, stepping away from May and closer to the Prince. "If need presses, if Dailgre comes against Mirddyn in too great a force, would you fight with us to preserve this land?"

"We are outside your world," the Prince said. "We can do no more to help you."

Kester nodded. "I thank you for the service you've extended to us. We must leave."

"Farewell, Prince," May said, fighting to keep tears from welling up. "I'm very grateful to you."

Kester slid his sword and knife into his belt. He walked May past the piled bodies. Prince Aidan and his clan already disappeared into the wood. Clouds scudded away. The full moon brightened the field. To her surprise, May spied her apple tree. Funny she was so near with almost everything she'd come with, including the pack on her back. Kester would need to recover what he left by the stream, so they headed that way. Before they passed it by, May needed to touch the tree and satisfy herself everything really happened, and she wasn't trapped in an evil dream.

Anticipating rough bark, she wanted the connection to her past that touch would give her. Her hand closed on a branch, *her stomach lurched, and the ground quaked.* Reflexively, she grasped the branch tighter. *A numbing sensation paralyzed her. As if on the edge of a steep precipice, May's inner balance took a tumble, completely disorienting her. Blackness swallowed her for several heartbeats. The ground rolled alarmingly beneath her feet, then rose up short.*

May fell with both hands outspread to save herself. Did

Aidan change his mind? Face down in the grass, May waited for the world to stop spinning.

***

Aidan hovered in the forest's canopy while his clan went ahead. May walked with the terran at her side. She turned in his direction. Moonlight picked out each delicate feature. Then she reached out to the apple tree. Aidan started. The air shifted, pushing at his wings.

Gone! One moment, May was right beside Kerriena's consort, the next, she disappeared.

The terran cried out. "Aidan!"

He pulled his knife from his belt. "Aidan! Let her go! She doesn't want you."

The fool ran at the woods and was nearly among the trees before he checked himself. Again, and again, he cursed Aidan, challenging him to a fight. Finally giving up, he raced back to the apple tree, searching about in the tall grass for any sign of where May was.

Understanding scorched Aidan. She played them all false. A rover! And now she was gone. What evil purpose brought her to the Realm? Aidan swore. She was far beyond his ability to reach now. He might never understand what her design was or when any damage she'd done would reveal itself.

Chapter 17

But in her way throws mischief and mischance,
Where by her course is stopped, and passage staid.

May rolled over. "Kester?"

He should be right beside her. "Kester!"

There was no trace of him.

"What have you done to him? Let him go, please, Aidan. Don't change your mind now."

Struggling with the lopsided pack on her back, she got to her feet. There ran a barbed wire fence alongside a country road. A farmhouse stood beyond it. May reeled.

"I'm back!" she cried.

She was, but Kester was lost. She'd never see him, couldn't help him. A tiny part of her whispered she'd never see Prince Aidan again either. What did she do? How did this happen? Could she undo it? Weak, May leaned against the apple tree for support. A slight shudder seemed to go through it, or was that just her? How could she be home now? In spite of longing for the relative safety her former world promised when she was on Illynd, now she was back, she didn't want to be here. Everything good in her life was just ripped from her grasp. For a long while, she hovered between disbelief and dismay. How would Kester manage without her? Gone was everything between them, just when it meant so much to her, when Kester meant so much. Prince Aidan proved he held her in some regard too, saving Kester and letting them both go. What should she do? She could think of nothing, do nothing.

For the rest of the night, she stayed with the tree. As dawn approached, May stumbled wearily through the field to her old life, her true life. Going to the side door, she found it unlocked.

She slipped inside. The house was quiet. If it were a weekday, her father would be getting up for work. May walked to the calendar hung by the refrigerator, flipped up the light switch. August; it was early June when she'd left. Feeling as if she moved on automatic, she took off her pack. As she bent, she felt the pouch at her waist and remembered the gems. She should hide them. There was already too much to explain about her absence.

She decided on the bottom junk drawer. Lifting her gown, she undid the bag from the shift's drawstring. She put the pouch in a paper bag of mismatched screws and hid it under other odds and ends. That done, May pulled out a chair and sat, too heartsick to do anything else. Her father saw her first.

"May?" he said, unbelieving, his unshaven face paling.

"May." He said it again, coming closer. "It's you. What's that getup? Where've you been? We've been looking everywhere. We thought you were dead. Ruby!"

His voice cracked. "It's May, in the kitchen. Call the police. She's home."

In minutes a patrol car was diverted from its post watching for early morning speeders. The cops, enthusiastic, barraged May with questions. 'Where was she all this time, was she kidnapped, did her parents do anything to hurt her? Why was she wearing those odd clothes, how did she get the cut under her chin and the bruise on her cheek?'

May said nothing. The energy required to speak wasn't there. Her head pounded. She was drained, uncaring of what happened. The cops called for an ambulance, and she was taken to the hospital. Doctors said she suffered from shock, the cut under her chin, and bruises. She required no stitches, just a butterfly bandage. They said she was slightly underweight, her blood iron poor. There was no evidence of any abuse. May submitted to these examinations without a murmur. Finally left alone in a white bed, given a shot of what she didn't know, she slept. Not until the next afternoon were her parents allowed to visit.

Her father came in first, clutching roses with ferns. Her mother carried magazines rolled tight. Surprisingly, her long absent Uncle Ray was also there. He acted as if he'd taken charge of her parents.

Uncle Ray's voice was falsely bright. "Look, she's fine, see? Hey, May."

He aimed his efforts at her. "We're all glad you're back. Everyone was really upset when you disappeared."

Her uncle pulled up a chair. Her parents perched on plastic seats. They kept looking to her uncle, but neither spoke. Taking their silence as his cue, he let out a breath.

"Whew!" Uncle Ray said. "You don't know what it's been like since you've been gone. What a mess. At first the cops thought your parents did something, I don't know," he said sheepishly, "something bad I guess, when they reported you missing."

He lowered his voice. "You know…the police came to the house, searched your room. For crikes sakes, you didn't even have a mattress, just that box spring. It made them suspicious your dad never fixed up your room, when all the others were okay."

Her uncle looked at his brother-in-law, who wouldn't meet his glance. "They found the empty booze bottles, no food, and the water heater busted. My god, the police even searched through the huge pile of garbage behind the garage, a private dump it looked like, but…you weren't there."

He picked at his trousers. "Your disappearance was in all the papers and local T.V. Everyone demanded to know how you could be living in those conditions."

Uncle Ray shifted in his seat. "I had to get your parents a lawyer and help them cleanup. Things looked bad; the lawyer was certain they'd be charged, but when the cops found the suitcase you left in the weeds across from the house, the theory of your disappearance changed. It was clear you'd run away. Why didn't you say anything, May?" he asked, his tone genuinely hurt.

"I realize our dad did what he could with his will, but if you'd called me, I would have helped too."

Hearing her uncle's concern, the wall May shielded behind crumbled. Tears ran down her face. "I don't know," she said in a whisper. "You were far away, I didn't think of asking you."

Her uncle handed her a tissue. "Well, don't fret. Things have changed. Your parents go to Alcoholics Anonymous three times a week, more if they need it. We gutted your room, your dad and I, put up sheet-rock and painted. You won't know the place. Your dad bought a new mattress, sanded and finished a set of second-hand furniture. You'll like it. Everything will be okay now, you'll see. And you don't have to tell us where you've been until you feel like it. We're just glad to have you back with us."

He gave her a hug. "I'll just leave you alone with your folks now."

Once he was gone, there was an awkward silence. Her parents made no move to be closer to her.

Her mother fidgeted with the curling magazines. "I got something for you to read," she finally said. "And…you look fine, May. The doctor said that cut shouldn't scar."

Her father handed her the flowers. "You always liked roses, May. I remembered that. Your mother and I are sorry. We haven't been good to you. We have a problem."

"I know you do, Daddy. I'm glad you're getting help."

She cast about for something to say about where she was. The truth was so strange they'd think she was crazy. She nearly believed she was. If not for the dress, gems, and her injuries, she'd have nothing to show it happened.

"I made friends," May said. "I can't say who. I don't

want to get them in trouble. I wasn't happy at home, but I thought I should tell you I was okay. It was a stranger who hurt me on my way back to see you."

"That's okay, don't talk about it," her mother said in a rush. "The doctor said nobody 'touched' you," she added in a lower tone. "Everything will be fine."

They both got up to leave.

"The nurse said not to stay long," her mother said. "The police still want to talk to you, but they said it was okay for you to come home tomorrow. Your father and I have to go to parenting classes, or you won't get to stay at home. We have to be there at eight o'clock."

"Bye, May," her father said.

They left May with rolled magazines and flowers out of water. Her parent's hadn't looked happy to see her again. Neither one kissed her hello or goodbye. May wasn't surprised, not when her running caused so much trouble, not when all she could think about was Kester and Illynd. Was he even still alive? What was happening there? She laid her head back on the pillow. The last time she saw Kester and Prince Aidan played out until she fell to sleep.

After rounds the next day, May was pronounced fit to leave. The car ride was too quiet. It felt as if her experiences made her grow apart from her parents and her old life. She didn't know them anymore, and they never knew her.

"See your room," her mother said.

The peeled paint was gone and the floor sanded and

glossed. New sheetrock walls were painted pale pink. The bed was covered with a quilt and matching pillows.

"Your father painted that second-hand desk and chair to match the bed," her mother added.

All May's schoolbooks were lined up on it, even her sketchpad was there. Everything was different. A plumber had been in. The bathroom gave out hot and cold water. The yard behind the garage was cut grass, nothing else. Her mother did all the cooking. The food cabinets were stocked, the freezer full. No one stayed up shouting, cursing, drinking, and throwing things. Her parents were a shadow of the people she knew.

They acted hesitant around her, as if they were afraid to put their foot wrong. Worse, even sober, they didn't say anything like we love you, or we missed you, not in any way May could believe was real. Later that week, they took May to her police interview, bringing along the lawyer her uncle got for them.

"Look, we saw what you had on," one cop said. "What kind of cult did you run away to?"

Her lawyer interrupted. "My client's daughter has done nothing illegal. She came as a courtesy, and to back up her parents as blameless."

He stood and indicated May should too. "We're done here."

Gratitude for Uncle Ray providing a lawyer filled May; if her uncle hadn't been in China and then Japan, Granddad would have gotten him involved long ago. Right now the last thing she needed was to tell the truth, and the lawyer speaking for her made that easier. When the police gave a statement saying her parents were freed of any suspicion in her disappearance, reporters, who'd called many times, stopped doing so. It was almost September. May was to return to school. Her mother took her shopping.

She found it strange to see plaids, floral prints, and colored jeans. May picked up a sweater set.

"That's nice," her mother said. "Get it."

Her mother held it for her. May ran her hand over cotton T-shirts, not as soft as spider silk, checked for her size. When she moved away, her mother picked up three in different colors, added them to what she carried. When her mother kept carting away stuff May seemed interested in, May stopped even lingering over what was on sale. Her parents never bought her so many new things for school before. That should make May happy, as if they were showing her how much they cared.

May didn't feel love in any of it, but fear that others were watching how they treated their child since her return. May dreaded the thought of school now the numbness she'd felt wore off. She cared what happened in her life more than ever. Illynd changed her; her relationship with Kester, dealing with Prince Aidan, pixies, and death made her different. She never knew she was a fighter. Thank goodness because since she returned, she had a lot to contend with.

While dusting the living room, May found a folder in the end table drawer. It was full of newspaper clippings about her disappearance. Every detail of how her family lived was in it. Familiar shame flooded her. Tuesday she'd be at school. School used to be her haven, a place that gave her normal. How could she face teachers and classmates now? Everyone in town knew everything about how they'd lived. The first day back, May got on the bus in front of her house.

She dressed in pressed new jeans, sneakers, and sweater. Her hair was in her usual braid. As soon as she reached the top bus step, the talk ceased. Everyone inspected her. May blushed and moved quickly down the aisle.

"Sit here," Renee said.

Renee Wilkin lived at the far end of her country road. A popular cheerleader, 'sit here' were the first words Renee spoke to May in all the time they went to school together. Even so, May settled on the seat. Several members of her class, John Hearn, Rich Lennon, and Bob, she didn't know his last name, but he was on the school's football team, were in front and back of Renee and May.

"So, tell us, May," Renee said, "Where were you all summer?"

"Yeah," John chimed in, "Tell us. It'll be our secret."

May held her notebooks tightly in front of her.

"Hey," Renee said. "I heard from Tim Johnson, whose cop Dad said you were in some kind of cult? That's cool. Were they Jesus freaks, tree huggers, or what? I'd love to see the dress they said you were wearing. I heard it was like something out of Robin Hood."

"That was wild, May, all the stuff in the papers about your house," Bob chimed in from behind her. "Funny, you always walking around school, your nose up in the air, not talking to anyone. And living in your own private dump," he snorted.

"I bet she was with hippies. Did they believe in orgies?" John said with a smirk. "All the guys really want to know."

May stood up, dropped her books.

"Driver," she called, "stop the bus, I have to get off."

May went to the front and waited for the bus to pull over.

"Are you okay?" the driver said. "Feel sick or something?"

"Yes," May said, looking at the foursome laughing and gesturing to each other. She left the bus and ran back home, anger building with every step that slapped the street. May wished she was far away from this life. For all its dangers, she longed for what she lost with Kester on Illynd. When she got back, no one was home.

Her license to drive reinstated, her mother left for her job just after the bus pulled away. May went to her room. The backpack was in her closet. She put it on her bed. Someone put it away, perhaps her mother. Not before she went through it however. Her spare clothes weren't there, but the outfit she got from Kerys was, washed and folded. Checking the pack's side pockets, she found the odd stick from the apple tree. Her mother must have been afraid to offend her by tossing it out;

both parents were so tentative with her now. A tingle enveloped her arm as she held the stick.

To her surprise, the flower still clung to the branch and held a light scent, the ripe and green apples still fresh. She put it back in the pack. Since she returned, everything that happened played out in the back of her mind. Her biggest question was how did it come about in the first place? What kind of power had seized on her? Could she make it back to Illynd again? She needed to walk.

May crossed the road to the field, the first time there since she got home. It was a fall day ripe with the nutty undertone of hay drying in an adjoining field, which a local farmer leased. May turned her back on the road and her house. Almost she could pretend she was in Illynd. A passing aircraft's drone ruined the illusion. Going to her apple tree, May sat with her back against its trunk.

Its low branches were heavy with over-ripe apples. Bees clung stubbornly to rotting fruit splat against the grass beneath. Had she been transported that night because she wanted so badly to leave? May tried to recall every detail of how she ended up on another world. The moon had lit the field and apple tree. She'd set down the suitcase and put her hand up to move aside a branch—that was when it happened. When she touched the tree, the earth shook.

May recalled a strange tingling sensation too. Excitement kindled because she felt something similar when she touched the apple tree and lost Kester. But she was leaning on the tree now, and didn't feel anything—her sweater was between the tree and her skin. Though she sat here so many times, those she actually had skin contact with the tree were few. May stood, afraid to test the difference with her bare hand. If she was wrong, she had nothing. She studied the grayed, peeling bark; just an old tree.

"Please be right," she whispered, "please, let me be right."

Lightly, May touched the tree. The pins and needles prickle filled her palm. She pulled her hand back and tried again. Testing again, and again, she lifted, touched, lifted, and then ran her hand up and down the bark. It wasn't just its texture, that's not what it was at all. May lightly pressed her cheek to the trunk. The same weird feeling spread into her face. Somehow, getting back to Illynd wasn't about how she touched this tree.

She had the desire to leave, she made contact with bark, but nothing more happened. She missed something. Both times an act or circumstance she didn't understand was involved. She must figure out what that was.

Chapter 18

But patience perforce he must abide,
What fortune and his fate on him will lay,
Fond is the fear, that finds no remedy;
Yet warily, he watches every way

May didn't leave the tree until she heard her mother return at about two-thirty in the afternoon. She wasn't going to give up. Life here changed, her parents reformed, and May was different too. She no longer belonged in this world. After hearing about the incident on the bus, her parents contacted the school board.

The board was aware of the gossip about May among fellow students. They felt her presence might be too much of a distraction and agreed May should finish her last school year doing independent home study. May was done with school and home. She didn't have to live without love. Someone cared about her, and she wanted that again. Getting back to Illynd was her only goal. She must know how Kester was.

He risked and lost everything important in his life for her. She would face danger to help him, but she had to puzzle out what the apple tree had to do with it. Every day she rushed through her required schoolwork and then sat in thought at her desk. On Thursday she wrote each step she'd taken that first time she landed on Illynd, but even in black and white, nothing jumped out at her to say how it happened or why. Friday, she just set aside her papers when she spotted the calendar in the desk's drawer. It showed holidays, high and low tides, sunrise and sunset times, and the phases of the moon. The new moon was already over. The full moon was due in days.

Wow; could that be it? Charged with the idea, May
flipped calendar leaves backward and forward. She couldn't
believe it, but she found a pattern. Each time she'd 'roved',
using Kester's word, going from her world to his and back to
her own, there had been a full moon. She tried to recall any
other time she laid a hand to the apple tree.

It happened often enough in the full light of day. Some of
those days would be during the full moon. Wait. Time, the
time; the moon had been right overhead, half as bright as
midday. Midnight! It was midnight. Thrilled at her
discovery, May got up, stared out her window at the apple tree.
This had to be her way to return to Kester. Thoughts of
leaving sobered her, considering the efforts her parents made
to undo the damage they did to her. How would they handle it
if she left again? But she must go back. Kester needed her.
Taking out a fresh sheet of paper, May wrote. Days later, with
her preparations done, it was seven o'clock on the night of the
full moon.

May sat with her parents watching a nature television
show. So far, her mother kept a full-time job. For that reason
or her AA counseling, she was dressing nicer, fixing her hair.
She even wore makeup and started exercising. Her father was
doing well too. Since he stopped spending his paycheck on
alcohol, he was able to save money. They cleaned up their act,
and were nicer to each other, but sadly, May felt the rift
between her parents and her would never heal.

How could they take back years of neglect? All the harsh words and fights were nothing to the lack of care they'd given May. While they were drunk, her childhood passed by both of them. She still would have left home when she was eighteen. The strain of what lay unsaid between them was too difficult to live with. Once, she thought all she wanted to hear from them was they were sorry, but now it was said, it wasn't enough. She didn't hate them, but they'd killed any respect May should have for her parents. When the show was over, May kissed them goodnight on the cheek; she hadn't done that for years.

No tears threatened though. By eleven-twenty, her parents were sleeping. Slipping down the stairs and out to the attached shed with her backpack, May carried leather boots in her hand. In the shed, she quickly dressed in the clothes Kerys leant her. She folded her other things and set them on a bench, along with a white envelope with her letter. Quickly, she made her way to the field in front of her home. Ground mist gathered in its hollows. The apple tree shone jewel-like with the full moon's glossing. Her pack was secured about her shoulders.

It was filled with food, water, and everything else she'd need, including the gems Kester gave to her. Having come here every day since she understood the apple tree's secret, May knew just where to put her hand. There was a notch in its thickest branch. She could grip it firmly and hang on for a long as she wished. Trying it out lifted her spirits the way nothing had since her unexpected return.

Latching onto it now, the tingle of contact shivered up and down her arm. That was it, nothing else. Alarmed, May stared at the moon as if would give her a clue as to what was going on.

Just then the pins and needles numbness intensified all through her body. An abrupt shift occurred, as if she pitched over a steep drop. Her stomach flipped. Her vision blacked out. The ground beneath her heaved and twisted, wringing itself tight and springing back flat.

May smacked against the tree trunk, dizzy, the world spun. Shutting her eyes, fearing she'd be sick, she hung onto the tree branch with grim determination. When the dizziness passed, May opened her eyes.

Night sounds were all around in the pitch dark. She slid down beside the tree and waited for what would come next. Much time passed with May uncomfortable, too keyed up to lie down. Light came into the sky, slowly revealing the landscape. When May didn't see her home, the road, or the barbed wire fence, she wanted to cry with joy, but the dangers of her last visit here did not allow it.

Dangerous men could be about. Prince Aidan's fairies might be on alert in the forest. It was too soon to crow over this victory. Ghostly wisps rose from the pond's surface. She patted the tree. The contact tingled.

"I don't understand how or why this happened," she said softly. "But I'm grateful."

Where was Kester? He had to be alright. She might be

able to tell how long Kester had been away from his campsite. She walked in that direction, breathing deep. May forgot how alive the air here was. Where the stream trickled into the pond, she slowed her pace. She feared coming across men who swore allegiance to Dailgre. Peering about the rock that hid Kester's camp, May got a shock. A man's form rolled in blankets at the campsite.

He was alone. She couldn't think what to do. After staring several minutes, she was about to creep away when the man turned over. Kester.

May went around the rock.

"Kester," she said, holding tight to the laughter and joy ready to explode out of her.

"Wake up. It's May. I'm back!"

Chapter 19

The silly man that in the thicket lay
Saw all this goodly sport, and grieved sore,
Yet durst he not against it do or say,
But did his heart with bitter thoughts engorge

Kester startled and sat bolt upright. Seeing who stood there, he relaxed somewhat, threw off his blanket and got to his feet. "Kester is the name, Lady. Have I your acquaintance?"

"Kester, don't joke. I've been horribly worried about you. What are you doing here? I thought you'd be in the north. Is everything safe now?"

Did he know her? No, he'd remember that hair, those bright eyes. Perhaps she was the younger sister of a former lady friend grown up.

"I'm well, Lady, though I should be beaten for forgetting your fair face, I can't recall our meeting," he said.

The pleasure in her expression drained away. Something was wrong.

"You honestly don't know me?" she asked.

"I wish I could claim the privilege, Lady, but sadly, I can't."

She'd gone white. Seeing her reaction, he took her elbow and led her to his blanket.

"Sit here. My mam always held things looked better for a cup of té. It won't take a moment to make some."

He scooped up fresh water in his pot while his company sat stunned. It wouldn't surprise him if he caught her speaking to herself, an unspoken argument was so apparent in her face. He built up the fire and set the water to boil.

"I'm called May McKinny," she said. "Can you tell me what this season is?"

"The same for everyone, the time of planting that comes after months of the long dark."

"The same day," she said. "Is it the same day? Kester, wow, I wasn't expecting this."

Kester sat down opposite her. A feeling of unease was growing in him. The whole meeting between them was uncanny.

"You don't remember me," she said. "But I know you. You saved my life more than once. Before you interrupt, hear me out. I know what I'm going to say is bizarre, but I have proof. For instance, you say you don't know me, but I know your real name is Lachlan of the family Mirddyn. You're the nephew of the King."

Taken aback, Kester waited.

"Kester," she said, "your country and king are in terrible danger."

"Now you must explain yourself, Lady."

"This is so hard," she said.

She frowned. "But you have to believe me…we were close, were friends and I came back to help you. There are strangers in Delain," she gestured in that general direction. "They're there to help attack it. Your friend Kerys and all her family will die if we don't do something now."

At the mention of Kerys, Kester started, and then checked himself.

"The King, his queen, their sons and even your father, Kester, will be killed in an ambush near Delain too," she said.

"What evil you spew!" Kester closed the space between them, grabbed her and shook her. "Why? I want answers!"

"I'm a rover," she said shrinking from him. "You guessed I was the first time I was here. You were right, though I didn't know or understand it myself. I was lost on your world until I met you by this pond. You swore to help me."

She shifted her shoulder; he did have a hard grip on her.

"That first night I followed fools' lights and was caught in the dance," she said. "You followed and got us out, but weeks passed while we were there. We got to Delain too late. You might have stopped it all from happening, if not for helping me. We were going north when Dailgre's men caught us. You fought to save me again. Afterward I roved back to where I come from. It was unintentional, because I had no knowledge of roving. I've learned a few things since then, so I returned to help you."

Kester skepticism built with each word out of her mouth.

"The water's boiling," she said.

He picked the pot off the fire and set it down. Té could wait.

"What is it you carry at your back?" he said. "I'd study it, if we're friends, as you say."

For an answer, she took off the sack and handed it over. "I brought food, water, and a few clothes."

Kester was interested in the packets wrapped in silvery sheets.

"I used aluminum foil," she said, as if that made any sense to him. "Plastic worried you the last time."

There was liquid in a round device, as she demonstrated for him, taking a sip.

"That's an aluminum water bottle, this," she said lifting her shift's sleeve, "was lent to me by Kerys the first time I was here. She was very kind, as were you. I want to help your family, your friends, and you, Kester. That's why I returned. You must trust me."

He handed her back her sack.

"I'm thirsty. Could you brew the tea?"

Nodding, Kester took out tin cups. He needed to think about what to do with this unexpected problem, so to stall, he started salt bacon and flat bread on the large rock on the edge of the fire.

"May, is it? I knew you as May? Not Lady May?"

"Yes," she said, smiling. She lost her smile when she looked at the woods beyond the field.

"Is it safe so close to the trees? I don't want to be snared by the Realm again."

He shook his head. "I can't credit I'd willingly be caught by fools' lights."

Glancing at her fair face, he knew that was a lie. He

might go after her. Her air of innocence held appeal. She sipped her té, easy in his company.

"This is weird," she said. "I know so little about how and why I've come here. My home should be right over there," she pointed opposite the forest.

"Why did I come back from a different time in my world to the same day I was here before?" She shook her head.

Kester was making his own calculations as he cooked. "If all is as you say, Lady...May, you'll have no objection to coming with me. I must bring the King this news. Delain's force of guardsmen is small. If you speak true, it will need reinforcement."

"Of course I'll go with you, Kester. You've proven I can trust you."

After they ate, Kester packed to leave. "We'll pick up horses at the nearest village, but a half day's walk."

Kester kept the stranger just slightly ahead of him. His senses were fully alert. She moved along as though used to going on foot. Harmless as she wished to seem, Kester wasn't fooled. Her sweet appearance could snare many a man. It was time for a noon meal, but he found the village's smithy at his sup and purchased two good mounts. The lady claimed no experience on horseback, so he gave her rudimentary instructions. At first she balked at riding sidesaddle, professing a desire to straddle the horse with her legs, but Kester pointed out it would be impossible to sit modestly in her long skirts.

"I feel like I'll fall off," she said. "If I was wearing pants, I'd ride like you do."

"Pants?" Kester asked.

"Trousers," she said.

A lady in trousers; he had no way to picture this. In spite of her fretting, she soon got into the rhythm of the horse's gait. They stopped only when Kester decided to make camp for the night. She made a show of being uneasy. It was the woods she feared, and faes.

"Must we stay under trees?"

"This bit of forest has no ill reputation as the one about Delain. I've slept here before, taking no harm from it."

Removing a tight roll strapped to the bottom of her sack, she unfurled it near the fire he built.

"Is there somewhere to wash?"

"There, to the left is a stream," he said. "Go downstream. We'll need fresh water."

While there was light to see, she left camp. He didn't like to let her go alone, but could do nothing until she provoked him. Coming back with her hair a halo about her shoulders, her face pink and shining, Kester saw further evidence of her appeal. He took out a length of cord and a net.

"I'm off to catch supper," he said brusquely. "Wait here."

Kester returned with three fish. Lady May helped him gut them, did it good job of it too. He greased a pan with salt bacon. The scents of frying set up his hunger.

"Have some of my bread." First, she bit a slice to show it was harmless.

Kester tried the other half. "Fine milled flour," he said. He finished the rest and took another.

The lady ate a whole fish, leaving the crisp skin, while he finished off the other two. Afterwards, she offered another foodstuff from her pack, once again eating some first. He picked over each piece, having no difficulty recognizing nuts and raisins, but suspicious of something called chocolate.

"What fruit are these?"

"They come from a cacao tree, but they wouldn't grow around here. If they were anywhere on Illynd, it would be farther south."

He sniffed one, tasted it. Flavor flooded his mouth. He quickly took another. "I've not had the like."

She laughed. "Where I come from, most people feel that way about chocolate."

Kester ate all his. Lady May gave him what was left of hers. "We face a hard ride on the morrow. We should retire," he said.

"Fine," she said.

She slipped off boots, got into her strange blanket, and pulled something along its side. She turned away from the fire and him. Kester banked the fire, unrolled his blanket and covered himself boots on. If trouble came in the night, he'd be ready. He watched Lady May for a long while before he felt he could sleep.

She was awake at first light; he heard her moving about, but Kester was already up. He had oats cooking while she braided her hair. He threw in berries he'd gathered this morning.

"Good morn, Lady May. It was a quiet night."

"Just May," she said. "Good morning. How long will it take us to reach your uncle?"

"Another two days. The oats are ready."

She accepted a tin bowlful. "Thank you," she said, after tasting them. "It's good."

He felt the strain of their stilted conversation as she must. He knew what worried him.

"I don't look forward to riding sidesaddle again," she said.

The countryside changed. Occasionally, they saw a homestead beside which, furrowed fields sprouted crops. There were herds of tough, hairy cattle watched over by men with dogs at their side. Once they spotted a wayward goat. Long after noon, Kester made a stop for a meal.

She contributed apples and a sticky substance called buttered peanuts. She cut and cored the apples and dipped them in the butter, then lay them on his tin dish. Kester was more than willing to try her food after the chocolate. He found the butter good but wasn't as fond of it as he was chocolate. Kester fried salt bacon with wild greens he found along the stream. Lady May praised his efforts but only ate the greens; the night before, she ate his fish, but no bacon. Faes did not touch meat. Were rovers related to faes? He'd never heard so.

It was something to bring up with the King. The day wore away with little passing between them. She made no suspicious moves, said nothing more to provoke him, yet Kester's wariness didn't fade. Why did she play at knowing him? Any spy could have told her what she knew of him. She required his trust, so it must be the last thing he'd give her. That night, Lady May asked to make the flat bread. When she turned it, her piece fell into the ashes. Kester quickly picked it up and slapped it on the hot stone.

"Can't waste supplies," he said.

When it browned, he brushed off the ash and ate it as his portion. The next day the mountains were visible. The town was below the King's stronghold in the foothills. They headed in its direction.

"Kester," Lady May said, "the last time I was here, you were concerned I'd be recognized as a rover. Is it safe to tell your uncle? Can I trust him?"

"Can he trust you, Lady? Rovers bring trouble. If you're what you say, a friend, your actions will prove it out. My uncle's a good man and a good king. I stand with him."

She was silent. Let her be afraid. If she brought misfortune to Illynd, she'd suffer for it. For his part, he had his own fears. Was he wrong to bring her to court? This was what she desired. Was it wise to give a rover what they sought? They passed thick walls that encircled buildings constructed of the same gray-brown stone as poked up everywhere. The town spread over a large area, with reed and daub fenced gardens to keep livestock out, stacked woodpiles, low now at the start of growing season. Many folk worked planting, hoeing, or feeding winter's debris to open fires. At the castle's gate, Kester spoke to a guard about his business.

They passed inside. He dismounted and grabbed Lady May's horse. She slid down into his arms and then to the ground, where she shook her skirts. The stronghold consisted of massive stone blocks. Wide, squat towers, one at each corner, were cut high up with deep windows. A wood door rising to a height of two interior floors fronted the edifice. A uniformed guard stood to the side of it. Kester was immediately hailed.

"Ho, there, Kester!" The guard winked. "It's pretty company you've brought. You're back sooner than expected too."

"My company, as you put it, won't find you as interesting, Tighe. Stick to tavern girls and farm lasses," Kester said. "Is my uncle in residence?"

"Aye, he's just come from a morning's hunt," Tighe said.

"Both eyes open to duty, Tighe."

Kester led her past the smirking guardsman. "This way, Lady, the King will need see us right away."

Kester kept hold of her arm, fearful she'd bolt now she was faced with her goal, or worse. Inside these walls, the interior was cool. At an ornate wood and brass door, Kester knocked.

Another guard opened it onto the throne room, but its high seat was empty. Several men sat at a table near the dais. Earthenware mugs held scrolls open. Pewter candle stands with stubby beeswax candles illuminated ink and water-colored maps. Sticks of wax, writing implements, and inkbottles cluttered the table's top. An older man, like Kester in looks but for furrows on his forehead and gray at his temples, dominated the table.

He stood when he spotted Kester, noted Lady May and smiled. "Lachlan, back so soon? Who do you bring to meet us?"

Kester came forward with Lady May in his grip.

"Majesty." He bowed, pulled her with him.

"We've told you a hundred times, Lachlan, it is uncle."

"Yes sir, Uncle." Kester hesitated to speak with the advisors sitting about the table. "I bring news, Uncle, urgent news, yet…I would keep it close for now."

The King nodded sharp at him. Suddenly, grim lines set in his face.

"Ministers," he said. "Please excuse us. We'll resume our business at a later hour. Come, Lachlan, we'll go to our private study. We're assuming your unnamed lady friend is included in this tale you wish to tell?"

"Yes, Maj. . . Uncle." Kester followed with Lady May in tow. The King opened a door beyond the throne to a comfortable room with wood shelves that stored leather-bound manuscripts and tied scrolls. Kester shut the door behind

186

them.

The King said, "Introduce us to this lady you're leading about, Lachlan. We're certain you can release her arm. We don't think she'll run away."

The King smiled at Lady May again, the warm, winning grin Kester loved at any other time, but not today, and not for this one.

"This is Lady May McKinny," Kester said. "Hers is a strange tale, Uncle. I'll leave it to her to begin."

"Your majesty," she said.

She coughed, and Kester didn't wonder the words she must say stuck in her throat, considering who she delivered them to.

"I came here with Kester to warn that your enemy Dailgre will attack your country. He'll land ships at Delain. Men acting as spies are already in the town. If you'd don't believe my warning, he might destroy that town; he means to wipe you out, including all your family."

The King jumped up from his seat. "What is this, Lachlan?"

"There's more to her tale, Uncle. Lady May is a rover. Her fantastic story has her passing through Mirddyn in a time when Dailgre's men slew your queen, your sons, my father, and you. The attack on Delain had already happened. She claims my friendship too, swearing I saved her life. Now, she says, she's come back at a time beforehand to repay the favor."

The King sat back in his chair and looked hard at Lady

May. "We assume you've searched her for weapons?"

"Yes, Uncle. She had none…so far her manner has been sensible."

His uncle sat without speech for several minutes.

"Do you offer your services to us, Lady May? In times of turmoil, it's known rovers stand at the side of kings. Is this our time?"

"In spite of how I got here, I'm an ordinary young woman," Lady May said. "I know little of roving. It happened to me by accident the first time here, and again when I went back to my world. I had to figure out how to rove on purpose. I had to get back to help Kester. When I left, he was the only member of the royal family alive. Dailgre's men attacked us, and Kester was severely wounded. His life was saved by fairies' healing powders."

Kester snapped, "You said naught of fae glamour to me."

"If we believe Dailgre will attack at Delain, my lady," the King said, with a warning glance at Kester. "Then we must send a force to secure that harbor. This would leave us weak in other places. Do you see our difficulty? If this is treachery, the attack will fall hardest in those less defended areas. We require more than the declaration of a stranger, a rover, no less, to make such vital choices."

"I know Kester's friend Moran betrayed you to Dailgre. He led Dailgre's men to ambush the King," May said.

Kester swore. "Impossible! Moran's been comrade to me since we were babes. You show your true colors now."

She managed to look hurt. "Kester, I know you trusted him, but he misled you. He was jealous of your station in life."

Kester turned to the King. "Uncle, these are base lies—"

The King interrupted. "How do you purpose we uncover this treachery, my lady?"

"Moran met with the spies near Delain," she said. "Have him followed. See where he goes, who he speaks with. His behavior should give him away. It must be soon, your majesty. Delain will be attacked in three months."

"Fair enough, Lachlan. It will do no harm to Moran if he's watched. If he's blameless, it will out in the end. We must look into this threat to our land. Other measures can also be taken."

Kester glared at this snake dressed as lamb, his anger held in only for his uncle's sake.

The King stood. "You must be tired, Lady May. We invite you to stay here as our guest."

The King pulled a bell rope near the fireplace. A guardsman opened the door. "Escort the lady to our best suite. Anything she requires is to be provided for her comfort."

She had the cheek to look relieved.

"Thank you, your majesty," she said, "My only wish is to help all of you. Dailgre and his men were butchers. What they did then…sickened me."

Unhappy with his uncle's decision, Kester stood.

"Be careful, Kester," she said in a low voice. "Moran

hated you. He hid his true self well, but I saw him stick you with a knife. He meant to kill you then, he still does."

Having done her best to convince them of her deceits, she allowed herself to be led away.

"You can't believe her," Kester said, as soon as the door shut. "Moran would not do me false. She plays upon her fair face, a pretty disguise over an evil package. A cell would be the suite for her."

"Until we gauge the truth of what she says," the King said, "it would be prudent to act with tact. A rover can offer an advantage in dangerous times. If Dailgre is preparing a strike, we may need her services. You're right, though. She does put a fair face on very evil tidings."

Chapter 20

His credit now in doubtful balance hung;
For hardly could be hurt, who was already stung.

Discouraged by Kester's mistrust, May followed the soldier up a staircase to the castle's next level, where bright rugs warmed its stone floors. Seeing a maidservant ahead, the soldier called her over, gave her the King's instructions, made a short bow in May's direction and left her. Smiling, the servant showed May to a double door and opened one side.

An ornate wood bed graced the impressive space. Carved wood chairs, table, freestanding wardrobe and chest finished the furnishings.

"My lady, I hope this suits you," the servant said.

May walked to a window. A walled garden in spring bloom filled her view. The hand-blown glass slightly distorted everything. She turned. "This is lovely."

The servant dipped a curtsey. "My lady, what may I do for you?"

"I need a bath, but I've only this dress with me. Can I buy another somewhere in town?"

"I'll prepare a bath, my lady, but a new gown must be tailored. I'll see what can be done. Are you hungry or thirsty, my lady?"

"Yes, thank you, I'd love tea."

"Very good, my lady. I'll return shortly with a tray."

"Thank you," May said.

She opened the wardrobe to put her backpack in it. Her

efforts to convince the King and Kester of their danger drained her. She sat at the table, laid her head on her arms.

"My lady."

May popped up her head. There stood no servant but an elegant woman, perhaps in her thirties. She had warm features, golden hair, and pale eyes that studied May with frankness.

"We are called Inis and are Lachlan's aunt," she announced regally. "We bid you welcome. Our husband told us somewhat of the purpose of your visit."

May scrambled up to curtsey. "Majesty."

"We wished to see for ourselves the young lady who carries this terrible caution. If you speak true, you are a friend whose coming saved our sons and our lord. If you speak false, and carry a threat to our sons and our lord, then not even hidden powers will save you from our wrath."

"I told the truth, Majesty," May said, head tilted from her curtsy. "I came to help the king and Kester."

"Rise, Lady," the Queen said, "That we can lock eye to eye."

May gazed into the fair queen's face.

"A man may ask why a thing is," the Queen said, "and the ways and means he studies involve power and plots. However, let a woman ask why and perhaps she will discover what a man will not. Why did you come, truly? What drives you to risk yourself?"

Tears spilled into May's eyes. The frustrations of

Kester's barely concealed hostility toward her were laid bare. "I care about Kester," she said with trembling lips. "We were close, he saved my life. I had to come back to help him."

The Queen considered this. "We believe you," she said simply.

A knock sounded. The servant returned with a tray. Another came behind her with an armload of clothing, which she lay on the bed, curtseyed, and left.

"We took the liberty of sending along gowns for your use. We were told you came with the clothes on your back," Queen Inis said.

The first serving woman waited.

"We wish you to take charge of Lady May, Imogen," the Queen said to the servant. "Lady May, please join us at supper this night. We'll send someone along later to escort you."

The Queen left. Had she found a new friend?

"My lady," Imogen said with a quick dip. "Will you wish to bathe or eat first?"

It was food first, then a deliciously hot bath. May chose a blue gown with an embroidered border and gold shift. She struggled to lace the gown's bodice with a gold cord, impossible to do alone. She saw a bell rope by the bed, pulled it. Imogen came to help her. After, Imogen used combs to pull the sides of May's hair back. She never sat down with a king and queen before, but May wished Kester to see her at her best. A knock came at the door.

Imogen answered. Attired in a formal tunic, hair brushed

and a new shine to his boots, Kester stood there looking uncomfortable and not just because he disliked dressing up.

"My aunt sends me to escort you down to supper."

Pleased, May strove not to smile.

"You look lovely, Lady," he said grudgingly.

"Thank you."

He held out his arm out for her. When they reached a timbered hall, Kester drew May to the Queen's side.

"Good evening, Lady May," the Queen said.

"Good evening, your majesties. I wish to thank you for lending me what I needed," May said.

The King stood opposite. "We hope you've found everything to your liking."

"I'm comfortable, thank you," May said, as they took their seats.

Just then, a flush-faced woman herded three boys into the room. "Say good eve to your majesties," she said.

The toddler, blond hair in his eyes, ran for his mother and grabbed her skirts.

"Sweeting!" the Queen said. She picked him up and kissed his round cheeks. The others rushed up. The oldest, perhaps six, dark like his father, and the middle son, with his mother's coloring, were enfolded in her arms and kissed next.

"Say goodnight to your da," Inis said. They walked more sedately to their father, who kissed the top of each head. The nurse-maidservant led them off.

"They're beautiful children," May said to the Queen.

"Yes," she said her voice a bit wobbly.

Recalling Kester's wrenching grief when he said his family was slain, May bit the inside of her mouth; she was here to stop that from happening. Servers set down dishes of soup. Bread, crocks of honey, jams, and butter were already on the table. The food was good, simple, yet hardy. May gazed about as she ate, but Kester avoided her eye.

Instead, Kester kept in whispered conversation with the King. Small stuffed birds made the next course. May moved pieces of fowl about, didn't eat any, but did enjoy the roasted potatoes, turnips, and carrots. Slices of cake dusted with sugar ended the meal. Throughout it, the Queen told May about castle life, but May keenly felt Kester's lack of interest in her. Now the Queen called Kester aside.

He came to May a moment later. "My aunt requested I show you about the gardens."

"I'd love to see them," May said.

He offered his arm. Moving around flowerbeds lit by torches, he was largely silent while May paused several times to look at a flower. Many of the blooms were tight for the night. Their perfume lingered however. At a stone seat, May asked if they could talk in private for a moment.

Kester took a seat next to her.

"Kester, I brought something that belongs to you."

"What would that be, Lady?"

May took out the gems. She'd already set aside the fairy recipes. "These."

He looked inside the purse. "What's this? You think to bribe me to treachery?"

"Of course not, they belong to you."

"How? I've done nothing to earn such," he said.

As hard as it was to tell this Kester, who disapproved of and mistrusted her, May related what passed while they were in the Realm. She left out her personal trials with Prince Aidan. Kester digested what she said. The bag of gems could be taken as proof of her story. He tied the bag shut and dropped it in her lap.

"You say it belongs to me, but I'd accept no reward from this fae who as you claim, tried to kill you. I would have thrown such 'payment' in her face."

"You wouldn't take them," she said. "That's why the gems were with me when I left."

"At last, a sour truth issues from your sweet mouth." He got up and stalked away.

She must be patient, stop trying so hard. Kester would find out she told the truth. May was up, dressed less formally, and sitting in the same garden the next day when she had an idea. Asking permission, she was escorted to where Queen Inis worked on embroidery while watching her sons play.

May curtseyed. "Good morning, your majesty, it's a fine day."

"Good morn, my lady. How did your walk with Kester go?"

"Not well. I'm afraid only time will help him to trust me.

I wanted to ask a favor...I'd like to mix up recipes for skin creams. This is a list of things I would need."

May gave her the recipes Bri wrote out.

Queen Inis studied them. "Dried herbs, pure lanolin, beeswax, almond oil...yes we have these."

"I would like permission to make the creams, Majesty. They are amazing. I had them from a pixy."

The real reasons for mixing the fairy concoctions went unsaid by her. May hoped to restore a touch of the magic she'd felt in the Realm, and rekindle the admiration she enjoyed from Kester while there. Considering the comments he'd made then, part of that was how she'd looked.

The Queen nodded. "We can't see harm in those ingredients. You have our leave. Imogen will assist you."

A narrow storeroom held most everything she needed, better stocked perhaps as it was meant for the entire castle's use.

"Thank you, Imogen. You're excused," May said when she'd showed her about.

May tied on an apron and rolled back her sleeves. She put dried herbs into the pestle and ground them to powder. With that done, she carefully measured amounts into a small kettle. Though she worked the morning away, it was hard to wait on the news from Delain about Moran. She finished her first effort. After cooking down the ingredients at one of the great kitchen's fireplaces, May brought it back to the apothecary.

She pressed the herbal stew three times through a sieve

lined with linen. After she mixed those distilled herbs with lanolin in a clean mortar, May found two small crocks and filled each with half the mixture. She set them aside to cool. She started the next recipe.

Imogen came to the door. "Her majesty requests your company in the solar for the noon meal."

May washed her hands, hung up the apron, and followed Imogen into a sunny balcony above the gardens.

"How are your balms coming?" the Queen said, after May curtsied and took a seat.

"I've finished the face cream and should be done with the rest this afternoon."

May had taken a crock with her, which she placed on the table. "After cleaning your skin, smooth this into your face and neck. It softens it, makes it look fresh."

"Well, it sounds wonderful. We can't wait to try them. How is it you befriended a pixy?"

Once again, May hadn't thought her actions through. She took a foolish risk having to explain this to the Queen, who had little reason to trust her.

The Queen spoke first. "You've been in the Realm."

"Yes," May said, relieved there was no accusation in the Queen's tone.

"It's said faes are striking," the Queen said in a more confidential tone.

"That's true," May said, recalling Prince Aidan, "So beautiful they're almost unreal, but it takes more than physical

perfection to make them lovely. They can be heedlessly
cruel."

The Queen placed her hand on May's. "We see you've
had some terrible experience of them. You're well away from
there."

After a surprisingly pleasant lunch with the Queen, May
went back to her work. Late in the afternoon, she found
Imogen and asked her take the other beauty mixtures for the
Queen. Each crock was covered with linen tied with twine,
and neatly printed, 'mouth', 'skin', or 'hair' on its tag. She
copied the recipes to go along with her gift. May took her
crocks up to her room.

After washing up, she tried out her face cream, hoping it
would work as it should. To her delight, she achieved the
smoothness and sheen of Goll's work in the Realm. The balm
and hair cream also worked; Bri said they were 'simples',
which perhaps meant they did not need fairy magic or
whatever to work. Would Kester notice? At supper in the
dining hall, May sat beside the Queen.

Several times, she caught Kester gazing at her, but he
turned away each time. After the meal, May had nothing to
occupy herself. The Queen was with her sons, so May walked
in the gardens. She had a new appreciation of herbs after
working with them. Tomorrow, she'd do sketches and tie
them into a booklet. With nothing better to do, she studied the
night sky. These were strange constellations with some
similarities, but she was no student of astronomy to identify

anything.

"My lady."

Kester stood before her looking grim.

"Yes?" she said.

"There's news from Delain. Come with me."

May stood. Kester clamped her arm in his and escorted her to the study where the King waited. How bad was his news? Anger vibrated off him. What would they do to her? The King's cautious reception didn't mean anything if they believed she lied. They might imprison her, or worse. Coming back to help Kester was risky, but this danger she only saw now.

Chapter 21

Whom Princes late displeasure left in bands,
For false letters and suborned wile

The King's expression gave no hint of what she faced. "My lady, we wished to have you close by when we read this report."

May dipped an awkward curtsy, as Kester wouldn't release her arm. What if her timing was off and Moran hadn't made any contact with conspirators yet? Would they torture her?

"Please sit," the King said.

Kester kept fast by her chair. The King lifted a small metal tube and tapped out a paper roll.

"We train birds to fly to points in our kingdom," the King said. "In this manner, we send and receive news of import quickly. A bird's just arrived with this."

Unrolling the message, he held it up to the light. He studied it silently, and then grunted. "There's a traitor in our midst," he thundered.

Kester leapt up and grabbed her shoulders.

"It is not she," the King said. "Moran slipped away alone to meet men who came to shore in a secluded cove. Moran unrolled a map and pointed out things to discuss with them. They then took it away with them."

"It can't be!" Kester released May as if she burned him. "She's twisted this to her advantage. I'd trust Moran with my life."

"We will not trust him with the life of our queen, our sons, or our people. We are vulnerable in Delain," the King said. "It is a prime place to attack, as it is less than a week's march to our seat here. If we were not also watching other trouble spots, we wouldn't be in this position. We must draw men back from our eastern and western borders, but we fear there's not enough time to stand with a strong force against Dailgre at Delain."

The King turned to May. "Is there other aid you can offer us, my lady? Rovers are said to master strange forces."

May shook her head. "I wish I could do more."

"Then we must hope your timely appearance here is all the warning we will need," the King said. "But we fear it may not be so. At least, we will see our queen and our sons safe. They're to leave this night for our stronghold in the east. We will go to Delain with the main force of men that can be gathered here on the morrow. We owe you a debt, Lady, for your warning. Might we ask what you will do now? Is there somewhere you would go? We'll provide you with a fresh mount and any supplies you need."

May was taken aback. Of course, the King would assume she was finished with them.

"I don't know yet, Majesty...I'll think it over."

"You go with our deepest appreciation."

The King gave her a nod. May was dismissed. She stood for a moment watching Kester, who pulled a scroll toward himself, paying her no mind. Feeling bereft, she left.

Back in her room, she lay across the bed. What would she do now? Kester had no use for her. She couldn't stay on with nothing else to offer. Suddenly, she was angry. Kester didn't even thank her. She risked her life to help him, and he did not care. May got up and took out her backpack. The gown she arrived in hung in the wardrobe. She took off the Queen's borrowed finery and dressed in that. What was the point of staying here? Kester hated her. The sooner she was away, the better. In the kitchen, May found Imogen sipping tea. She jumped up with a start when she saw May.

"I've come for supplies," May said. "The King said I could take what I needed."

As Imogen looked on, May picked out hard loaves of bread and rounds of cheese. She also took dried apples, oats, a half-pound of tea, a small pan to cook with, tinder and a striker; she had a pot, tin cup, plate, and utensils. She just managed to fit everything in her pack.

"I was promised a mount," May said. "Please lead me to the stables."

At the stables near the castle's outer wall, May shocked the groom by insisting the horse be fixed without a sidesaddle.

"I'll ride like a man," she said.

May was off without a backward look. It was dark, few were on the streets. It was a good thing, as a great deal of leg was exposed by the manner in which she rode. Once out the main gate, May was well into the countryside before she stopped for the night. The loneliness of her camp bothered her. Every sound was suspicious. She kept her horse tied close by. Lying in her sleeping bag, she was sure she wouldn't be able to fall asleep. Now Kester didn't need her, May must consider her future.

It hurt more than she imagined losing Kester's good opinion, but without it she couldn't stay here. Another full moon would see her back on her world. Until then, she'd stay at the village nearest the apple tree. She had the gems; she'd barter or sell one to take a room at an inn. Closer to the time she must go, she'd hide near the tree until she could leave. It was painful knowing what she had to go back to. You can't go home; the saying was true.

She would not stay with her parents. Having had her granddad's love, having known Kester's kindness, May had to believe something better was out there for her. The hardest thing to face was being alone, no one to share with, and no one to care. She sunk into sleep.

Pain startled May awake. Something bit her. It was too dark to see what. The arm outside her sleeping bag stung with fiery pain near the elbow. Was it a snake?

"A-ah!" she cried. Something bit her neck. She struggled with the bag's zipper, freed herself, jumped up. "Ow!"

Another bite throbbed at her ankle. She hopped about. Nearby, her horse whinnied in pain. Something was biting him also. A light kindled in the night. A flaming torch waved about. May heard small, fierce cries of distress.

"Away with you, filthy imps! I'll scorch you."

Kester! What was he doing?

Kester came toward her with the torch. Several bug-like objects fluttered around her. They shrieked shrilly when the torch's flame got close to them.

"Did those nasty imps get you?" he asked.

"Yes," she said.

"Take this," he said handing her the torch. "I'll build a fire. Never pass the night without a fire by your side. Even a small one keeps them at bay. It's human blood they feast on, the filthy creatures, but horse blood will do. Cowardly too, like to catch you asleep. Don't you know aught of imps?"

The campfire he made flared up when he had her set the torch into it. "Let me see those bites. They turn foul if they aren't tended."

May showed him the spot on her arm, neck, and the bite on her ankle. Kester retrieved his horse, boiled water and took linen out of his saddlebag. When the water steamed, he soaked the cloth and cleaned her bites. The heat was soothing.

"That's a nasty one on your arm. Better keep an eye on it."

"Why are you here?" May said.

"You left before I could thank you. I was outraged over Moran... couldn't face you right off. I can barely believe he did this. It's a hard thing when a man you've known all your life turns on you. You wonder if you can trust anyone."

"I'm sorry, but I had to warn your family and you."

"Why did you leave?" Kester said. "Don't tell me…I was hateful, and you said we'd been friends. Where will you go?"

"Back," she said. He'd softened, but they were still too strained with each other. "To do that, I must be near where I found you."

"I'm going ahead of the King to Delain, so I can come with you. It's not safe for a young lady to move about alone."

"Thank you, Kester. I'd like your company."

Perhaps he was embarrassed by his hot attitude up to now, because he busied himself laying out a blanket on the other side of the fire. Once he settled, he banked it so it would burn through the night.

"Kester, do you think there's a chance you'll beat this attack at Delain?"

"We may not have enough guardsmen, so we'll call on the locals to fight with us. At least surprise and treachery won't aid Dailgre's cause. Moran's movements are watched, thanks to your warning."

"I just wish I could do more. Tell me, Kester, what kind of weapons do your soldiers' fight with?"

"The sword, the double ax, dirks for close fighting, and archers for a longer reach. Why?"

"You don't use cannons or explosives?"

"What arms are those?" he asked.

"Cannon shoot iron balls a far distance, for instance, out to sea at a ship to sink it, or at an army before they're too close to fight back. Explosives can be set in a place to spray out debris and cause a lot of damage."

"I've never seen arms as you describe," he said. "If we possessed such, it could give a great advantage against Dailgre. Is this an example of your powers? Could you create such fearsome means for my uncle to fight with?"

May was quiet for a moment.

"Of course," Kester said, "he would reward you...handsomely...your services, I mean."

"You think—" She sat up. "I left my world, came back here fearing Dailgre's men were in charge, with no idea what would happen to me. It wasn't to make a profit...whatever you think."

The hurt she'd held in exploded. "We were friends...you were the first real friend I've ever had."

She didn't trust herself to say more. Several minutes passed.

"I can only beg pardon," Kester said. "I wish...I regret my harsh behavior."

"Forget it," May said with a sigh. "The first time we were together, we had different experiences, we had to help each other, trust each other...it's not your fault."

Everything was against them this time.

"As to weapons," May said. "I couldn't make cannons fast enough to use, even if I knew how. Gunpowder might be possible. Is there a yellow rock here? It smells bad, like something rotten."

"There's such. It breaks apart easily."

"That's it," May said. "I don't know what else I'd need, but I believe it could be found here. Gunpowder is the only thing I can think of that might help you."

"You can make this?"

"I must go back to my world to learn how," May said. "No…it won't work. I left and returned to a time before we'd met. I just about managed to convince you to hear my warning this time. What if I fail next time or Moran is not exposed? Without your trust, I risk everything."

"But you managed, Lady May. It's just taken time to put aside my stubborn refusal to accept you."

"I can't take chances with your life, Kester. I won't risk your family either."

The fire sizzled as it bit into green wood.

"A token," Kester said. "I'll give you a token I'd not give to anyone except for dire need. On your return, show it to me. I'll have to believe you."

He put more wood on the fire. Then he pulled out a gold chain from about his neck. "This I wear close to my heart."

A gold ring with a square ruby dangled at the bottom. "This was my dear mam's. Since her death, I've not removed it."

He slid the ring off the chain. "Give me your hand."

May held it out, meaning just to look at the ring, but he put it on her third finger, smiling when he saw how well it fit her.

"By this token, I'll know you speak true. There's no way for that to lie on your finger, unless by my hand," Kester said.

Looking at the ring, May softly promised. "Then I'll do it."

The next morning, May surprised Kester at her boldness in riding as a man. If he was uncomfortable seeing her bared leg on each side of the horse, he hid it well.

"I wonder that we became such friends," Kester said, "in so little time."

May had not wanted to get into what happened in the Realm, but now gave him a clipped version of what happened to them there.

"Sounds as if you outfoxed a fae," Kester said.

"We did," she said.

That night in camp, May wondered if she made a mistake promising Kester so much. Now she'd committed herself, she feared more than anything failing to keep her word. How did men like Kester and the King carry such responsibilities? What they decided, did, or didn't do meant life and death to their subjects. She could barely promise to leave Illynd and come back with an archaic bit of knowledge. Kester had been right to wonder if he could trust her. In the morning, she switched to riding sidesaddle.

They were coming close to the village and were sure to encounter the odd farmer along the way. Even this way, May was getting used to riding, to enjoy it. Kester acted easier in her company too.

"That's rye grown for bread," he said of a field they passed.

"And that pretty yellow flower smells foul; don't doubt me, or the scent will make your head ache," he said.

"I believe you," May said.

Once in the village, they stopped at a tavern and ordered a meal. Later in the day, they neared the pond and her apple tree. She felt familiar dread of fairies and hated to sit on her horse so exposed to view.

"It's too soon," she said.

She explained what she learned of how she'd roved, recalling what she'd read about the phases of the moon. The same as on Earth, full moons here were roughly thirty days apart. Last evening she pointed out the waning crescent moon, telling Kester it meant the moon was shrinking to the naked eye.

"Ride with me to Delain," Kester said. "You can stay with my friend Kerys until it's near time for the next full moon. You said you'd met her, so you'll know her quality. If I can, I'll bring you back to the tree; if not, I'll send you with guardsmen I trust."

"I'll go to Delain, but don't say anything about our time in the Realm to Kerys. She's a good person, but I'd rather not explain that to her twice," May said.

Passing so close by the forest, May kept turning about, staring in the direction of any sound. "Fairy spies could be out," she whispered.

Then she relaxed; Prince Aidan would not be looking for her. Since her return, she was nothing but another terran peasant to him. As long as she avoided fairy rings, she'd be fine. Nothing went amiss, and they arrived at Delain the next day in the canoe. Kester introduced May to Kerys as a friend of his family. May knew she surprised Kerys with her tight hug and teary eyes, but it was wonderful to see her unhurt.

"I must slip out to meet with my uncle," Kester said to May in private. "Moran and his men will be taken before they can tip off Dailgre. Then we'll fortify the town against assault."

After settling in the room she stayed in before, May went down to the kitchen and offered her help. Kerys seemed quietly pleased to share the work. Peeling potatoes in the kitchen while Kerys served in the dining room, May heard a voice that made her freeze.

"Who's this pretty poppet doing scullery?" Moran bellowed, as he pushed through the shutters with a mug of ale.

May dropped a potato and hurried toward the back hall. His thick hand caught her arm.

"It's lonely duty this." Moran pulled her toward the corner table.

May tried to jerk out of his grasp. "Let me alone."

"Don't go timid. You just want a bit o' company." He pushed her down onto the bench, sat fast by her side, his great arm wrapped about her.

May turned away from his muggy breath. "I'll scream."

"I'll keep that stopped," he said, clamping her chin, taking her mouth. Squirming and struggling, May felt the slip of his wet lips. He was mountain, not man. Digging her nails into his arm and neck made no impression.

"Moran! Get off her."

Kester shot into the room.

"Kester! You dog!" Moran roared, and then laughed as he released May. "Just having a bit of fun."

Once freed from his grip, May slapped him as hard as she could.

Moran didn't flinch.

"She doesn't like you, Moran," Kester said, his hand at his belt.

"Go and come back, Kester. I hadn't time to warm her properly."

"Leave me alone," May said, trying to get past him.

"Let the lady by, Moran."

With a shrug, Moran got up from the bench. May rushed to the washbasin in the corner and scrubbed his foulness from her. Wiping herself on a towel, May registered Kester's hands clenching and unclenching. Any second he'd strike. The last time they fought, Kester nearly died. May went to Kester, pulled his head down, and kissed him. She felt his surprise, but after a moment he held her waist, taking to her trick with enthusiasm she hadn't expected.

"Ah, so you've staked out that territory, you dog. When you're tired of young pups, girl, come find me."

"Our room is upstairs," she said in a low voice. "Let's go."

She took Kester's hand and pulled him away. Moran's coarse laughter followed them. Once inside, May bolted the door; her legs were balloons losing air. "That pig," she cried. "If you didn't come—"

She had to sit down.

"One wrong word...I'd have gutted him," Kester said.

"Don't try it," May said. "He nearly killed you before. He's a dirty fighter. Let the King's soldiers take him in."

Kester came forward and studied her face. "Did he hurt you?"

She shook her head. "I...I feel sick."

"Be calm," he said.

Kester placed a log on the hearth's hot coals and poured water from the jug for her. May held herself up with quivering arms, sipped, and waited for the nausea to pass.

"I should wait here," he said. "He may take note otherwise."

Her neck and cheeks flushed.

He took the chair across from her. "The King's guardsmen will be here tonight. Strangers about Delain are marked to be picked up, along with Moran. You'll be safe."

He placed a hand near hers. After all this, they were finally getting along. If she'd known more about roving that first Kester would have asked, must you leave, May? She would have found out what it meant to him if she did stay. But she had this version of Kester. Later, as he was leaving, Kester told her to keep the door bolted until he told her it was safe. May climbed into bed, but rest was impossible.

She kept recalling the fighting at the docks, Kerys' abused body. That could not happen again. Most of all, she worried if Kester would wait for the soldiers to deal with Moran.

Chapter 22

But he the more with furious rage was fired

Someone banged her door. May ran over in her night shift. "Who's there?"

"Kerys, quick! Kester's fighting Moran. They'll kill each other."

May undid the bolt and threw open the door. Kerys stood wild-eyed, a lamp in her hand. May grabbed the cloak hanging by the door and threw it over her shoulders. Barefoot, she followed Kerys down stairs, through the kitchen, past the empty tavern and out into the night. By the light of torches held aloft by Kery's brothers and Da, Kester and Moran struggled. Nearby one of the King's soldiers held his head, blood streaming into his eyes.

"That guardsman came to arrest Moran, but Moran clouted him with his mug and ran. Kester caught him in the street," Kerys said.

Blood stained Kester's left sleeve. Moran circled him. Kester's sword arm was up. Suddenly Moran rushed him, but Kester back-stepped, and then leapt sideways. This made Moran miss his sword thrust and overbalance. Kester smacked his teetering body with the flat of his sword. Moran dropped hard. Kester planted his blade's tip against Moran's neck.

Sweating profusely, Moran twisted his head. "You can't consider I've done treachery, Kester," he gasped. "We've been mates forever."

"I could sever your ugly head from your shoulders with no regret," Kester said.

Heavy footfalls hurried up the street. Four soldiers parted the crowd. Their leader kicked Moran's blade away. "We'll have him now, sir."

Kester hesitated, and then took his sword up. Moran's arms were tied behind him. Kester moved toward Kerys and May.

Kerys grabbed at him to help him inside. "You're cut! We'll tend to you."

In the kitchen, May boiled water while Kerys took out herbs for healing. As they waited for the water, they ripped strips of clean linen. Kester slumped on a chair.

"I have to take off this tunic, Kester," Kerys said. "It's ruined, anyway."

She and May helped Kester remove the slashed garment. His chest still heaved. Kerys washed all about his wound with water steeped with herbs. Then she examined the injury.

"Not so deep, but a nasty cut. The skin won't stay together to heal if you move it about. I must hem it shut."

Kerys took out a length of linen thread and a needle from a sewing basket. Just before she made to plunge it into Kester's skin, May stopped her.

"Wait! Sterilize it first," she said. She snatched the threaded needle and threw it into the boiling water.

"What are you doing?" Kerys cried.

"It must be boiled several minutes before you use it. It

could make Kester sick otherwise."

"This is something they do where you came from?" Kester said to May.

She nodded.

"Let her do it," Kester told Kerys.

May waited until she felt it was long enough, and then she fished out the needle with a clean spoon. She laid it to cool on a square of linen. In the meantime, Kerys held a fresh cloth to Kester's wound to staunch the bleeding.

"Try it now," May said.

Kerys picked up the needle and made ten neat stitches to close Kester's cut. His face was a mask, his lips tight. When she was done, Kerys put a thick pad of linen on it, and wrapped it with another length of linen and tied it. He sighed with audible relief.

"I'll check how that's healing come morn," Kerys said. "Help him to his room, May, while I clean here."

May held Kester's good arm and escorted him to a room down the hall from hers. She bid him lie on his bed. Then she pulled off his boots and covered him with the blanket. "I was so frightened for you."

"I waited to be sure Moran was taken," Kester said. "When he ran, I was hard after him. His hair will go white in prison," he said, "thanks to your courage coming here to warn us. We owe you a great debt, May."

In the morning, the King rode openly into Delain. In the square, he spoke to townspeople about the threat they faced.

Work began immediately to fortify Delain. Fishermen still came and went to bring in their catch, but kept watch on the water for Dailgre's ships. The tavern and dining room were full up with soldiers. May worked with Kerys and another newly hired girl every day in the kitchen. Kester kept busy with the King's business. His wound was healing clean. Nearly every night he supped with May. They spoke of everything but her leave-taking. It was drawing near to the full moon. Each night before retiring, May walked by the shore to watch its progress.

She noted the waxing crescent, then the first quarter, as the moon grew toward the full. Almost time. Nervous energy jangled her stomach. Just how was she to accomplish what she needed to do when she got back? As this moon's twin wavered on the sea, she considered and rejected ideas until she was satisfied. When she must leave, Kester rode with her to the apple tree.

His arm was stiff, but he insisted on going. May had provisions from Kerys for both of them. She hugged Kerys goodbye and wished her family and her well. Most of the older women and all of the children were leaving Delain with a soldier escort to stay at the castle's town. Kester and she were going on alone. A soldier rowed them upriver, as Kester's arm was not up to the work. For most of the day, her departure weighed heavily between them. Having left the soldier at the river to wait for Kester's return, they made camp, ate, and then watched the moon together.

218

"Will you be safe in your land?" Kester said.

"Yes. It's just I'm worried about all of you. If something goes wrong and I can't get back, what will happen to you? I know so little about this roving…like how many times I can do it. What if I never see you again?"

Kester took her hand. "We're prepared as can be, and that only due to your coming. Don't fear for us. Are there other troubles to you besides your parents?"

"Not really." May shook her head. "Bad things happen at times, accidents, illness. We have our share of evil. Don't worry about me. I know what I must face when I get back. I promise to do everything in my power to return to help."

Kester moved closer. She laid her head against his shoulder. They sat thus for several minutes. Kester began to tell funny stories of his childhood, then about his time in his uncle's guard as a very earnest soldier. She laughed, a good, cleansing feeling coming over her. Later, as she lay in her blanket, the small fire between them, she swore to herself she would come back to Kester. The next day, May cringed at every mushroom they passed, and kept a wary watch for fools' lights. No way did she want to risk the Realm again. At the pond, they stopped at the campsite and made a meal. Nothing should go wrong, but her stomach was unconvinced, and she barely managed a bite of food.

She kept gazing at Kester, sipping tea, wanting to say more but found nothing on her tongue. After supper, she went around a rock to change into a T-shirt, jeans, sneakers, and a sweater. She packed her gown and boots and made sure of the purse Bri gave her by tying it to the belt loop in the front of her jeans, then tucking it down inside the front pocket. When she was ready, she went to wait with Kester until it was time to go to the tree.

It stood alone in the field. One thing May was glad about was her familiarity with it. Almost she felt the tree was an old friend. The full moon gave the twisted branches and leaves a soft shimmer. They were beside it now, but May hesitated.

"If all goes well, I'll see you in a month. I wish you could come with me." Her voice broke. "You won't...even know who I am."

Kester took her into his arms and stroked her hair. "If not for the troubles threatening our land, nothing would keep me from your side. I believe in you," he said. "Don't forget. You wear my ring."

She wiped her teary face, and he lowered his head, the warning enough to send an anticipatory flush through May before he kissed her. It was bittersweet, as May wanted to linger in his arms, but must pull away.

"I have to go."

Kester stood back. "Farewell."

She placed her hand on the notch between branch and trunk. Contact sent *a pins and needles tingling into her arm and throughout her body.*

Chapter 23

Next was November, he full gross and fat,
As fed with lard, and that right well might seem...
And after him, came next the chill December

Kester was far, far away.

The ground shuddered beneath May, everything tilted;
her insides rode an elevator up to a penthouse, and then
plunged down to a basement. Strong stinging pinpricks
engulfed her toe to tip. The darkness was total.

She fell against tree bark that felt cold and slick. May
shivered. Opening her eyes, there was just enough light to see.
A sharp pain stabbed her ankle.

"Ah!"

May made out two imps; one sat above her painful foot.
She shook that leg hard, threw it off her. They must have
come through from Illynd with her. The imps darted up and
circled about her face. She smacked at them with open hands.

"Eeiii!" they cried, high and shrill.

Together they spun and buzzed off toward the woods.

She could only hope it wasn't a male and a female. Here
was a hazard of roving she hadn't considered; cross-
contamination. May turned away to gaze across the field. Her
parent's house was difficult to make out. Hard rain pattered
the apple tree. Steeling herself, she walked home. Once
again, the side door was unlocked. May slipped inside. She
turned on the kitchen light, grabbed a paper towel, and blotted
her face as she checked the kitchen calendar. The days were

crossed up to November tenth. She took off her backpack. In the cabinet over the stove were boxed matches. She grabbed several. In the junk drawer, she got the ball of white twine— now for the hard part. Gingerly, wincing at each creak, she went upstairs.

Her room was as she left it. She pulled sweaters out of the closet, undergarments and socks from the dresser along with two pairs of jeans. Taking them out to the hall, she left them in a pile by the top stair. Then she went to her parents' room.

She pushed the door open. Her father snored, her mother too. Her father's wallet was on his bedside table. Tiptoeing there, she picked it up and backed carefully out of the room holding her breath. May took the wallet and her clothing to the kitchen. She opened the wallet. It must be Friday or Saturday because his store of cash was large. May kept five one-hundred dollar bills, making sure to leave two twenties. Then she got the pad by the phone, a pen, and sat down to write.

Dear Mom, Dad,

I'm fine. I came back for my clothes. I also borrowed cash, but I'm leaving two diamonds to make up for it. They're picked out from an inherited necklace belonging to a friend who wanted to help me. Please don't worry. I just can't stay here anymore. It's not your fault; I'm glad you've stopped drinking and are doing well, but I would have left when I turned eighteen anyway. Please, if you love and trust me at all, don't look for me, just let me go. That's all I ask except, make a good life for yourselves.

Love,

May

And please, lock the side door from now on.

May hoped they believed the lie about the diamonds. Taking out two from the purse, she guessed they might be three carats in weight apiece. Certainly, worth more than the five hundred she'd taken. She set the diamonds on top of the wallet, which weighted her note. May put everything she gathered in her backpack and added two bottled waters, granola bars, and bananas. Shutting the kitchen light, she slipped out the door, turning the lock first. It was raining steady. There was a lot of walking ahead of her. Going to the garden shed, she got her father's old army jacket and a baseball cap he kept there for yard work.

She adjusted the hatband to fit her head, donned the jacket, then the backpack. Zipping the jacket, she turned up the collar and left the shed. Shoving her hands into the pockets, she set off without a backward look. No cars went by, civilian or police. 'All the cops in the donut shops sing hey o, hey o' May sang softly. After the tension she felt being near the fairy woods, walking alone on this dark road was nothing. The sky lightened.

The rain lessened. A few cars passed in the last half-hour. Up ahead was a diner, Laundromat, and combination package/grocery store that catered to the summer vacation crowd. Lake Owo-nee offered boating, fishing, and swimming. Nearby Camp Owo-nee rented slots for R.V.'s, tents, and cabins for inexpensive summer fun. Her parents brought her to swim here before their drinking got out of control. Tired now, May was also hungry. The diner was open twenty-four seven.

Early risers parked out front. Shaking rain off her hat, she folded it, shoved it in a pocket and went inside. From a booth in the corner, May studied the menu. Right away, a sleepy brunette appeared with a thick white mug and poured hot coffee without being asked.

"Thank you," May said. The coffee smelled wonderful. "I'd like the trucker's special with wheat toast and hot cereal instead of sausages."

The waitress yawned, said, "You can put all that away? Little thing like you?"

"I'm very hungry."

"How'd you like those eggs?"

"Scrambled," she said.

When she left, May fixed her coffee. The taste was heavenly, just what she needed. The cooking smells made her mouth water too, but it was everything; the advertisements on the diner's walls, the black and white tiles on its floor, the eyeliner smudging the waitress' eyes, and the oil-heated air of the place that made May tear up. This was home, Earth; she was safe. Swallowing past the swelling in her throat, she blinked to clear her vision.

When she recovered, May studied the old-fashioned

jukebox's selector. Instead of the top-ten hit list, these were golden oldies. If she had a quarter—it was a long time since she heard music, except for the Dance. The waitress placed a laden white platter, bottle of catsup, and hot sauce in front of her.

May dug into eggs, hash browns, toast and the oatmeal.

The waitress topped off her coffee. "You were hungry, weren't you, honey?"

She laid the tab on the table and was about to turn away, but May was ready and gave her a hundred-dollar bill.

"You don't have anything smaller, honey?"

The bill for breakfast was four ninety-five.

"Sorry," May said with a shrug.

The waitress went to the register, held the bill to the light to examine it, was satisfied, and made change. She walked back and counted out May's money.

"Thank you," May said.

May left a dollar tip under her coffee cup. Out in the late fall air she drew in a deep breath. There were only darker reds and browned leaves left in the trees, the rest having dropped. Once again, time passed differently here, roughly two months here to one on Illynd, but they'd been added onto the time she was here before. Why it was this way, she had no clue. She crossed the road and entered Camp Owo-nee.

A rustic clapboard house was the camp's main office. Going to the unmanned counter, May rang the bell for service. A white-haired man, who'd left the diner before her, walked out of the office behind the counter.

"Good day, young lady. How was Gus's cooking?"

"It was fine."

His smile was friendly. "What can I do for you?" he asked.

"I'd like to rent a cabin near the lake for a month. I'll pay in advance."

His eyes lit up. "Don't get much business this time of year."

"I love the shift between seasons," she said. "I'm going to do nature studies, draw the lake, the trees, that kind of thing. I'm an art student."

"Well, you look like some kind of student, awfully young."

"I look younger than I am," she quickly made-up. "I'm nineteen."

"As old as all that?" he said. "Take cabin six. It's private and has the prettiest view."

"That sounds great, how much?" May held her breath.

"Give you a student discount on top of our out-of-season rate, which would make it two-fifty for the month."

May was relieved. There would be enough left over for food and supplies. She took out three hundred-dollar bills and accepted back five tens in change. She gave her name for the register as Kerys White from Marlborough, an upstate art college. Mr. Martindale, having introduced himself, showed her the cabin after he wrote out her receipt. Cabin Six stood on a spit of land reaching into the lake. Pine trees screened it from the other cabins. Its fireplace would be welcome on cool nights.

"There's wood in that crate there, with kindling and old newspapers. More wood on the porch," Mr. Martindale said.

The cabin walls were chinked. A couch faced the fireplace and an old trunk was the coffee table. A bookshelf held used National Geographic magazines, boxed games, and decks of cards—rainy weather pastimes. Windows overlooking the lake weren't curtained. A counter divided the kitchen from the sitting area.

Mr. Martindale opened the refrigerator, a model so old it had a circular motor on top. "Nice and cold...the stove drawer holds pots and pans," he said.

The bathroom was off the bedroom. Everything was clean. "Thank you, this will be fine," May said.

"There's a pay washer and dryer in the main house. There's no maid service off-season. You'll have to wash your sheets and towels. I'll give you a dollar in quarters a week to do the linens," Mr. Martindale said.

He gave her the cabin key and left. She located pencil stubs and recycled paper in a kitchen drawer, made a list. May left her backpack, tucked the purse in her jeans, and took all her cash too. Now she was on her own again, her cautious streak took over. The campground was quiet. She might be the only one renting a place. Wearing the jacket and cap, May walked to the nearby store, took a basket and located toiletries.

Then she picked up canned goods, fresh bread and a pastry gooey with apples and cinnamon. At the meat counter, a man with a part white, part bloodstained apron came closer when she drew near.

"Chuck is ground by order," he said. "Our customers say it makes the best burgers."

"Do you carry soy burgers?" May said. They didn't have those on Illynd.

He made a face, but pointed toward an upright freezer. May thanked him, got her soy burgers, picked up the fixings. It took no time to get everything else she might need in the basket. Last of all, she grabbed a drawing pad, pencils, and a gum eraser. If she forgot anything, the store wasn't far. At the checkout counter she added licorice and sour tarts to her order. Who knew when she'd have her favorite candies again? The register was run by a wiry twenty-something whose hair was an oily buddy to spotty skin. He lit with an interest in her that was unmistakable. He lingered bagging too, his mouth open part-way, swallowing several times.

Finally, the butcher yelled from behind the meat counter, "Speed up, Johnny. The lady doesn't want to stand there all day."

"Right, Dad," he drawled, red-faced.

Johnny moved marginally faster. "Carry your bags?" he asked when done.

"No thanks," May said.

As she walked toward Camp Owo-nee, May glanced

back. Johnny was on the store stoop watching her. May put away her purchases, then had a long shower. Afterward she carried drawing supplies outside. The day was an autumn treat. Canadian geese glided to a graceful landing on the water. May sat on a rock in the sun. Back on Kester's world, she had planned to stay here until the next full moon. Then she wouldn't be grilled by cops or forced to explain her absence to her parents. The heat made her pleasantly drowsy. A vivid memory of Prince Aidan, his intensity as he told her he would have no other for his consort, flooded her.

Now she was away from him, she lingered over what she felt in his presence. Was it fairy glamour that drew her against her better judgment? In spite of his declaration, he respected her wishes by the apple tree. On top of that Prince Aidan saved Kester's life, though he'd suspected Kester helped May escape. Was the prince a cunning player in a power game with Princess Kerriena, who used May like a piece on his board, or something else? Strange to think all those possibilities disappeared when she returned here the first time. Opening her eyes, she gazed at the lake.

Ducks bobbed near shore. Being here with no responsibilities was like having her first vacation. Lifting the top of the pad, she started to draw. When hunger gnawed at her, she went to try out the deck grill. Soy did not perfume the air. But she fixed her bun, added chips to the plate, came back out with a soda and the burger was done. In the afternoon, cars pulled into the campground. The weekenders were here.

The other cabins filled, along with a few tent sites, and five RV's parked in slots. Unwilling to be drawn into small talk, May went in.

She was sorry to share the lake, but at least her cabin was farthest away from the rest. May started a fire. Taking a deck of cards, she played solitaire. As the sky leached of light, she felt a sense of unease she couldn't shake off. She got up, checked to see if the door and windows were locked, and sat back down. Like a black eye, the curtain-less window across the way stared at her. No one would be on the lake in the dark. Rubbing her goose bumps, she leaned back into the couch.

Chapter 24

But if thou may with reason yet repress,
The growing evil, ere it strength have got.

May felt so alive this morning, so full of purpose knowing what she did here would help Kester. She wore the jacket and cap to walk to town. Spotting a stick in the brush, she tested to see how strong it was. Satisfied, she peeled bark from it as she walked. She felt safer holding a sturdy hiking stick. A car drove toward her, passed, and stopped. No other cars were coming along. She kept moving.

"W-would you like a ride?"

It was Johnny from the store, grinning despite stained teeth.

"No thanks. It's a nice day. I'd rather walk," she said.

Johnny nodded somewhat stupidly, if she were unkind. Not much later he must have turned around, because his car passed her going away from town. In an hour she was on Main Street. She went into the Victorian home turned into a library hat on, brim low. Someone might recognize her here. She stopped at the card catalog; computers hadn't reached here yet. At G, she looked up gunpowder, jotted sources, found them and carried two books to a secluded carrel.

When she had what she needed, she went to the copy machine, put in dimes, and copied pages. She folded them, put the papers in her pocket, and then put the books back. The walk to camp was warm in the army coat, but she left it on. By the time she neared Camp Owo-nee, she was thirsty. She stopped at the store for orange juice.

The store was busy with campers buying supplies for picnics. May got her juice and added a carton of ice cream. Good old John, or was it Johnny, was back at work. He didn't try small talk, just nodded at her. May went to the cabin and made another burger. She ate outside even though the camp was noisier, because the lake was beautiful. Later she walked the trail with her hiking stick. Several times, she thought someone followed her.

She twisted about, but each time saw no one. Stepping as they did, deer sounded human-like. It must be deer. Leaves spiraled down, and she chided herself for being spooked. No wonder, as being back reminded May about the person she hoped to be, which was different from her parents. They had been so involved in themselves. She never wanted to be that way. Was what she planned to do morally right?

Taking Kester the knowledge to make gunpowder didn't seem so simple here. May was uneasy about the destructive power she would introduce to Illynd. Though she feared its fairies and conflicts, so much was unspoiled on that world. What would gunpowder do to it? She hadn't missed the noise, pollution, or conflicts of this world. Would gunpowder be the start of worse on Illynd? Having already given her promise, how could she not keep it? She trusted Kester; she'd have to trust him with this knowledge too. Back at the cabin, she cleaned the fireplace, crumpled newspaper and lit a match to a new fire.

Once the kindling caught, May dished up ice cream, something else she'd missed on Illynd. Perhaps she could take that recipe back, as well as one for pizza. Afterward, May pulled out her photocopied page. She wanted to memorize how to make the gunpowder since anything written could be taken from her. She read the formula repeatedly, then got scrap paper from the kitchen and put down facts she remembered. After a few days keeping behind the pines that screened her cabin from the others, May wished she could be friendly with her fellow campers. She was so alone here.

This is what her life would be without Illynd and Kester. Back when she planned to live on her own, she had no clue how isolated that would feel. There was no one she could talk with, let alone share her troubles with here. If anything happened to her before she got back to Kester, there wasn't one soul to even take note of it. With her research done and food recipes gone over from an old cookbook in the cabin, she took solitary walks, sketched, and read all the old magazines. Each day, like a shadow, the niggling feeling something wasn't right fell on her.

She'd check out the windows and rattle the cabin's lock, or stare forward and back along the trail, hoping to catch whatever it was. Nerves, she told herself, wanting to laugh, wishing she had someone to share her unnamed fears. A few times, May treated herself to a meal at the diner just to be near others. Thankfully, the moon was a waning crescent. She'd be leaving.

May would to walk to the apple tree and wait by the pond on the day of the full moon. Now the time was here, she kept checking her finger, adjusting the ruby ring Kester put there. She hoped it would be enough for him to believe in her. If felt terrible to have lost his faith the last time. In spite of those qualms, she couldn't wait to see his honest, handsome face. May retired early.

At four-thirty she was up, ate, and washed dishes. May left a note thanking Mr. Martindale for his kindness. It was December so the weather turned chilly. May was glad for the army coat. She zipped it up, slipped on her backpack and cap, and left the door unlocked. It was early for the office to be open, so she slid her cabin key through the door's postal slit. Out on the main road, she turned toward her parents' house, home to her no longer.

If she made it back to Illynd, would she return here after helping Kester? She honestly didn't know.

Chapter 25

And drew her on the ground, and his sharp sword,
Against her snowy breast he fiercely bent,
And threatened death with many a bloody word;
Tongue hates to tell the rest, that eye to see abhorred

When the girl from the store this morning looked up, Johnny almost jumped. It was as if she looked right at him. After a minute, his breathing calmed. With the light on next to her, she couldn't see him, not considering how dark it was outside. It was his luck she rented this cabin hidden by pines. He could watch her as long as he liked. The stack of wood outside its front kept the noisy bunch of brats who were running around from seeing him too. When she got up to go to the bedroom, his breathing sped up.

He slipped around the cabin to the bedroom side. He already knew he could see in those windows just fine. When she drew the shutters without taking off so much as her sneakers, he cursed under his breath. Minutes later the light went out. He went back to the other side and wiggled the door knob—locked. Profoundly disappointed, he walked back to the store. The next day the usual torture greeted him.

His pop kept at him for any little thing. Finally, when Johnny thought he was done for the night, Pop got on his case again. He let him go only after making him scrub and hose out the garbage cans out back of the store. He hated the job and mouthed curses and threats under his breath the entire time. At the cabin window once more, he forgot everything when he saw his girl sitting on the couch, long hair hanging over her T-shirt.

Johnny liked the way her hair shone when it moved. She was real pretty with a figure she hid under that baggy old coat. Her breasts were high and her waist narrow. When she turned from him in the store that first day, his mouth filled with saliva watching her tight bottom. Johnny wanted her badly. Pretty girls like her never talked with him, not when he was in school, not since he dropped out. He knew he was a geek, a 'skinny freak', his pop called him. He hated Pop.

He hated living at home like some kind of slave, working in the store twenty-four/seven. The only thing that kept him going was his fantasies. Those were usually confined to the hot chicks gracing his porn stash. Now there was this girl, his girl. He wondered what she was doing all by herself renting a cabin. According to nosy old Mr. Martindale gossiping to Johnny's dad when he came by the store, she was an art student. The second night he was back.

Johnny watched her read papers over, and over, writing stuff down, and finally, she threw her notes away. The fire must be warm because she pulled her sweater over her head, her T-shirt riding up her bare stomach, bra showing—shit, she pulled the shirt down. She was killing him!

Like she knew he was watching. Then she shut the light and went to the bedroom. Johnny followed fast as he could in the dark. Take off the T-shirt, he silently begged. She kicked off the sneakers, unzipped her jeans, tugged them down and he was in heaven. She made a face, hurried to the window in those white panties and closed the shutters. Damn! Johnny almost kicked the cabin wall. The light winked out, and he reluctantly dragged his butt back to his family's apartment over the store.

His girl settled into a routine, with Johnny alert to her comings and goings, so he could find her wherever she was all day long. No one ever came to see her, and she never used the public phone. None of those old cabins had one either. His fantasies about her grew.

He saw himself approach her. She'd smile at him. They'd talk. He'd kiss her. In his mind, things went pretty hot and fast from there. Of course, he was pissed when she didn't accept his offer of a ride to town.

What did she think; he was out to rape her? He was just a guy trying to be friendly. Damn. It aggravated him every time he thought about it. Tonight, alarm filled him. She took things from the kitchen to pack with clothes and other stuff in a backpack. She was leaving. When? He'd ask Martindale in the morning, casual like. If he didn't jump on this he'd never get a chance with her.

As soon as he could whine his way into an early coffee break the next morning, Johnny ran to check on his girl, Kerys; got her name when he sneaked a peak into the check-in book at the camp office. This time her door wasn't locked when he tried it. Damn! She already left.

Suddenly he got an idea. Maybe there was an address, a

phone number in the garbage. He went to the wastebasket and dumped it out. At the bottom were handwritten scraps. Johnny remembered she'd written all those. Reading them, he got a shock. Wow, what was this chick up to? Gunpowder— was she gonna blow up something? Excited, Johnny stuffed the papers into his pocket and left. Johnny's pop would be pissed he didn't return from his break, but he didn't care. He had this chick in the palms of his hands. He got in Pop's car and drove off. Scanning the road ahead, he had to keep letting his foot off the gas, going too fast in his hurry to find her. Finally, to his relief, Johnny spotted her in a field alongside the road. Perfect. He pulled over and watched.

She headed toward a wooded area, climbed a stonewall that bordered it, and soon disappeared from sight. Where was she going? He stared at the trees, waited for her to reappear. Ten minutes passed, fifteen. His break was way over. Come on. Come on, he urged. Where are you? He scanned the woods. The trees went up alongside a grassy hill. There was a pond over to the left. He gazed back and forth again, and then stared hard.

There, showing in a gray line just above the pond was smoke. It had to be her. What was she up to? He wanted to make a move. What if she was meeting someone? She was out there with her stuff. The cabin was empty. She had to be meeting someone. He'd wait to be sure. As dark fell, so did the temperature. The sky lowered. Long before Pop could find his car pulled off the roadside, Johnny had driven it into a field opposite the woods, hid it behind its heavy brush border. His window was rolled down. He sniffed, the air smelled like snow. He smiled. She wasn't meeting anyone. It was getting dark and too late for that.

He got out of the car, made his way toward the pond. Johnny warmed to the welcome he expected from her now he knew what was up. She'd be real grateful to stay out of trouble. A wet flake hit his face. It was snowing. He crossed a swampy area. Suddenly, he saw her coming his way. A tree stood between him and her. That explained why she didn't see him right off. He halted. Pulling his hand out of his pocket, he clicked on his flashlight, froze her in her tracks.

"Hello, m-m miss, Kerys, isn't that your n-name? It's J-Johnny from the s-store. Remember?"

After her initial shock, she spoke fast. "Johnny, what a surprise, I was out for a walk, I just love the snow."

He smirked, kept the light in her eyes. "You're a l-liar. I s-saw what you wrote. I kept your p-papers to prove it. What are you planning to b-blow up?'

Her face changed again. Not so snooty, now she was afraid. This wasn't the way she thought it was supposed to go.

"I was just doodling, Johnny," she said. "I write a lot of stuff. You should see my sketchbook."

"I don't think the c-cops will believe that, Kerys," he said, a little smile dawning.

"N-now, I want something from you. I got my car parked up the road. Y-you just come with m-me. I'll k-keep your secret and give you back your papers if you're real nice," he said.

Her eyes widened. This was better than he hoped, but if he had to, he'd show her he wasn't kidding. She started to move toward him, but sideways.

"I can't go with you, Johnny. If you'll promise to go away and leave me alone, I'll give you something better, something worth a lot of money."

He was suspicious. "What have you g-got?"

"A gem, Johnny, a big diamond."

"You think I'm s-stupid and ugly?" He shouted this, anger and frustration bubbling up now he was so close to his goal.

She moved toward the tree, all the while fumbling at her jacket. Mouth open, he watched her hands at the waistband of her jeans. She pulled something up and held it out.

"See?" she said, stretching the palm of her hand toward him.

Johnny trained his light on it. It sparkled.

"I'll give you this if you'll go and leave me alone."

Was that a diamond? Shit, she was giving him a diamond. Wow. This was crazy. He couldn't believe his luck.

Johnny lunged for her. "I'll have that and y-you."

He grunted as he rammed into her, smacked her flat. He heard a crack, like a stick breaking.

"Ah-h," she cried out.

His flashlight dropped, illuminating the tree in its beam.

When he bent to grab her, she kicked at him, rolled toward the tree. Johnny hung onto her leg and pulled in the other direction.

She sat up and struck out with her good arm, smacking his face hard, breaking his nose. Stunned, blood gushed out and dribbled into Johnny's mouth. He spit hot coppery snot. Lurching forward, he laid his weight on her, pinning her hips. She couldn't buck him off now.

"Bitch!"

He screamed, red filling his vision as he squeezed her neck. He'd show her. He'd show them all, especially Pop. He'd take this bitch, then take her diamond and blow this place with Pop's car. She flailed away with her unbroken arm, trying to grab something.

There was nothing to grab, no sticks or rocks. Johnny hung on tighter, more excited than mad now. She threw dirt and snow in his face. He shook it off. She wasn't fighting as hard, just flailing her good arm. She'd pass out. It'd be easy to do whatever he wanted when she was unconscious. She reached further, grabbed something and *a strange tingling spread from Johnny's hands to his arms, flashed all through his body. The ground beneath them heaved violently. His insides shifted as if he teetered on a high point before he took a swift fall that shot him back up again. At the same time, everything went black.*

"What the hell?" His fingers let go of her throat.

She retched and gasped for air. Johnny kept her pinned.

"What'd you do?" he cried.

"Kester!" she screamed. "HELP! He's kil—"

Johnny got her throat again. She had been waiting for someone. All along, she was somebody's girl, pretending she was alone. Fresh anger filled him. She was his, his. She lied, though. No one was coming.

"Ain't no one but us, bitch. And you're d-dead."

He started choking her again. She clutched at, clawed his fingers, gave up when he squeezed harder. To his delight, he felt her go limp. Pulling at his belt, the rush of blood in his head and groin roaring, Johnny didn't feel the blow that came.

Chapter 26

Death with a most grim and ghastly visage seen,
Yet is he naught but parting of the breath

Incensed, Kester smashed the attacker on the back of his head, laying him out. He pulled the brute off the woman. Holding his torch aloft, he was sickened by her purpled face. Quickly, Kester tied the villain's hands tight and bent to examine her. So young she was.

He swore; it was a vicious way to die. Tentatively, he touched the red mark about her neck. A low gasp escaped her lips—still alive. Sticking the torch into the ground, he picked her up and retrieved it. The beast that savaged her could wait. At his camp, he built up the fire. Her swollen face was speckled with red dots. Her neck had white handprints tellingly standing out. He set water to boil. For the first time, he registered her strange garb.

She wore mannish trouser and white boots of a sort he never saw before. She was muddy and wet, yet it was a fair, dry night. He carefully removed the sack on her back and the heavy tunic. The odd shift beneath it was shoved up, her trouser front opened for the foul act he'd interrupted. Her left arm swelled alarmingly below the elbow, the forearm broken. To spare her pain, he'd set the bones while she was unconscious.

He broke green sticks into splints. Afterward, with her arm seen too, her face and neck bathed, he sat back. He'd done all he could. He must hope she would wake from her deep sleep. Gently, he covered her with the other half of his blanket. Light seeped into a new day. It must have woken his prisoner, as loud moaning came from where Kester left him trussed by the tree. Rape and murder carried a harsh penalty in Mirddyn. Kester went to him.

"Get to your feet," he said.

"Hey, look, mister, you gotta help me out," the fiend said.

"Up" Kester said. He pulled his knife, and the fiend scrambled to stand.

"Go to the pond," Kester said.

"Is she your girl?" the fiend asked. "She said she was mine, I mean, I'm sorry, I didn't know, you know?"

He turned about, walked backwards, tied hands out like a beggar's. "Untie me, and I'll be gone, man. I won't tell anyone what you and her were doing. Okay?"

"On your knees," Kester said.

His prisoner paled, dropped down, shoulders shaking while Kester tethered him to a tree near the pond's stream with stout rope, making it so he could reach water to drink but couldn't escape. It would do until soldiers from town could be sent. Kester walked back to his camp, his prisoner quiet for the moment. As for the young lady, Kester wouldn't leave her. He fashioned a travois to drag her with him to Delain. He was settling her on it when she moaned, brushing her face with her good hand. The ring on her finger made him hold his breath.

Kester bent to examine the gold and ruby ring.

Wonderingly, he pulled the chain out from about his neck. His mam's ring wasn't there, but on this lady's finger. How was it a stranger had on her finger a ring Kester never took off the chain about his neck? Not since his mam passed and his da gave it to him as a remembrance. He pulled the chain over his head. There was no break in it. If this was not his mam's ring, it was its twin. He slid the ring off the lady's hand. She moaned again. Inscribed inside was his mam's name. There was no mistaking it. For now, he put the ring back on the lady's finger. He hoped he'd be able to get this story out of her. Kester did a last check on her attacker.

"Hey, you're back, gonna let me go now?" the beast said.

Kester glared at him and then walked away.

"Come on! You can't leave me like this!"

Kester ignored the increasingly panicky shouts, went back to his horse, and hooked up the travois. Those sounds died away the further they went. Surprisingly, the jostling and bumping did not wake the lady. Kester passed through the forest to the river. He shied the horse home; it had been this way before and always returned to its stable. At his boat, he carefully placed the lady in, along with her sack, and covered her with his blanket. All the day he watched her face, hoping for signs she would waken. Kester reached town late.

He pulled the boat up onto the bank below the inn and went to seek help. After dispatching guardsmen to collect the lady's attacker, he went with Kerys to fetch the lady from the boat. Kerys took over.

"Come upstairs," Kerys said, "careful, set her down here."

Kerys eased off the stranger's odd boots, put the cover over her.

"Jud," Kerys said, "run fetch the healer. Kester, you're done in. Go to the tavern and get somewhat to eat. By the look of you, a strong drink won't go amiss. I've got her in hand."

Early next morning, Kerys was cooking when Kester came into the kitchen to speak with her.

"I was with her earlier," Kerys said. "Whoever did that to her was an ogre. Her neck's ringed with bruises, poor thing. I undressed her before the healer got in. She wore the strangest garments, never saw her about either. I'd guess she counts sixteen summers. What do you know of her?"

"Nothing," Kester said. "I was sleeping when a cry in the dark woke me. I lit a torch and made for the noise. A brute was straddling her, choking the life out of her. He already broke her arm. I clouted him and tied him up. The guardsmen were in an ugly mood when they went to fetch him back. With so many tempting trees along the way, I cautioned them not to take the matter into their own hands."

Kester shook his head. "Kerys, I don't know her, but I think I should. There's something familiar about her."

He didn't mention his ring on the lady's finger, as Kerys had never seen it on him. Kester went up with Kerys, carrying the pitcher of hot water. She opened the shutters wide, flooded the room with light.

"Unh."

"She might be waking." Kerys rinsed a cloth in hot water and wiped the lady's face.

Her eyelids fluttered, then opened, shut, opened again. "W-water—" she said.

Kester poured a drink from the other pitcher on the table and gave it to Kerys, who held it to the lady's lips. She gulped, coughed, and Kerys pulled it away. "Easy, take it slow."

Kerys helped her drink more.

"Kester," the lady croaked, staring with wide eyes. "I've found you."

"You know me, lady?"

"Questions will wait, Kester," Kerys said. "Keep her quiet while I go brew té. I've herbs to soothe pain."

Kerys left. The lady tried to sit, but her broken arm prevented it. Kester helped her, putting the pillows behind her back.

"Kester," she said in a rasp painful to hear. She held her throat with her good hand. "Where—"

"Don't speak, Lady. Let me try to answer your questions. You're safe at the Sundowner Inn at Delain. The man who did this to you will be dealt with. Rest. Everything else can wait."

She did not speak again. Her expression said the pain was too much. Kerys came in with a mug of doctored té. She helped her patient take it in small sips. After a time, it started its work, for she relaxed against the pillows.

"Better now," Kerys said with pleasure. "I'll be back with broth."

When she was gone, the lady tried to speak again.

"Kester," she whispered. Kester moved his chair nearer to hear.

"Kester...I've brought...what you need."

Kester was puzzled. She reached her good hand out to him, laying it on his arm.

"I've got...tell you...hard to believe. Please...let me."

He nodded.

"Rover," she said, her voice harsh, "Don't know much . . . I've been...twice by apple tree . . . not far from your camp."

She took another sip of the nearly empty cup before she spoke again.

"First time...you saved my life...friends." She gestured from her to him. "Then this town...attacked by Dailgre."

At mention of the name, Kester's skin tightened.

"Your friends...killed. Dailgre massacred King...your father... an ambush...betrayed by Moran."

She paused, but he nodded for her to continue.

"Please . . . water?"

Going to the pitcher, Kester filled her mug and handed it to her. She took several swallows and coughed, wincing.

When she spoke again, her voice sounded clearer but she could not speak above a low whisper. "Went to my world, returned the same day...I don't understand roving. You didn't know me. It was hard for Lachlan...to trust me."

He started hearing her speak his true name.

She took another sip. "Moran met Dailgre's men, proved I wasn't lying. To help, I wanted to get you a...weapon."

She drank more water. "Afraid to go back, but you said you'd trust this."

She held up her good hand to show him the ring.

"I noted the ring," Kester said. "And your garb made me wonder just where you came from. But how else can you prove yourself?"

"No time...alert the King about Dailgre, watch Moran."
She studied his face.

"I see one flaw in your story. Where is the weapon you speak of? There were none on your person, or in your sack."

"In my head...how to make the weapon. Almost didn't make it myself," she grimaced. "That Johnny jumped me. He wanted to—"

"I know what the creature wanted," Kester said grim.

Coloring, she shut her eyes. Tears slid down her cheeks. "Kester...my rescue again."

She opened her eyes. "Thank you."

"I did what a decent man would, Lady," he said, his voice gentle. "Might I ask, just what does this weapon do? Will there be time to use it if we need defend Delain?"

She nodded. "I'll teach you...simple...sulfur, a crumbly yellow rock, saltpeter, charcoal."

She shut her eyes.

"Forgive me for pressing you, Lady. Speak only one

word more, and then you must rest. Your name...I would know the name of a friend I trusted with my mam's ring."

Her smile was shallow but there. "May...McKinny."

"Rest, Lady May. I'll take your warning to my uncle...and watch Moran."

At the mention of his old friend, she paled and squeezed his fingers. "Careful...Moran hurt you last—"

She coughed, couldn't stop. Kerys rushed in with broth, giving him a look that chased him out of the room. Kester was allowed to visit Lady May that evening. She confessed she felt weaker than she would have believed. Satisfied she was doing well considering the ordeal she survived, Kester told her he received word from the King. He was coming to Delain.

"I wonder at your weapon...the materials you named are common," Kester said, "Are they used in a magic?"

Her voice recovered everything but strength, was still soft to the ear. "No, but together they can cause a lot of damage."

"I brought other things to make charges," she said as she took a chair by the fire, "twine and matches. Where's my pack?"

Kester found the sack in the wardrobe.

"In the side pocket," she said.

Kester took out a ball of slender rope. She reached into the sack and pulled out a small box. From this, she took a stick of wood with a blue tip. He watched her scratch it across the side of the box. When its tip flared like a tiny torch, he jumped.

Holding it up, she smiled. A strange scent filled the air. He watched fascinated, until the flame burnt close to her fingers and she blew it out. Then she handed the burnt remnant to him to examine. He sniffed it.

"That's a match," she said. "They won't work if they get wet. We'll practice with the gunpowder, fuses, and matches before you rely on them in a fight."

Kester sat back and shook his head.

"A rover," he said, marveling at the burnt stick. "You talk of battle and weapons with such sureness, yet you must keep what you are secret. My uncle knows, of course, my lady," he said.

With her bearing and knowledge, she merited the title lady

She leaned back. "I...can't tell you how worried I was you wouldn't believe me."

"How could I not?" Kester said going to fill her mug with water Kerys left. "I would not give out that ring to one I did not trust."

She took the mug, smiled. "It's served its purpose, please, take it back. I know how much it means to you."

Kester glanced at the ring; it fit as if it belonged, and shook his head. "It feels right you keep it now. My mam would approve."

She was teary-eyed, and turned away.

"Rest, Lady May. Tomorrow you will be stronger."

She would need that strength.

Chapter 27

That may not hope by flight to scape alive,
Still waits for death with dread and trembling awe

The next day, early, Kester knocked at Lady May's door.
At her soft, 'come in', he cracked it. She was not out of bed
yet, but pulled the blankets up close, exhibiting a natural
modesty.

"I've folk that must meet you," he said.

She nodded, sitting up awkwardly, while keeping the
covers high. Kester stepped in with three men. He introduced
them; the burgess of Delain and two of the town's elders. Like
them, he was somber.

"How do you mend, Lady McKinny? Kester's told your
story and vouched for you," the burgess informed her gravely.

"I'm much better, thank you, sir," she said.

"Have you family we can send to, my lady?" the burgess
asked.

"No, sir. I've been on my own for years."

"How many summers have you, my lady? You seem very
young."

"Seventeen, sir."

The burgess nodded.

"These gentlemen must examine the tale of how you were
attacked," Kester said, his face a mask. "I've told what I
observed."

"I was coming to Delain to find Kester," Lady May said
in her ruined voice. "I was surprised by Johnny, the son of a

shopkeeper in the village I stopped in far south of here. I didn't realize it when I left, but he followed me. When he showed himself, he said he wanted me to . . . come with him, be with him. I wouldn't. I said I'd give him something valuable if he would leave me alone," May said. She paused to sip water.

"I had taken out my purse," May said, "but he knocked me down, broke my arm. He said…he would take my purse and me. He sat on me, choked me. When he let go for a moment, I cried for help. Then he choked me harder. I blacked out."

The burgess frowned. "Did this villain . . ., I'm required to be indelicate, my lady, did he force you? Did he spoil you?"

Her face burned. "No," she said. "I blacked out, but no, I'm sure he didn't."

Kester broke in to explain. "I pulled the brute off the Lady," he said. "He meant to violate her; that much was clear."

The burgess coughed. "You're safe with us, my lady. We don't tolerate villainy in Delain. We've your story and Kester's, a man well known and respected hereabouts."

The burgess turned to the elders. Each one nodded. They all moved a bit closer, studying May's fair skin dotted with red pinpricks from the strangulation, the finger marks raw about her throat, her bruised and broken arm in its sling.

"Your attacker will be dealt with," the burgess said. "Thank you, my lady. We'll leave you, wishing good health on you."

Kester went out with them. He didn't come back until late. Lady May sat at the table near the fireplace arranging wildflowers and herbs in a bowl with water.

She smiled. "Kerys helped me walk out in the garden today," she said, "and let me pick these."

Kerys had come up with té for May as well as his supper and then left, busy with the dinner trade.

Kester sat, but he would not eat this night. He knew he must look grim. "It's been a hard day, my lady," he said.

"What's happened?" Alarm raised her tone.

"Late this afternoon we questioned that...Johnny. He was full of complaints, 'Why was he here? Who were we? Why did we lock him up?' When confronted by my account of his attack on you, that he planned theft and rape, having broken your arm and choked you near death, he shut up."

She dropped a sprig of mint to put her hand on Kester's, flinched because it was icy.

"When he spoke again," Kester said, "it was as if that meant nothing. He asked over, and over, who were we to lock him up? He had rights, we couldn't tell him what to do. The burgess and elders came to a swift decision; guilty of mayhem on a female, highway robbery, and attempt to murder."

He paused.

"I've just come from his hanging that was carried out at sunset."

Lady May went white. If she wasn't seated, Kester was

certain she'd fall over.

"Be strong," he said. "This evil was not yours. I only just saved your life. If I wasn't at my camp you'd be dead now, not him. Do they allow killing to go unpunished where you come from?"

She shook her head. "No," she whispered in a small voice. "It's just . . . so quick."

"When a death decree is made, it's cruel to put off the punishment."

Kester brushed back hairs from her face. "There are finger marks on your neck yet."

Shuddering, her good hand went to her throat. "Something else happened today, didn't it?" she said after a long stretch in which they sat silent.

"I followed my lifelong comrade Moran this morning when he left town," Kester said, "to where he met a skiff full of Dailgre's men. I've got proof Moran betrayed Mirddyn. It's truly been an evil day."

Kester would not detail the scene he recently left. Johnny did not face his end well, but screamed, writhed, and thrashed about. He was wrestled down and gagged. It was no surprise a man who'd spoil and kill a slip of a female would die a coward, but as necessary as it was, his death was a horror to witness. The King's guard and town leaders were at the hanging along with Kester, as the grave occasion warranted. It took place inside jail walls, so the sight could offend no one else. Weary, he rubbed his head.

Lady May gripped his fingers. "I'm so sorry about your friend…but you had to know."

"The King's on his way. Moran and his men will be taken in."

"Kester, Moran attacked you twice and both times, you were injured. Swear you'll stay away when it's done," May said.

Kester had no answer for that. Going to Kerys privately before coming up to speak with Lady May, he'd made certain she doctored Lady May's té. Both feared Lady May would suffer over the news of the hanging. Before he left her, she was drowsy. Kerys slipped in and helped her to bed.

The next few days, Kester met with Lady May to share what was happening in town. He was pleased she made trips to the kitchen to watch Kerys cook. When he told her Moran was taken without mishap, she brightened. The King was in town preparing for the coming conflict. Kester came to Lady May to work on her weapon. She had an arm in a sling, fading bruises, but was speaking much clearer. Before they began, she told him they must guard the secret she shared with him.

"We should work in private," she said, "and it's dangerous to work with. I made of list of what we need."

Kester took the paper and came back for Lady May after lunch. He walked her to a storehouse near the edge of town cleared out for their use. A table was set up there, along with the supplies.

"Let's start with the fuse," she said. She instructed Kester to take twine she supplied and dip it in melted wax. When they finished sample lengths, she asked him to lay a piece on the cleared table.

"Light one," she said.

Kester held the match pressed against the darker side of the box and pushed. The flame made him flinch, but he quickly held it to a piece until it caught. Straightening, he forgot the match. Lady May blew it out for him. The waxed twine burned steadily.

"I guess it will do," she said. "This part is dangerous. Make sure not to mix the ingredients together until we're ready."

Kester ground sulfur first. It stank. When he got it to a fine consistency, she told him to pour it out into the waiting crock and make sure to wipe the mortar and pestle clean. When he was done, he ground saltpeter and set it aside, then cleaned up and ground the charcoal.

"I don't really know what to expect next," she said, "Or how dangerous this part is. Gently stir a small, equal amount of all three powders and pour it on this square of linen."

Kester did so sweat trickling, not liking Lady May's insistence she stay.

"Now tie it up," she said.

He made a bag of what she named gunpowder.

"The next part should be done away from the village so no one sees what you're up to. Lay the bag in an open area and insert a long fuse so there's enough time to get away. Light it, and then run behind a big boulder or tree you've picked out beforehand. If it doesn't flare up right away with loud noise and smoke, stay away, give it time."

Kester nodded.

"Once you see what it can do, you can judge how much gunpowder you'll need to use to protect Delain."

"I should return tomorrow, Lady May" Kester said.

"Please, call me May. We were friends, Kester. I hope we're friends still."

"Of course, May, as you wish. I'm pleased to be counted friend to you. You've been nothing but brave, risking much to help us with this," he said lifting the muslin bag.

"Thank you," she said. "But be careful, Kester. It's dangerous work."

Yet she was here to do it with him.

Chapter 28

But be of cheer, and comfort you to take...
...Assure yourself I will you not forsake

If Kester was hurt trying out charges, May would be responsible. She should have gone with him, here, nothing could take her mind off him. She couldn't work with one arm, so she sat and watched Kerys do everything. Time passed slowly. The next morning May ate so little Kerys wondered if she were ill. Kester should return soon, but by noon May could not bear sitting, so she walked by the water to watch the seabirds.

"May! It worked."

Kester hurried toward her, smiling broadly.

"It made a terrific noise and smoke," he said excitedly. "One little bag of the powder, yet it left a pit in the rocky soil. It's a fearsome weapon."

Enthused, he kissed her. She felt a pleasant stirring inside. He moved back a step.

"Didn't expect that," May said, her smile matching his.

"I did," Kester said.

This time, Kester held her gently, his fingers in her hair. May had no idea a kiss could be sweet, thrilling, and comforting all at once. Inside his arms was a haven. He drew away but she didn't want him to stop.

Kester whispered, "This is not the place. I won't hurt your reputation."

She flushed. He held her good hand and walked with her

toward the inn.

"I was thinking...while you were away," May said, "Of how to use the gunpowder. Please tell me what you think."

"Go on."

"First, it should look as though nothing unusual is going on in town. Let the fishing boats go out, have men walk about, that sort of thing. Dailgre mustn't know he's expected. In the first attack, men landed at the docks with silent ships after night fell. Hide charges of gunpowder on the docks ready to be lit. They can be put anywhere else you can lure Dailgre's men in force. It's dangerous work for the person who's to light the charge. They should plan a route of escape."

"Good suggestions, I'll share them with my uncle. We'll make you a guardsmen, next, May. You might have saved Mirddyn."

They'd reached the back hall by the kitchen.

"I could...see you to your room," Kester said.

Where her reputation would be in his hands, but more important, what would Kester think of her afterwards?

"I...I don't need help, thank you," May said.

Kester let her arm go. "Then I should leave."

"Kester?" May could not move.

He smiled, kissed her cheek, said, "We have time."

The King must be keeping Kester busy, because he did not see her that evening or the next day until late. He said they'd done trials of the powder with fuses of differing lengths to get an idea of how long it would take for an explosion. The

King was so impressed that he personally thanked May. To her dismay, both the King and Kester insisted any women still in Delain leave town for the north.

It was doubly dangerous now they'd use gunpowder charges. May wanted to stay, so did Kerys, but both understood it would give the men more to worry about. Packing to leave, May found her old clothes in the wardrobe. The purse of gems she always kept on her person. Leaving this room felt like leaving her first real home. It was funny to think of this alien place that way, but having become a valued person here, as well as being near Kester made it hard to go. Kester waited for them in the kitchen. How could she safely sit in the north waiting for word of how the fight went in Delain? Kester must sense her reluctance.

"We'll be fine, May. You've done all you can. Now you must settle my concerns and be safe."

He put his arm around her good side and kissed her cheek.

"Is that your best?" Kerys said, laughing as she left the kitchen.

Kester didn't need more prompting. His mouth was warm, tender, as it took May's and held it. Here, in his arms, was where she should stay. From his response, she knew Kester felt the same, but having won back his good opinion must be her consolation.

"Goodbye, Kester. Please, take care."

"Soon together, May, you'll see," he said.

Kerys said farewells to her pa and brothers out front, and

they joined the other women who stayed behind to help. An escort of two soldiers was to take them as far as the next village, where it would be safe to leave them. They would make their way to the castle from there on their own. The women were a silent group, helping at turns to paddle upstream. As evening called them to make camp, they built up a large fire and cooked fresh fish caught in nets. May lay awake, telling herself her arm in a sling and a blanket between her and the hard ground was the cause, but really it was the dark forest.

Passing through these woods, the Realm and its fairies were prominent, especially Prince Aidan. His sapphire eyes mocked her even in memory. She should feel relief, but any moment feared he'd appear. Finally, stiff and sore, she fell into a fitful sleep.

At first light, she washed at the river with Kerys and the other women. Kerys helped May put her backpack past her broken arm. After it was secured, she put the sling for her arm back over her neck. They struck out on a deer track. The day was fair. The women picked wild flowers as they walked. Late, they stopped at an open space to make a meal. May spotted bright pink at the edge of the meadow, a flower she'd never seen before. A sweet scent came off them. She bent to pick. Once she gathered a handful, she turned back to the fire.

"May," Kerys called. "Look what I've got."

Kerys held a tin dish of ripe berries out in front of her.

May smiled. "That's—"

At that moment, May was enveloped in a glittering cloud that rose from the ground near her feet; *Kerys, along with everything within view, grayed out.*

***

"May! May! Come back to us, May!" Kerys called in shock. Dropping the berries, she ran to the last spot she saw May under the trees. The dust cloud thinned.

Stopping short, she looked down with horror. Nearly hidden by a profusion of pink flowers was the fae ring. Before her shocked eyes, its glowing mushrooms shriveled. The last of its spores drifted away.

Chapter 29

His blazing eye, like two bright shining shields,
Did burn with wrath, and sparkled living fire

"Look what we've got." Aidan gripped May's uninjured arm firmly. "You appreciate our flowers?"

He felt shock ripple through her. She swayed. The pink bouquet slipped from her fingertips.

"Let me go," she said.

"Not happy to be caught?" he said.

She stopped struggling. He watched her slow her breathing, glance about. They were in the Hall of Dance with many clans watching. Aidan's was nearest, circled about them both.

"My prince," Rais said near Aidan's ear. "It would be better to conduct this meeting in private."

"Come along, little sweet. You've been naughty," Aidan said.

On those words, his treacherous consort's face changed. Shock was writ large in her gray eyes. "You remember everything!"

Aidan laughed. "Not experienced after all. We exist outside of time. Our long memories can't be fooled by your tricks."

He clamped her waist and half-supported, half-dragged her out and down the corridors toward Guilly hall, his men on alert before and after them. Once inside, they shut the door and set a guard. He then escorted her into his private study alone, pushed her none too gently into a seat. Aidan sat opposite and considered her. Reaching out, he tilted up her chin, brushed her hair aside. His consort's neck bore traces of bruising. His eye fell on her sling.

"What's your lover been doing to you?"

"Kester would never hurt me," May said. "I was attacked by a man who'd followed me. Kester stopped him."

"He swore at our last meeting to keep you safe," Aidan said. "We were foolish to accept a terran's word. Our physic will see to your injuries shortly."

He stood and paced. "We were unwise in many things where you were concerned. Your youth, beauty, and seeming innocence were a distraction. Now your nature is exposed. The day we allowed our physic to heal your lover, we watched afterward. Imagine our displeasure when you disappeared before our eyes; a rover!"

He stopped before her. "There hasn't been a rover in the Realm for hundreds of years. Recently we had reports of mischief outside our forest. What evil did you bring to Illynd?"

"Help for my friends," she said proudly. "An unfair fight between Kester's people and Dailgre's men is coming, and...Kester needed my help."

She dug her fingers into the bed cover. "I didn't trick you, Prince Aidan," she said. "Everything about Illynd was new to me when I met you. I didn't know how I came to be here. I didn't lie to you."

"Please, don't bother," he said, as he crossed his arms.

"We're alert to your deceits now, little sweet. No innocent would bring such destructive power here as you have and just give it to terrans. Or are you so green, you believed that once you gave over this power you could take it back? Terrans' will find an excuse to use it again, and again. Eventually their enemies will uncover its mysteries."

The emotions playing across her face could be entertaining; certainly she made the effort to make him believe she was distressed.

"This game amuses us, but first things first. Come," he said.

He helped her up and escorted her to another door. It opened on his suite. The bedroom door stood ajar. He went in, she moved as if reluctant to follow. May was dwarfed by its massive gold bed, each corner fashioned like a slender tree with a canopy of leaves as in Guilly Hall.

"Sit on the bed," he said.

"My prince," said a voice at the bedroom door.

"This is Derec, our personal physic. Come in, we have your patient," Aidan said.

Derec carried a tray of pots and other items he placed on the bed.

"Take special care of our consort, Derec." Aidan moved away to give Derec room to work.

May's face was prettily flushed. Derec lifted her hair from her neck. "When did you first receive these injuries, my lady?"

"Ten days ago," May said. "I was nearly killed."

"I see that. I'll help with these."

Derec helped May take off her pack and sling, setting them aside. Then he looked over his pots and chose a cream. Lifting her hair again, he rubbed it into her neck. Aidan watched his consort's eyes widen. Never having been treated this way, she couldn't know the effect. As its powers' worked, it sent a flush of heat through the injured area.

"There, the remnant of bruising and underlying damage is gone," Derec said.

Aidan was gratified to watch the yellowed bruises replaced by smooth, fair skin. Derec lifted her broken arm, lightly touching the forearm where the break occurred. "Lay back," he said, helping her to be comfortable.

"Your arm will feel numb at first," Derec said. "Heat will spread from the center of the injured bone and itch, and then you will lose all feeling in the injured area. In a few hours, that numbness will wear off. You'll have full use of it again. It will be difficult to maneuver it until then, however, for the lack of feeling."

Derec carefully took the splint off. May winced as he rested her arm on the bed. Opening a packet of powder, he rubbed it over the injured site, the pain of his manipulation making her bite her lip and go white, but she didn't complain. Again, she reacted with surprise as the powders took her pain.

"Ah," May said, her body trembling, and then relaxing. "It feels so strange."

"You have the effect of the healing now?" Derec asked.

"Yes," she said.

"Good. Your arm is sound. If you discover another problem, please ask for me, my lady," Derec said.

"Thank you," May said, awe in her tone. "Derec, thank you for my friend too, I haven't forgotten."

Derec made a nod to her and left. The pixy Bri arrived, peered in, and then quickly gave Aidan a curtsy.

"We'll leave for now," Aidan said.

He went out. The door was cracked. Standing close to it, he waited to hear how this meeting went.

"My lady!" the pixy exclaimed.

"Bri," May said, "I never thought I'd see you again."

"Does the Prince suspect me?" Bri asked in a lower voice.

"Why should he? Oh, Bri, I'm glad to have your friendship, but I'm afraid. He won't let me slip away as easily as the first time."

"No, my lady," the pixy said. "The vents to the outer air are laid with traps. None could enter or leave by those routes now. I was so worried, my lady. I heard you were injured."

"Don't worry, I'm healed now, Bri, thanks to Derec. Are you here to take me back to the Rose rooms?"

"Oh no, my lady. The Prince sent me to be your servant, seeing he's still unaware of…my part, but you're to stay here. He won't let you out of his sight."

"How can he?" May said.

Aidan smiled on hearing the distress in her voice.

"Surely Princess Kerriena won't agree to have me here? She hated me before. Now they're joined, it would be impossible," May said.

"Oh, my lady," Bri said. "The match between Clan Guilly and Clan Maich never took place."

"But I heard the ceremonies as I was escaping."

"The Prince's courtier Rais interrupted with the news you disappeared. Prince Aidan accused the Princess. She was insulted and withdrew her clan. The mood since is uneasy. Both clans wield great power here."

For a moment, neither of them said anything.

When the pixy spoke again, her tone was falsely bright. "I'll draw you a bath, my lady. You'll feel much better after."

May did not argue. It was as Aidan suspected; his consort escaped with help. She would try again. It didn't worry him the pixy exhibited more loyalty to his consort than to himself. He knew their secrets. Keeping this little sweet was still amusing, but he must decide what to do with her. Quietly, he moved away from the bedroom door and left his rooms. Derec waited on him in his study. Rais was there too, pouring wine.

"Well," Rais said. "Has she confessed? Did she share the nature of the weapon she brought to the terrans?"

"Patience, Rais," Aidan said. "Our spy got a sample of the powders. We are studying it. It appears to be a simple. We will know everything soon."

"You think to play with her?" Rais said. "She's no toy."

"Her body is fragile as any terrans'," Derec broke in. "It's clear she has enemies."

"She's fully recovered?" Aidan said sharply, unable to mask his concern.

"Of course; I know my craft," Derec said.

Aidan relaxed.

"Aidan. Let me question her. I'm immune to this fascination for a red head," Rais said.

Aidan responded to his faithful courtier with coolness. "That amuses us, Rais, considering it was you that came with the tale of a terran beauty new to the dance who might serve our purposes. Now she is ours, we will decide what will be done."

"Of course, my prince, forgive my poor attempts to protect you. I would see Aidan, Prince become Aidan King of all Clans fairy. I hoped to spare you any missteps on that path," Rais said.

"It is our path…don't forget that Rais," Aidan said.

"When you are King," Rais said, "we will see the end of fairies' trifling with terrans. What happened in the Old Realm must not be allowed to spread through Illynd."

"Yet the Lady May is terran," Derec said. "That will prove an obstacle, if you keep her as your consort."

"She's no terran…physically close perhaps, but she possesses knowledge and powers that elevate her, Derec. When I'm done with her, the clans and both of you will understand that distinction," Aidan said.

Aidan left them to walk along the halls, annoyed he was

short with Rais and Derec. He ended back at his suite and
went in. Bri carried a basket full of items for his consort.

"Leave that for now," he said.

Ducking her head, the pixy hurried out. Just then, May
came into the sitting room. His breath caught. That amazing
hair, laced with lavender ribbons, complemented the gown that
skimmed her appealing figure. Her exposed arms, neck, and
shoulders were tempting as cream to a cat. The subtle perfume
warmed by that skin preceded her.

"The report from our physic assures us you are sound,"
Aidan said curtly. "You look a fair little flower, despite your
trade. Come with us."

He led her back to the bedroom. "Let's see what a rover
carries about on her back."

He dumped out her bag's contents. Odd garments and
boots, a leather purse, and assorted other items. Taking up the
purse, he weighted it in his hand speculatively, then opened it
and spilled gems onto the bed. "What are these?

"They're not mine," May said. "They were given to
Kester by Princess Kerriena for services to her when he was in
the Realm."

Of course they were fey gems; Aidan recognized the pixy
quality cuts. "And now you have them."

"He didn't want payment from her. She tried to kill me."

"Noble." Aidan's eyes narrowed. "What's on that hand?"

Aidan lifted it and examined a ring.

"It's a gift from Kester," she said, blushing.

"A large ruby set in gold, from a friend?" he said, letting her hand fall.

He inspected her bag. There was a blanket lashed at the bottom and a piece of branch in the side pocket. He examined it carefully. "Flower, bud, and fruit, all on the same branch, alive, yet not attached to a tree. This throbs with inner power, old power. What do you do with this?"

"I don't do anything. It's just a stick from an apple tree."

"So that is the Gate," Aidan said, as understanding dawned. "Really, my lady, you've given yourself away too easily."

"I don't know what you're talking about," she said, fear tingeing her voice.

"We see you're sorry you spoke so quickly. Almost we could believe the lie of your inexperience."

"These are harmless," he said of her other things spread about the bed. "But this bit of stick we will keep."

He smiled knowingly. "Just in the case you possess more understanding of its use than you let on."

"Aidan, wait," she said.

Distress appeared to make his consort forget reserve.

"Please, Aidan, you must believe I came to help my friend Kester. If you remember everything, you'll know his land is in danger of attack. I need to learn how the fight goes...and if all is well with him."

Aidan registered her intense expression—there were things left unsaid in her entreaties.

"So you care that much?" He turned and left her.

Aidan's consort in love with a terran after she'd been in his arms; how comic Kerriena would find this if she discovered it. Worse was how May had taken him in. Aidan had known consorts of other fairies. Long ago even Rais favored an attractive terran that bored Aidan every time her mouth opened. But May was different from the start. Intelligent, well-spoken, and seemingly not afraid of anything but her desires. Trembling at his kisses, fearful of his passion for her, he held back his glamour the first time she was in his realm, enjoying the slow dance between them when he knew how it must end. Yet she had lied, he had believed, and for that his little sweet should feel the full force of his glamour.

Chapter 30

But soon the knights with their bright-burning blades
Broke their rude troupes and orders did confound

Aidan passed the smoky quartz fireplace, from which a red glow emanated, surprised to see his consort nearby. Curled on a brown velvet chaise, she slept. Perhaps she felt safer here. He carefully lifted her soft, warm body. She stirred and turned toward his chest. Under her tightly shut lids, her eyes made quick movements, dreaming. For a brief moment, he felt strangely protective. He carried her to his bed, laid her down, drew the cover up. She rolled in her sleep, pulling it with her. Undressing, he slid under sheets on the bed's other side. He rarely used this bed for rest, but listening to her soft breathing, he found rest enchanting. Early, before she stirred, he was up, bathed, and dressed.

He went to meet with Rais, kept that short, and returned to his suite. Bri was dressing May's wealth of hair with crystal beads. Today she glowed in a white silk gown. It was simply styled, but with such youth on her side, May needed little to grace her form.

When she saw him, pink crept into her cheeks, her throat flushed. She didn't expect to wake in his bed.

"Lady May," he said. "We require your company. Our clan needs to see you by our side."

"Why? What's going on?" she asked.

"Nothing we can't deal with. Come."

He stood a head taller, was used to stately female fairies. Tentatively, she put her hand on his arm. He put his other hand over hers, enjoying everything different about her.

"In the future, Lady May, call us Aidan. No formalities need lie between us," he said, alluding to their sleeping arrangement.

"In that case, Aidan," she said, "call me plain May. I was never a lady before."

"As you wish, plain May, though calling you plain is at odds with nature."

She said nothing, had to hide her pleasure.

In Guilly hall, the entire clan assembled. Aidan escorted May to the seat besides his. Staying on his feet, he addressed his clan. "Clan Guilly, as rumors run rife, we've decided to speak to your concerns. Our consort is a rover, loyal to us. If trouble comes to the Realm we will face it together."

He glanced at May. She quickly covered her surprise. Good.

Once seated, Aidan offered her herb wine. With a slight hesitation, she sipped. Better; she was going along with him enough to drink in his presence. She ate the dainties he offered her. She even picked out a few for him, which he accepted. Since his announcement, Rais and he watched to see who came and went from the hall. This news would fast be known by Kerriena. With a nod, Aidan signaled for the musicians to play. He turned to ask May to dance. She consented. Holding her close, breathing her scent, he could almost forget she was dangerous. Rais was right. She was no simple terran and he was done with play. After the dance, Aidan escorted her back to their suite.

He stopped while she continued to the fireplace. "You had the wit not to disappoint us before our clan."

He was going to another gathering for clan leaders, but instead walked straight to her. Without a word, he pulled her into his arms and put his lips firmly on hers. Just as suddenly, he let her go. "We've meant to do that since first we had you back with us, plain May."

When he left, she had a bemused look on her face. Aidan returned to a council full of argument. The clans were excited and angry at turns.

"This ploy with your consort is too dangerous," Rais whispered. "If my love and loyalty are not wanted any longer, I will step aside."

"Nonsense," Aidan said low. "Have patience."

To top that drama, threats were issued from Kerriena's quarter. The other clans chimed in. The answers demanded were the same. Did Aidan plan to seize control? Was this why he harbored a rover? Had he rejected the union between Clan Maich and Clan Guilly to please his consort? Would he fight Kerriena? Was it a Kingship he sought? Kerriena started what came next.

Under her orders, a contingent of Maich soldiers challenged Aidan's Guilly soldiers in the Hall of Dance. Though their words were heated, fighting began only when a

Maich lieutenant drew his sword and struck down a Guilly soldier. The Maich soldiers ran, hotly pursued by the Guilly contingent. Heavy fighting broke out near Maich Hall. As soon as he heard the news, Aidan ordered his long planned remedy to Maich aggression, though Kerriena was just as prepared.

Her traps were sprung, one after another, squeezing Clan Guilly, fomenting much anger against them with the other clans. If not headed off soon, Aidan's power base would disintegrate. Clan Guilly must escape. Aidan set his grumbies and pixies to recovering the Guilly treasure. He sent his personal pixy to Bri, to charge her to get his consort out to safety. Donning his armor, Aidan took up his sword and ran with his courtiers to join in the fight.

When he got to the worst of the combat, the silver-armored Maich were beating Guilly fairies back. All was confusion, shouting. Leaping in, he countered a fierce press aimed at Rais. Recognizing Aidan by his crowned helm, several soldiers turned their attentions on him. He rammed his blade through one, then another fairy, piercing the armor at the required angle, but as he drew back his sword, a hard blow landed on Aidan's shoulder.

Blood flowed from that gusset. A booming crack reverberated through the corridor. His enemies reeled. Thick smoke roiled to the high ceiling. Con had done his job. The pixy enlisted Guilly grumbies to lay the powders while the fight ensued. Stunned by the unexpected concussion, the

Maich were beaten for now. Aidan gave a shout. Rais and he would guard the retreat. His men came running with him toward Guilly Hall bearing their wounded.

Aidan, rounding a corner, was shocked to see May struggling madly as two Maich fairies carried her out of his clan hall. Confronted with a furious Aidan and his soldiers, the one on the left released his hold of May and fled. The other, determined to carry out Kerriena's revenge, whipped out a silver dirk. Aidan rushed at him with his sword, but Rais pitched his needle thin dirk into the Maich fairy's neck. The spray of hot blood hit Aidan and May. Ignoring it, Aidan shoved the mortally wounded fairy aside, grasped his consort, and in a moment, they were past the doors of his hall.

The bulk of his soldiers filed in. All the gold, silver, copper, and gems of the hall were stripped. Only dirt walls, ceilings, and floors remained. The hall's columns were revealed as the root system of the forest overhead. His servants did their work well. This measure of Guilly treasure would not line Kerriena's coffer.

"Now!" Aidan boomed.

Dust rained down, everything grayed out. Night sounds and cooler air greeted them. As Aidan's vision adjusted to starlight, his clan and he unfurled their wings. Holding May tight with his uninjured arm, he soared into the treetops, his clan following.

"Thank you," May whispered trembling.

"Hush," Aidan said. "They follow."

While they raced along, Derec sailed up. Gold wings held close as he hovered, Derec sprinkled healing powders into Aidan's wound. Then he darted off to attend to others with injuries. Fairy small still, the clan skimmed treetops, looping left or right while keeping watch for the Maich. Stars sparkled back from the river on the forest's border. There were calls of nocturnal animals, and the faint whir of the clan's collective beating wings. His consort's face was tight, as if she worked not to cry. He squeezed her waist.

"I have you safe," he whispered.

There was a thin line of light at the horizon. Soon black clouds swallowed dawn. Aidan signaled his clan to descend. Scouts discovered a rock hollow that would hide them. A watch was ordered. The clan settled inside. Aidan gave May the flask from his belt, wine to give her strength.

"Please," she said, touching the dried blood on her neck. Specks dotted her face and more crusted her arm. He nodded and sent a fairy for water. When she received a water bag, she ripped the hem of her gown, wet it, and scrubbed until no blood marred her. When she was clean, she was too pale. She settled on a pile of dried leaves that blew into the space. Done giving orders, Aidan came to her.

After removing his armor, he lowered himself and pulled her close wordlessly. She didn't protest, but fell asleep with her head on his arm, snugged tight for warmth. Later without disturbing her, he rose to see the rain. Near the opening in the rocks, a small fire had been lit. Several fairies stood about it.

He sniffed roasting wild mushrooms. His consort stirred. For seconds she looked confused, then seeing him, stood and brushed off her gown.

"My lady," he said, "We've wild mushrooms, a treat we no longer indulge in unless out hunting."

There were several mushrooms not yet cut and cooked; while they were so small, one could feed half the clan. He handed her a large slice held in a fresh leaf.

"Thank you," May said.

She blew on it, prepared to taste it. Suddenly she dropped it.

"Burn your fingers?" Aidan asked.

"Grumbies…they're why mushrooms aren't served," she said.

Aidan smiled. "You'd think they were offspring, the fuss Grumbies raised about not gathering or cooking wild mushrooms." He bit into his piece, broke off some for her.

"No, thank you," May said. "I'm with grumbies on this point. I'll never see a mushroom the same way."

"There's no other food," Aidan said.

"I'll drink water, and then I'd like to clean up," she said.

He led her outside, pointing out a streamlet where she could wash her face, telling her not to go far for 'the necessary.'

She came back minutes' later, face damp. Though she was slightly bedraggled by the rough night, he suppressed a smile. He pictured her living as the ancient wood fairies, naked, all pale limbs and masses of red hair. It was a sight he wouldn't share with any. Turning to duty, he gave orders. They would be moving again in spite of the storm. The fire was put out. His clan packed their meager supplies. The Guilly pixies and grumbies had gone on ahead with everything else. Once he donned his armor, Aidan came to his consort and held her, taking them both up into the covering clouds. They were far away from the Conclave of Clans heading east. He felt his consort shiver.

"What's wrong?" Aidan said.

"It's cold."

"He gave her his flask again. "Sip this. It will warm you."

"Aidan, I thank you, and Rais, for saving my life. Can you tell me anything now of where we are going. Is it safe?"

"We're safe enough now, but it's not good to be out in the open. We're headed for a secret stronghold of the Guilly Clan. We can't tell you more than that. We'll be quite comfortable there."

"What of Bri, the other pixies, and the grumbies? And where did the precious metals in Guilly Hall go? I was shocked when I left the room to find Bri and all was dirt."

"Our loyal pixies and grumbies took anything of value on ahead of us. We stayed behind to give them time to escape. Now answer our question. Why were you in the hall?"

"Bri gathered my things and told me to wait, but I heard fighting. I had to see who might be in danger—"

She faltered, didn't wish to admit she'd been fearful for him. Grassy lands opened under them. Here and there were rude terran homesteads. At times, a light would shine in the night. Cattle moaned. Finally, the rain ended. A rising sun illuminated the flanks of hills. Above those, great mountains loomed, to the left an endless slice of beach was washed by the sea. Seabirds flew near the band of fairies out of curiosity.

"This is a lonely place," May said.

"None come here," Aidan said. "The foothills are too rocky for crops. Bear and wolves prowl them for food. Wild goats, sheep, deer, and other game draw the predators."

Hillsides were a tangle of growth. Wild flowers bloomed with abandon, taking over whole slopes. The strengthening day lit a foamy green sea. Sharply-cut, the mountains stood in a gray-blue haze, tops touched with snow. Aidan breathed deep of the tangy air. They soared higher, the earth rose to meet them. He signaled for the clan to land.

"We've avoided detection," Aidan said. "The last sighting of Clan Maich was late the first night. Let us away to our new home."

He had plans for his little sweet. This was the perfect setting to put them into play.

Dust flew up and fell on those assembled. *A fog of gray, brief but total, enveloped them.*

Chapter 31

Into this world, to work confusion,
And set it all on fire by force unknown,
Is wicked discord—

When they got the news from the guardsmen's bird, Kester heard roaring in his ears.

His uncle put his arm across his shoulders. "You can't help her, Lachlan. There's no door you can beat down to get into the Realm. She'll have to find a way to save herself."

Kester breathed as if he'd just run miles. What did those cursed faes want with May? He feared he understood that answer too well. How May would deal with this fresh peril was more the point. The stories she related of the time she'd spent with him in the Realm skirted over faes plying their seductive glamour. Since their goodbye kiss, Kester had another reason May sacrificed so much to get back to Illynd.

She came back for him, hard as it was to credit, but now he felt as she must; he would go anywhere for her, do anything for her, but the Realm was shut to him. His uncle was right. Yet Kester struggled with the overwhelming need to cast off responsibility and race after May. Find a fae ring, go in armed, fight for her. Every fae warrior with its bright sword and fantastic armor mocked him. Swallowing the bitter taste in his mouth, he rushed out of the inn anyway.

At the end of the day, Kester stayed in Delain.

Days later, crouched by the side of the Sundowner's courtyard, Kester gauged the advance of Dailgre's guardsmen.

Reason forced him to stand with his uncle and da in Delain. The King had sent messages to every village. If anyone suddenly showed matching May's description, he would learn of it, and so would his nephew. It was the best comfort the King could offer to him. For May's sake, Kester hoped it would be enough. He watched the wharf. The ideas May shared for battle was surprisingly good.

Dailgre's guardsmen were moving toward the traps they'd set. Underneath the docks, just out of the surf, lay one of the King's guards. A low whistle, the signal, sounded. A band of Dailgre's guard topside the docks hesitated. Hearing nothing else, and seeing nothing, they started forward again. One of May's matchsticks was set to a line of powder. Fire snaked to the charges placed near the dock pilings. The guard who lit it was to slip into the sea. He was a strong swimmer with less than a minute to get to a safe distance. The sudden boom from those charges was deafening.

Bits of wood pier and grimmer debris flew in all directions. Even from where he waited, Kester felt the explosive shock wave, ducked when blast rubble landed too near. Dailgre's guardsmen not killed or injured by that blast, collected themselves and poured into Delain. Running with several bags of gunpowder in his pockets, Kester watched for the next bottleneck of Dailgre's guards. As planned, heavy carts were overturned when the charge at the wharf blew, blocking the three main routes from the sea. Quickly setting up two bags of gunpowder, Kester waited on his enemy's advance. When he judged a goodly number were coming his way, he laid a line of gunpowder.

"There's one!"

Arrows hit the stones near where Kester knelt by a cart. Moving backwards, he shook a longer line of powder, making for a place of cover. Enemy guardsmen were gaining his position. Lighting a matchstick, he set the line afire. To his right, more enemies raced up the street parallel to this. Another pile blocked it. Kester spotted his third cousin running away. How close to where he hid were his cousin's charges laid?

Kester risked the open, dashing up the street to get away. More arrows flew at him. Just then, two explosive roars filled the air with stone chips, parts of the carts, everything flew up, out and back down. Agonized cries and frustrated shouts went unmarked by Kester. Face down on the flagstones, oily smoke curled lazily toward his unmoving form as he blacked out.

***

Consciousness was ill-defined. Kester drifted, coming painfully aware only when a female healer bathed stinging, raw scrapes on the fleshy pads of his hands. He received the wounds when the shock wave of his third cousin's charge blew up parallel to his position.

"Those injuries," the healer said, "will heal."

Did she have to speak so loudly?

"You were hit here," she said touching the wound on the back of his head. The pain made him flinch. "By flying debris, a bloody mess, but the cut wasn't deep, closed…two stitches—"

He faded away until a groan issued from his mouth, waking him. A cool cloth wiped his neck.

"Un-nh." he moaned. His eyelid was lifted. Light registered in his brain. When the lid was released, he opened both eyes. Shutters were wide. Fresh sea air circulated. Fully awake, Kester struggled to sit, but a small hand pressed him back against the pillows.

"What the outcome?" he croaked.

"Hush," the female healer said.

"Tell me," he said, wincing at his throbbing skull.

"You're in a good bed and not a cell," the healer snapped, as her fingers found the blood-beat at his wrist. "That should tell you everything you need to know. Now hush."

His healer was surprisingly young, and way too pretty to have devoted herself to a life of study, though it was obvious she must have or else wouldn't be ministering to him. Her shining, gold hair was pulled into a twist, perhaps to give her the illusion of age or severity, but freckles sprinkled across her fair face ruined the effect. When she glanced up, he noted piercingly blue eyes. The healer went to her tray and started mixing herbs in a pestle.

While she worked, Kester lay quiet. Given the pain in his head, it was enough. Still, it didn't keep him from appreciating the healer's lush figure, which was barely hid by the white apron she wore to protect her traditional blue healer's shift.

"Take this," the healer said, bringing a cup to his mouth. She held his head to help him drink. Kester choked the foul brew down grimacing.

"That's horrible," he said when he was done.

"I could have made it taste better, I suppose," the healer said. "Perhaps the vile flavor will remind you in future not to take so much risk with yourself."

"You'd tease an injured man?" Kester said.

"I was here when your third cousin brought you in," she said, her face full of disapproval. "He thought he carried a dead man. The King was frantic. He harried the poor fellow until he admitted you recklessly held back setting your charge off. He was already well away, he said, when he saw you struck down. Don't you value your place in Mirddyn?"

Her tone was insufferably prissy.

Damn his cousin for lying. "Who are you to question me?" he said trying again to get up.

"Be still." Embarrassing as it was, she held him down.

"You wouldn't remember me," she said, "Though you harassed me unmercifully when we were at lessons together. I'm Fianna."

No, not little Fianna? The shining hair and blue eyes whisked back into that skinny, freckle-faced girl. The companion of his youngest sister, Fianna was a bothersome pest who took tutoring with Kester's sisters and him. Nosy, opinionated, and smart; Fianna always knew her studies.

While his knuckles were rapped for his failures, she smirked unbearably. He'd gotten his revenge.

Once he slid choke root into her meat pie. She didn't notice until she chewed. She was coughing and retching, while he laughed so hard his side hurt. Furious, she called him a green-eyed horror. Another time, he mixed rock salt into her milk. She gagged and sprayed the passing tutor with the mouthful. For that, she was given three whacks on her backside. Now he was at her mercy, it seemed.

"Sir," Fianna said sternly. "You've been under these past two days. If you try to get up, I'll call a guard to tie you down."

Kester did not doubt she would do that very thing.

The next day was little better. Fianna checked him over, tight-lipped, as if angry with him. He bore it as well as he could. Finally, he asked for his uncle. She assured him she'd pass along his request. His uncle came to see him not long after.

"Lachlan," the King's expression said more of his concern for his nephew than he need put into words. "Your da will be along later. He's been at your side several times while you were insensible. You gave him a bit of worry."

"I'm fine, Uncle," Kester said. His head ached still, making it hard for him to keep down solid food. Not that the evil Fianna, as he'd taken to calling her to himself, would allow him anything decent; just broth, té, water or her witch's brew of herbs.

"I heard others talk about the fighting, Uncle, but I must know, have you word of Lady May?"

His uncle's face darkened. "No. At least, not news you'd welcome. The weapon Lady May taught us to construct couldn't be kept secret once it was used in warfare. Several of Dailgre's men escaped. Yesterday our guardsmen caught one of his spies. Concealed on his person was a letter with Dailgre's seal. He's put a price on the rover's head. Dailgre doesn't know her identity yet, but it's certain he soon will. He wants this rover alive, or dead otherwise. The sum Dailgre set was five thousand gold coins."

Kester paled. This was evil news for May. Perhaps she was better off in the Realm. At least it protected her from what lay in wait for her here.

His uncle patted Kester's arm. "You mustn't let this disturb you, Lachlan. She's a rover. She'll know how to defend herself."

When his uncle was gone, Kester tried to think how he could help May. The King didn't know Lady May as he'd come to. She was brave and fine, yet vulnerable. She had no experience of men like Dailgre, nor the danger he presented, of that, he was certain. Groaning softly, he shifted in the bed. It took all his effort, but he pulled himself upright. His head throbbed. For a second, his vision grayed.

He waited for it to clear. Carefully, he set first one, then the other foot on the floor. Holding the side of the bed, he pushed himself upright. Mustering his resolve, he took several steps. Suddenly, the door opened.

Fianna rushed in, putting her arm about his waist. He sagged against her.

"What are you up to?" she said, helping him back to the bed. He lay against it unresisting.

"I've got to get fit," he said. "There's something I must do." He'd broken out in a sweat.

"You're in no shape to leave this bed. Your da's just outside. Do you want to give him more pain? What if he'd seen you in a heap on the floor just now?"

He said nothing. Very quickly, she made him presentable, wiping his face with a cloth, covering his legs with the blanket and tucking it tight. She propped the pillow behind his head.

"Stay put. I'll tie you down yet."

She left to get his da. Weak all over, his head paining him, it hurt worse to know she was right, evil woman. What help could he offer May in his condition? Recalling the help she'd said a fae prince gave them after one of Moran's attacks was his only consolation now. As he recovered from his concussion, Kester protested loudly over the diet she ordered and the enforced rest, irritating Fianna no end.

"You've not changed," Fianna said, "Still a horror."

He, in turn, was often vexed with Fianna. Drink this muck, no more than a half-hour exercise today, early to sleep.

"You're worse than my old nanny when I was a babe!" he told her. "Perhaps you're in the wrong profession."

When she grudgingly pronounced him fit, his headaches

were gone. Though he was a bit soft for lying abed, he could remedy that with training exercises in no time. Dressing in his travelling garb, he was surprised when Fianna came into his room without knocking. Hastily, he grabbed his tunic to cover his exposed chest.

"Oh," she said. "Thought you'd gone, I left some herbals here."

She smiled at his effort to cover himself. "I've seen everything already, a hazard of my trade."

Annoyed by her amusement at his modesty, he quickly pulled the tunic over his head.

"Can't wait to be off? Looking for your pretty little friend?" she asked.

"What can you know of her?" Kester said.

"I've Kerys as my source. We talked when she'd done visiting you. So you pine for this Lady May?" Fianna said.

"It's no business of yours."

"As your healer, I think of your welfare. Forget my own efforts. Your king and your da are concerned. You throw their care into their teeth in your haste to save this fae consort."

Kester came close to Fianna. "Don't speak of things of which you have no idea. May risked her life to save Mirddyn. She's also the kindest person you could hope to know, healer. You were an imp as a youth, and I see no improvement now. Don't ever make the mistake of maligning her in my presence again."

Collecting his pack and scabbard, Kester left. He didn't

witness the tears his harsh leave-taking started.

Chapter 32

In the other was, this mischief, that mishap;
With the one his foes he threatened to invade,
With the other he his friends meant to enwrap,
For whom he could not kill, he practiced to entrap.

May swayed, disoriented. Only Aidan's grip kept her on her feet. When she could see, May registered a granite floor speckled with mica. This space itself was huge, its walls supported with wood timbers. Overhead, a groin vaulting framed the ceiling. Fantastic chandeliers of rock crystal filled it with light. The clan dispersed. Aidan walked away with Rais, leaving May by herself.

"My lady, your new home," Bri said from behind her. "Not extravagant as the Gathering Conclave of Clans, but comfortable."

May was glad of any relief, so she let Bri lead her along without comment. Hangings depicting stag running through trees, birds wheeling near the shore, and flowered hillsides graced the walls.

"The clan's ladies fashioned these," Bri said.

They put May's humble stitching to shame. Bri opened a door onto a room where real sunlight streamed in from a skylight of blown glass. For all the beauty of the Gathering Conclave, May missed seeing the sky.

"How is it there is a window?" May said.

"Natural openings in surface rock," Bri said. "Once again, you're sharing the Prince's rooms."

The walls were warm cherry wood. With a finger, May

traced an acorn and its leaf so perfectly carv d on the fireplace panel she thought it grew there, before she gratefully sank onto a chaise.

"I'm starved, Bri. Could I please eat before I see the rest?"

"Of course, my lady."

Bri was back quick with a tray, from which May ate without speaking.

"I'm exhausted…I'll need herb wine," May said when she was done.

"Things are different in a clan home, my lady. We don't revel endlessly here. Sleep if you wish."

"You don't know how thankful I am to hear that," May said.

Of course the bed was kingly, its headboard towering. A row of candlesticks glowed on the bedroom's mantle. May let Bri show her the pink granite water closet. Another window, set high on the wall, allowed a swath of sunlight in. A deep pool cut into the stone floor. Two gold taps arched over it.

"Why are there four knobs?" May asked.

"Hot and cold fresh water, and hot and cold seawater, my lady," Bri said. "We're near the ocean. Seawater's wonderful for the skin."

"I guess I'll find out. I need a bath," May said. "I wish I had a fresh gown, but I'll settle for this one cleaned."

"My lady, your gowns are here, as are all your things," Bri said as she ran bathwater. "We brought everything, including the Guilly gold."

When she left, May slipped into foamy green seawater that fizzed and bubbled along her skin. She sighed, floated for a time. Finally, she washed her hair out in fresh water and left the pool. Slipping into the gown Bri put out, she went to the bedroom. She piled pillows behind her on the bed, got comfortable. What would Aidan want of her now?

He knew about gunpowder or used something similar during the fight with Kerriena, and when he saved her from Dailgre's men. She was no help to him that way. She must make him believe it was her only weapon. Perhaps it would help if she turned the fairy weakness for frill on Aidan.

"Bri," she said.

The pixy appeared at the door. "My lady?" she asked.

"I want to wear the prettiest gown you have for me."

Bri appeared thrilled. She helped May change into a blue-bell colored gown, which crisscrossed over her bosom, and tied about the waist with blue crystal flowers. Bri did her hair up with matched crystals, allowing tendrils to escape.

"May."

Aidan walked in. Suddenly the room was too small.

"We are stunned," he said.

"Were there problems with your clan?" May asked, instantly regretting she resorted to this tactic with Aidan.

"We're all here, and there were no injuries Derec could not address. This hideaway's been ready for a long time. The Maich Clan is a fierce lot, all the more so for their ambitious head Kerriena. Nothing less than a Queen-ship will satisfy her. Now she's been thwarted, she is beyond angry. She means to destroy us."

"If I'm so offensive to her, Aidan, why take me back?"

"We will not be dictated to. She seeks to rule us, not join with us."

Aidan looked tired, if that was possible.

"Why don't you rest," May said. "Perhaps, if you allow it, Bri can show me this conclave."

"It's perfectly safe here," Aidan said. "You're free to go about."

He left her for the bedroom. The first place May wanted to find was the apothecary. She needed to know where fairy powders were kept. Goll, loyal to Clan Guilly, was busy at a worktable.

"Pleased to see you, Lady May," he said as he bowed.

May had no way to inspect the area too closely at present, so they accepted fresh creams and left. After looking over the public spaces, Bri showed May the treasury.

"See, my lady, "these stacks are the gold walls stripped from the Gathering Conclave," Bri said.

There were also copper, silver, and tiles of cut gems neatly piled. Other treasures, jewels in cases, uncut stones, and raw gold had its home here.

"There's so much wealth," May said

"This is nothing," Bri said. "The Guilly clan has mines all over Illynd, and greater treasuries than this little pile."

And perhaps, what she needed wouldn't be missed. The possibility of escape was heightened. "Could I see the kitchen?" May asked.

In the kitchen, grumbies cleaned and polished silver and gold plates. A pair of grumbies pressed fresh butter in molds. When they noticed May, every grumby stopped what it was doing and bowed her way. May smiled, pleased the fairies were here.

"Never seen them do that," Bri said, as the grumbies went back to their work. She shrugged.

Lia, Bri's friend, whipped meringue. "My lady," Lia said. "Do you have a request? Perhaps you'd like a picnic prepared?"

"A picnic?" May asked.

"Yes, my lady, on the seaside or under the twisted pines," Lia said. "Others go to the mountaintop. Of course, you'd want furs for the snow. Bri can get anything you'd need."

How wonderful it would be to go outside here. The lands they flew over would be marvelous up close. Asking Aidan for a picnic was impossible, given how she came to be in his custody again. He knew she wanted to run. Remembering the lonely stretches they flew over to get here, how would she defend herself if she escaped? Aidan mentioned bears and wolves. Even with the powders to restore her normal size, where would she go? Aidan would easily find her. Bri took her past storerooms filled with supplies.

The new home for Clan Guilly had been well-prepared.

May liked this place much more than the Gathering Conclave of Clans. Here and there, light filtered in from outside, which made the spaces homier, more real. Back at Aidan's rooms, May peered into the bedroom. Aidan may not sleep, but his eyes were shut. Carefully closing the door, Bri took out embroidery threads and taught May stitches. Much later, the bedroom door opened. Aidan, fresh and dressed in black silk and leather, nodded at them and left. Not long after, however, he returned.

"Bri, bring a tray. We will dine here with our consort."

Bri returned with a laden tray and carafes of water and herb wine.

"You may leave us," he said.

Aidan looked somber since he came back. "May, our spies turned in reports. We've just got them out of Rais. There was fighting in Delain. Clan Mirddyn was victorious."

May slowly breathed out. Kester was safe.

"This is not good news for you," he added brusquely. "Dailgre, known for brutality, learned a rover had a hand in the weapon used against him. He offered a high price for your capture, but if that isn't possible, he'll pay for your head. He won't allow his enemies to keep such a prize at their disposal. We understand you will seek to escape and rejoin your friend. If you do, this Kester won't be able to protect you. In fact, your presence will threaten his life."

May held her head in her hands.

How did she end up in this mess? Her unhappy home life

paled alongside of being hunted by this evil man. Aidan was right. If she ran to Kester, he'd be in danger. He'd defend her no matter what. Her only hope was to leave Illynd forever, if she could manage to do that much. It would be hard to wait for the next full moon without catching someone's notice, though, maybe impossible.

Aidan waited. Only when she looked up did he continue.

"There's more. Princess Kerriena knows you're a rover, which gives Clan Guilly an advantage over the Maich. Your presence here threatens her standing among the clans. She won't hesitate to destroy you. You've landed yourself into more trouble than you can handle."

May's hand shook when she tried to sip wine. She set the glass down wrong, it fell over. What could she do?

Aidan sat, put his arm about her, and pressed her face to his chest. She was crying. Gently, he put his other arm about her.

"Almost we believe in your inexperience," he said softly after holding her for several minutes in silence.

"We have a proposal, May. Our clan risked much to flee the comforts of the conclave. We're renegades in the Realm now. Of course, eventually other clans will treat with us, even ally themselves with us, but in the meantime, we are cut off."

What did this mean to her?

"Our clan would be strengthened if we form a new alliance. We offer ourselves to you as a mate, plain May. Your rover's gifts will be your settlement, as our clan and its protection will be yours."

Marry Aidan! It would mean staying in the Realm with him. May would lose Kester just when they'd become closer. May hadn't dared admit this to herself when she prepared to leave Earth again, yet the tiny hope Kester might care for her carried her through. She'd made so many missteps since the one that thrust her into Illynd. This choice would ruin her hope of any happiness forever.

"We pledge with our life you'd be well cared for, safe, and in time, perhaps even happy as our mate."

Bad as things were, May was astonished Aidan was sincere. It was one thing to hope Kester could like her, but she never thought of marriage. She never wanted to be trapped in a relationship as her parents had been. Nevertheless, her practical side whispered, what choices did she have now? She'd been troubled about bringing gunpowder to Illynd; here were the consequences. She saved Kester, his family, and friends—she couldn't regret doing that.   But she would hate herself if gunpowder was misused because she brought it to Illynd.

She could hate Illynd for ruining her hope of being happy, but she'd done that to herself. Though she didn't deserve it, Aidan offered her protection. She glanced up. Something altered in his astonishing blue eyes. May's heart squeezed harder, blood heated her groin; she felt more exposed by those responses than when learning there was a price on her head. Would he kiss her? She was in his arms, why didn't he?

She put her mouth on his. He was fast to respond.

She wanted the madness his lips on her neck, throat, and between her breasts stirred in her, but it would end in his bed. She suddenly recalled Kester saying, 'resist this Prince'.

"Aidan, stop."

She pushed at his head. "Aidan, do you expect this...match to be real, or in name only?"

"We do not please you?"

She adjusted the front of her gown. "I must know how you mean us to be joined, Aidan. I," she faltered, blushing. "I don't want to lie to you, because you're right. I don't have anywhere else to go."

"You would join us in name only?" he asked.

May hated his sudden remoteness.

"If that is what is required," Aidan said, "consider our bargain sealed. Once again, your true nature is revealed. How coldly you can calculate, even heated by desire. If a union of power is your wish, it only takes the ceremony in front of the clan to make it complete."

Aidan went to the outer door.

"Good night, plain May."

Bemused, May tried to sort out what happened. She forgot everything important, everything that mattered, was ready to give up herself. Any time she was close to Aidan, reason fled. Whether it was fairy allure or the force of his personality, Aidan was too much for her. Now he was gone, she couldn't believe it, but she was disappointed. For the first time she wondered if she should allow herself to explore these feelings for him. She stared up at the ceiling. It was impossible to stay here with Aidan, who expected things she didn't have to give him. It was worse thinking of leaving Kester, but she had to get out of Illynd. Once, she wanted to run from home for good, never to return.

Back on Earth, the idea of staying on Illynd had appeal. Now she'd ruined things on Illynd again, just when the relationship between Kester and her had such promise. She wished she'd made love with him back in Delain. He'd wanted her, she'd wanted him, but inexperience made her cautious. Kester would have been considerate. She trusted him. Now she was trapped with Aidan, and everything about him was out of control. She didn't have faith in herself around Aidan either, and that frightened her. Right now she had no choice, she allied herself with Aidan, and Kester would not understand.

She swallowed past the tightness in her throat. She was on her own from now on. Even if it meant she never saw Kester again. If there was a possibility of escaping this place and going back to her world, she would, but she was afraid. There were many dangers laid in her path. Yet Aidan was dangerous too.

What had she done, saying yes? Already she was drawn to him. She couldn't imagine acting as Aidan's mate without any feelings between them. A heart-stopping thought brought her up short. If they made love, they might have a child. May had been warned by Bri, though she hadn't meant it that way; Aidan would stay beautiful, while May would wither. When he tired of her, it would destroy May to leave a child in the Realm. With or without love, whether the union was sexless or not, she agreed to be at Aidan's side. These were not comforting thoughts, but because no one disturbed her, eventually she fell asleep.

She stirred at a soft knock. Bri bustled in before she answered. "My lady, it's so exciting. The clan is abuzz with news of your union with the Prince."

May made the effort to smile. From now on, she must act as if she wanted this. "Thank you, Bri. I'm guess you're surprised."

"Well, my lady, you didn't like it here before."

Bri lowered her voice. "Some were unhappy when the ceremony with Princess Kerriena fell apart. That union was meant to elevate Clan Guilly. Dark words were said about the Prince's interest in you. Now it's known you're a rover, they see his wisdom. Of course, power is not everything. It's plain the Prince adores you."

"Bri," May said, feeling awkward. "How is it I've never seen fairy children?"

"You have, my lady. High fairies gain full height in their first year. Of course, given our long lives, there's little pressure for offspring. But as head of his clan, Prince Aidan will secure his line."

"But when they don't want children, when they're not

ready," May said, "How do they keep from getting pregnant?"

"Herbs powders are taken in drink. From the first dosing, they prevent childbearing. The mix is altered for terran lovers. You desire them?"

May nodded.

"Then I'll get them for you," Bri said.

"Thank you....Bri, I'd like this kept between us."

Bri hurried off. It was one thing to be in a position that might lead to intimacy with Aidan, but having his child was impossible. May was certain she could not make a life in the Realm. If she found a way to escape, she would take it.

Chapter 33

Tell then, O Lady tell, what fateful price
Hath with so huge misfortune you oppressed?

May nibbled a breakfast roll. Before she shoved aside the rest of the tray, Bri showed her a packet of the powders she requested.

"I went to Goll, who's to be trusted, my lady. He'll send a supply as needed with no one wiser for it," Bri said.

May took the first dose in tea, had a hard time swallowing it too, though it did not alter the taste. What was wrong with her, going along with Aidan's proposal? Bri drew a hot seawater bath. Afterward, May donned a new gold gown. Bri arranged her hair, telling May she must make an impressive appearance before the clan. There was a knock at the sitting room door.

"Yes?"

Seg, Aidan's pixy, was there. "My lady," he said. "The Prince asks you wear this."

Seg opened a case. Inside was an extraordinary necklace of teardrop diamonds.

"These belong to Clan Guilly. The Prince felt they would do your youth justice, as it is not as heavy as other pieces."

It was an impersonal way to receive such a gift. Once she had it on, May was struck by her reflection. Her transformation into something she didn't recognize was now complete; it was her life that was unreal. Aidan came in, and it was impossible to do anything but watch his every move.

"The Guilly jewels become you, though you require no gilding," he said.

He went to the water closet, came out minutes later changed into a gold tunic. They went to the main hall where musicians played. The Prince walked May to a spot near the great fireplace. Rais signaled for quiet.

"Clan Guilly," Aidan said, "we present the Lady May McKinny, who consents to be our mate. Issue of this union will be the heirs of Clan Guilly. The match will take place under the quarter moon."

He turned to May and held her hand to his lips. "Not soon enough, my lady," he said in a tone honeyed with seduction.

May blushed, and the clan broke out with laughter and clapping. Aidan led her to their seats. Playing at being in love with Aidan was easier than she would have thought. She could smile, laugh and accept his attentions without caution here. The hard part would come when they were alone. Aidan introduced May about the clan. They danced together, and then May accepted dances with clansmen. Rais claimed a turn leading May about the floor.

"My prince is taken in," Rais said. "What magic do you own, my lady, beyond the very obvious?"

"I know what you mean, Rais. Everything's happened so quickly."

"Just as long as you're sure, my lady," Rais said, "To remember the Prince's moods are mercurial. He's not one to play with, nor am I."

Unsettled by Rais' comments and the clan's scrutiny, May was glad when Aidan escorted her to their rooms. Once inside, he dismissed Bri.

"It would be strange if we spent time away from you this night. We promise not to disturb your rest," Aidan said.

May was uncomfortable. This was something she must get used to, but she hated it that Aidan was frosty as soon as they were alone. She nodded, left to get ready for bed while Aidan waited in the sitting room. Once prepared, she pulled the outer door ajar, then ran to the bed and got under the covers. Aidan came in, May turned to her side. In a few minutes, he was in the bed. There was plenty of space between them but she feigned sleep. Soon, exhausted from playacting, she did fall asleep.

May woke to find Aidan still nearby. She slipped out of bed, grabbing a gown and going into the water closet. She bathed quickly. When she came out, Seg was coming in with a tray for two.

"Ah, darling," Aidan said. "Join us for refreshment?"

"I'm not hungry."

"Oh, but you must be after last night, little sweet," he mocked, "Sit with us."

May did as he asked. Aidan moved over to share the tray.

So close when Aidan was naked under the covers was unbearable. Where his arm brushed hers, her skin burned. How was she to spend day after day this way?

"You're quiet," he said.

"Why do you bait me?" May said. "I've agreed to the match. I'm doing my best." Tears slid down her face.

"Desperate when you've got what you wanted?"

"I haven't anything...I've lost everything. I'm a prisoner here. If I could go back to my world instead of doing this, I would. My only friends on Illynd will be in grave danger if I go to them, so I won't. I hate what's happening, I don't know how I'll stand it," she said in a small voice.

Aidan was silent. May didn't move to wipe her face.

"Surely, things are not so dark. What might please you this day?"

May dabbed her face. "I would like to be outside," she admitted after a minute. "Perhaps to be on the beach, or the mountain, although you won't allow it. I just want to see more sky. I feel so confined."

"We will take you, and you won't escape from us. Tell Bri to get you warm furs. We'll see the ocean and the peak."

Heartened by his offer, May left for Aidan to dress and bathe. When he came out, he informed her he must first see to clan business. In the sitting room, Bri arranged her hair in a simple style. May asked for furs.

Bri came back with them as well as fabrics draped over her arm. "My lady, you must choose for your gown."

"What gown?" May said.

"Why, for the union," Bri said.

She spread out a beaded gold silk, a white silk-satin that crinkled when May touched it, and a pale embroidered cloth.

Bri draped each across her shoulder so May could see it against her skin.

When she laid the silk-satin, Bri beamed. "Against your fair skin and auburn hair, it's perfect."

May had to agree it looked lovely.

"What style should the gown take, my lady?"

"I don't know Bri. You understand these ceremonies better. I'll trust your judgment."

"It's an honor, my lady. I'll arrange it to suit you."

"Thank you, Bri."

The union was fast coming. May wondered if she should make it a physical one too. What did she gain by holding back? It seemed this was going to be her life. Once wed, Aidan would not lose his hold on her, but clamp tighter. It was up to her to make something of what she faced. So far May had her unwilling fascination with Aidan, and his desire for her. Kester would blame fairy glamour.

To be sure, it was heady to be the object of Aidan's attention. She sighed. If she gave in, those feelings might grow, she might even believe she loved him. If making love helped Aidan to care about her, everything would be easier. Aidan was May's protector now, and unlike Kester, could save her from the evils of this world. She couldn't help but compare what Aidan offered to her old life on Earth.

There she was an afterthought, unloved. But to be stuck here without love was more of the same. May would prefer the simplest home she'd seen among Kester's folk. Kerys' was filled with family who worked together and kept a circle of good friends, Kester being but one of them. Kester's uncle was blessed in the same manner with his queen and their children. It was family and friends May considered important. This was lacking between Aidan and her. Once they made love, what would replace that excitement between them? How could she chain herself to a union with no friendship?

It could turn into a repeat of her unfortunate parents, hateful and spite-filled. No matter what, May would not subject a child to a loveless home. Her gaze fell on the silk-satin cloth. It was late for regrets. Too much depended on how Aidan behaved from here on.

Chapter 34

Whereby close fire into his heart does creep:
So, he then deceives, deceived in his deceit,
Made drunk with drugs of dear voluptuous receipt.

"You're ready?" Aidan said.

She nodded. At times when he considered May, Aidan believed in her innocent pose. This intrigued him. What was the truth and what was the lie in her? Standing there with auburn hair spilling over white furs, she was bewitching too. He led them to the main hall. After appraising Rais of his plans, he took May's arm. Bri set down the basket for them and stepped away. He threw up powders, everything *grayed*.

Daylight, abrupt and bright, revealed they stood on the cliff. Freed from the transportation powder's grip, he tossed up enlarging powders. *Skin, bone, muscle and blood vibrated*; they attained full height. Unfolding his wings, Aidan beat the air. He held May with one hand and the basket with his other as he flew over the cliff to the beach. When he reached a cove, he landed on sun-warmed sand. May took off the fur, left it on a rock.

"Can I walk near the water?"

Aidan nodded, leaned back against the furs, content to watch. Removing slippers, holding up her gown, her shapely legs skipped in the surf as she avoided the spray. She stopped to gaze across the sea. Water wet her gown when she picked up shells. Seabirds circled. Finally May sat on the sand, spreading the gown to dry. It seemed she communed with the forces of this place, water, earth and sky. Time passed and she

311

turned to him.

"I'm ready to see the mountain," she said, coming over to where he got to his feet. "I've never been to the top of one before."

"Put this on," he said, draping fur over her shoulders. "We don't feel cold, but use furs to picnic on…you, however, are meant to wear such."

He put his arm about her once more, grasped the basket, and flew up. He skimmed low over brush, stony ground, and finally snow-clad slopes. At a level place, he set on untouched, blue-bright snow. May looked all about with delight. She shivered and drew the furs closer. Aidan brushed snow off a mossy bank.

"Let's picnic."

He opened the basket and poured wine. Tiny sandwiches and cakes were unwrapped from leaves. The sea air perked appetites. When done, he closed the basket.

"Come here, close to us," Aidan said. "See this view."

May hesitated, but sat beside him. He put his arm about her. The mountainside appeared to slide precipitously toward wildflower-covered lowlands.

"Why do you do this?" Aidan asked.

"What do you mean?"

"The union, why agree to it?" he said.

"You gave me the answer to that yourself. I'm alone on Illynd. Believe me or not, I don't know where to turn. Though you won't consider I'm telling the truth, I'm frightened. Kerriena hates me. Dailgre wants me dead. I won't put Kester in danger for my sake, though I know he'd help me."

"When you talk like this, almost we believe you," Aidan said.

"Why can't you? Am I so terrible?"

"Very," he said. "You speak sweetly and simply, but honeyed words cannot cover your acts. You hid your true nature the first time you were in our realm. It took cunning to do so. Then you reappear on Illynd with a dire weapon. It seals a victory for your supporter Kester's clan. Rewarded with gems and what else, we have yet to discover. Then, when we catch you unawares, we find a piece of Gate in your possession. Though we don't know how you use this wand of power, eventually we will learn the truth."

In spite of the serious charges he laid, she had the nerve to laugh.

"Are you so very confident?" Aidan said.

"No," she said. "It's just you think I'm all this...I wish I could make you understand me. Perhaps if we took time to get to know each other better—"

Aidan played with a piece of her hair. "We do much for our clan," he said, "but not all."

He kissed her cool mouth. This must be his way to discover her. She responded, her sweet lips warming, opening, tickled by his tongue. His hands slid inside the furs to cup her breasts. She shivered but didn't push away. After he'd had her quivering beneath him, he could press for any truths he wished revealed. Fairy allure could drive a terran to depths of desire unheard of between fairies, the fascinations of such unions were the original reason the Dance of Fools was established. As he learned from previous encounters, May was vulnerable to his lovemaking. Yet Aidan was proud. He'd held his glamour in check; the advantages in such unions were too much on the side of the fairy.

Aidan desired clever partners with whom lovemaking was a mutual exploration, not an over-matched seduction. He also held back because his clan must see his consort as his equal, a power to contend with, or they would not respect her. The clan must believe in May's gifts. Kerriena had been unable to give Aidan what he wanted most; control through kingship. His little sweet would give him all he desired. Yet once kindled, May's responses shook him in ways Aidan didn't expect.

He took her mouth again, pulling her tight, fingers pressing into her back, finding the hooks of her gown and corset. Breasts sweetened by mint and lavender rubbed into her skin responded to his touches. For a brief moment, he left her exposed to throw off his tunic. When he lay over her again, she moaned and clasped him tight, the silk of her body lovelier than any finery. He must see more.

He pulled garments away. When he caressed her body, a thrill rushed through her and him. Now it was his garment in the way. He peeled off trousers, made ready to bring them both the delight held off too long.

She gasped, "Aidan...be careful...I'm a virgin."

He held still. "You've taken no lover?"

"No," she said, her voice faint.

Groaning, he rolled off and tossed the furs over her nakedness. Quick, he drew on his discarded garments, keeping her out of his sight, hearing her scramble to dress herself. When he turned back and found her in the act of drawing her gown over her corset, her averted eyes spoke for her. She was inexperienced and embarrassed. She did keep her secrets well.

"We'll go back," he said, quashing his anger. Long-held traditions kept him from going further, though she had desired this as much as he, but there was more to gain than this moment's passions. In fairy unions, virginity held a prized place. Considered a part of the dowry, a ceremony must seal their joining. He landed on the cliff and threw up the powders. At the main hall, he sent her to their rooms, saying only other business called him.

Days' later, Aidan was closeted with Rais in his study. A bottle of wine stood on the table along with two glasses. They'd discussed how the upcoming ceremony should proceed, as May had no clan to stand with her. Rais would take May's side in the ceremony.

Aidan took a sip and set down the glass. "She's different," he said, speaking informally with Rais. "And as lovely as she is, she's unconscious of that aspect of her charm, as if such considerations matter not. Her speech is full of helping her friends. I see one thing, and then she does the unexpected, revealing more of her nature than she should, if one is to believe the façade she projects. I'm intrigued by this."

"I thought this a union of powers, my prince? It might be one way to a kingship, but be on your guard with her. I fear her."

"She is dangerous, Rais. I'm drawn to her against my good judgment. I felt the attraction the first time I took her hand in the dance."

"I advise against this, Aidan. It's not too late to break the contract. Her powers are yet unproved. As a rover, any loyalty Lady May pretends to is suspect. You told me earlier she draws you in and rejects you almost as quickly. Can she be relied on?"

For several minutes, Aidan considered how to answer.

"If she's using me, Rais, I'm also using her. She needs my protection. For whatever reason, inexperience, greed, or sheer stupidity, she's made many enemies on Illynd. A month is a long time to wait in uncertainty, hoping your back is not too exposed to a blade before you can escape to other, safer worlds. Knowing her need, I pledged my clan's strong arm to her. It can't be unsaid. In turn, she's promised to use her power in aid of the clan. Would you make me a liar? Or do you think me such a fool I can't deal with her tricks?"

Rais gave him an unflinching gaze. "I've known you well

and long enough. You've never been a fool. But don't let this fixation you've developed for her fog your good sense. You've never allowed appetites to lead you."

"Don't fear for me, friend," Aidan said. "I've haven't fallen, and this lady's not in this for love. Of that she's most convincingly assured me."

In spite of what he'd said to Rais, as Aidan walked to his suite, he felt a sense of having accomplished what he meant to. Rais would confer with Derec over his concern Aidan was infatuated, then they would speak quietly with the few other fairies they trusted most, and the tale of Aidan's grand passion for his intended would fix her worthiness in every fairy's mind. Since the incident during their picnic, he'd kept away from his consort, though he found it a difficult task, especially when she rested.

Then he'd slip in quietly so as not to disturb May. Each time he would study her. He longed to explore every part of her, to teach her about giving and taking pleasure; he was, as she'd dared to say once, used to getting everything he wanted. But when they were joined, he would explore her newly kindled feelings and his own. The ceremony drew near. On the day before the union, Aidan called Bri to his study. He never considered disciplining her, though she helped his consort escape the Realm. Better to exploit a flaw than squash it. The pixy was dwarfed by his great desk. He suppressed a smile.

"How is the Lady May?"

Bri swallowed. "To be truthful, Highness, nervous, though I showed her where she'll stand and move during the ceremony, as you wished."

He nodded. He'd seen the hall this morning. Living wildflowers now covered its floor while its chandeliers were hung with ropes of sparkling gems.

"When I told her she would be Princess Consort, she did not believe me," Bri said. "I said a princess may be born royal, or become one by marriage."

"Did she have other concerns?"

"She asked about fairy children."

"Why?" Aidan said.

Bri realized she gave something vital away, was upset, strove to hid it. "Curious."

It should not surprise him May thought of this or that the pixy kept her mistress' wish not to have a child quiet. "Your mistress will need such loyalty as you've shown, Bri. You're dismissed."

Once again, Aidan misread his consort. She was prepared to bed him, but not to bear his child. A princess consort was a vessel for an heir. What else wasn't May willing to do to honor their contract?

Chapter 35

She is the mighty Queen of Fairy,
...She is the flower of grace and chastity
....my life, my liege, my Sovereign, my dear

The night before the union, May paced, sat in a chair, got up, checked the outer hall, went back to pace again. She'd felt so stupid when Aidan rejected her. Aidan never took a terran from the dance, but must have thought she was more sophisticated than she actually was. No wonder he preferred fairy lovers. They would know how to please him, would enjoy their bodies and his. Any day she expected to be kicked out to fend for herself in the wilds of Illynd. Bri did her best to cheer her, but May couldn't confide how Aidan treated her. Today, Bri was more excited by the union than May could bear.

"You must eat, my lady," Bri fussed. "You've lost weight."

May tried. Tea at least, soothed her. Afterward, Bri came in with something bulky wrapped in cloth.

"Your gown, my lady, try it in case it needs adjustment."

The first piece was a skirt, the second a strapless corset with a tracery of silver beads. The corset showed off cleavage May was unused to displaying. The beads repeated along the hem, weighting the silk-satin that flared from her hips. May was amazed at Bri's creation.

"Oh, my lady, just right for your youthfulness," Bri said. "With the Guilly tiara, you'll be an elegant match to the Prince."

"What is the Guilly tiara?"

"When the Prince was to wed Kerriena," Bri said. "The Guilly tiara was remade to suit Kerriena's demands. The Prince instructed it redone for you. Oh! Perhaps he wished to surprise you. Please, don't let on."

May remembered the last gift Aidan sent for her, the diamond necklace.

"I'll act surprised, Bri."

When her pixy left, May wondered why Aidan hadn't sent her away. What would happen once they were wed? He swore to honor the agreement; that might mean sex was still on his agenda. To be safe, May took the powders to prevent pregnancy. What if all he wanted was to exploit her supposed powers?

That was not good. He appeared to understand more about roving than May did. If he wouldn't see her, speak to her, tell her what he wanted, everything she came up with was useless speculation. She made her choice with Aidan, giving up the slimmest hope of a life with Kester or an escape to Earth. She shivered.

If her body didn't please Aidan, what would? She was using him, taking advantage of the security he offered. When he understood she couldn't summon any powers, who would save her from him? May tried to relax in a hot seawater bath. Once in bed, her thoughts whirled like a spinning top. In the morning, Aidan still wasn't there.

"The Prince sends regards, my lady." Bri said, as she

carried in breakfast. "He ordered this for you. He bids you eat all, as you'll need it for the long ceremony. He's with his clan preparing."

May forced herself to eat and drink. Afterward she took pains bathing, using the creams. At last, she slipped into the dress and sat at the dressing table. Bri perfumed and shined her hair, drawing the top up, curls about her shoulders. She pinned the hair so nothing showed to detract from the Guilly tiara. There was a knock at the door. Bri answered it.

Aidan stood there so elegant and aloof, May feared she might cry. Clad in his gold breastplate, black hair tied at the neck, the crown on his head was unneeded. No royal stamp could surpass that demeanor. Bri slipped out of the room.

"Stand," he said.

Knees barely obeying, she managed to rise and smoothed out the gown.

"Incredible," he said.

He came nearer, and she was enveloped by his intensity. "In our heart we are one, and so shall we go forward."

May was stunned; he meant it.

"Aidan," she said, but he stopped her with a finger on her lips. "Come, plain May."

May accepted his arm when she should run, lock herself in the water closet, and beg for the mercy of being cast out of the Realm altogether. Instead, Aidan was leading her to the main hall. Once there Rais took her aside, making no comment on the tremors she couldn't hide. Here was one

who'd help her flee.   Having quickly changed into a sweet
dress, Bri fluttered excitedly with the other pixies. The
mediator hushed the gathering. Aidan stood beside two gold
thrones. Rais escorted May to Aidan and bowed low, taking a
station nearby.

"Hear me, Clan Guilly," the mediator began. "This is a
contracted union of two powers, Prince Aidan of Clan Guilly
and the virgin Lady May McKinny, Rover."

Blush painted May. How could Aidan share that here?
The voice of the mediator cut through the buzz in her ears.

"All the forms have been obeyed. We ask you to draw
near and witness this pact. Prince Aidan pledges his treasure,
clan name, and fidelity to the Lady May. For her part, Lady
May pledges her faithfulness, her rover's powers, and offers
up her virgin state to Prince Aidan. Is this agreement
contracted by your unbound will?"

Hearing all the promises she must swear to, May was
horrified with her lies to the Guilly Clan and to Aidan. For
several seconds she fought a fresh urge to flee, but these fierce
fairies would hunt her, perhaps kill her for her treachery.

"It is a true agreement of our unbound will," Prince Aidan
said.

Now was May's last chance, but when she gazed at Aidan,
she caved.

"It is a true agreement of my unbound will," she said, in
as steady a voice as she could manage. The weight of her
promise settled on her. She thought she'd been foolish before;

what she did here was irrational.

"Set your mark as witness to your oaths," the mediator said.

Nearby, a table held a handwritten scroll that outlined Aidan's wealth and both their pledges. Aidan signed first. May took the gold pen, dipped it, and added her name though her hand shook. Witnessed and sworn to—what had she done?

Rais came up to the mediator with the Guilly tiara on a cushion. The clarity and sparkle of the gems laid in the lacy gold-worked crown astonished her.

"With this union, the Lady May is elevated to Princess Consort," the mediator intoned.

"For ourselves and for our clan, we crown you Princess Consort May of Clan Guilly," Aidan said in a clear voice. He took the Guilly tiara and set in firmly on May's head. Rais lifted May's right hand and held it out.

"I release the Princess Consort to your care," he said to the Prince. Rais bowed to her as Aidan took her hand.

"Clan Guilly, your princess consort," the mediator called out.

Aidan tucked her arm close. A long column opened in the hall. On either side, fairies stood. Aidan led her down that corridor, turned them about and ended back at the thrones. He bid her take her throne and took his. She was grateful to rest her quivering legs, but this elevated seat could never feel easy given all it signified. One by one, fairies stepped forward to renew loyalty to Prince Aidan and May, Princess Consort.

This was an important part of the ceremony, Bri had said. A child of this union would one day rule, so these vows affirmed the clan's loyalty to that issue. May was coached to make a slight dip of her head to each fairy. Gifts of gems, gold and silver bars, rare essences, cases of special wines and champagnes, rich cloth embroidered or intricately beaded, gorgeous tapestries, and fine crystals were presented. Aidan accepted everything with a nod. The process was slow, as the entire hall came before them. May was relieved when glasses of herb wine were brought to them. They stood.

The mediator toasted, "To the glory of Clan Guilly, Prince Aidan and the Princess Consort. The Guilly fairies welcome their new sovereign."

Glasses were raised and sipped.

"Now, plain May," Aidan said so only she could hear. "We will get through this together."

They walked to the adjoining gallery for the feast. Afterward, they danced barefoot amidst flowers carpeting real grass with the room's attention fastened on them. She moved closer, and Aidan tightened his arm about her. Others joined in. May was partnered with different clan members for hours.

Finally, Aidan intervened. "Bri will escort you away, my princess. There's something we must do first, then we'll join you."

Whispers followed her out. On their bed was a gown May hadn't seen before.

"A gift from your prince," Bri said.

It was fashioned of lace.

"Thank you, Bri," May said. "I won't need you tonight."

Smiling, Bri left. Herb wine on the table, flowers twined about the head and the foot of the bed, candles on the mantel lit. Removing the Guilly tiara, May pulled out hair pins, took off corset and skirt. Quickly, she slipped on the bed gown whose lace left little hid. She felt she must be mad. How could she live like this? A tap came at the door. She rushed under the bedcover.

When he came into the room, he'd already put aside his crown. Aidan glanced at her and shrugged off his tunic. He poured a drink, came and sat next to her. "You need this."

She took the glass with a trembling hand. "I'm afraid," she breathed softly. "You don't wish to keep this in name only."

"No, princess, we keep true to our union."

"I hate to say this now, Aidan, but I shouldn't have let things go this far."

"Oh?"

She sipped the wine. "I really am sorry…I lied to your clan, to you."

He brought her glass back to the table and sat next to her again.

"You'll be right to be angry," she said.

Ignoring her, he kissed her softly. When his practiced hands caressed her hair, her skin, May didn't want him to stop, she was his. But his mouth left hers.

"Aidan, I . . .

"If you want me to leave, say so now. I have only so much control."

He wanted her…why didn't matter, but May didn't have the courage to say yes or no. She felt heat in her neck, her cheeks.

Aidan's breath released. "I'll go."

She touched his chest lightly, leaned forward and brushed his mouth with hers. He answered her tentative kiss with his own deeply fervent one. His need and hers overwhelmed May. For a brief moment, Aidan left her. In the next, he was naked in their bed. She moved into his embrace. Coaxing with mouth and hands, May didn't protest when he slid her gown away. Blushing hot all over for her nakedness, she couldn't keep his gaze. He moved so his body touched hers, the shock of that sensation destroying the last doubt that she wanted this to go on. Aidan used his hands and his warm mouth to break down her defenses. May returned his lovemaking with hesitant explorations. Aidan's reaction was maddening, restrained, yet passionate. Finally, when neither one could bear holding back any longer, they sealed their union in flesh. Afterward, Aidan nestled her body. Tears slid from May's eyes. Feeling moisture on his arm, he turned her to face him.

"What's wrong?"

"I . . . can't help it," she said in a low voice. "I'm happy."

As if touched by her words, he kissed her tenderly. She

felt her heart was never so full.

In the morning, May huddled next to the sleeping Aidan smiling. His sensitivity the night before delighted her. His beautiful body, unashamedly naked, was powerful muscle rippling under smooth skin. A glow that had nothing to do with the bright shaft of sunlight streaming in enveloped her. Last night Aidan revealed things through his lovemaking that surprised and thrilled her. Further, her response to him was equally strong. Tears came to her just thinking of it.

Did she dare believe Aidan in love with her? Could she admit she loved him? She slipped from the bed and went to the water closet. May knew they slept late. Drawing hot seawater, she filled the pool. She wanted to be fresh this morning. Slipping into the foamy bath, she relaxed until the door opened. Aidan joined her in the pool, took up a sponge and began to wash her back in lazy circles.

"I can bathe myself," she said.

"But it's much more delightful if we do it together."

Strong, wet arms slid around her soapy body. Aidan was right.

Much later, sated with lovemaking for now, May dressed and combed out her hair. Aidan left after giving her a lingering kiss, saying he would return later. When he'd gone, Bri came into the room to clear away the tray she set out for them while they bathed. May donned a pale saffron gown. Bri wound her thick braid with gold cord. To May's surprise, Aidan was back.

He complemented her beauty, kissed her. "I hate to do this now, my princess, in fact all I wish is to stay shut in these rooms with you in our bed," he said against her neck, dropping the formal 'we' during their first night together.

"But, Kerriena is a threat to our clan," Aidan said. "It's time I see what you can do with your powers."

Why did he ask so soon? It would ruin what they began.

"Come and sit with me away from this bed." He smiled. "So I can concentrate on the task at hand."

They went to the sitting room.

"It's time for truth telling," he said. "What is the extent of your abilities?"

"I don't have any, Aidan. I don't even understand how the power I stumbled on works."

Aidan's eyes narrowed.

"I will tell you everything," May said. "The first time I came here, it was because I grabbed an apple tree in my world during a full moon at midnight. When I figured out those conditions for roving, I went back to my world to help Kester fight Dailgre. You don't understand about the world I come from, Aidan. There is power there, but not the kind that you experience here. The forces I speak of are in weapons. There are many kinds."

She got to her feet. "Any number of arms from my world would have helped Kester, but I chose one I could not carry with me, but make here. I knew I was bringing destructive knowledge to Illynd, but I saw my friend's brutally murdered body, learned all Kester's family had been killed, even the little children. I couldn't let that happen again. Fairies hold themselves apart, but Kester and his family are like me, vulnerable in a way you can't understand. Still, it was a mistake, I see that now."

She took a breath before she continued.

"To help your cause, Aidan, I could fetch horrific weapons. Guns that shoot lead bullets from so far off your enemy wouldn't see the killing blow. There are bombs more destructive than gunpowder. They ruin large areas along with everyone and everything on it. Men have made bombs that kill with sickness too. One device explodes and rains fire on those below, clinging to the skin as it burns. Poisons fill weapons that can wipe out everything in nature. Gas to choke the air you breathe. What terrible bludgeon would you want me to carry here for your use?"

Aidan sat silently.

"What of the tree?" he said finally, without any reproach for her deceit. "Is the apple tree the only Gate to your world?"

"Yes," she said, greatly relieved at Aidan's reaction. It would not have surprised her if he handed her to her enemies for using him as she did. "At least, as far as I know."

"It's too close to Kerriena and her clan. To use that Gate exposes you to many dangers."

He sat for a while thinking. "I have an idea," he said. "It may save us both."

Chapter 36

That love is not, where most it is professed,
Too truly tried in his extremist state;
At last resolved likewise to prove the rest

Aidan returned with something in paper. Un-wrapping it, he held it out the stick May kept from the apple tree.

"This is alive with power," he said. "It was why I took it from you. The flower, bud, and fruit mark the apple tree's true essence. It is against nature for the tree to bear all three at the same time, even more so for this branch to survive detached from its tree. Like Daione Sidhe, that apple tree is a power outside of the world. Perhaps you are new to your understanding of Gates, but you must learn to tap into this power, my princess. I know something of Gates. Long ago, Illynd's fairies roved here by way of another Gate."

Why hadn't he told her before?

"Our former world, Cett, had become too small," he said. "The great clans of our sires and dames would not hold all our ambitions. A rover's services were taken to transport us here. Illynd was wide and fresh, so we brought terrans with us too, to help fill it. We made the Gathering Conclave of Clans on Illynd to consolidate our control here. I tell you this because I can teach you to tap this power. These Gates do not open to just anyone, May; you were called. Only rovers make the Gates' work. A mystery lies within you and it answers to the Gate. Of that I'm certain."

May knew Aidan was wrong. She was a teenager, and before all this, had an ordinary life. It was an accident she ended up here. Nevertheless, he needed her. Since making her vow, she owed it to him to find a way to help him. Aidan put away the stick and led her to a small room off the apothecary's workshop and bolted the door. Taking out a mortar and pestle, glass jars, and a yellowed paper with writing on it, he was ready.

"Power is born with us but it doesn't come fully realized. This is an example of what we had to learn for ourselves, the recipe for acceleration," he said, "a powder we use to speed plant growth. Created with the right mix of herbs and essences, it taps into the natural world's energies."

"I don't know how you mean," May said.

"The natural realm is imbued with vital forces our inborn gifts act on. Some powders have been refined over thousands of years. Their capabilities must be uncovered with skill and patience, as yours must be understood by you. You'll start by recreating the acceleration recipe. Come here."

Aidan moved so she could take his place at the table.

"Measure these ingredients into the pestle, and then sift them together with your fingers, concentrating your will. You'll feel it if you press hard enough."

May was willing, though she felt foolish. She measured, stirred, tried to picture the ingredients working as she wished them to. "Is this what you mean?" she asked.

Frowning, he sifted the dust through his fingertips. "No, this exhibits nothing. Can't you tell?"

May shook her head.

"Try again," he said. "Remember any plant will grow faster with this in its soil. It's how our kitchens get fresh vegetables and fruits year round."

"Alright," May said hating to disappoint him. When she did all that was required, Aidan tested the result.

"You're not concentrating," he said, shaking his head. "Do you feel a shift of power from you to what you're creating?"

"No, Aidan, I don't. The apple tree holds this mystery. It was only when I made contact with the tree I felt anything. Aidan, I've been forgetting what any child knows. The moon's gravity affects sea tides, is stronger when the moon is full. It must be the same here."

"What is this gravity?" Aidan said.

"An invisible force that pulls objects, it keeps the moon moving with our world, this world too. Perhaps the Gate's power is strongest during full moon because it's concentrated then. But why just at midnight?"

"Many things are like that," Aidan said, "power that's tapped in an exact manner, such as our powders." Aidan's face suddenly brightened.

"Stay here," he said.

While waiting, May noted essences in crocks, ingredients in wood boxes, roots, shoots, and funguses pickled in jars. There were packets the same as Aidan used for enlarging. Another was transportation powders.

Aidan returned, bolted the door, and pulled the apple tree

stick from his sleeve. "Try again using this. Perhaps you require the connection to tap your ability."

Suddenly May didn't want him to be right. She shouldn't feel that way, but if she could do what he expected, it would change everything about who she was. Using a length of linen, he fixed the stick against her lower arm. Her skin tingled where it made contact with it.

"Now, try mixing growth powder again," he said.

May measured and stirred because he told her to, not because she wanted to. This time, however, she did not keep an image of the powder growing plants. Sweat beaded her upper lip as the peculiar prickle enveloped her entire arm.

"I'm done."

Aidan picked up her powder, rubbed it, let it fall from his fingers.

"It's not working," he said.

May leaned her elbows against the table, hoping he did not sense her relief.

"You're tired," Aidan said. "Let's put this aside for now. We'll try again later."

He carefully undid the stick and put it back into his sleeve. Then he unbolted the door and escorted her out. Along the way, fairies greeted them. Back at their rooms, May sank into a seat.

"What if it never works for me, Aidan? What will happen?"

"It will work," Aidan said.

Aidan left to see Rais. He was so supportive, no, enamored was a better way to describe how he treated May since they'd wed. She appreciated the restraint Aidan used before their union. He had honored her virginity, elevating her status before the clan. And she was afraid to do her best to help him. That evening they must put in an appearance in the main hall. May dressed in a gown embellished with gems along the hem. Aidan lit up when he saw her.

"Perfect," he said.

The occasion was formal, with pixies and grumbies serving and taking away. May listened to the talk about the table. Aidan spoke with his courtiers about the patrols keeping watch for the Maich. None was reported beyond the old forest. As she listened, May overheard speculation about her role in the clan. A few wondered what her contribution would be. What would they say when found out it was nothing? Afterward, they retired to their room.

Feeling shy might be silly now, but May went to the water closet to get ready for bed. The sheer gown Bri left out earlier was too revealing, so she hesitated coming out. Aidan left her to get ready to join her. Settling under the silk sheet, she didn't realize how tired she was from the night before. In minutes, she fell asleep listening to the crackling fire. Rising late again, she freshened up as Aidan rested. Coming out, she went to her wardrobe for a gown.

"May."

Aidan was sitting up. "I like what you're wearing now,"

he said.

"It's morning, Aidan," she said.

He got out of bed, turned her all the way around and pulled her to him. His hands slid down to caress her buttocks. Much later, after hours of slow, delightful lovemaking, they bathed and dressed.

"I must take a meeting to hold off those in the clan who expected a show of what you can do," Aidan said. "I'll join you when it's over."

He was doing everything he could to protect her, and she was afraid to understand why she was able to use the Gate. She was wrong to hold back. If she had any ability, it might be easier to face without Aidan. Remembering where he put the apple stick in his wardrobe, she put it in a basket, laid a cloth over it, and left. Bolting the door of the workroom once more, she took out recipes and ingredients. She wrapped the stick to her arm. The familiar tingle wasn't unpleasant. Determined, she visualized the ingredients coming together as she measured and mixed. When done, she felt nothing but dry softness. She took down growth powder Aidan showed her and opened the packet. May dipped her fingers.

A spark flew off her fingertips. She tried it again. There was a jolt of energy. She carefully folded up the packet and put it back, taking down another packet, this time the one used for conveyance. She just touched her fingertip to it and immediately felt a current of energy flow to her finger. She'd never be able to do this for Aidan. May cried silently, head across her arms, sobs shaking the workbench. Despite Aidan's belief, she was useless unless she went back to find something on her world he could use. After putting everything where it belonged, May then returned to their rooms.

She worked at embroidery with little interest. Bri had told her other ladies would soon ask her to join them at sewing. May had liked the idea then. Now, without anything to offer but bad needlework, what was she doing here? It was a mistake joining with Aidan. Her fears for her safety clouded her thinking. Since she'd come to Illynd she'd made terrible choices. Lying to Aidan had been wrong. Aidan didn't return. It was late when she retired without him. She cried a little again, then gave up tears, as weeping would not help her.

A soft touch woke her. "Yes?" she murmured.

"May, I need to speak with you." Aidan was standing by the bed.

She rubbed her eyes.

He held his candle closer. "Were you crying?"

"No," she said, getting up and slipping on her robe. "Let me splash my face."

When she joined him, he was by the fire with tea for her.

"I've been in dispute with the clan," he said. "I told them I was satisfied with your loyalty. There were challenges made and answered, but not to everyone's satisfaction, I'm afraid. For now, we're at an impasse. It won't last for long. Rumors are circulating Maich fairies scour the lands all about. It's feared we'll be discovered. Of course, we've taken precautions against this, but a skilled spy may see through these."

"What will they do if when they find I have no powers, Aidan?"

"They think to annul our union and force you out," he said. "I will not hear of it. They'd have to cast me out too."

May shook her head. "I could help you, Aidan. I could go to my world and find something, not a weapon perhaps, but a defense against Kerriena."

"No," he said. "You'll stay at my side and trust me to shield you. I have other means to deal with the clan."

He stroked her hair. "Don't think of leaving me," he said in a husky voice. "I couldn't bear it."

His manner touched her. "Once," he whispered, "you said I could not love. My love for you is fierce. I would crush anyone or anything that tried to take you from me."

He took her mouth, kissed her deeply. May answered his passion, tears wetting her cheeks.

"Will I always make you cry?"

He wiped her face, and she nodded. "Yes, because I love you, Aidan. Strange, when I was sure you'd trample my feelings. I can't believe you love me too."

"My plain May," Aidan said as he carried her to their bed. Admitting they loved each other heightened every caress, every kiss. This, May knew, was what she longed for, a life with someone who truly cared for her, whom she could freely love in return. The realization made more her determined nothing bad would come of the lie she told to Aidan.

Chapter 37

And forth he fares full of malicious mind,
To work mischief and avenging woe

Bri came in with a tray while Aidan left to speak with Rais.

"Please, Bri," May said, "Sit a moment."

The pixy did, gazed at May expectantly.

"What's being said by others in the clan about Aidan and me?"

Bri clucked. "Gossip, my princess…fools will say anything. I wouldn't repeat it."

"Please, Bri. I must hear it."

She looked down at her hands, up at May. "You won't keep your promise. Prince Aidan was taken in, passion clouds his reason. If they could see how you love him."

"What do they want to do about this?"

"Some want you out," Bri said. "A few say both of you should go. Prince Aidan's ambitious cousin Cuill stands to gain. He had an eye for Princess Kerriena. She wouldn't consider him. He wasn't head of the clan. If Aidan is ousted, Cuill is next in line."

It was worse than May feared. She couldn't let Aidan lose his position. He was so proud. It would hurt him terribly.

"Not to worry, my princess. The Prince is a match for Cuill. Show the clan what you can do. There'll be no more talk."

May was not able to meet the pixy's eyes.

"You may go, Bri," she whispered. "Take the tray away."

If Aidan were forced out, how vulnerable would he be? How many would go with him? It was easy to imagine Princess Kerriena's vindictiveness extending to crushing Aidan. Shaking off such thoughts with difficulty, May did a mental count. Eight days before the next full moon; not much time. With Aidan away, May went to the treasury.

Precious things were stacked everywhere, including gold coins. She took two handfuls and put them in her pockets. Then she went to the kitchen on the pretense of arranging a private dinner for Aidan in their rooms. May filled a basket with breads and cakes that looked like they would keep, as well as cheese and bottles of herb wine. Then she picked up apples and figs. She needed a few more items.

At the apothecary, May bolted the door to Aidan's workshop. She took a bag for the gold, the packets she wanted, and slipped them under the linen covering the basket. Then she left for their rooms. Opening her wardrobe, she took her old clothes and sneakers, along with the things Kerys lent her. She dressed in that outfit, tied the gem pouch securely. May filled her backpack.

Going to Aidan's wardrobe, she added the apple-stick to her pack too. Aidan could return any time, but more likely, his clan meeting would keep him away. How would she stop him from following her? This was her most difficult task. She must convince Aidan she used him, and now wanted no more to do with him. If he lost his place as head of the clan for her sake, or worse, his life, she couldn't bear it.

Just thinking of any harm coming to Aidan because of her stupidity made her queasy. Everything that happened since she first set foot on this world was a warning bell. She knew how dangerous life here was, but kept taking for granted things would work out to help her. Still, how could she leave Aidan?

His passionate declaration of love swelled her throat. She could only hope he'd forgive her for doing this now. She unearthed parchment in a drawer. Taking sheets, along with pen and ink, she composed a letter. It was a struggle not to give herself away by her tears. Twice she threw splotched papers into the fire. Angry over indulging in self-pity with Aidan's life at stake, she wiped her face with the back of her hand.

Aidan,

It was amusing playing fairy queen, but I've lost interest. Now Clan Guilly is at odds with the Conclave, I'm forced to take what I wish out of Illynd by other means. Already I am far beyond your reach.

May

The lovemaking was marvelous.

May hated to think of how Aidan would take this note, but had no choice if she was to keep him from coming after her. To soothe her sore eyes, she rinsed her face in cool water. Afterward, she went to the outer door and opened it. From farther off came footfalls, muted talk. Back in the bedroom, she settled the backpack on her shoulders. May tossed the contents of a packet over her head before she could stop herself. *Frozen in gray nothingness,* in the next second, May was out on the cliff.

Late sunlight gave the beach below a golden hue. If fairy scouts were out, she hoped they were nowhere near her position. Taking out the other packet, she sprinkled it over her head, felt the *twang as her body stretched.* It was disorienting to morph to her true height, but she felt much less vulnerable. As soon as she trusted her feet, she began to run down the rocky slope toward the lowlands.

***

Rais tapped the bedroom door, waited on an answer. Aidan sent him to fetch the Princess Consort to the counsel. The Prince would have her back up what he'd said to them. When Rais got no response, he knocked again. Perhaps she slept; terrans loved to lie abed. Softly, he turned the handle. The fireplace lent enough light to see the room was empty. The door to the water closet was ajar.

"My princess?" he called softly, then louder, "Princess?"

Having no answer, he peered in. She wasn't there. He made a frenzied search. A paper lay on the bed. Taking it up, he lit a candle off the fireplace and read.

"Imp fire!"

With this note, Aidan would be branded a fool. Bad enough she used them all. He'd warned Aidan. If only he'd listened. There must be a way to deflect her betrayal and the anger the clan would heap on Aidan when they learned she'd fled. To work, it had to make the Princess Consort out as bad as possible. This spiteful note was no help to his prince. How completely the wretch betrayed Aidan's faith in her. Frustrated, Rais took the paper and threw it on the fire, watching until it was ash. How might he protect the Prince? His hand unconsciously brushed his dirk, and an idea was born.

He must make this look good. Taking his dirk, he held it behind him and threw himself backward onto it, landing heavily against the bed. Wincing, pain like fire burning his vitals, he staggered toward the door smearing his bloody hand on the wall as he went.

Out in the main hall, Rais made it halfway across the floor bleeding heavily before he collapsed with a cry. Several fairies ran to his aid, calling for a physic. A moment later, Aidan was at his side, turning him over carefully.

"Rais! What treachery is this?"

"Ah-h…stabbed me." Rais moaned.

"Who? Who did this?" Aidan asked.

Aidan's physic Derec knelt at Rais' side and cut away his tunic. The dirk sunk deep. Gently, he pulled it out. Blood flowed freely. He poured powders into the open wound and pressed a pad of linen to it, holding it firm.

"Will he recover?" Aidan said.

"We can't know yet, my prince," Derec said. "He's lost a large volume of blood."

Rais' hand fell away from where he'd grabbed Aidan's tunic. The gathered fairies murmured with alarm. Aidan glanced up. They went silent.

"My prince," Rais ground out. "I went for…Princess . . . caught her…escaping. Stunned me…wave of hand, grabbed my dirk…stabbed me. Waved…other hand . . . gone."

Shouts resounded in the hall. Satisfied he had done what he could, Rais allowed himself to faint.

Chapter 38

Of lovers' sad calamities of old,
Full of piteous stories do remain

May ran until a stitch jabbed her side. Panting heavily, tears streaking her face, she switched to a fast walk, but the night was close. Aidan spoke of bears and wolves in the hills. There were too many noises, a crackle, rustling in brush she passed. Strange animal calls made her flinch, what made them, and why? She hadn't thought to bring anything sharper than a kitchen knife. She was moving west. Run again, walk, run more, don't think, don't cry and don't look back. May pushed between two small trees and something exploded up in front of her, flapping, leaves and feathers flying.

She stopped, bent her head to her knees, and let her body recover from the sudden spike in blood pressure the large bird caused her in its panic to escape her stumbling across its perch in the dark. May kept moving after that, but exhaustion made her trip one too many times. She found clear space under a wide bush, decided she must rest there. It was harder to leave Aidan than she realized. How could she do this to him?

She'd already done her worst by lying. Now she must undo that damage. Taking out a round of cheese, she ate half of it with bread and a fig. She was exhausted, but dare not linger, so she sipped herb wine. After splashing her face in a pool, filling her water bag and checking her compass to head the right way, she kept moving. All day she pushed her body with herb wine, ran, walked or jogged into the lowlands. A painful, persistent ache above her eyes replaced tears she didn't shed. Truly, no one came here save for the animals.

In her progress, she disturbed deer, birds, even a possum that immediately played dead. Occasionally May glanced back at the mountains expecting Aidan or his fairies to swoop out of the sky. That none reached her yet didn't mean they weren't after her. Late in the afternoon, she spotted a corral-like enclosure to a farmstead. May washed her face, combed her hair, and shook the dust from her skirts. At the farmhouse door, she knocked and a white-haired woman cracked it.

"I'm sorry to bother you, mistress," May said. "But could you tell me where I can buy a horse? Mine went lame. I'll pay gold."

When May mentioned gold, the woman pulled the door wider. "We've two horses, me lady, one in the fields, and the other in the corral. It's a good horse broke for riding...I could part with it for a gold coin."

May had already put a few coins in her pocket. It wouldn't do to reveal how much she carried with her. She placed one in the woman's dry palm. The woman rubbed it, smiled, and led May to an old mare perhaps already retired, but May couldn't be choosy. She ran her hand down its legs to be sure it was sound. She knew little of horses, but in four days, she must be back at the apple tree.

"I'll need a bridle too," May said.

The woman placed the bridle on the horse while May

watched to see how it was done. She even laid a blanket on its back for May to use. Before she left, May gave her another coin for sheer gratitude.

Straddling the horse like a man, May rode away with the old woman waving with a large grin. Two gold coins for a half-copper horse, if that. What a bargain the farm wife struck this day. The horse had a lumpy back, but was tougher than it seemed. Dismounting hours later in the dark, May tied it near a clump of grass it happily munched. May kindled a fire to keep away imps, banked it, and unrolled her sleeping bag. Having gone on herb wine until now, she fell to sleep almost instantly.

A whiskery nose tickled her face the next day. May pushed the mare away and got up. Stretching, she looked around. Away west was the beginning of the forest. To her right, a stream wended through the grass. She led the mare to the water and weighted the bridle with a stone so it could drink. Downstream, she washed face, neck, and hands. Knowing Dailgre placed a price on her head, she wouldn't risk villages to buy supplies.

She rationed what she brought and ate. All day she rode, giving homesteads a wide berth. At least her help brought Kester and his uncle this peace. When her stomach gnawed at her, she didn't stop. By early evening, she had to sip herb wine to keep on. That meant she could forgo sleep. Once it was dark, she got off the horse and led it. Traveling that way was safest with the price on her head.

Especially with Kerriena's spies searching for the Guilly Fairies' conclave too. Worse for her, they might know she was being sought. She sipped herb wine to keep sharp. At times, Aidan's face swam before her, his amazing blue eyes tender. This was the hardest thing May had ever done. She'd changed since she run away from home. If she'd stuck it out there to finish school, gotten advice from a counselor about college; but she hadn't the stomach to stick up for herself then. Illynd was teaching her to fight. She'd braved Aidan back when he mocked her, risked everything to help Kester. Now she was nearing the apple tree, the idea she must leave again stabbed her.

What if she never made her way back to Aidan's side? She'd never be able to tell Aidan why she did this to him, to them. Things went wrong for her before. Tears blurred her vision. This effort was all she had to give him. It had to work. Nearing his old camp, she wondered where Kester was now.

Would he be with his uncle, or south with Kerys? She didn't want to cross his path. He didn't need her kind of trouble; Kerys had been right. Her difficulties proved dangerous for Kester, and so far, disastrous for Aidan. White streaked the heavens, a meteor shower. Finally May reached the pond. She no longer needed the horse. Its presence might give her away. Taking a stick, she shied it away. No doubt a farmer would realize it was a stray and keep it. May was careful to stay out of sight of Kester's campsite. Getting closer, she checked and found it empty.

She breathed out heavily. The last thing she needed was to run into Kester and be forced to explain her presence. May must hide for the rest of the day. Kester's camp wouldn't do, nor would the forest. She chose to wait behind a large rock on the other side of the pond. She made no fire. Her head pounded dully. Sipping herb wine and eating stale bread, she waited through the day. When the light failed, May crept to the stream to clean up. Then she changed into jeans, T-shirt, and sneakers. She packed the other clothes. In the side pouch was the apple stick, which she took so Aidan would believe she lied about it too.

After all this time, the apple was red, the flowers blush, and the budding apples green. If only she did know how to use it. May shoved the stick into her back pocket. Ghostly white and round, the moon showed above the hills. All she needed was midnight and the apple tree.

As May moved into the swampy end of the field toward the tree, her heart made a painful hop. Like an old friend expecting her return, the apple tree stood. There were hours to wait until midnight, but she needed to be closer. May crouched, scanning the forest fearful Kerriena's clan would burst out. A prickle at the back of her neck made her twist about, as if Dailgre himself reached to grab her. Mostly, she feared Aidan. He knew of the tree, and the full moon's effect. What if he came for her? Nothing stirred in all the land about. Swallowing, May passed into the darkness under the apple tree's canopy. A hand closed over her ankle, pulled her down, another stifled her scream.

"May."

Kester!

"Don't be afraid."

She nearly collapsed as joy and alarm filled her. May hugged him, trembling. "Why did you come, Kester?"

"After all you risked to help my family...me, how could I not?"

The danger to Kester was greater than she could bear.

"I've hid in the wood all this day, waiting, hoping you'd show," he said. "When it was dark, I slipped over here on the chance you'd be here with the full moon...Thank the stars you've escaped the Realm, May. So you mean to leave Illynd...and me."

"I must," May said.

How could she tell Kester she'd turned to Aidan over him? She'd wanted to believe her choice wouldn't mean as much to Kester as it had to her, that he'd forget what they'd shared, but here he was, risking himself again. Kester would have done this because he was honorable, but she knew his being here meant much more.

"Things...are changed, for me...us. There's been a rift in the Realm," she said. "Prince Aidan's position is threatened. I need to return to my world."

"Not tonight." The voice came from above. "Seize them!"

May was dragged up. Lights flared. Kester struggled in the grip of two Maich fairies. Another fairy fluttered from the tree. Dusted midair, she gained full height, Princess Kerriena in a silver breastplate and armed with a sword.

The Princess shook her silvery head. "It's not like Aidan to neglect his consort so. A pity he won't see you meet your end."

Cold sweat broke out all over May.

"Why did you come to our realm?" the Princess asked in her sweet voice. "So far as we can tell, your business was to thwart our plans to become Queen of the Clans fairy. Of course, we nearly repaid your interference."

Her laugh was lovely too. "You'll not escape our wrath this time. Tell us, consort, did you think to dally with our castoff terran there?" the Princess asked.

"I did not," May said, "I'm a rover."

She made a fist, squeezed her nails so they cut the palm of her hand. "I came to exploit this world, Princess, and gain advantage for myself, as strong women will do. I'm disappointed with Illynd though. You must have heard what I said before you made yourself known. Prince Aidan lost standing in his clan, so I left him to attend to my business."

"What would that be, rover? We saw the destructive power of the weapon you brought to the terrans. You wouldn't return with a weapon to help Clan Guilly?" the Princess asked.

May shook her head. "By losing his power, the Prince also lost his appeal. Now I've seen what this world offers, I'm not impressed. Illynd is too primitive. Worse, it bores me."

Curiosity blossomed in the lovely Princess' face.

"On my world," May said, "we snap light on and off with a fingertip. Our food is hot in seconds. We fly, but in luxurious carriages while we enjoy food, drink, and are amused by performances or music. We have well-appointed ships that sail warm seas; we can fly to our moon. As for other entertainments we indulge in, well, there's nothing like them here. I found myself shocked by the Realm's lack. For the ambitious, there are weapons in my world to make the one I secured for Kester a child's toy," May said.

She shrugged. "I don't plan to return here."

The Princess laughed. "Poor Aidan's proved twice unworthy, first of us, then his lowly consort. However, this world you describe interests us. We would see it."

"Send Kester away then," May said. "My business with him is done. I offer my services to you, Princess. A rover is always ready to price a job."

"You will do what we ask," the Princess said coolly. "And keep your skin. As for this terran, we remember him fondly."

"Still your servant, my lady," Kester said, bowing awkwardly, held as he was by Kerriena's soldiers.

"Why did you come?" Princess Kerriena asked. "My spies followed you."

May was quick to answer for Kester. "In my bag, there's a purse full of gems he got in payment from you. He, in turn, used it to secure the weapon for his town."

"See if she speaks the truth," the Princess said.

A fairy fished the purse out and handed it to the Princess. She peered inside. "They are the same." she said.

She closed the purse, handed it back to the soldier, who put them in May's pack.

"So," Princess Kerriena said slowly. "Now you work for us."

She turned to Kester. "You're not needed longer. Go."

The soldiers released him. May was able to stand anything Kerriena did if it kept Kester safe. She squeezed her fist tighter as she watched him walk into the night.

Chapter 39

Whereat she wandered much, but would not stay
For gold, or pearls, or precious stones an hour,
But them despised all; for all was in her power

Run, Kester and don't come back—May hoped a thought so deeply felt could be communicated without words. He could not rescue her but might try. Thankfully the moon was nearly overhead.

"Princess," May said. "If we're to go, we must ready ourselves quickly or wait for another full moon. But perhaps you have to discuss this with your clan first?"

"We please ourselves," the Princess said.

"Will you come alone, or with soldiers?" May asked.

"A guard of ten should be sufficient," Princess Kerriena said.

She pointed out ten fairies, including the two who held May.

"You must all have contact with me," May said. "I'll need a hand free to rove."

The Princess nodded. The soldier on May's left released her arm.

"If anything goes amiss," the Princess said, "if our clan senses danger to us, your life is forfeit."

"I understood you've done this before, Highness," May said. "So you'll know it's somewhat like your conveyance powders. Everything will go dark, but it is transitory. When we arrive in my world, I will be pleased to introduce you to its wonders."

Sweat prickled May's spine. Johnny was an accident, but this was a huge gamble. There was no time to think, no other help she could count on. Her pack was returned, and she strapped it on while Princess Kerriena's escort held hand to hand, the last in the line the Princess, who clasped May's right hand. Given the nod by the Princess, May grabbed her favored branch with all her might, simultaneously wrenched her other hand free of Princess Kerriena's grip but; *a swifter surge of power than ever before coursed throughout May. The ground roiled. Nausea rose as the sensation of plummeting out of a great height pounded through her. The world blacked out. Violent blue light flashed crackling and spitting. How long had no measure here, but in that space a corona of blue-white fire outlined Princess Kerriena and her fairy soldiers.*

Aghast the Princess and her soldiers were sucked into roving with her, though she'd tried to immediately fling them off, May clung fiercely to the tree.

Her skin crawled in concert with a shockwave rippling just under the tree's surface, in that instant, earth beneath May's feet boomed like a thunder-wave. Dirt and dust billowed. She slipped hard against the tree, her right arm scraping down its rough trunk. She cried out as sharp splinter stuck deep in her flesh.

The wound pulsed. Warm blood flowed down her skin. The apple tree was suddenly searing hot. May pulled her hand up, stumbled back. The shaking beneath her feet subsided.

Aghast at the chilling fate she'd orchestrated for Princess Kerriena, May collapsed, retching, her body hot and cold alternately. Terse orders were shouted, someone was fighting. She dragged herself around the tree.

The Maich Clan's silver armor flashed in the moonlight. She was close to the main contingent of them. They didn't notice her as they fought with fairies in gold armor, Clan Guilly. Aidan!

May sat up, blood rushed back to her brain. The crowned helm made Aidan a prime target. Several Maich surrounded him. Aidan caught a Maich fairy's sword with the guard of his sword's blade. Two other fairies came at his front. He jabbed one with his gold shield's sharp center point. Aidan kept punching with his shield, wielding his sword, furious and fast. Another soldier was behind him, raised a sword above Aidan's exposed neck. May screamed. Her right arm flew up, energy tore out of it.

The jolt tossed Aidan's assailant several yards. Thrumming with power, May turned toward the other Maich soldiers, pointed at each of them in turn. The force ripping out of her knocked them flat. Acting on instinct, she mowed down the rest of Kerriena's clan. Aidan's fairies seized on this turn, disarming the Maich and tying their hands with cord while they lay stunned. Panting, May refused to believe what she'd done.

A hard arm came across May's throat from behind. A triumphant voice crowed above her ear. "Got her!"

Rais pulled May against his armored chest, his dirk at her throat. "Give the word and she's dead."

"Hold!" Aidan thundered.

He strode over to where Rais held her. "So," Aidan said, breathing heavily. "We've caught you cold in the act of betrayal. How will you wriggle out of this, consort?"

He snatched her jaw and held it. This Aidan was wounded, full of fury and ready to pounce.

"What did Kerriena promise? It must be rich to suit you. What evil will she bring from your world to contaminate this one?" Aidan said.

She tried to shake off his cruel grip, failed.

"We will know what you've done this night," Aidan said. "If we must use torture, we will to learn what Kerriena bought to use against our clan."

He pushed her face away as if it burned him to touch her. She gasped. The imprint of his grip pulsed. Beyond Aidan's livid face, May read hate in those of his clan nearby watching. Aidan would never believe her. She'd set this up by leaving him that horrid note. She couldn't have dreamed it would end with Kerriena adrift in that terrible emptiness. No matter what happened now, May achieved from sheer desperation what she set out to do.

Pacing before her, Aidan said, "You lulled us with your contrived innocence. Does your terran lover know you sell yourself, consort? Tell us of the bargain you struck with Kerriena."

Almost grateful Rais held her upright, May said, "I was going to my world, found Kester waiting for me on the chance I might return. Unfortunately, the Princess was already here. I convinced her of my world's wonders...offered her my services, she agreed to let Kester go."

Rais' knife hand shifted against her neck. "You have your confession, my prince. Let me slay her."

"No!" Kester came running out of the dark. Two of Aidan's fairies easily caught him.

"Kester! Don't fight," May said.

"Bring him here," Aidan said.

Kester, knocked down to his knees and dragged over, appealed to Aidan. "She's telling the truth. Kerriena forced May to rove. I was here. I heard everything."

"Really?" Rais said. "Let's see."

He used his left hand to pull the pack off May, still holding his dirk to her neck with his right. May shuddered when it pricked her skin. He threw the pack to a fairy that dumped out its contents. Aidan had seen the gems.

He jangled the coins. "This gold, consort, surely was a down payment? Say not you are bought so cheaply."

"I'll confess, Aidan," May said. "And someday you might even believe it. It doesn't matter now you're safe. I did that much."

"We are past finding your tales amusing, consort," Aidan said. "Tell us how working for Kerriena helped us?"

May shrank from speaking of it, the horror was so fresh.

"The Princess, I didn't mean for it to happen that way."

Pausing for a breath, she steadied her voice and then continued. "Princess Kerriena and her soldiers held onto me...I tried to leave them behind but...we all roved. The forces were stronger than any I've experienced. When it was done, I was on this world instead of my own."

"What's become of the Princess?" Aidan said. "Where is she?"

"I don't know," May said, still shocked at her desperate act. "The circuit from this world wasn't completed."

"You know where she is," Aidan said. "Tell us."

"Gone," May said. Her last sight of the Princess was terribly vivid. "Lost in-between this world and my—"

Several fairies gasped. Aidan appeared stunned; every eye trained on the apple tree, which was visible now dawn approached. Aidan stepped toward it. May shook her head unbelieving. The tree was a ruin, its leaves shriveled black, its bark ashy. He broke off a branch. It crumbled into dust. Even if Kerriena survived, she couldn't come to this world using a ruined Gate. Aidan laid his hand on the tree's trunk.

"There's nothing," he said. "Whatever force filled this tree is gone. It's naught but a shell."

May sagged. Rais squeezed her tighter. Her apple tree, May's only way back. She'd never see her parents or her home world again.

"So, consort, whatever your motives, you've overreached yourself, it seems," Aidan said. "Your gate is destroyed.

Princess Kerriena will not return. You've done us a favor, though we doubt it was your true purpose. We can see by your expression you're not happy with this turn."

Aidan hated her. May truly lost everything.

"Let me end her, my prince," Rais said. "Princess Kerriena is no threat now, no matter what they meant to accomplish. Let me be avenged for her treachery."

She steeled herself for Rais' blade.

Chapter 40

And foul blaspheme that Queen for forged guile,
Both with bold speeches, which he blazed had

"Aidan," Kester said. "How can you kill her? She saved your neck, or did you forget Princess Kerriena's guards were struck down?"

"Yes," Aidan said, "You swore you were powerless. Why save us? Did you decide we would be useful yet? Where's the apple stick? You made sure to take it when you escaped."

Rais patted down May roughly, easily finding the stick in her back pocket. "Is this what you seek, my prince?"

Aidan took it and held it as if he were testing it, his expression severe. "This hums with power even with the tree dead. You've lied about everything, but your scheming's caught up to you. You're able to use this power when you will."

"I didn't use it, Aidan," May said.

"She's telling the truth," Kester said. "She held up an empty hand when your enemies were struck down."

Several of Aidan's clan concurred nothing was in her hand when the Maich soldiers were hit.

"Let me," Aidan said to Rais. He stepped closer and twisted May's left hand up to inspect it, then her right hand. "What's this?"

A trail of blood ran from the underside of May's forearm to her fingertips. Deep in her flesh, a black splinter showed clearly under the pale skin. May had forgotten the wound, though it throbbed.

"Derec," Aidan said. His physic came forward.

"How did this happen?" Aidan said.

"Roving," said May, trembling. "I fell against the tree after...Kerriena. This broke off in my arm."

When he felt her quiver, Rais pressed his dirk harder. "Don't try me," he warned.

"Remove it," Aidan said, "before she can turn its power against us."

Derec searched through a leather bag tied to his belt for what he needed. He put thin blade against her skin and probed the opening of her wound. He slid the instrument in, lifting the splinter. May broke out in sweat. The physic grasped the end of it and pulled. It felt like Derec yanked on raw flesh instead of the jagged fragment in her arm. She moaned through her clenched teeth.

"What's the problem?" Aidan said.

"I can't get it," Derec said. "It's hung up in her flesh. It will have to be cut out."

"Do it," May said. "It will make him happy, so do it."

May shut her eyes. Cool steel touched her forearm. She gritted her teeth against more pain to come.

"What is that?" Derec gasped. The knife he held fell from his fingers.

Aidan still had her arm, but something was happening. The entry of the splinter knitted up into a white, star-shaped scar. Clearly visible under her skin, the splinter went from appearing dark, nearly black, to silver. Then it vanished. Where the splinter had been, a silver tracery spread under her skin, traveling through it like a root system with many branches going up her arm. There was awed silence as the tracery appeared again; May saw it in her left arm and hand. The sensation of thousands of angry bees, stinging and buzzing, rode with it. An agonized scream ripped from May as the charge hit her heart with shocking violence making her body leap.

Aidan's grip was ripped away, as was Rais'. Only this electric, terrifying shock rooted May's feet to the ground. For a moment, the entire tracery gleamed within her exposed skin, and then slowly settled back into her flesh until it could no longer be seen. The only sign it was ever there was the star-shaped spot on her forearm. May panted in the phenomenon's aftermath, unable to credit what she witnessed or felt. The pain was gone too.

"Unbelievable," Derec whispered. "Never have I seen such power."

Stepping in to renew his grip, the hand that held the dirk shaky, Rais begged, "I have to kill her, my prince."

Aidan said nothing. Like the others, he appeared dumbfounded by what they'd witnessed. May was petrified, of Aidan's wrath, Rais' hate, and of what just occurred.

"Hold off, Rais!" Aidan said at last. "Answer this, consort. How did you escape our realm?"

"You should know," May said, "You kept powders in

your workroom. I took what I needed…food, and those gold coins from the treasury. Then I wrote the note and left. I didn't want to hurt you, Aidan. That letter was cruel, but I had to keep you from coming after me…to convince you of my treachery so you'd think you couldn't stop me. For your sake, I was going to my world, determined to find something to help you against the Princess. I was right to risk it, Aidan."

"Such desperation," Aidan said. His next words fell like stones. "There was no note. Did you think to trick us with such a patent lie?"

He turned away. "Rais—" he said, nodded.

He took a few steps away from them both. Rais twisted his dirk. Kester stared, a horrified expression frozen on his face. Glancing from Kester to Aidan, May squeezed her eyes shut. Waiting to feel her throat cut, her mind swirled. Was Rais trying to torture her?

She whispered. "I love you, Aidan."

Rais let go of her. May buckled, ending half-upright. She didn't feel anything, when would she feel it?

***

"My prince," Rais called.

Aidan turned, the deed was done. He took in the slender neck bent forward, almost obscenely beautiful hair covering what he couldn't bear to see, though knowledge of the red smile hid there would stick with him forever.

"She told the truth," Rais said. "She's telling the truth."

"What do you mean, Rais?" Aidan said.

May pushed back on her haunches with quaking arms. Aidan was before her in a flash, grabbing her, pulling her up, brushing hair out of her white face. She sagged against him without strength.

"My prince, there was a note," Rais said. "I found it on the bed when I went to fetch her to the clan meeting. I was fearful, my prince, the clan would blame you for her flight, punish you for trusting her. I burned the note in the fire. Then I fell on my own blade so she would take their ire and you would be spared."

Aidan held May to him. "You lied to me, Rais? I trusted you with my deepest confidences. How could you lie to me about her, when you knew what no one else did?"

Rais looked at him squarely. "I meant to protect you, my prince. The clan threatened to oust you in favor of Cuill."

Suddenly, the body Aidan held went limp. "May, May?"

Chapter 41

Yet pity often did the gods relent,
To see so fair things marred, and spoiled quite

A blue patch widened until May could recognize it as sky. Close by, a bird called. Derec wiped her face with a cool cloth. She shivered violently.

"Don't speak, Princess," he said. "You've had a shock. Sip this."

She drank from his flask and a warm glow spread through her, though weariness seemed rooted in her. Derec spread a cloak about her. Aidan stood apart, staring in their direction while speaking in low tones with Rais and Kester. She could hear everything but her vision went in and out.

"We should leave this spot," Rais said. "More of the Maich clan will come soon. We can sort everything at a safer distance."

"Make ready," Aidan said. "We'll leave the Maich trussed here."

He addressed Kester. "Terran, you've been a loyal friend to our consort, a better one than we have. Take this gold as a reward for faithfulness. Go with our blessing. We will protect her now."

"Will you?" Kester said. "From what I've witnessed, she needs saving from you. I can't believe you have any regard for her welfare."

Aidan didn't respond.

"Let me take her to my people," Kester said. "I need no gold to love her. She'll be safe there and much happier."

Aidan turned to May. If he wanted her answer, she couldn't speak, didn't want to speak. Nothing mattered now.

"That is impossible," Aiden said. "May is the Clan's Princess Consort."

On hearing this, Kester's eyes narrowed. Aidan continued. "We've sworn oaths to each other. They might not hold now; that's a matter for the clan to decide. We promise you this. When she recovers, if she desires to leave our realm, we will send for you ourselves and let her go with you."

May shivered so hard her teeth clicked together. Derec bent over her again, tried to give her another sip out of the flask, but everything faded.

***

When she woke, May was in Aidan's bed. Things began to come back, her flight, Princess Kerriena, the terrible confrontation with Aidan. She pushed herself up.

Bri jumped out of a nearby chair. "Princess, you're awake. The physic said you would soon. He ordered me to call him right away."

"Wait, where's the Prince?" May asked.

What did he plan for her? He'd already given Rais permission to slit her throat.

"He's…elsewhere, my princess." Bri went to the door. "I'll be right back."

Bri rushed off. Fresh flowers were on the table, warmth spread from the hearth, yet May felt no comfort in the setting. Bri came back with Derec.

"Princess," he said with a smile. "You're looking much better. Do you have any pains?"

May shook her head. "No," she said, as Derec picked up her right arm and examined the curious scar on its underside. He gently probed the skin with his fingertips. It was strange she felt no trace of the splinter. Though she remembered what happened, she couldn't believe it was gone. He held her arm for a moment frowning.

"Is something wrong?" May said.

"No, not now you've rested," Derec said.

"What happened back by the tree, Derec? What was that strange thing that happened beneath my skin?"

"Not just under your skin, Princess, but burrowed into your very being. As far as I can understand it, the power of the Gate, some or all of it, transferred into you, became part of you when your body absorbed its splinter. We believe the splinter concentrated the burst of energy that saved the Prince," Derec said.

It was impossible, yet May saw it happen. Now all she had was this scar. "What do you think this means, Derec?"

"I'm not certain, Princess. My best guess is it's altered your terran nature forever. There's no way I know of to separate this power from you, not now it is a part of you," Derec said.

May touched the alien scar. She felt the same, flesh and blood and warm.

"You haven't taken food for days, my princess. I thought

it best you sleep away the shock of what occurred at the tree. Please, try the soup and té I ordered for you. If you can manage more, feel free. Have Bri call me if you need anything. You may get up and walk later, but only if you eat first."

"Thank you, Derec," May said, laying a hand on his arm. "Before you go, please tell me what Aidan did about my friend Kester?"

"He was allowed to go back to his kin unmolested, my princess."

Thankful, but afraid to ask about Aidan, May settled against the pillows. When Bri returned, May managed the soup and two cups of tea. Later, leaning on Bri, she walked to the sitting room. Sunlight filtered in, but that pleasure dimmed for her too.

"What happened here, Bri, after the clan found I'd gone?" May said.

"Oh," Bri said. "It was uproar. The Prince was furious. The clan made ready for an attack. It wasn't certain Rais would recover. The Prince wouldn't leave his side. Then the powders did their work, and he was whole. They left not long after, Rais insisting he go too. 'To avenge himself', he said. I couldn't believe you a traitor, Princess. Not seeing how you love the Prince."

"Bri," May asked, "how angry is the clan and the Prince? Has there been talk of how I'll be punished?"

Bri looked shocked. "My princess, when you destroyed

Kerriena, you saved the Prince's life, fulfilled your vows as Princess Consort."

May was barely able to believe no punishment seemed in the offing, but Aidan's absence at her bedside showed his feeling for her. Later May bathed and dressed with Bri's help. She felt ready to brave the clan. Out in the main hall, her presence caused all talk to cease. Everyone made curtsies to her. Rais appeared before her and bowed lower than any.

"My princess," he said, knee still bent, speaking loudly. Those in the room drew closer.

"I owe you the deepest apology," Rais said. "If my continued presence will be too painful for you to bear, I will leave the clan immediately. I only waited on your verdict. My actions caused the Prince and you much grief. When I heard your last words of love for my prince, I knew how terribly I wronged you. I pressed the Prince not to trust in you. Lay the blame for the rift between you at my feet."

She was touched by his admission, more so because he'd placed his fate in her hands. "You wanted to save Aidan. So did I. I don't blame you for doing what you did…there was no reason for you to trust me. For such loyalty, you deserve to stay beside Aidan."

"Thank you, my princess," Rais said, breathing out heavily. "You've proven yourself a princess worthy of Clan Guilly." He held out his hand. "I pledge to support you while my fairy blood flows."

Pleased by his gesture, she grasped Rais' hand tight.

"Thank you, Rais. By telling the truth, you saved me."

He straightened, his honor restored by her acceptance of his hand and pledge.

"Where is the Prince?" She'd expected Aidan to show himself at any point during this drama.

Rais shook his head. "He's in a dark mood, Princess. He's shut himself away, won't speak with anyone. He blames himself for what happened at that tree, though I held myself responsible, told him so repeatedly; he wouldn't hear it."

Aidan was sorry? "Please take me to him, Rais."

Rais offered his arm, led her to the apothecary and knocked on Aidan's private workshop. "My prince."

"Go away, Rais," Aidan growled.

"Aidan," May said. "Will you let me in?"

After a long moment, the door's bolt slid. Rais nodded at May. She pushed inside. Aidan settled on a stool by the worktable. A candle stub burned next to him. His eyes were glazed, he appeared lost.

She shut the door. "Aidan, why do you stay away?"

"You wonder this when I sanctioned your death?" he said hoarsely. "I did not keep faith with my plain May. I knew you, innocent and loving, in my arms. When Rais. . .still, it's no excuse. I should have recognized the truth of you if no one else did. I was without honor."

May moved closer. "You had less reason to believe in me than anyone," she said softly. "I betrayed you, left when you were certain I loved you and you could trust me."

"You were right to go," he said roughly. "I've been a fool where you're concerned."

"I was wrong," May said. "If I believed in you as I should, I would have tried harder to convince you to take me to the tree. You would have protected me from the Maich. Kerriena—"

The shocking deed she'd done reared up at her. Swallowing, she made herself continue. "She might not have died in that horrible way. I'll never forget what I did, what happened because I didn't have faith in your love and your strength."

She touched his face. "I love you, Aidan. Please, never stay away from me again."

"You love me? Do you understand…Rais could have killed you?"

"I used everything, Aidan, to convince you not to trust me, so why should Rais or you believe in me? I took the stick so you'd doubt me. I ran off when I swore to stay. I left that note so you'd hate me. It did its work too well. Rais was convinced of my guilt and so were you. The pain I caused you was unforgivable. I don't blame you for striking out. Please…say you still love me…you forgive me."

Blindly, Aidan grasped her arms. "Are you real?" he whispered. "Can you truly love me?"

"Yes," May breathed, leaning into him.

He kissed her softly at first, then with rising passion. He pulled back to look at her, as if to prove he didn't dream.

Tears slipped down her cheeks.

"My plain May is crying…things must be well between us…she cries when she is happy."

He held her a long while. When they collected themselves, they went arm in arm to the main hall. As they walked through, Rais began to clap. The clan joined in. May smiled, unable to credit her mistakes hadn't destroyed what Aidan and she shared. Aidan stopped and raised his hand for quiet.

"Before Clan Guilly," he said solemnly, "We, I attest the agreement made with the Princess Consort was a true and binding one. She risked her life and my wrath. She brought down our sworn enemy, Princess Kerriena of the Maich…and she saved my life. I present the Princess Consort, May of Clan Guilly."

He turned to May and bowed. Cries of Aidan, May, ran about the hall. A small contingent did not cheer, those allied with Cuill. Aidan led her to their rooms. Bri set out wine, dainties, and wisely retreated. After a long conversation, Aidan soaked in the bathing pool. May waited naked in their bed, and when he joined her, she pulled him into her arms.

Chapter 42

And in the thickest of cover of that shade,
There was a pleasant arbor, not by art,
But of the tree's own inclination made

Days later, Aidan took May on a picnic to a secluded spot in the foothills where wild roses scented the air. "May," he said as he set down the furs and basket, "I had long talks with Derec and Rais while you slept away your shock. We came to conclusions I must share with you."

"What is it, Aidan? You're so serious."

He walked to a dell protected from the wind. "This will do, I believe."

He pulled May's piece of apple branch out of his sleeve. He could see she'd forgotten about it. He held a packet of powder in his hand too. Her face changed; she knew why they were there.

"Derec said you should do this part. This stick wasn't destroyed when you broke the circuit to your world. It's alive with power still. We believe it may be possible to open a new Gate to your world with it. Are you certain Kerriena never reached it?"

"Yes," May said.

Aidan was convinced. He had to be, to allow May to do this. When he'd pressed her for details of Kerriena's death, May hated to talk about what she'd done to that Princess. In the past he might not have so readily believed her, but after the lengths she had gone to help him, he was sure she told the truth.

374

"Two queens can't occupy the same nest," he'd said to soothe her guilt. "Have you seen one bee attack another, clinging to its back, stinging again, and again? When Kerriena was done with you, she'd have set one of her drones that job."

"May," Aidan said now, holding out a small shovel. "You're the rover. You must plant the stick."

Animated by the possibility of seeing her home world again, May took the digging tool and broke up the soil. When she made a decent hole, Aidan put a hand on her shoulder.

"Here, sift this it into it."

May sprinkled the powder and positioned the stick in the treated earth, said, "Ouch," but kept on tamping the soil around the stick so it held firm.

"Stand back," Aidan said.

Brushing soil from her hands, Aidan spied a drop of blood on her finger.

"Aidan?" May said sounding odd.

The stick began to sprout slender branches.

"Aidan, do you see this?" she said of her finger.

"Pinch it," he said. "It will stop bleeding."

Already this tree grew taller and wider, the branches getting thicker.

"Blood, Aidan, just now my blood mingled with the tree's growth. Something like this happened on Earth. A cut re-opened and my blood was absorbed into the old apple tree's bark. Afterward the tree felt different when I touched it. For the first time I felt a current of something I didn't understand in the tree. Could that be how I was made a rover, through the tree imprinting on my blood?"

"It could be," Aidan said.

"The first time," she said, "my mother was responsible for my injury, though it was an accident. Just now was chance."

"Was it?" Aidan asked.

Already they stood in shade made by leaves and budding flowers. Then the growth slowed. The tree ended nearly a foot higher than May was tall. May and he stepped around the tree. One branch close to the trunk held two perfect red apples, two buds, and three sweet-smelling flowers. It was the stamp; the sign the apple tree was also a Gate. To test it, May and he put a hand on the tree. Contact tingled. Chance or design, it meant one thing.

"Aidan, I can go home."

"Yes," Aidan said. This was the last trial of whether she forgave him. "If you wish to go back to your world with the next full moon, I won't stop you."

"Aidan, I will want to go back, but not now, not even soon now I have your trust and love. In the future I'll go to see if my parents are alright, but just knowing I can—"

She put her arms about him. "I'm very happy, Aidan. I've never been happier."

"Are you certain, May? I swore to Kester if you weren't, I would send for him."

"Though you aren't wrong to think I felt more for Kester once, Aidan, I love him now as a friend. In time I'll see him again, to assure him I'm well, and ask after his family too. But it's you I adore, Aidan. After all we've been through; you must know I love and want only you."

"There's more, May. Derec didn't tell you his suspicions about the splinter in your arm, did he?"

"He talked about something to do with it," May said. "Why?"

"As you slept, Derec did tests, May, all perfectly safe to you, let me assure you. You're more like us now, May. The Gate's power is yours. As it is with us, your life force is out of time, your aging processes done. Always you'll be as you were when the power filled you; seventeen summers gone. As far as Derec can determine, a killing blow is the only way to end your existence now."

"That can't be true, Aidan! I'm like Kester, human, terran…we grow older and die, if an accident or illness doesn't take us sooner."

"There can be no mistake, May. The splinter acted as a transfer of old power, whose force we can't understand fully. Think of it May. You'll always be at my side now, my love. You can't know how it tortured me to think I would lose you one day, as your body was terran and frail. Having fallen in love with you, I could never turn you out for growing older, as you feared. My love for you is not so shallow. But it will never happen now."

He'd made her cry.

"It's too much," she said. "I can't believe this . . . my life, will go on . . . so." She shook her head.

"Time will teach you to trust this gift, my plain May."

May walked to the young tree and stroked its trunk. "All those times I talked to myself as I sat under the tree that's been reborn here, somehow it understood me, Aidan, and gave me the means to rove. I wish, hope whatever forces are at play in the Gate understand how much I appreciate that gift."

She took Aidan's hand.

"And now my plain May, I'd like to test that you're able to direct your power again, as you did when you saved my life. There is still dissent among a few clan members, mostly due to my cousin Cuill. If we make a public demonstration of your power, so those who didn't witness it first-hand could be convinced, it would put an end to Cuill's machinations."

"Of course, Aidan. I helped create this problem."

After landing them on the beach, Aidan set large rocks near the shore and walked back to her.

"Derec advised on this point," Aidan said. "Lift the arm that bears the scar. See if you can direct power at those rocks."

"What should I do? Break them or throw them?"

"Just concentrate on shifting them," he said.

Raising her arm, May pointed it. Nothing happened. She let her arm fall. "I don't know, Aidan," she said. "When you were in need, I was desperate to save you. I'm not desperate enough to throw rocks around, I guess."

"Strong emotion is not all that's required," Aidan said.

"It's strong will that counts. You must want to do this. Master the power. Move the rocks."

May nodded, lifted her arm. They were both astonished when the rocks stuttered up and flew back into the surf.

"It worked, Aidan! I did it!"

"I knew you could." He had to be sure she retained the ability. "This can't be the only use for the power that lies within you. What else are you capable of, my plain May?"

She slid her arms about his waist. "I have no idea, but isn't this enough for now? Let's go up to the mountaintop for our picnic," she said. "We never finished dessert the last time."

Aidan unfolded his wings laughing.

That evening the clan gathered on the beach. This time, Cuill and his followers placed the rocks. Aidan wanted them, and by proxy the Clans fairy, to be satisfied what happened next was not a trick. May bared her arm, twisted it, and blasted three rocks to powder. The next three she threw back into the waves. Surprised cries came from many fairies. Even those who'd seen her against Kerriena's soldiers were impressed. Then a battle was in play, and they couldn't fully appreciate what occurred.

"This is the fulfillment of my vow to Prince Aidan and Clan Guilly," May said solemnly. "I show you this by way of proving my promise to you. I will stand with Clan Guilly against its enemies. I will support my lord, Prince Aidan."

Taking her right arm, Aidan raised it to his lips and kissed her hand.

Just then, Bri and a flock of Guilly pixies and grumbies arrived and quickly set up tables. Hundreds of candles were lit. Trays of food and carafes of wine were laid out. To celebrate her mistress, Bri sought permission from Aidan and then arranged the whole affair with help from the grumbies, who volunteered to do so. The clan, except for Cuill, stayed on well into the night, dancing, flying along the beach; the revel ended after the sun rose. Later that day, Aidan asked May to help with a special project in his apothecary.

Aidan was bent on teaching May. They distilled essences and simmered herbs. For the next week, he taught her how to recognize other natural substances needed for the powders of fairy. The first time May was successful in transferring her power into a powder, Aidan was certain there were other avenues her power could take. Alone in in their rooms, May brought up something new.

"Aidan, a long life seems a wonderful thing, but I wonder what I can do with this gift. I was used to working. I can't spend all the time stretching before me in an endless party, there's more to life than that."

"As head of this clan, I'm occupied with more than you've seen," Aidan said. "But I sense you're leading up to a point. Please, tell me what you'd like to do?"

She could surprise him still.

May waved her hands about as she spoke. "We can do so much good on Illynd, Aidan. It's a beautiful world, untouched compared to the problems my world created for itself. But it does have dangers. This Dailgre for instance, he's no threat to Kester and his people at this moment, but what do you know about him?"

"That he's a petty tyrant who bullies his subjects and heavily taxes them. He keeps a large force of terrans to support him. Why?" Aidan asked.

"If Dailgre were to come here to conquer Mirddyn, it would threaten the Realm's peace. Why not stop him before then?"

"Fairies stray not into terran affairs," Aidan said. "He cannot harm us."

"Aidan, Dailgre could cut down the forests, mine our mountains for gold, abuse our peaceful terran neighbors and, in other ways ruin the peace around us. Why should we let things go so far?"

"What do you propose?"

"Let's stop Dailgre before he can do any more damage," she said.

He should give her this and see what she made of it. "It would take the clan to agree on such a course," Aidan said.

May smiled. "We can speak to them together."

Clan Guilly agreed to remove the problem Dailgre presented, but insisted it be handled without warfare. Since her display of power, Aidan's clan was in a mood to agree with almost any idea of May's. Word circulated of her loyalty to Clan Guilly. Since then, Clan Maich sued for peace

negotiations. A pact was made. Other clans welcomed Clan
Guilly, and they were free once again to enjoy the Gathering
Conclave. As a precaution, Clan Guilly would keep the
hidden conclave by the sea as a permanent base. May dreaded
returning to the Gathering Conclave, and Aidan was thrilled
such a small thing as staying here pleased her. She was more
enthused when her plan was put in motion; Guilly scouts were
sent to spy on Dailgre's fiefdom across the sea.

They reported Dailgre imposed oppressive taxes. His
soldiers were well-armed and well-fed, while his people
existed on the edge of starvation. His seat of power was
heavily fortified and guarded. Aidan held a council where the
maps and information the scouts brought back were shared.
May's plan was worked out. The main force of Guilly fairies,
Aidan, and May flew to Dail in two long flights under the
cover of night, resting in-between on a small island. Frosty
stars reflected in the deep, black ocean, the sight thrilled May.

"I used to think if I was trapped in the Realm it would kill
me inside, but now couldn't imagine living any other way, in
any other place," May said.

"If all goes well," Aidan said, "other designs we have for
Illynd will find a better reception."

In Dail, they hid in trees overlooking Dailgre's massive
castle. Armed with the powders needed to pull everything off,
they dispersed at midnight. The next morning as Dailgre rose
to break his fast, cries of alarm greeted him. Aidan and May,
fairy-small, stood on a high beam in Dailgre's bedchamber.

"Shut this noise!" Dailgre said, neck-rolls propping his red face. He stalked about in a nightshirt, hairy legs showing.

"My lord, forgive me." A courtier rushed in, tugging his tunic to rights, wearing one boot, its mate tucked under his arm.

"What's this halla balloo all about, Cumberland? Where are my six eggs and pound of bacon? My toasted loaf and butter?"

"Strange doings in the night, my lord," Cumberland said.

"What, man?" Dailgre said. "Say it straight out!"

"My lord," Cumberland said wonderingly. "Overnight all the doors to the castle were taken away. Right now, they're burning in a bonfire by the lake. What's worse, my lord, every castle guard has lost their weapons. Most of them look to be burning up in the very same fire."

"WHAT?" Dailgre said. "Pull them out. My soldiers want weapons."

"Impossible, my lord," Cumberland said. "The fire is too hot."

"Water the fire then, idjit!" Dailgre roared.

"The soldiers are trying, my lord."

Dailgre pulled pants up under his nightshirt. "Show me this catastrophe."

Cumberland went out while struggling to put on his second boot. Dailgre halted by a hanging door hinge, and then stalked after him. Following discretely above, Aidan flew with May. At a high balcony, Cumberland pointed. A blazing fire at the lake shore didn't spread or fizzle, though a brigade threw bucket after bucket of water from the lake on it.

"What sort of an attack is this?" Dailgre said. "Where's my enemy?"

"My lord, we're not attacked," Cumberland said, his head bobbing. "No army is without the castle, or indeed, within. This is a mystery, my lord."

"I wake to find all the doors and weapons afire, and you tell me I am not attacked?"

Dailgre stumped off to his room, followed by the bewildered Cumberland. He pulled things out of the chest at the bottom of his bed. "Mark me," Dailgre said. "The attack is a begun. My enemies won the first stroke, but I have my army, navy, and great treasury to fall back on."

"My lord, there is more to report," Cumberland said, his expression grave.

When Cumberland didn't elaborate, but only stood sweating and wiping his face repeatedly with a handkerchief, Dailgre screamed.

"Tell me, fool!"

"Your treasury is empty."

"Impossible!" Dailgre said. "A great store of gold, coin and precious items lie there. You must be mad."

"I'm not, my lord. All the doors are gone, including the treasury doors. Every coin, every precious plate and cup...all gone."

Not waiting for his courtier, Dailgre ran out of the

bedchamber and down flights of stairs to the deepest levels of the castle. Aidan and May kept high overhead. Along corridors and through openings that should bear locks, bolts, and braces, Dailgre ran puffing and blowing. When he reached the treasury wide open with no guard, Dailgre gaped. Bags that should be stacked high with coins lay deflated as empty bladders. Gold plate and silver cups were not crammed on the shelves. Jewelry chests lay upside down, contents missing. The vast treasure so savagely extracted from his people and enemies alike gone. Dailgre sank to the floor.

Minutes later, Cumberland rounded the doorway, alarm writ on his face. "My lord, we must flee. The villagers know about the weapons and the doors. It's not safe here, my lord. They're headed this way, shouting about taxes and the forced draft of their sons."

When Dailgre failed to respond, Cumberland turned and ran, bent on saving his own skin, most like. Aidan, the clan, and May flew over the fiefdom of Dail all night, merry and celebrating as much as the citizens of Dail. The chief delight in all the revels was the strange doings that greeted them with that day's dawn.

When Dail woke that morning, its people found sometime in the night gold, silver and copper coins appeared on their tables. Some had a gold plate, or silver cups, still others costly jewelry. After securing their newly found riches in safe places, the citizens of Dail met in the streets. They heard strange reports of doors gone, weapons burned. 'Faes' whispered some, but most scoffed at such notions.

Faes scorned terran affairs. Taking the advantage given however, villagers living in the castle's shadow stormed in to find their great ruler blubbering in his empty treasury. On the next day, he would stand trial for oppressive conscription and excessive taxation. Dailgre's army and navy were bereft of weapons; other bonfires raged about the kingdom that day, all at the same time. Soldiers and sailor stepped away from war to go home. Seeking to fill the leadership void were once respected leaders cast down by Dailgre.

They counseled a return to Dail's old customs; fishing, trade, and peace. A relieved and war-weary populace was more than prepared to vote them back. Dail would never learn that using sleeping powders, Aidan and his clan kept Dailgre's soldiers unconscious while their weapons were taken. Doors were stripped off the castle's hinges with none awake to raise an alarm. Special powders made the bonfires too hot to recover anything of Dailgre's war gear but lumps of molten metal. Without injury, without danger to Clan Guilly or the people of Dail, Dailgre was defeated. Aidan was extremely proud of May's strategy.

The clan was equally impressed with May's cleverness and Aidan's choice of a Princess Consort. When they'd returned to their clan home, and these happenings became known throughout the Realm, whispers that Aidan should take on the mantle of King were everywhere. When Rais told Aidan this, he laughed and kissed his plain May.

Chapter 43

Then shrilling trumpets loudly began to bray,
And bade them leave their labors and long toil,
To joyous feast and other gentle play

Knowing May wed Aidan dogged Kester all the way to
his uncle's castle. Until he met her, he'd never taken any of
the relationships he enjoyed seriously. In his own way, he was
a rover; a wanderer finding more pleasure in traveling about
for the King than being stuck at court. If he had May at his
side now, he'd be ready to settle into a life with her. Her
defection for the elegant fae did not touch his pride however.
It was hard to feel rivalry with Prince Aidan. He was
powerful, imbued with fae mystique. Kester couldn't consider
he was a competitor in such a contest. Not that those things
would sway his May.

No. If she fell in love with Aidan, perhaps the Prince was
a better fae than Kester knew. Surprisingly, Aidan did
promise to let May go if she proved unhappy. It was a faint
hope, but the only one Kester could see for the two of them.
Weeks later, when news filtered into Mirddyn's harbors of the
strange doings in Dail, Kester had reason to think things had
changed. He discussed this with the King.

"Faes have only ever used us. May did this for Mirddyn,"
Kester said.

"I believe you are correct," the King said. "We are still
impressed with the lengths Lady May went to aid us, and now
Dailgre is beaten down so sorely, and his country is so

changed, it is doubtful Dail will attack Mirddyn or anyone else in our sons' lifetime. Will the lovely Lady May visit us in the future?"

Kester frowned. "She's wed Prince Aidan. He's sworn to be her protector too."

"Ah. I'm sorry, nephew. I feared the lady wasn't right for you. She was quite different, with a forward personality not seen in our young females."

"Yes…I found that endearing in her," Kester said.

That night, his aunt prevailed upon Kester to come to supper. To his surprise, Fianna was seated near the Queen. When Fianna spotted Kester, she colored as if embarrassed. For his part, seeing the fiery healer was no treat. He made to ignore her for much of the meal. Afterward, his aunt roped him in to give Fianna a tour of the gardens. At least his aunt was consistent in her matchmaking efforts. Once he'd lent his arm, Fianna was quiet. After they walked several minutes, she took her hand away.

"I need no guide," she said coolly. "Thank you."

A bit ashamed he snubbed her, Kester relented. "Fianna…I apologize for my hot words to you the last time we were together. I never thanked you for taking care of me. I was a poor patient."

"Yes, but I had no right to say anything personal. Please pardon me," she said.

They were both silent for a moment.

"Am I truly terrible still?" she said. "Looking back, I was

insufferable when we took lessons together. I loved showing you up. I'm afraid I acted as if we were in a sort of contest. You'd be surprised to know how hard I studied so I could beat you. I guess I was still seeing you as I did then."

"For my part, when you scolded me about my concern for the Lady May, I was already very worried for her sake," Kester said as a way of explaining his own temper. "As things stand, I suppose I've no right to fret over her welfare now."

"Why?" Fianna said. "I mean, if you wish to share your thoughts with me?"

In spite of his concerns, he smiled at her sudden tact.

"Let's walk," he said, offering his arm again. She took it, smiling.

"The Lady May is far from my sphere now. In fact, she's Princess May. She wed the powerful fae Prince Aidan." He sighed. "I pray she'll be happy. She wasn't fond of the Realm the first time we were caught there."

"You were there?" Fianna looked surprised.

"I see my aunt didn't share everything," Kester said.

For another hour, Kester spoke to Fianna of his adventures with May in the Realm, though he knew only what May had related, his recent encounter with the Maich and Guilly faes gave him added insights. As he spoke, he couldn't keep the longing out of his voice. Later, in his room, Kester lingered over his last sight of May. Before he fell asleep, the picture of Fianna all grown up filled his mind. She'd become a lovely young woman of fine character. For the next weeks, her matchmaking transparent to them both, the Queen found any excuse to put Kester together with Fianna.

She was his partner for family gatherings, court picnics, and the dance the King arranged to celebrate the new trade agreement with Dail. The more time Kester spent with Fianna, the less his thoughts turned to May. There was no word from Prince Aidan. Weeks passed and still no message came. Yet the first time things changed between Fianna and Kester again, it was more her doing than his.

Coming back late from an errand for the Queen, Kester acting as her escort, Fianna's pony limped. He checked the pony's hoof. A sharp stone embedded itself between shoe and nail. He tried to pry it out with his knife, but couldn't shift it.

"This needs a blacksmith, I'm afraid," he said. "The shoe must come off. You can ride behind me. The pony won't bear your weight without pain."

Looping the pony's bridle around his saddle horn, he got on his horse and helped Fianna up. She leaned into his body as they rode. The scent of sachet warmed by her heat was hard to ignore. When he stopped in the courtyard to help her down, she slid into his arms. Boldly, before he could speak, she kissed him. His arms went round her waist. Minutes later she drew back blushing as if ashamed at her daring and ran into the castle.

Two days passed since then. When a messenger came with a small scroll for Kester, he leapt up. Unrolling it, he was thrilled to see the signature at the bottom. After reading the script, he hastily readied himself to travel. Day dawned bright and fair as he reached his old camp. May was waiting by the pond where they first met. When he saw her, he spurred his horse.

"Kester!" she called from her perch on a rock. Ethereally lovely, a circle of fresh flowers in May's glorious hair fit her better than any crown of fae gold.

"You look a rare beauty, May, I mean, Princess May," he said, as he got down from his horse to greet her. "Much better than last we met."

"I'm well, Kester and happy. Will you give me your hand?"

He reached up and grasped her arms to help her down from her perch. This was the moment he longed for and feared; would he see his May fogged with fae glamour? Her grey eyes were as bright as he recalled.

"How have you been?" she said, keeping his hands in hers.

"Fair for a man who's missed you...life with Prince Aidan is agreeable?" His heart and breath stilled as he waited for further proof one way or another.

"Aidan treasures me, Kester. He loves me, and I him. I felt an attraction to him the first time we were in the Realm, but my dearest friend was right to help me escape. So much is changed since then." She smiled. "I had to see you, Kester, to be certain you're well, and so you would see for yourself how I am."

Kester knew the worst for himself from her shining face. "Could May McKinny been meant for a simple life, I would have had my happiness secured, but I can't be sorry you've found such joy. It was no accident you fell into this world, and Prince Aidan was no fool to make you his princess."

"For your sake, Kester, I hope you find what I have now. I owe you my life, my love, and my respect. I'm indebted to you for all you've done for me."

May pulled the ruby ring off her finger. "Here," she said with a tremulous smile. "You used to carry this to remember your dear mother. Take it now and remember us both. If ever you need help, send this. I vow to answer your need."

She kissed him, sweetly, gently, and too briefly. "Goodbye, Kester, my first, best friend."

"Fare you well, May. I'll miss you."

He took out the gold chain about his neck and fixed the ruby ring on it, putting it under his tunic.

"Look for me, Kester. From time to time, I'll visit as friends should."

Tossing the crown of flowers from her head, a spray of glittering dust flew up. Mushrooms developed with amazing speed into an enchanted circle. Stepping into the fae ring, May smiled, tears glistening as the spore cloud separated them.

He watched long after she'd disappeared, then bent and picked up the flowery crown, a bittersweet token, slipped it into this tunic and rode away. On the lonely trip back, he let his sadness and loss fill him. In his first sight of May perched on that rock, she appeared more fae than he'd ever seen her in the past. Loving May was a recurring, delightful dream he must shake off. His path was to live with the realities of terran life, not in the field of fantasies that inhabited the Realm. That was her world now.

Having accepted this loss, his thoughts went to the kiss he shared with the lovely Fianna and stayed there, as they had much of late. Days' later, having arrived at the castle well past midnight, he entered his room and lit a candle. To his surprise, Fianna was there in a chair asleep. She'd been crying.

"Fianna," he said softly.

He laid a hand on her shoulder and gave her a gentle shake. She woke confused for a moment and then her fair face went pink.

"Oh," she said. "I . . . I was sure, I mean, why are you here?"

"Isn't that my question?" .

"I thought you were with her," Fianna said. "You went to her, didn't you?"

He crouched down next to the chair and took her hand. "Yes. I had to go. I had to see how Prince Aidan treated her and if…she needed anything. She's well. And she's staying in the Realm."

He smiled ruefully. "My heart knew she wasn't coming back. It's taken a long time for me believe it. Thick in the head, I fear."

"You love her," Fianna said in a small voice, hurt.

"I always will."

"I should go," Fianna said, rising from the chair.

She tried to pull her hand away, but Kester kept it. "Why do you run? I can't tell you how enchanting you looked sleeping."

He pulled her close. "I've let go of a dear friend, but must you leave me, Fianna? I've become so very fond of you."

"Fond? You think I could be happy with that?"

"No," he said, drawing her into a passionate kiss. Fianna didn't summon any resistance. When he finally spoke again, she was flushed.

"I'm fond enough to admit I've been falling in love with you, imp," he said. "Admit you've been feeling the same for me, or I'll kiss you again."

Fianna was silent.

"All right," he said, before he claimed her soft mouth. When they parted, they were both breathing heavier.

"Pax," Fianna said softly. "I give up. I do love you, you green-eyed horror."

Though sorely tempted, he did not take Fianna to his bed that night, or even in the weeks that passed. Instead, he did something she didn't expect. He asked her to be his mate. To his joy, she accepted.

Midwinter, Prince Aidan and Princess May arrived along with many others to a wedding. Mirddyn's castle was ablaze with lights for an evening ceremony. Outside, as if on cue, snowflakes drifted down the sky. Kester suffered a fancy black tunic. Fianna was enchanting in ivory lace. After the vows, the new couple danced alone. Then Princess May danced with Kester, and the Prince twirled Fianna. They brought exquisite fae gifts for them. The finest Kester received all that day, however, was Fianna's hand as she pledged to be his. After the revels, Kester and Fianna were fae-kissed by the Prince and Princess before they rode to an estate on the north shore to begin their lives together.

***

May discovered when flying high up in the storm, its forming flakes tumbled, struck each other, clumped up and blew apart again. Wrapped in furs snug by Aidan's side, they were alone in the darkened sky returning to their clan home. She tried not to, but May kept gazing in the direction of her last sight of Kester and his bride riding away. She had not met with Kester since they parted by the pond. Things were unsaid by both that day.

He knew as well as she that if events had gone differently, they would be together now. Aidan was her great love, but May never forgot those feelings shared with Kester. She also understood something of Aidan's dilemma before she was imbued with the Gate's power. From a distance, May would see dear Kester age until death finally claimed him. Meanwhile she must go on such a long time she couldn't grasp it, but without him in the world.

"You've changed my thinking," Aidan said.

"Was I trying to?"

Aidan squeezed her waist. "I thought little on terrans before I pulled you from the Dance. You make me understand how many ways we are alike. For example, Kester and I share something profound."

"I'm surprised you say so," May said.

"How can you be?" Aidan said. "When we both love you?"

ABOUT THE AUTHOR

Maureen Ungar writes Young Adult and Adult Fiction. She resides in Litchfield County with her husband, daughter Shaina, their cat Mocha Cappuccino, rabbit Samwise, and a flock of silly chickens.

Realms

Realms

Realms

Realms

Realms

Realms

www.ingramcontent.com/pod-product-compliance
Lightning Source LLC
Chambersburg PA
CBHW051547250626
47157CB00001B/220